T0204945

THE
WHISPER
SISTER

ALSO BY JENNIFER S. BROWN

Modern Girls

THE
WHISPER
SISTER

A NOVEL

JENNIFER S. BROWN

LAKE UNION
PUBLISHING

Published by Lake Union Publishing, Seattle

www.apub.com

Amazon, the Amazon logo, and Lake Union Publishing are trademarks of Amazon.com, Inc., or its affiliates.

ISBN-13: 9781662521232 (paperback)
ISBN-13: 9781662521249 (digital)

Cover design by Caroline Teagle Johnson
Cover photography by Richard Jenkins
Cover images: © Bruno Bleu / Shutterstock; © Jitalia17 / Getty

Epigraph from the Billy Sunday Archives, used with permission from Archives & Special Collections, Morgan Library, Grace College & Seminary, Winona Lake, Indiana.

Printed in the United States of America

For Melissa T. Brown
You'll always be the Max to my Minnie

The rain of tears is over. The slums will soon be a memory. We will turn our prisons into factories, our jails into storehouses and corncribs. Men will walk upright now, women will smile, children will laugh, hell will be for rent.

—Reverend Billy Sunday, in a sermon in Richmond, Virginia, January 17, 1919

February 29, 1932

When Mama fretted about us contracting polio, a streetcar crushing our limbs, a fall down the stairs, or whatever other *tsuris* she might invent, I threw her words back at her: if you're fated to drown, you may die in a teaspoon of water.

Maybe this was meant to be.

Maybe I was his teaspoon of water.

∽

As if nothing were amiss, I asked, "A drink to seal the deal?"

He grinned and took a seat. "What's the special?"

"The Whisper Sister." From the well, I picked up a bottle. *The* bottle. The label read Sam Thompson Pure Rye Whiskey. The label lied. I poured a few ounces into a shaker, twice the alcohol I'd normally serve. Before I set down the bottle, he grabbed my arm. My heart sped up so much I couldn't hear the phonograph over the sound of throbbing in my chest.

"You've always been stingy with the pour."

I added another ounce.

From a jar, I spooned a generous heap of honey. Three dashes of Bénédictine and a splash of cognac. I cracked an egg, the yolk dancing from shell to shell as the white streamed into the shaker. After scooping in ice, I closed the lid and shook it vigorously so the honey dissipated and the liquor chilled. The colder the booze, the harder it was to discern the bitterness of the alcohol. I set a strainer over a cocktail glass and tipped the drink in. The egg white floated on top, a creamy coda. I twisted in a lemon peel before sliding the poisonous concoction across the oak counter to his outstretched hand.

The cocktail would be delicious. Even if the bane had a scent or taste, it would be undetectable. I couldn't be sure it'd do the job: wood, or methyl, alcohol could simply blind a person or make him ill. But if you imbibe enough, death is a risk—or a benefit, depending on which side of the bottle you're on.

From my personal bottle of Old Forester—the real stuff—I poured myself a glass. Always straight bourbon for me.

He closed his fist around his glass, flashing me that half smile. For a moment, I thought to knock it out of his hand, to blame clumsiness and mix him a proper one.

But I didn't.

"To our understanding," he said.

"To our understanding."

In two swallows he downed his drink. "Nice tang," he said. "Though maybe a bit more honey."

I stood frozen before realizing he meant me to make him another.

I forced a smile and began pouring.

Part One

Chapter One

January 17, 1920

The ship rumbled, a growing noise that roused us from sleep and hammered in my ears. My older brother, Shmerka, and I hopped from our bunks and bolted to the deck, certain we were about to crash. Instead, we found people laughing and crying. Old men in prayer shawls recited blessings. Catholics crossed themselves. And ahead of us, a sight like I'd never seen: a massive green woman emerging from the sea. A ragged man said, "Say a blessing! It's Lady Liberty!" When we stared blankly at him, he said, "Lady Liberty! Welcoming us to America! We are in America." I had no idea who this Lady Liberty was, and the sheer immensity of her terrified me.

"America!" I whispered, trying the name on my lips.

Shmerka grabbed me none too gently. "We've got to get Mama," he said in Yiddish.

Dodging other passengers, we ran to the hold, where hundreds of us had eaten, slept, and lived for the ten days of our journey. The stink of vomit and urine was suffocating. Mama was folding our blankets and tidying.

"Mama! We've arrived!"

Even on the boat, far from home, Mama found work to be done. "We may be in America, but we don't leave a mess." She brushed the thin mattress on the bottom wooden bunk I had shared with her.

Shmerka had slept above us, with a bird's-eye view of the rows of beds housing other steerage passengers.

The ship ground to a halt.

Mama rubbed her hands on her floor-dusting skirt, straightened her jacket, and picked up a carpetbag. She passed a second one to Shmerka and handed me a wicker basket. "Let's go see what this America has in store."

On the deck we waited for the barge shuttling passengers to Ellis Island. Mama gazed beyond the ship. "Look at this!" The throng of bodies prevented me from seeing, so Mama thrust me closer to the railing. The water churned angrily, small whitecaps dotting the enraged cobalt water. "Isn't that something?"

Buildings staggered, one after another, so many Towers of Babel jumbled together, as if striving for God above. I squinted, searching for the glimmers that would surely reflect off the streets paved with gold, but all I saw was smoke rising in the sky and grayness. So much grayness.

~

The building on Ellis Island was cavernous, the line never ending. We were inspected by doctors, interrogated by immigration officials, and spit out with the rest of the teeming masses. We emerged dazed, anxious to find my father.

My nose filled with the harsh odor of coal. *So this is what America smells like.*

Behind a fence stood a throng of Americans. The men had clean-shaven faces, and the women wore wide hats with ribbons and flowers, more decorative than practical.

"Where's Papa?" I asked.

Mama's eyes skated over the crowd.

Papa had made his way to America at the end of 1913. Within a year, he sent for us, tickets and instructions arriving by post. But two months before we were to depart, news reached Bratsyana of a man shot in Austria, which delayed our trip by six years. Papa had been in America longer than I'd lived with him back home. I couldn't remember the feel of his beard or the sound of his evening prayers. I didn't know what Papa looked like outside our family photo. Mama said this was normal—seven years was a long time for anyone, never mind a child—but it worried me that I wouldn't recognize my own papa.

"Feige! Feige!" a man called.

Mama glanced up, first in confusion, then in relief. "Yitzhak? Is that you?"

The man pushed his way through and wrapped his arms around Mama. "Oh, Feigela! You're here. Let me look at you." He stepped back to appraise Mama, taking in her head covering, the skirt that had been mended too many times, the grooves of hunger on her face.

"Yitzhak, what happened to you?" My mother caressed Papa's bare cheeks. "Where is your beard?"

Papa's rumbly guffaw touched a memory. He rubbed his chin. "Americans don't wear beards."

He hugged her again before turning to me and Shmerka. The man standing in front of me didn't resemble the man in the photo. His clothes were strange, a large overcoat with a belted waist and many buttons and a gray hat with a brim. Where was the rounded black yarmulke of home? Where were his sidelocks? He knelt down before us. "Come to your old papa."

Shmerka and I hesitantly stepped forward. Papa swept us into a bear hug. My body stiffened in the embrace of this stranger. He held on for longer than was comfortable. I took in his muskiness, the smoothness of his skin.

When he released us, Mama peered at him. "How is a beard not American?"

My eyes flitted to the people around us. Those of us off the boat—with skirts to our ankles, headscarves, bushy beards, caps—appeared nothing like those waiting. A girl about my age on the other side wore

7

a ruby coat with a fur collar, her hair curled below her ears. My braids stretched to the middle of my back.

"Feige, you just arrived. You will see how America works. Everything is different."

Different? I pulled Shmerka close, putting my arm through his.

"Come." Papa picked up the carpetbags. "We will catch the ferry to Manhattan." He looked at me. "A new life awaits you!"

America.

Chapter Two

America. How I longed for Bratsyana.

New York was . . . I didn't have the words to describe New York, even in Yiddish. The forest of buildings, the crowds of people, the layer of dirt that settled on the back of my neck. New York dirt was different than Bratsyana dirt, the way it seeped into my skin, filled my mouth. And the stench! The odor of stale bodies, rotten food, dung, gasoline, and smoke clogged the air, choking my throat.

Then there was the stranger we were living with.

"He's not a stranger." Mama's tone was sharp. "He's your papa."

Still I side-eyed him.

America. More would happen in a single year on the Lower East Side than in my entire ten years in Ukraine.

The school had placed me in a baby class. Not even the teacher liked me. On that first day, she'd said, "Malka?" as if smelling three-day-old herring. It was the only word she uttered that I recognized.

When she realized I didn't understand her, she switched to Yiddish. "This class is conducted in English. Study hard, and you'll move into a grade more suited to your age. Otherwise, you'll be here the entire year." She pursed her lips. "Malka is an old-world name. Wouldn't you like an American name?"

"An American name?" I repeated in Yiddish. A name was a name.

"An American name." She put her pencil in the corner of her mouth. "Minnie. You'll be Minnie." She wrote something on a paper. "I'm Miss Kagan. Minnie, when is your birthday?"

"Birthday?"

"The day you were born. It's a date Americans need to know. Ask your mother, and tell me tomorrow." She gestured toward the rows of desks. "Have a seat, Minnie."

Minnie. What a terrible name. I missed the hard crunch of the *k*, didn't like how the *e* sound could be drawn forever, but I couldn't protest in English, so Minnie I would be.

~

Mama worked sewing blouses until after six, so I cooked dinner.

The American kitchen befuddled me, with its gas stove and icebox. The first day we'd arrived, I had stood at the sink, turning the water on and off until Papa had chided me. Running water inside. Who could've imagined?

Our apartment consisted of one room, divided into two. In front were the kitchen and parlor. Behind a half-wall divider was a living area. Shmerka and I slept on a mattress near the stove; Mama and Papa slept in the back.

After using the coin Papa had left for me to start the gas, I cooked buckwheat for holishkes. Once dinner was simmering, I opened the book from Miss Kagan. It was filled with strange marks. Shmerka had one too.

"Will this ever make sense?"

He shrugged. He wasn't in my class, but he was also with kids much younger. We stared at the books gloomily.

I rolled the buckwheat in the cabbage and baked it. When Mama and Papa returned, I removed the holishkes from the oven.

At the table we helped ourselves. The cabbage was tough, the buckwheat crunchy.

"Ah, Malka," Mama said. "How will you be a proper wife if you can't cook?"

"Minnie," I said.

"What? Hand me the salt."

I set down my fork. "My name is Minnie."

My brother swallowed his mouthful. "And I'm Max."

"What is this nonsense?" Mama dumped salt on her food.

"My teacher said Malka was old-world, so now I'm Minnie."

"And you . . . Max?" Papa asked.

"A boy at school, Leo, suggested the name."

"How did you understand him?" I asked.

"He spoke Yiddish."

"No one would speak Yiddish to me." I stabbed the cabbage with my knife.

Papa stroked his chin. What would our American father think of our American names? "Minnie and Max."

We nodded.

"I like it," he pronounced.

I dropped my gaze to the table so he couldn't see my relief.

"Why on earth would they need new names? They have perfectly fine names."

"It's America, Feige. Everyone gets an American name. I have one."

Mama pointed with her fork. "Yitzhak, what are you talking about?"

"I'm Isaac here. Or Ike."

"Ike? Ridiculous. Changing your name is an insult to your ancestors." She waved her fork in the air. "Don't expect me to use those *farkakte* names."

The cabbage took a lengthy time to chew. I swallowed before asking, "Mama? When's my birthday?"

"Birthday?" She hacked at her food. "In the spring."

"My teacher said I need a date. Americans have birthdays."

"You're not an American; you're a Jew," Mama said.

"She can be an American *and* a Jew," Papa said.

Mama was about to say something sharp, so I pushed on. "My birthday?"

"I need one too," Max said.

"Tateh had already passed." She poked her knife toward Max. "That's why you have his name."

"But what year was that?"

Papa picked the buckwheat out of his cabbage. "About a year after Anshel, *alav hashalom*." Anshel. The brother we left in Bratsyana. The brother buried next to my grandfather in a graveyard marked only with ragged fieldstones rising at odd angles from the dirt. "1907?"

"Remember how hot it was when Shmerka was born?" Mama said. "My feet swelled like knaidlach in chicken soup."

"Let's say August," Papa said. "Max, pick a number between one and thirty-one."

"Twenty-three?"

"Your birthday is August twenty-third, 1907."

"What about me?" I asked.

"Well, you were born two years after Shmerka, a bit after Passover," Mama said.

"How about the first of May?" Papa suggested. "You'd have a May Day parade every year on your birthday."

Mama said, "How lovely."

"So May 1, 1909?" I searched Mama's face for approval.

"That makes you almost eleven. Sounds right."

It was agreed. We had birthdays, and we had names. Were we now Americans?

Later, Papa settled me into bed. "Did you like school?"

"No."

He laughed. "Things will get better when you learn English."

"But the lines make no sense."

12

Papa picked up my schoolbook, which was next to my mattress. "I can help. See this?" He pointed at a triangle shape with legs. "This is the letter *A*."

"*A.*"

"*A* is for *ape*," Papa read. "I'll tell you what. We'll practice every evening. For now, go to sleep."

He kissed me on the forehead and made a cozy, warm packet of sheets to tuck around me. It was nothing like the thick quilted spread I had back home. I yearned for the comfort of my bed in Bratsyana. *You're in America now,* I reminded myself.

"In English," Papa said, "you say, 'Good night.' Good night, my Minnie."

"Good night, my papa."

I chanted softly, "*A, A, A,*" and wondered how long it would be until I dreamed in English.

Chapter Three

Never had I worked as tirelessly as I worked on learning English. For the next year, Max and I competed to see who could learn more. I was better at speaking, but he mastered reading first. As promised, Papa sat with us each night, patiently teaching us our letters. Sometimes I'd sit on his lap, my fingers tracing the words in the newspaper. Papa's scent became familiar, the scratchiness of his stubble against my cheek comforting. That first summer in America, Max and I were permitted to take English classes at the settlement house instead of working, so by September, the beginning of the next school year, I'd moved up two grades. Because Max already knew his numbers, he moved up three.

Max and I used English with each other and Papa, but Mama insisted we speak Yiddish with her. "I have no need for English," she said. "The butcher speaks Yiddish, the grocer speaks Yiddish, the rabbi speaks Yiddish, my friends speak Yiddish. If Yiddish is good enough for them, it's good enough for you."

During school lunch, I gravitated toward girls my age. Mama was thrilled that Max's friend Leo turned out to be the rabbi's son. She insisted I make respectable friends as well. "Honor is dearer than money."

For her, I befriended Leah, though she bored me. Her mother was also from Bratsyana, which pleased Mama. Leah kept her dresses clean and ate the kosher lunches her mother packed.

I preferred Sylvia, though. Sylvia climbed the fence and played kick the can at recess. We'd rough and tumble until the teacher bellowed at us to stop. Sylvia was a year older than me but grades ahead, yet she didn't mind. She taught me important skills, like how to buy food from a pushcart and the kind of English I didn't learn from schoolbooks: *bee's knees, copacetic, ritzy.*

At the beginning of our second summer in America, Max and I no longer had the luxury of classes; we needed jobs. As a twelve-year-old, I cut fabric at a factory. Ten hours a day, I hunched over a table, my fingers calcified around the handle of my scissors. I cut piece after piece for the seamstresses. My hair glued to my neck, a scarf strangling me. I longed to bob my hair like the women in magazines, but Mama wouldn't allow it.

"Mama, please," I begged. "Like Irene Castle's bob. She's famous."

"Only *nafkas* have short hair," she said.

When I pointed out the prostitutes on our street had long hair, Mama swatted my bottom for disrespect.

My hands swelled in the heat. I constantly wiped my brow, because if sweat dropped on the fabric, the boss docked my pay. We weren't allowed to speak, so in my head, I told myself stories in English. At night I soaked my hands in Epsom salts, rubbing them to work out the kinks.

Mama and I fought regularly. "Malka, help with the laundry." "Malka, sweep the room." "Malka, chop onions."

"But my hands hurt."

"You think my hands don't hurt? My back? My feet? Housework still needs to be done."

Sometimes, on Sundays, when Mama ordered me to do the marketing, I'd sneak to the picture show with Sylvia. It meant a *potch* on my *tuchus* when I got back, but it was worth it.

Max worked, too, but for an associate of Papa's. Papa delivered things for a powerful man, a Mr. Rothstein. Mr. Rothstein needed someone he could trust to run errands, so Papa offered up Max. Max spent the day outside and had the freedom to use the toilet whenever he wanted.

"Why can't I do what Max does?" I asked my father.

"It's not a job for girls," Papa said.

One evening, my eyelids sagged as I circled a brush leisurely on the floor, making no effort to scrub. Mama ironed Papa's shirts, as if the kitchen weren't hot enough.

"Malka, use elbow grease. A lazy person has to do a task twice."

Papa read his paper and smoked at the table. "She's a child, Feige. Let her be."

"A child? At home, she'd be running the house. Here her breads are half-raw, the floor is streaked, and yellow rings stain her collars."

"New York is our home."

"Home is where your people are."

"Lots of people in New York. Feige, it's 1921. Things are different. When Minnie is grown, she'll have a job in an office. She'll buy her bread from the bakery and hire a washerwoman to do her laundry." The paper rustled as he turned the page.

Mama reheated her iron on the stove. "A lady needs to know how to care for her family. Even if she were the czar's niece, she should know."

"My Minnela did not come to America to be a laborer. She'll be a fine lady."

"A fine lady who wears dirty rags because she can't clean the clothes on her back."

"Our luck is changing, Feige."

"Our luck is as bright as the new moon." Mama muttered curses at Papa under her breath as she moved the hot iron across the shirt. "May all your teeth fall out except one to make you suffer." In Bratsyana, curses and blessings were tossed like chicken feed. Mama's tongue-lashings reminded me of home.

I didn't want to be a laborer. I didn't want to work in sweatshops. I didn't want to be a *balabusta*, a housewife, slaving endlessly for my family. I didn't know yet what I wanted to do, but the list of things I didn't want grew daily.

What could I do? Back home, I could milk the cow, tend the fire, pluck weeds from the garden, feed the chickens, collect the eggs. But here? No cow. No fire. No garden. No chickens. In America, I was useless.

~

On a Saturday in July, Sylvia waited for me outside the factory. In Bratsyana, Saturday was a holy day, a day on which we refrained from work. In America, it was another day to earn a buck.

Sylvia bounced. "Come on!"

"I'm so tired."

"You'll wake up."

She grabbed my hand, and I moaned, wanting only to soak in Epsom salts and crawl into bed. She dragged me into an empty alleyway. "Look!" From her pocket, she drew a pack of Lucky Strikes.

"Where did you get that?" I snatched it from her, the soreness of my hands forgotten.

"I swiped it."

I opened the box. Twenty sticks poked out. I ran one under my nose. The smell was earthy, like the loam of the fields back home. "Matches?"

She passed me a booklet.

In my mouth, the cigarette drooped awkwardly while I used both hands to light the match. I cupped one hand around the end of the cigarette, as I'd seen my father do, bringing the flame closer. The tip crackled. How daring of me. How utterly American of me. I inhaled deeply.

Too deeply. The smoke spewed from my mouth. I coughed the cough of a tuberculous patient. It was as if someone had taken a flaming feather duster and shoved it down my throat, tickling me with fiery plumes from the inside.

"You okay?" Sylvia pounded my back, as if I were choking on gristle.

I held up a finger to indicate she should stop.

"I'm not choking," I managed to say between hacks. "Stop hitting me." With a few deep breaths, I composed myself. My mouth tasted ashy and metallic. "Your turn."

She looked at the cigarettes in her hand dubiously.

"C'mon."

"Do you feel anything?"

I considered. "No." I brought the cigarette up and inhaled again, this time more slowly. Still burned. Still coughed. But not as much.

Sylvia lit hers. She, too, hawked loudly.

On my third inhale, it still hurt, but I watched the smoke flow from my mouth. It danced daintily as it rose. On my next inhale, lightness cascaded through my body. My head was pleasantly wobbly.

"This isn't bad." Sylvia took another puff.

My throat was singed, but I wanted one more inhale. With practice, I thought, I could be a decent smoker.

As the cigarette reached my lips, a door in the alley banged open. Men's voices echoed in the narrow space.

"Quick, hide it." I stashed my cigarette behind my back, but Sylvia said, "No one cares what we do."

She would have been right if one of those three men hadn't been my father. He did business all over the Lower East Side. Just my luck he was doing business there that day. Could I run? Before I could escape, his eyes bored into mine. My stomach clenched. I dropped the cigarette.

"Minnie, what are you doing here?" He scrutinized me, then Sylvia, noticing the cigarette in her hand and the lit one at my feet. "What is that?" he roared.

He bent down and picked up the still-burning butt. "A cigarette?" He flicked it toward me. I dodged to keep it from hitting me. His face ferocious, he spit out a slew of Yiddish, as if he was too furious to formulate English words. "What kind of girl smokes? It's low class, disgusting. Did I raise a whore?"

My eyes widened. *Beg for forgiveness,* I thought, but what came out was, "You smoke!" Why was it okay for him but not for me? Sylvia gaped at me. I made shooing motions with my hand. She got the message and shot out of the alley.

Papa puffed his chest, as if readying to punch me, but one of the other men placed a hand on his arm. "Ike, she's a kid. Kids do this."

The man was lean, lanky, more boy than adult. Probably not much older than Max. Short. Like someone who'd be beaten up for protection money. And yet his hand stilled Papa.

Papa closed his eyes, and when he opened them, he was calmer. "I am a man. A provider. I smoke because work is hard and I need to relax."

"My work is hard too," I said. "I need to relax." The two men laughed. The second man was more substantial, with dark hair and caterpillar eyebrows over hooded eyes.

"Whatta you do?" asked the slender man.

"Cut fabric." I kicked the ground. "Ten hours a day. Till my hands are claws." I held up my hands squeezed into talons.

"I'd need smokes too," the second man said, his words thick, the accent muddled, Italian and Brooklyn.

Seeing an opportunity, I pounced. "If you'd let me work with you, Papa, I wouldn't need a cigarette at the end of the day."

"Why, you—" Papa's hands clenched into fists.

"She can work for us," the slender man said. Why wasn't he afraid of Papa?

"She's a girl." Papa seethed.

"This is America." I parroted the words he'd spoken to Mama, knowing the storm I would face but counting on the other men to prevent Papa from whaling on me. Later would be another story, but for now, I held my ground. "1921. Things are different."

"You wicked little—" Again Papa was stopped by the slender man.

In Yiddish, the slender man said, "Wasn't it Job who told us it's the wicked who prosper?" He switched to English. "Why shouldn't your daughter have her fair share?"

"Meyer—" Papa said.

Meyer interrupted him. "How much you make cutting fabric?"

"Eight dollars a week."

Meyer turned to Papa. "She can make more."

"Charlie." Desperation flooded Papa's voice as he turned to the larger man. "Talk some sense into him."

Charlie shrugged. "Meyer does what Meyer does."

"What's your name?" Meyer asked.

"Minnie."

"Minnie." He rubbed his chin. "Come by the cigar shop on Forsyth Street tomorrow morning, eight a.m."

"Really?" I peeked at Papa, scared to look him straight on.

Papa's lips pursed; his nostrils flared. "If Meyer says you can, you can."

"Thanks, Meyer!" I stood in awe of this younger man whom Papa obeyed.

"That's Mr. Lansky to you," Papa said.

"Mr. Lansky doesn't sit right," the young man said. "Call me Meyer. Or Lansky."

"Thank you"—I didn't dare use his first name again—"Lansky."

I shuffled, unsure what to do, until Papa hissed, "Shoo!" and I ran away as fast as I could.

Chapter Four

Another of Mama's sayings: anger and rage turn a man into a beast.

Papa's wrath would come.

At dinner, I picked at my food, waiting for the apartment door to fly open. Every noise from the hall sent me three feet into the air. Washing dishes, I dropped a plate, shattering it in the sink.

"Malka," Mama chided, "take more care."

Papa wasn't back at bedtime. I didn't regret that cigarette for one minute, but I definitely regretted allowing myself to be caught. I should have run as soon as I'd heard the alley door open.

I drifted in and out of sleep, alarmed by the tiniest of sounds: water running in the next apartment, the faint noises of the street, a sniffle from Max. I was too terrified to be excited about my new job.

At close to midnight, the front door slammed against the back wall. Papa bellowed, "Minnie Soffer, outta bed."

I leaped up.

"What's going on?" Mama asked.

"I have work tomorrow," Max said, burrowing under his sheets.

"So, apparently, does your sister," Papa said. "How dare you go over my head!"

"Work? What work?" Mama asked.

"Deliveries," he said.

"I'm sorry, Papa." I hunched my body, preparing for blows. I wasn't expecting what came next.

"Sit." He pulled out a kitchen chair.

My brow furrowed. I sat. Papa slammed a pack of cigarettes on the table. "Smoke," he ordered.

"Yitzhak!" Mama said.

"I caught her smoking this afternoon."

Mama clutched her chest.

"Smoke." Papa pointed to a new box of Chesterfields.

Slowly I opened the lid, undid the foil, and removed a cigarette, darting glances at Papa, waiting for him to stop me. What was he doing?

Papa lit the cigarette for me, with a sneer. "Inhale."

I did. The smoke scratched my already raw throat. I hacked like I had croup.

"Yitzhak, isn't this enough?"

"Inhale," he said again.

I inhaled again. The cigarette didn't taste as sweet as it had earlier that day.

"Keep going."

I smoked the whole cigarette. Ashes swirled through me, clogging my head, roiling my stomach.

"Another one."

"I can't."

"Yitzhak, please," Mama said. Max stared as if watching a picture show.

"Another one."

After my fifth cigarette, I bolted up. "I'm going to be sick."

He slapped his hands on my shoulders and pushed me back in the chair.

When I retched, it was not only on the kitchen table but on myself.

"Yitzhak!"

"Another." He refused to let Mama clean me.

The stench of vomit mixed with smoke made me heave again. My lungs had been sandpapered. My head couldn't have hurt more had I pounded it on a concrete wall. My heart beat so rapidly it threatened to leap out of my chest.

After an hour, Mama said, "Yitzhak, no more." Mama's stricken face was enough to stop Papa.

He snatched the pack after I'd finished my tenth cigarette. "You like smoking, do you?" he said.

I shook my head, bashing my brain against my skull.

"Don't ever do it again."

I nodded and stood to go back to bed, but Papa collared me and walloped my *tuchus* but good.

～

I was wide awake. Everything hurt: my skin burned like I'd extinguished the cigarettes on my arm, my eyes as if they'd been rinsed with bleach. Papa's wheezing gnawed at me like a mosquito. The heat threatened to smother me. My hair hung limply, reeking of smoke. My chest closed like a fist of anger.

I rose to use the toilet. Down the hall of the building was the shared lavatory. I peed and returned to the apartment.

Whistles of sleep greeted me as my eyes adjusted to the darkness. There, on the sideboard. Mama's sewing basket.

I winced as I caught a whiff of my hair. Papa hadn't let me bathe before going to bed.

I was twelve years old. Too old for Papa to be telling me what to do. The hell with Papa.

I seized Mama's sewing shears. Grabbing a hunk of my hair, I sliced. The blade didn't slide smoothly, so I hacked at the hair. A few minutes of sawing, and I held a ponytail's worth of my mane. I peered into the mirror by the door but saw no reflection in the dark. Someone fidgeted, and I froze. When the snores resumed, I continued. Soon my head lightened, a pile of hair in front of me. As silently as possible, I returned the scissors to the basket and gathered the fallen hair. I shoved the strands underneath my mattress. *I've shown him,* I thought, drifting to sleep.

~

Two hours later, I awoke to my mother yelling. "What is this? What is this mess?"

I didn't know what she meant, until I rolled over. A coolness wafted over my neck.

"Feige, calm down." Papa sat to wait for his coffee. "What's this on the table?"

"Exactly," Mama said. "What is this?"

"Horsehair?" Papa asked. "Why is there horsehair in the kitchen?"

I placed the pillow over my head.

No one said anything for a moment, and then Mama's voice roared to life. "This is no horsehair!"

A swift kick to the side of my mattress made me pull the pillow tightly around my head. "Malka Soffer, take that pillow off this instant."

I removed it. Max jolted up in bed.

Mama gasped. "*Oy vey iz mir!* Malka! What have you done? You are no better than the girls on the street corner. Your own children, they become your worst enemies." She took my chin in her hand and twisted my head to see all sides, tears bursting from her. "If your brother Anshel were alive to see this! What a disgrace."

I needed to humble myself. To beg for mercy.

But my anger at both of them flickered like the tip of a cigarette touched by the flame of a match. How dare Papa order me around? How dare Mama throw Anshel's name at me? Didn't we come to America to do as we pleased? "It's a free country." Speaking was painful, my throat shaved from the inside. "And it's my hair."

The vein in Papa's neck throbbed.

"Your hair?" Mama said. "Why you good-for-nothing little—" She lunged, her hand open to slap, but Max pulled me toward him.

24

"Mama, stop. It's just hair," Max said.

"Just hair? This godforsaken country where children think they know best. I'll show her who knows a thing or two."

"Feige!" Papa's voice thundered, silencing the room. His eyes pierced me. "Minnie, this insolence is becoming a habit with you. Fine. Have short hair. She looks like a stray dog. Going out with that hair is punishment enough."

Punishment? My hand stroked my head as I hurried to the mirror. I shrieked. I'd made a mess. Strands jutted at uneven angles, and with my natural wave, my hair ballooned from my head. Forget Irene Castle. I was Brownie the Wonder Dog.

"I can fix it." I reached for Mama's shears, but Papa slapped my hand.

"You will do no such thing. That hair stays. Go to work." Papa sat and lit a cigarette.

"I can't go to my new job like this!" I spit on my hand and tried to tame the flying pieces.

"Ah, but you'll have to." Papa sounded smug. "Out of here. Both of you."

Mama said, "But their breakfast, their lunches—"

"Off!"

And with no breakfast and no lunch, Max and I rushed out the door.

Chapter Five

When Max and I reached the sidewalk, he stopped, grabbing my arm.

"Ow!"

"Minnie, what are you doing? The guys Papa works for are not good guys."

"Whatta you mean?" The street buzzed with cars, horses, people. Yet New York, so noisy, so dirty, was growing on me.

"They're messed up in narcotics. Bootlegging. The protection racket."

I must have looked blank, because he said, "Drugs. Alcohol smuggling. Making people pay so you don't hurt them. All of it is illegal."

"I'm just working for that kid, Lansky."

"That *kid* is nineteen years old. You heard of the Bugs and Meyer Gang? Lansky is *that* Meyer. People get hurt."

The Bugs and Meyer Gang? Papa was in with them? I shuffled my feet. "So? Papa doesn't seem to mind."

"Papa's in as deep as they are."

I didn't want to admit that Max was scaring me. Papa had said, more than once, I couldn't work for his friends. But the factory was horrific, and whatever went on in Papa's world had to be better. "No one is going to hurt a girl. What's the worst that could happen?"

"Jail?"

"I'm twelve. No one is sending me to jail."

"You're twelve. You know nothing." He squeezed my arm tighter. "Minnie, turn around, go back to the factory, and cut fabric. It may be miserable, but it's legal."

"I'm not worried." I tossed back my shoulders. "I'm going to work."

I wrenched my arm from his grasp and stomped off. But as soon as Max was out of sight, I leaned on a wall and rubbed my sore arm. Was what he said true? Could I go to jail? Could Papa? Exactly *how* bad were these illegal activities?

Maybe Max was right. Maybe I should return to the factory.

But if I did, that would prove Papa right. That I couldn't do this kind of work. I'd never get another chance.

Papa was a smart man. If he thought it was safe to work with these men, then it must be safe for me.

I pushed myself from the wall and walked to my new job.

～

At the cigar store, I peered through the window. My throat still hurt, my head pounded, and I'd had so little sleep. The door flew open, nearly hitting me.

"You coming or what?" said a young guy with a newsboy cap.

No going back now. If I left, I'd forever be marked a chicken and truly be stuck at the factory. "I'm here for Lansky."

The boy laughed.

"I'm going to work for him." I crossed my arms and squinted, trying to look tough.

A double-chinned guy behind the counter said, "Didja hear that, Lefty? She's going to work for Lansky."

Lefty shook his head. "You're working for me."

"But—"

"You work for me. I work for him"—he indicated the other guy with his thumb—"and he works for Lansky. Got it?"

I choked back my misgivings. "Got it." Guess Max had been right. This guy Lansky wasn't just some kid.

"What's with your hair?" Lefty asked.

My hand reached up. I'd forgotten about the disaster of my hairdo. "Nothing," I mumbled. "What am I gonna do?"

"Definitely not modeling." The two of them chortled. "What's your name?"

"Minnie."

"Okay, Minnie. You're playing craps."

"Craps?" My skin tingled, and I woke up a bit. Boys played craps on almost every street corner. It was a game. I'd be doing it as a job?

The guy behind the counter said, "A girl? You sure 'bout this?"

Lefty shrugged. "I'm not sure about anything. But guys'll figure if a Jane can win, they can win."

"My name's Minnie."

"I know your name."

Sometimes my English still failed me. Especially the slang.

"Okay, time to teach you how to win at craps."

~

The swindle was perfect. The first person to play won. Easy money. Crowds would form. Coins and bills tossed down. When the first gambler stepped away, boys would clamor to be next.

My job? I was that first person. By switching the dealer's dice with a pair of weighted dice, I rolled winners. After my turn, those wins didn't come as easily. Every few hours I moved to a different game—there were hundreds of them—jumping in to be a winner, showing there was money to be made.

I'd had no idea street craps were organized. Every game on every corner of the Lower East Side was run by Lansky or someone like Lansky. One of his men would show up, stand at the edge of the circle, and collect money from the dealer.

Working craps was a first-rate job. Not only was I outside, but the jack was swell. The craps dealer let me keep my winnings, so I made two to three bucks a day. Way better than the eight dollars a week at that job that turned my hands into claws. Each night I handed most of my pay to Mama, who thought I was making deliveries, but I'd keep a quarter for myself.

My job lasted exactly five days.

~

Late Thursday morning, I knelt on Hester Street, shaking my dice, playing the part of someone hoping to win big. The chatter quieted. My money was on the pass line. I rolled the dice. A four and a three. A winner. Yet when I glanced up to crow about my luck, all I saw were backs. Feet stampeded, and everyone scattered.

"What's going—"

A hand clamped down on my neck.

"Well, what do we have here?" The voice was Irish and languid.

He lifted me off the ground, like a cat picking up a mouse he'd just killed.

A cop.

My stomach wrenched as if a hundred pairs of dice were being thrown in it.

"What's your name?" he asked.

How was I the only one caught? Every one of them had run like they'd been tipped off.

"He asked you your name." A second cop, also Irish.

"Bertha Klein."

"Bertha, is it?" The cop smirked at the other, who gave him a nod.

"Okay, Bertha Klein, let's get you home."

"Home?" The thought of what Mama would do to me made me hope they'd take me to jail. "I'm not telling you where I live." I couldn't puff up my chest because of the way he held me, but I sounded defiant. My insides, though, were shakier than Mama's calf-foot jelly.

"You don't have to, Bertha Klein. Everyone knows how to find Ike Soffer."

Ike Soffer? He knew Papa? My brain swirled as I tried to make sense of how he knew I wasn't Bertha Klein.

The cop cackled as he led me away.

~

Oddly, both Mama and Papa were there when the copper half dragged me up the stairs and tossed me into the apartment.

Mama paled. "What's going on?" she asked in Yiddish.

"Can I help, Officer?" Papa spoke in English.

"Collared this one gambling."

Mama wrung a dish towel, the veins in her arms popping.

"Thank you, Officer," Papa said. "I can take it from here." Papa stuck out his hand to shake. My eyes narrowed as I caught sight of a bill passing from Papa to the cop. So that's how the cops knew who I was. Why everyone else had known to run. I'd been outsmarted. By Papa. I was furious. And, I admitted, a bit impressed.

"Yitzhak, what did she do?"

In Yiddish, Papa said, "Apparently, Minnie is now a low-life gambler."

"That's not true." My jaw clenched. It wasn't gambling if you knew you'd win. And low life? I worked for the same men he did.

Yet I cowered at the look Papa shot me. "She gets a little extra money, it seems, and she spends it on craps. All that time she has between deliveries."

"That's it," Mama said. "You're not working that job anymore. Back to the factory tomorrow and straight home after." For the first time I questioned whether Mama knew what Papa did. Papa had lied, said I was making deliveries when he knew I was playing craps. He clearly didn't want her to know. What else didn't she know?

"But—"

"But nothing," Papa said. "Listen to your mother. You're lucky they didn't haul you to jail. You should be getting a *potch* on the *tuchus*, but I'm feeling generous." Then in English, he said, "I take it you've learned not to cross your father?"

With a smirk, he put on his hat and strutted out.

Mama *potched* my *tuchus* anyway.

~

Cutting fabric. No more freedom. Hair like a wet dog's. Sylvia had offered to trim it, but I hadn't dared.

I was not having a great week.

On Sunday, though, at breakfast, Papa sighed. Setting down his paper, he said, "Let's go."

"Where are we going?" I asked.

"I'm tired of looking at that horror."

I followed Papa out of the apartment and onto the street.

As we walked, I said, "I was good at that job."

"I know."

"Then why did you stop me?"

"Minnela, it's a dangerous game."

"Craps?"

"The *Undzer Shtik*."

"Huh?"

"The men who run this business are not to be trusted. You're too innocent. You trust too easily."

"But you trust them."

"I do *not* trust them. But they pay well, and I know how to watch my back."

31

I thought of what Max said about people getting hurt. I glanced up at Papa, worried something could happen to him, but before I could ask, he stopped in front of a barbershop.

"C'mon." A bell jangled when Papa opened the door.

A barber trimmed the sideburns of one man while another waited. The three men chattered about Babe Ruth—would he break his own record?—but when they noticed us, a hush fell. The barber's hands dropped.

"Mr. Soffer." The barber's eyes blinked rapidly. "I wasn't expecting you till next week."

"Relax, Sam. I'm not here for that." Papa placed a hand on my shoulder. "My daughter needs a haircut."

The man in the chair, who had only had one sideburn sheared, sprang up. "I can wait."

Papa smiled. "Kind of you." He patted my head. "Hop up."

I crept over, unsure if this was a trick. I knew how it went: Children last. Always. But no one stopped me as I climbed into a chair dusted with tufts of dark hair.

The barber asked, "What do you want?"

"A Castle bob."

The barber waited for Papa's nod before grabbing scissors.

What to make of this? These men spoke with New York accents. They carried themselves like Americans. Yet they deferred to Papa, with his thick Yiddish accent.

The barber pulled and tugged and cut. Tiny wisps danced, floating to the floor. I'd never had a haircut in a shop.

After fifteen minutes, the barber set down his shears and spread brilliantine through my hair. His hand trembled. "Do you like it?" He spoke to Papa, not me.

I hardly recognized the face in the mirror. The girl reflected was almost attractive. My nose was a little broad and my teeth too big, but the short hair highlighted the angles of my face. "And how," I said. The difference in appearance was the difference between each side of the fence at Ellis Island. No longer did I belong with the headscarved and sidelocked immigrants; I clearly stood on the side of shaved faces and flowery hats.

In the mirror, Papa's eyes found mine. "Well, I'll be. You look American."

American? I wanted to sit there all day gazing at myself, but Papa helped me from the chair.

"How much do I owe you?" Papa asked.

"Nothing, Mr. Soffer. On the house."

Papa tipped his hat. "Kind of you, Sammy." He led me to the door. "I'll see you in a week."

"Of course, Mr. Soffer," the barber stammered.

Walking down the street, I shook my head, enjoying the airiness.

"You keep doing that, your head's going to fall off."

I kept shaking. "Why didn't you have to pay for my haircut?"

"He was showing his gratitude."

"For what?"

"I protect him. Mr. Rothstein and I, we make sure nothing happens to his shop. It's a service he pays for."

That didn't sound so bad.

"What about Mr. Lansky?"

"He works for Mr. Rothstein too." Papa put his arm around my shoulders, and I understood all had been forgiven. "You didn't cry."

"Over a haircut?"

"Over the cigarettes. You got sick. You got angry. But you didn't cry." He ruffled my hair, and I worried he'd muss it. "You've got a bit of your papa's toughness in you." He peered down his nose at me. "Unfortunately you also have some of your papa's stubbornness. You'll need to watch that." He gave me a little squeeze. "Come, my Minnela. An American girl like you needs an American treat. Let's get an ice cream."

I floated down the street, like an American.

Chapter Six

In the fall of 1921, Mama started humming. Sweet Yiddish melodies filled the apartment. When Papa heard her, he said, "You're humming."

"Am I?"

"The last time you hummed as you worked . . ." Papa tilted his head in my direction.

Mama pecked his cheek with a sly smile.

"Oh, Feigela." Papa pulled her in and kissed her in a way that made me need to leave the room.

We'd moved into a better apartment, one with two bedrooms beside the front parlor and the kitchen, plus our own toilet. I'd entered sixth grade, only a year behind other twelve-year-olds, and Max was in ninth. Mama had stopped working as Papa's job had expanded. Mr. Rothstein had given him a bigger territory to cover, more responsibility. We now had chicken every Friday. And not the scrawny ones either.

Mama glided with a new calm. At times she'd stare into the distance, hand resting on her stomach, lips curved, as if thinking of a joke only she knew. When I questioned her, she beamed and said, "You will understand soon enough."

The photo of our family from the Old World sat by Mama's bed. She began carrying it with her as she did her chores, narrating her day, a one-sided conversation with Anshel. "Anshel, see all the marvelous food your father has provided for us." "Anshel, Shmerka received a one hundred on his history test." Sometimes it seemed Mama spoke to my dead brother more than she spoke to us.

The day before we had left Bratsyana, Mama had gone out alone. Out of boredom I had followed her. The mixture of snow and rain made the ground slushy. She held up her skirt as she trudged, a doomed attempt to keep it unsoiled. My boots sucked up mud, soaking the layers of newspaper stuffed where the soles had worn away. We headed, I realized, toward the cemetery. I dodged behind trees, but Mama muttered prayers as she walked, oblivious to me.

At the desolate ground, where grave markers listed, as if ready to be toppled by the slightest breeze, Mama placed a small rock upon her father's grave to ward off the golems and the demons. She closed her eyes and silently moved her lips before turning to the smaller grave beside it. She rubbed the gravestone, stroking it like the cheek of a baby. She cried. "A mother doesn't desert her child. My Anshel. I will never forgive myself for leaving you behind."

Anshel's face had faded in my memory. The typhoid had taken him quickly, when he was about seven. Mama missed Anshel fiercely. Sometimes she'd hug me so tightly my breath would catch, as if that might keep me from perishing too.

$\sim$

Now, though, Mama radiated joy. To add to her happiness, Uncle Aaron arrived in America. The reunion between Mama and her younger brother was a noisy affair. Mama wanted him to move in with us—"We have all this room now. Two entire bedrooms!"—but he moved to the Upper West Side with a friend from his old yeshiva. He might as well have lived in California for how long it took to travel there from the Lower East Side. Uncle Aaron found a job with a shoemaker and took evening classes at City College. Yet every Friday he made the trek to our apartment for Shabbos dinner. When the five of us sat at the table, I thought Mama would burst with pride.

But, as Mama often said, pride lies on the dung heap. Papa's work took up more time. Instead of visiting shops during the day, he was doing deliveries at all hours. A phone was installed so Papa could run when needed. Mama gave the phone a wide berth, as if fearing a dybbuk might leap from it. Papa stayed out until late at night, missed Shabbos dinners, ran with men she called questionable.

Yet things remained harmonious until mid-December, when Max and I arrived from school to find Mama in bed. That alone was cause for alarm—Mama never rested. She lay on her side, clutching her stomach, keening in pain.

"Bring Mrs. Oberman." The words were barely more than gasps.

"I'll go," Max said before I could volunteer. He flew out the door, his footsteps clomping down the stairs.

I slipped my hand in Mama's. She clutched mine hard. I bit my lip to keep from crying out. Whatever wave of pain gripped her passed.

"Oh, Malka," she said.

I brushed the hair from her forehead with my free hand. "Sh, sh, Mama."

"My Malkala," she said. "What a wonderful mother you will make."

After what felt like hours but probably wasn't more than twenty minutes, Max returned with Mrs. Oberman. Until that moment, I hadn't wondered why she'd called Mrs. Oberman, a midwife, instead of a doctor. The midwife hurried in, shooing me out of the room. Max left to search for Papa.

Mrs. Oberman didn't stay for long. "Minnie," she said. "I'm sorry. I can't save it."

"Save what?"

"The baby."

Baby?

"Your mother needs rest. You need to care for her."

I poured Mama a cup of tea, but my hands shook, and it splashed my dress. With a deep breath, I tried again, returning to Mama with the tea and a damp cloth so I could wipe her tears away.

~

That's when the humming stopped. That's when Mama and Papa fought in earnest. Mama didn't like Papa's job: the late hours Papa kept, the nature of his work, the company he associated with. It confused me: Would Mama prefer no Friday-night chickens and a drearier apartment? Wasn't she happy Papa's job meant she no longer had to work? I, for one, was relieved to be out of that factory. That, to me, was worth whatever he was doing.

The fiercest fights came after Shabbos. Mama cooked from Thursday afternoon right up until sunset on Friday, the eggy scent of challah and the soothing aroma of chicken soup reminding me of home. Before dinner, Mama sent Max to the synagogue to drop a few coins in the *tzedakah* box. Uncle Aaron would arrive, minutes before the lighting of the candles. Mama and I made the blessing over the flames, and then we'd idle, hoping the door would open, that Papa would appear. Mama and Uncle Aaron discussed his classes, his work. He always had a new cut on his hand for Mama to bandage or glue on his shirt for Mama to remove.

As dusk turned to darkness, we'd sit for dinner without Papa. Uncle Aaron recited the blessings in Papa's stead: kiddush over the wine, *hamotzi* over the bread. After the last bite of apple mohn, he led us in *benching*, the after-dinner prayers. Mama gazed at her younger brother with adulation, and when he left, so did the little of her good cheer.

I longed for the happy Mama to return.

Chapter Seven

On a chilly Friday in April, Mama and I welcomed in the Sabbath. As I guided the match to the Shabbos candles, the front door opened. In walked Papa.

"Home on Shabbos?" Mama said.

"Home on Shabbos," he said.

"Who knew? Miracles do happen."

Instead of gruffly making a snide remark about miracles and religion, Papa surprised me; he caressed Mama's cheek. "Sometimes they do."

Mama nudged me back to attention. We waved our hands over the flames to welcome in the light of the Sabbath before covering our eyes and saying the prayer that sanctified the holy day.

Papa stood at the head of the table and lifted the wineglass. When he sang the prayers in his baritone, the sound slid all the way into my toes.

If you had asked me if I remembered living in Bratsyana before Papa left, I'd have said of course not. Yet when he chanted the prayers, I was transported. I pictured us at the table: me, Max, Anshel, Mama, Papa, Bubbe, and Zayde. The wood walls, the draft from the windows, the scent of snow, Papa reciting these exact words in that exact tone, with a bearded face and short side curls.

When the prayer ended, Papa moved to the sink to perform the handwashing ritual before blessing the challah. He ripped off a hunk, dunked it in salt, and ate it. The loaf passed to each of us, and we did the same.

When the bread returned to him, Papa tore off more. "Ah, Feige. No one bakes a challah like you."

To hide her blush, Mama busied herself serving the mushroom barley soup. In the center of the table, she lay chicken, cabbage, and lokshen kugel.

We dove in. Papa chatted with Uncle Aaron about his apprenticeship, Max about school, me about the books I was reading. He lavished praise upon the food.

Mama twitched she was so curious. Finally she asked, "So, Yitzhak, to what do we owe this visit?"

"Visit?" He laughed. "I live here, you know." Papa poured a generous serving of the sweet wine. Drinking for religious purposes was permitted during Prohibition.

"Go slow on that," Mama said. "Wine is difficult to come by."

Max and I exchanged glances. In Papa's world, wine wasn't hard to find.

Papa drank a healthy swallow. "I have news."

"News? What news? Did someone die? Did Mr. Rothstein fire you? Don't keep me in suspense, Yitzhak!"

"Why do you always jump to the worst? I've good news."

"So tell us!"

Papa's voice boomed. "I am trying to!"

Mama threw her hands into the air, as if to say, Who's stopping you?

"I'm going into business for myself." Papa cut his chicken.

"For yourself? Doing what? Driving your own car?"

"Think bigger, Feige. I've bought a soda shop."

"A soda shop? What on earth do you know about a soda shop?"

He knew nothing of soda shops.

"In my work for Mr. Rothstein, I've encountered a number of businesses and have had a chance to learn about them. A soda shop makes sense."

"It's an existing shop you've purchased?" Uncle Aaron asked.

"More or less."

"What does *more or less* mean?" Mama's fork froze midair.

"It means the structure is there. I need to bring it to life."

"So it's a soda shop that failed?"

Papa threw down his napkin. "Feige, I know what I'm doing."

"How are you paying for this soda shop?"

"I borrowed money from Mr. Rothstein."

Mama gasped. "You borrowed money? Borrow brings sorrow. What if you don't make enough to pay him back?"

"I'll make enough."

"I want to see this soda shop."

Papa smiled. "I expected nothing less."

～

On Sunday, Mama ordered us into our Shabbos clothes.

"Do I have to?" I tugged at the bottom of the dress, which was short for me, as I'd grown another inch. "We're looking at a building."

"We're looking at your papa's new business."

He'd worked the previous night—until the shop was successful, he'd continue his job with Mr. Rothstein—but Papa met us at the apartment, his grin not quite masking his fatigue.

Together we paraded to the shop, Papa in the lead, Mama right behind him, puffed up like a Passover popover.

A broad plate glass window declaring Baxter Street Sodas revealed a narrow store, with a steel counter and five high stools. Two small tables with metal chairs perched in the front.

The soda shop was real? Papa was going legit?

"The soda shop used to be part of the drugstore next door, but when the owner died, he left it to his two sons. The boys didn't get along. They split the store in two."

"Tsk-tsk," Mama said. "Like Solomon splitting the baby."

"Precisely. The brother who owned the soda shop tired of New York. He sold it and moved to California." Papa jangled the keys. "What are we waiting for? Come inside."

We filed into the store. Mama ran her finger over surfaces and knocked on the counter and walls. "Could use a scrubbing. Too bad it's not bigger."

"When the stock arrives, we'll open."

"I'll come this week and clean it."

"No, Feige, I couldn't ask you to do that." Papa's voice rang with insincerity.

"Of course I will." She turned and spread her arms. "See, children? See what happens when you work hard and save your money?" No one reminded her that Papa had taken out loans, that he could no more save money than sprout wings and fly. "You can own your own business. This is what we came to America for." To Papa, she said, "Let me check behind the counter."

~

After dinner, as Max and I lay in our beds, I asked, "Is Papa really running a soda shop?"

Max rolled on his side and propped himself on his elbow. "I can't imagine."

"What do you think he's doing?"

"Something illegal."

"Yes, but what?"

"Laundering money. Selling drugs. Taking bets."

"Or fronting a speakeasy!" I bolted up. "Do you think it could be a speakeasy?"

"What do you know of speakeasies?"

"I saw that picture show. The Mack Sennett one. A speakeasy would be the butterfly's boots."

"It most certainly would not." He slid to my mattress. "Minnie, Papa's work is illegal. He could end up in jail."

"Papa's too smart for that." Papa was the cleverest person I could imagine.

"No one is too smart for that."

"You don't like Papa much, do you?"

Max sighed. "I love him. But his work scares me. When I did deliveries, I saw things."

"Like what?"

"Drugs."

"Oh." I ripped off a cuticle, leaving a small trail of blood. "Papa doesn't take the drugs, does he?"

"No, but I delivered them. The guys put them in a violin case and sent me off, because no one stops a kid with a violin. If I'd been caught . . ." He closed his eyes and took a deep breath. "People get hurt in this business, Min. When I grow up, I'm going to be a lawyer. Make sure things are right in the world."

"If you become a lawyer, you can defend Papa if he has trouble."

Max returned to his bed. "No, Min. When I'm a lawyer, I'm going to help innocent people."

"How will you know they're innocent?" What was *innocent*, anyway? We both had school friends who stole penny candy. Sylvia regularly pinched things from the store. I occasionally spied a pushcart seller placing a finger on the scale. Leibe from downstairs said he was fourteen so he could quit school and start working, but he was only eleven. Did this make them bad people? Not innocent?

But Max had crawled under the covers and turned his back to me, the conversation apparently over.

∼

For the next week, Mama spent every day at the tiny soda shop, dusting and mopping and polishing until the chrome sparkled and the glass twinkled.

While Mama scoured, Papa hired a soda jerk and ordered barrels of ice cream and seltzer, and soon a grand opening sign beckoned the neighborhood folks. Mama beamed from the sidewalk.

"Look at all the customers," Mama said. "We'll make a living with this store."

"Indeed." Papa picked up Mama's hand and kissed it. "Indeed."

~

On a Sunday morning, I sat at the table, grumbling about homework.

Papa emerged from their bedroom. "I'm headed to the store." He pecked Mama on the cheek. Ever since the store had opened, he and Mama had gotten along better, touched more, kissed when they thought we weren't watching.

A minute after Papa left, I hopped up. "I almost forgot. Sylvia needs me to return her book."

Mama stood at the stove and waved her hand, dismissing me. I ran out the front door, no book in hand. I leaped down the stairs, two at a time, then headed toward Baxter Street. Within a few blocks, breathless, I spotted Papa. Trying to stay hidden, I shadowed him to the store. Sure enough, he walked past the soda shop and down the alley.

The alley held no cover, so I was exposed when Papa turned to unlock the door. "Minnie!" His eyes shone with fury. "Go home. Now!"

"I want to see the bar." It was a gamble, but one I was willing to take.

"Who said anything about a bar?"

"I'm no dumb Dora," I said. "I can figure things out."

"You can, can you?"

"Please? I want to see what a bar looks like." We had arrived in America just in time for Prohibition, when drinking went underground.

On the street, boys talked about making their own coffin varnish or where to buy the cheap stuff. Occasionally one would make it inside a joint, but for a girl, it was near impossible to get in.

"How old are you?"

"Thirteen in two weeks." I threw back my shoulders, trying to stand taller. "In the old country, I'd practically be married now."

He chuckled. "That's not exactly how it worked." He put his key in the lock, and I deflated until he said, "If your mother learns of this place . . . well, I wouldn't want to be you if your mother learns about this place." He opened the door. "*Nu?* You coming?"

I bubbled with excitement. "Hell, yes!"

With a half smile, he held the door.

We walked into a black corridor, where he unlocked another door. It swung to reveal a dark room that didn't illuminate much more when he flipped a light switch.

I'd seen bars in movies. Speakeasies with glitter and shine. Chrome counters, fancy-dressed bartenders, flappers flirting with sheiks, the tinkle of fine crystal.

This was not one of those establishments. This was a gritty gin joint, a blind pig, with peanut shells and sawdust littering the ground. My feet stuck to the floor as I walked farther in. Behind the plywood bar was a row of bottles, glistening under a pale bulb. A few rickety chairs and tables dotted the room. It smelled sour, yeasty, like Mama's bread dough.

I loved it.

I wandered the room, touching everything: the tables, the chairs, the bar. At the counter, I looked at Papa, and he nodded, so I slipped behind it. The bottles were cool to the touch, as the basement held the chill of spring. I grabbed a balled-up apron and pulled it over my head. I placed both hands on the bar and leaned toward Papa. "So." I used a gruff, deep voice. "What'll you have?"

The front door opened, startling me. The word *illegal* flashed in my mind, so I hunched, trying to make myself small.

The man spotted me. "Replacing me already, Ike?"

I stood back up.

"Riley, this is my daughter, Minnie. Minnie, this is my barkeep, Riley."

"How do you do." I didn't say his name because I remembered how Papa had yelled when I'd called Mr. Lansky by his first name. Riley was short and compact with pitted skin and beady eyes.

"Minnie was about to pour me a drink."

Riley joined me behind the bar. "A whisper sister in the making." Something in his tone made me take a small step back.

"What's a whisper sister?"

"A woman who runs a bar," Papa said. "So, my little whisper sister, I'll have a bourbon. Neat."

I took umbrage. "I can pour without spilling." My tone would have earned me a slap from Mama, but here it only made Papa snicker. I liked this place.

Riley handed me a bottle of brown liquor and a short glass. "Neat means straight up, no ice, no mixers."

I pulled the cork from the bottle and tilted it over the glass. The booze gushed out. Riley said, "Whoa!" while Papa said, "Trying to get me blotto?"

Riley took the bottle from me. He held up the glass. "See where the design changes?" I nodded. "Stop pouring at the line."

I'd filled the cup to the brim, as if it were a juice cup.

Papa pushed the overfull glass toward me. "Would you like to have this one, Minnie?"

"Would I!"

Riley pulled out another short glass and filled it a third of the way. He gave that one to Papa. Papa lifted his glass to clink with mine, like they did in the movies.

"Cheers," I said, and he replied, "*L'chaim*."

I gulped the liquor as if I were drinking the sweet Shabbos wine. Half went down my throat like a lit match. The other half I spit on the counter.

"Watch it!" Riley jumped back as I spewed bourbon.

"What was that?" I stuck my tongue out as if I could sputter out the fire.

Riley and Papa both reeled in laughter. "That is bourbon." Papa caught his breath. "You sip it." He demonstrated. "Try again."

I didn't want to try again, but I didn't want him to think I was a cream puff. I picked up the glass and took a sniff. The odor singed my nostrils. I sipped the barest of sips. The alcohol was still fiery, but in a more pleasant, warming way. I drank a little more. Tasted like burning rubber. If I held my breath, the bitterness was less harsh. I moved to take another swallow, but Papa touched my hand. "Nurse it." At my confused expression, he said, "Drink slowly. Take time between swallows."

I counted to three out loud. "Long enough?" I drank without waiting for an answer, once again sending Papa and Riley into guffaws.

"Minnie, you have three servings in there."

I drank more.

Riley said, "Quite the family resemblance, Ike. She drinks like you."

I liked the comparison. "In the movies, people have cocktails with fancy names."

"Mixers mask the flavor of the alcohol, so you can't be sure what's in it. With straight bourbon I know what I'm drinking, even if what I'm drinking isn't very good. Trust no one. Especially when booze is involved."

I nodded, drank more, and decided I, too, would drink my bourbon neat when I had the chance to drink again.

The bourbon didn't sting as much. My body turned into a balloon, airy and light. I drank more.

"You're going to wish later you'd nursed that," Papa warned.

"Why?"

He shook his head.

Papa let me finish my drink before shooing me off. "I've work to do. Remember, not a word to your mother." He stroked his mustache. "Maybe don't mention it to your brother either."

Not tell Max? I told Max everything. But if Papa wanted it to be a secret, I'd keep it a secret. The bar was just mine and Papa's.

My steps were buoyant, my limbs loose on my walk to the apartment. I smiled and waved to folks on the street before skipping up the stairs. A whisper sister. Perhaps that was the job for me.

"How are Sylvia's parents?" Mama asked when I walked in.

"Lovely. Simply lovely."

Mama shot me a queer look. "Do your homework."

I sat across from Max, who scrutinized me.

Focusing was difficult, the letters in my reader dancing across the page, so I took the book into the bedroom to read lying down. After a few minutes, my eyelids were too heavy to stay open.

～

I woke up a few hours later, feeling not so buoyant. Or loose. Or sweet. My stomach churned, and a hundred tap dancers shim-shammed in my skull.

I groaned as I tried to prop myself up.

Max raised his head from the book he was reading in bed. "Bet you feel good now."

"Whatta ya mean?"

He made a dramatic show of sniffing. "You reek of booze."

I groaned again.

"Here." On the table next to the bed, he'd set a glass of water and headache powder and on the floor a soup pot. "Where'd you get the stuff? Sylvia?"

"Don't tell Mama, okay?" Best he think it came from Sylvia. I had a promise to keep.

47

"I won't. You were passed out. I told her you'd had fish that tasted funny at Sylvia's. So when you throw up, she won't be suspicious."

"Throw up?" The minute the words were out of my mouth, a cold sweat gripped my neck, and my midsection convulsed. I must have turned green, because Max grabbed the pot and held it as I emptied the contents of my stomach.

"Oh, Minnie. At least you've learned your lesson."

Oh, I'd learned my lesson all right. Fill a bourbon glass a third of the way. No mixers. Nurse the drink.

But Max didn't need to know any of that. "I have, Max. I really have."

Chapter Eight

That summer, Mama's humming returned. This time, I understood why she hummed, why she cradled her stomach.

My own body also underwent a change. Over the previous year, my torso stretched and lengthened as my hips and bosom blossomed. On an August afternoon, sweat drenched me, even between my legs. When I went to the bathroom, the grisly scene greeting me brought a scream to my lips.

Mama hurried over. When she spotted the soiled panties, she slapped my cheek and cried, "Mazel tov! You're a woman. May you be blessed with health and fertility." She took my chin in her hand, her eyes turning ferocious. "Don't open your legs until you're married. Don't bring shame upon yourself and your family." Then she hugged me. I was so confused.

She taught me how to use rags in my knickers, and that was the end of it.

Two days later, on a Sunday, Sylvia and I sat at her kitchen table, a Ouija board she'd received for her birthday between us.

"What do we ask?"

"Whatever you want," Sylvia said.

The questions I needed answers for weren't ones I could say, not even to Sylvia. *Will Papa go to jail for his bar? Will Mama keep this baby? Why do I need to keep my legs closed?* "Um . . ."

"I'll go first," she said. We put our hands on the planchette. "Will I marry someone rich?"

Our hands slid around the board. I wasn't sure if it moved on its own or if Sylvia guided it, but she chirped in glee when it landed on yes.

"Your turn."

The pins holding the rag to my undergarment poked, making me fidget.

"What's up with you?" Sylvia asked. "You're jitterier than a street bum without hooch."

"This thing . . . happened."

Sylvia put her elbows on the table. "Yes?"

"I have to wear this rag, because . . ."

"Oh." Sylvia sat back, interest lost. "You got your period."

"My what?"

"Your period."

"You know about this?"

Sylvia squinted. "You don't know about this?"

I shook my head.

"You know how babies are made?"

I shook my head again. "Do you?"

"Okay, listen." Sylvia told me a tale that sounded as wild as Mama's *bubbe-meise* stories. It involved the private parts of men and women and bleeding once a month.

"Once a month!"

"Every month."

"How do you know all this?"

"From Sadie." Sylvia's older half sister lived in Newark. Sylvia's father, Mr. Goldwasser, had been a widow when he'd married Mrs. Goldwasser. Sadie was grown and wed before I had met Sylvia. "She also taught me how to use Kotex."

"Kotex?"

"You've seen the ads in magazines, haven't you?"

I had. But I hadn't understood what they were for.

"Hold on." She disappeared into her room, then returned with a strange belt with tabs hanging down and a box. "This is a sanitary belt. You wear it around your waist and fasten Kotex to it. When it's soiled, you toss out the Kotex." She demonstrated how it pinned into place. "You need one of these."

"I don't have any money."

"We'll nick one."

I'd never stolen anything before, but I wanted to try this Kotex. As we walked, I scrutinized people on the street. Did they all know about . . . well, the things Sylvia had described?

At a ladies' store Sylvia guarded while I grabbed a sanitary belt and stuck it under my shirt. Sylvia browsed through a rack before saying loudly, "I don't see anything I like," and we slipped out. I'd stolen!

"Okay," Sylvia said. "Now Kotex."

We giggled our way to a drugstore a few blocks down, where the druggist didn't know us. "Kotex is kept on the counter."

"How will we get it?"

"Leave this to me."

The druggist stood behind the counter, helping a customer. When his back turned, Sylvia sidled up and placed her hand on the counter near a stack of Kotex. A sign read **5 CENTS EACH; 60 CENTS A BOX.**

Her hand slipped off, a napkin in it. The druggist hadn't noticed.

With an exhale, I walked to the door, but before I could leave, a hand clamped on my shoulder. "Looks like your friend forgot to pay."

The druggist apparently had an assistant.

Fear billowed through my veins. I stood as still as if I'd been cast in iron.

Sylvia tried to discreetly drop the Kotex, but the assistant saw her. "That's five cents."

"We don't have the money." Sylvia stared at her shoes.

"Who's your father?"

Sylvia looked at me. I looked at Sylvia. Which one of us would crack first? My eyes blinked rapidly. I knew the answer, as much as I didn't like it. She had stolen for me. I should take the fall. I said, "My father is Ike Soffer."

The druggist and the assistant exchanged an undecipherable look.

"I'll phone your father," the druggist said.

He put us in a corner while he called the number I'd given him. The whole store heard his side of the conversation. I'd never felt more ashamed.

Twenty minutes later, Papa roared in.

"What were you thinking?" he yelled at me in Yiddish.

I was too frightened to respond.

"What were you stealing?"

"Kotex," I whispered.

"What?"

"Kotex."

I'd never seen my father at a loss for words. Was he blushing? He stammered before getting out, "Couldn't your mother take care of this?"

"She wants me to . . ." I couldn't complete the sentence, too mortified to discuss such things with Papa.

He tapped his foot while I squirmed. At last, he pulled coins from his pocket. "Buy what you need."

Without lifting my eyes from the floor, I handed the druggist coins. He handed me a bag with a box of twelve inside. I didn't dare look anyone in the face.

"Mr. Soffer, out of respect to you, we didn't call the police," the druggist said.

"Thank you for letting me handle this."

"Of course, Mr. Soffer."

Papa pushed us out of the store. To Sylvia, he said, "Beat it."

Sylvia sprinted without looking back.

"You always seem to get yourself in trouble with that one." He held me by the upper arm. He walked fast enough that I was dragged along. "The only thing worse than a thief is a thief who gets caught. Now I owe them a favor." He gestured toward the heavens with his free hand. "Like I need a *ganef* for a daughter."

Shame made my limbs heavy. I forced back tears because I knew I had to be tough, just like Papa.

"This doesn't happen again, you hear me?"

I nodded.

"Say it."

"This won't happen again."

"We won't tell your mother about this. She has enough troubles without this *balagan*."

"Yes, Papa."

"What will I do with a daughter such as you?" he mumbled.

~

The next morning, he woke me early. "Come."

I clambered out of bed and threw on my clothes. In the bathroom, I slid the belt over my waist and pinned on a fresh napkin. As all American women did.

"Let's go," Papa said.

"Where are we going?"

He responded by walking out. I hurried after him. We didn't go far, only to the corner drugstore.

The bell tinkled as Papa opened the door.

"Mr. Soffer," the druggist said. "What can I do for you today?"

"Mr. Aaronson. You know my daughter, Minnie?"

"I do indeed."

"I'd like for her to be able to shop on credit. Whatever she needs, the bill is sent to me."

"Of course, Mr. Soffer."

Papa turned to me. "That works?"

I grinned. No more rags. "That works."

~

The end of the summer whizzed by. Papa, over Mama's protests, allowed me to buy dresses better suited for a young lady, the loose ones that skimmed my hips, stopping shy of my knees. Mama was too busy with her humming to put much bite into her arguments.

The tranquility lasted through the fall.

Once again, Mrs. Oberman was called.

Once again, the humming stopped.

Chapter Nine

Fall 1923

Life moved in fits and bursts: slowly, then quickly, and then slowly again. Mama fluttered in a dither because Uncle Aaron made a *shidduch*, a match, and everything had to be just so. On a Thursday in October, after Sukkos, Mama scrubbed my skin raw before forcing me into an emerald green dress with ruffles down the front that she had sewed for the occasion.

In his work car, Papa drove us to the Upper West Side to witness Uncle Aaron marrying our new aunt. Aunt Sara, soft spoken and American born, beamed dewy eyed at Uncle Aaron. In the rabbi's chambers, the two married under the chuppah. Aunt Sara's parents hosted the wedding dinner at their apartment. Mama blazed with pride, her younger brother with an education, a job, and a wife. It was what she wanted for me and Max. Mama splurged on the gift, a bone china creamer-and-sugar set fancier than anything we owned. The only sorrow was that Uncle Aaron no longer made the trek to the Lower East Side for Shabbos dinner; he spent the Sabbath with his wife and her family.

~

In late January, Mama grew skittish. Nervous. Every slam of a door in the hall startled her. When we shopped, her head jerked at the screech of cars. She went to bed earlier, took naps in the afternoons, and moved sluggishly. A red ring appeared on her thumb.

"Where did that come from?" Mama didn't wear jewelry other than her plain gold wedding band.

"I borrowed it from Mrs. Shifman."

"Why?"

"Pu pu pu." She spit three times.

Not until I saw her at the stove, her hand on her lower belly, did I piece it together. Mama was pregnant. The ring was a talisman to ward off the evil eye.

I said nothing but took on more of the chores, allowing Mama to rest. I shopped after school, woke early to make breakfast buns, and washed the dishes after dinner.

"What a lovely *balabusta* you're becoming," Max said. I smacked him. I couldn't tell him why I was doing it; saying the words out loud tempted fate.

~

On a February afternoon, Max and I walked home from school together. School wasn't quite the misery it used to be because, at fourteen, I was finally in a class with kids my own age.

Max and I passed under the Second Avenue El. Dark swaths of shadow punctuated the slight stripes of daylight, which jumped when the train clanged overhead. Every time we passed this way, I questioned more and more my memories of home, of fields and sunshine and grass to luxuriate in. I thought of Anshel, forever in the outdoors, and I wondered if he was happy, if happiness was something he could feel. *Anshel,* I thought, *guard over Mama. Protect her.*

We strode briskly, the asphalt sidewalk crumbling beneath our feet. Women in garish makeup and low-cut dresses lingered in doorways. Loitering men sneered, hungry and vicious.

Max nattered on about his classes. I ignored him, listening to the noises of the street, the snap of a striking match, the throaty voices of the painted ladies, the clacking of rolling dice, the rumble of the tracks as a train in the distance slowed and started.

Max halted abruptly. "Oh shit."

My head shot up. "What?"

"Is that?" He squinted. "Let's—" But before Max finished his sentence, three boys emerged from the alley and blocked the sidewalk.

"C'mon." Max gripped my arm, leading me into the street, but the boys slid over, obstructing our way.

"What's the hurry?" the tallest one asked. He wore a brown newsboy cap, a hank of dark hair peeking out. He was sinewy, with one hand balled into a fist, which he used to hit his other hand.

"Yeah," said the boy behind him. What this boy didn't have in height, he made up for in breadth. A scar twitched at the corner of his mouth.

The third boy, small but wiry, stood and watched.

"What do you want?" Max spoke with a sneer, but his body trembled. He put his hand on my back and drew me toward him.

"What do we want?" The tall one was the spokesman. "What do we want, Vinnie?"

Vinnie, the stocky boy, said, "Well, Gino, it appears these Yids think it's permissible to walk on our street."

The hair on the back of my neck prickled at the word *Yid*. The word *Yid* meant we weren't going to be allowed to walk away. The word *Yid* meant we were in trouble.

A sudden urge to pee gripped me. I wanted to kick those guys and flee to Mama, but I'd never outrun them.

"What do you want?" Max asked again. I hoped I was the only one who detected the tremor in his voice.

Vinnie reached out and touched my hair. I jerked away, and Max yanked me closer.

"Your girl doesn't look half-bad for a kike."

My bladder bored into my stomach. I swallowed hard. I wouldn't pee in my dress. I wouldn't cry.

"I've had enough." Max tugged me toward the street.

The third boy snaked in front of Max. "Not so fast."

Viciousness oozed from him. One of his eyes drifted, though the other drilled into me. The pressure on my stomach intensified, and despite the chill, sweat dampened the back of my dress.

Gino lost all tones of teasing. "Yids want to use my street, they need to pay for the right. Shouldn't be a problem. Yids control the money, right?"

"This isn't your street," Max said. "It belongs to Moishe's gang."

"Does it now?" Gino said. "Vinnie, Paolo. You seen Moishe around lately?" The three made an overly dramatic show of looking around. "Nope. I don't see Moishe. Must not be his street anymore."

Max's fingers hurt my arm.

"A nickel to use our street," Gino said.

Swallowing hard, I tried to keep my voice steady. "Our mistake. We won't use your street again."

Gino snorted. "Didja hear that, Vinnie? They won't use our street again." His odor was rancid, like spoiled milk. "Listen, Yid. Remember this: all the streets are ours."

"Give him our nickel," I whispered to my brother.

"You heard your sister, Yid. Give us our nickel."

Max reached into his pocket to pull out the coin Papa had left us to buy dinner. Gino snatched it.

"That's one," Gino said.

"You asked for a nickel," Max said.

Gino wormed so close his spittle hit Max as he spoke. "From each of you."

"We don't have any more money." Max's voice cracked.

Don't cry, don't cry, don't cry, I recited in my head.

"Yids always have money. Paolo, check them."

Gino stepped back. Paolo shoved his hands in Max's pockets. "None here." His voice was dry and slightly accented. Without any warning, Paolo hauled his fist back and shot it forward so fast that it wasn't until Max hit the ground that I realized what had happened.

"I'll check the girl," Vinnie said.

Max's nose bled as he leaped up, only to be knocked back down with a punch to his eye.

I braced myself to be pummeled. Instead Vinnie yanked at my coat, ripping off the buttons. A clammy hand pulled up my dress and slid down my tights. I gasped. A finger pushed its way into me, into a place no one—not even I—had ever gone. It hurt, and I had to pee, and it took everything I had not to pee on him, as I was sure if I did, they would kill us. Vinnie's eyes half closed as his other hand moved up and rubbed my chest, the chest I'd been so proud of, the most visible sign I'd left girlhood. Now I wished it gone, wished I'd never changed.

Tears fell fast as I tried to wriggle away from him, his fingers prodding, scratching as they violently pushed, toying with my pubic hair, but it only made him groan and slip closer. He pressed his body against mine, thrusting his hips against me. He smelled sweet, like fresh bread, which confused me. My arms shook with the effort of trying to push him away, but he held tighter and thrust harder.

Max struggled to rise, to reach me, but Paolo kicked him in the side a couple of times, then put his foot on him. I didn't know what hurt more: Vinnie or Max's whimpers.

"Let her go, Vinnie," Gino said.

Vinnie opened his eyes and stared into mine as he squeezed my chest. His cold gaze scared me more than what he was doing. Gino spoke louder. "Let her go. We don't need that kind of trouble." Paolo released Max, then pulled Vinnie off me.

I ran to Max and knelt next to him, both of us crying.

Gino snarled, "Tomorrow you have a nickel for today and two for tomorrow. And the day after. And the day after that. You give us a nickel, you can use our streets. Don't have a nickel?" Gino shrugged.

"Well, let's hope you have that nickel." He gave Max a forceful kick. "Understand?"

Max groaned, clutching his stomach.

I choked out, "Yes."

"Don't think you can avoid us. We'll find you."

I shivered, frozen and brittle.

"What are you waiting for?" Gino said. "Get lost."

I heaved Max to standing. He and I, clasping hands, sprinted as best we could. Each step must have been agony for him. By the time we arrived home, my lower half was soaked with urine, and all I wanted to do was throw away the dress and tights, which that morning had been among my favorites. They were spoiled now. Everything was spoiled.

~

Outside the front door, Max waited. We didn't want to shock Mama.

Mama sat at the table, massaging her temples. I held my breath, hoping she wouldn't notice my soiled dress, which I tried to hide behind my books.

She was distracted, though. "I'm tired, Malka. I'm going to lay down. Can you handle dinner?"

I nodded, not trusting my voice. The minute the bedroom door closed, I let Max in.

"Let me clean you," I said.

"Let me be." He stumbled into our room.

I hauled out a pot and boiled water to wash my clothes. With a rag, I scrubbed my body. A layer of scum coated my skin. I dunked the cloth in the boiling water and almost scalded myself, rubbing, rubbing, rubbing. I needed a proper bath, but I couldn't take one without waking Mama, and she couldn't know what had happened. Not in her condition. I put on nightclothes, though it wasn't even dinnertime.

A nastiness gurgled inside me. I ran to the toilet. In that dark, tight, narrow space, I emptied my stomach, praying Mama wouldn't hear. I was depleted, a carcass, yet I couldn't stop heaving. At last, my body stilled. I sank to the icy tiles and rested my head on the cold seat, trying to understand what had happened. I thought of Mama telling me to keep my legs closed. I thought of Sylvia's crazy stories about private parts. Was this what they were talking about?

A trio of roaches scurried from behind the toilet. I clenched my hand into a tight fist and slammed it on one of them, relishing the pop.

After returning to the kitchen, I wet a fresh rag. I entered our bedroom on tiptoe.

Max lay on his back.

I sat next to him and sponged the dried blood from his face. He recoiled but allowed it. His eyes were striped with red, and I couldn't tell if it was from the thrashing or the tears.

"I'm sorry, Min." His voice was raspy, a murmur.

"Shh." I continued to clean. "Wasn't your fault."

His Adam's apple bounced up and down. "I should have . . . I mean—"

"Stop talking." I finished cleaning the best I could.

In the kitchen, I threw the rag in the pot with my dress, watching as the blood mixed with the water. From the icebox I pulled out herring, made a quick salad, and sliced dark bread, which I left for Papa to eat.

It was too early for sleep, but I didn't want to be awake anymore. I didn't want to be alone.

I crept to Mama's room and pushed open the door. An earthy smell hit me, the smell of dank sheets and unwashed bodies, but a comforting smell. Mama snuffled in her sleep, so I shut the door and, in the pitch darkness, made my way into her bed.

She stirred and rolled over. "Malka." Her voice thickened with sleepiness. "My Malka."

"Mama, I don't feel good."

"Come to Mama, my Malkala." She wrapped her arms around me, and I curled into her. I inhaled the milkiness of her skin and let myself believe, for just a moment, we were back home, in our small house with four walls, with a window on each one.

As I drifted off next to Mama, I prayed the baby stayed safe in her belly.

~

The next morning, I woke disoriented, unsure where Max was. Not until I heard the deep snore of Papa did I remember I was in Mama's bed. My body ached, and when I used the toilet, it burned when I peed.

I sat at the table. Could we avoid Gino and his gang? It might be possible for a few days, but the neighborhood wasn't that big. He'd find us eventually.

The thought that tortured me weaseled in, the one I didn't want to think about, the one that made me tremble: the hunger on Vinnie's face, the roughness of his fingers, the places he'd touched. My stomach churned anew, but there was nothing left to come out.

I scratched at the table with my fingernail. Papa emerged from the bedroom, his body straining beneath the buttons of his nightshirt. Since working for Mr. Rothstein, Papa had grown bulky, his belly shrinking, his arms and chest broadening.

"Minnela. Up early." He put water up for coffee. "What is this cooking?"

On the stove was the pot with my dirty clothes. "My dress was soiled."

Papa's brow furrowed. "Your ma couldn't do that?"

"Mama was tired."

Papa gazed toward the bedroom. He shook his head, smiled at me, and pulled the dress from the pot and squeezed it in the sink. Teasingly, he said, "These won't dry if you don't take them out of the water." He held them to his face, his nose wrinkling when he sniffed. "They'll smell better if you use washing powder."

I shrugged and took bread from the basket, left over from last night.

After placing my dress back in the pot, Papa sat and opened yesterday's paper.

I tore the bread into pieces, eating the crumbs one by one like a bird. Every now and then, Papa lowered the paper to glance at me, but I wouldn't meet his eyes.

After he'd turned the last page, he said, "What's bothering you, Minnie?"

"Nothing's bothering me."

"Never, in all our years here, have you let me read in peace. You chatter, pester me with questions." He patted my hand. "It's late, and you're not dressed for school. Are you going to tell me what's wrong?"

I bit my lip. "How can I make money?"

"Why do you need to make money?"

"For things." I stared at a spot on the wall behind him.

Papa chuckled. "For candy and the pictures? All you need to do is ask, Minnela." He pulled a handful of coins from his pocket. "How much is the cinema these days? A nickel?"

"Seven cents," I said. "But I need a nickel a day, and Max needs one too."

"A nickel a day!" Papa laughed his rumbly laugh. "You'll get sick if you eat a nickel's worth of candy a day."

I pulled the newspaper toward me and folded the corner back and forth, like a fan.

"Minnie." The newsprint blackened my fingers. "Minnie, look at me."

I looked at Papa.

He cocked his head. "Minnela, why do you need a nickel a day?"

I shrugged.

"Minnie, is the nickel a day for you?"

Shaking my head, I forced myself not to cry.

"Who is the nickel for?"

"Some boys."

Papa's face changed, his eyes flinty, his cheekbones sharper than they had been moments ago. "Why didn't Max stop them?"

"He tried."

Papa bounded out of the chair and stormed into the next room. "Max! Get up!"

"Is everything okay?" Mama called from behind her bedroom door.

"It's fine, Mama. Max overslept. Papa's waking him up."

That must have satisfied her, because she said no more.

A moan came from our room. I hurried in. Papa knelt beside Max. Max's eye was a fierce yellow, pus oozing from the corner.

"Oh, my Max!" Papa sounded both tender and furious at the same time. "Let me check you. I'll try not to hurt you."

He softly ran a hand over Max's body. Max struggled to hold back a cry.

"I don't think they broke anything." Papa sat back on his heels. "Who did this to you?"

"There were three of them." Max had difficulty speaking.

"Who were they?"

I jumped in. "Italians. Gino, Paolo, and Vinnie."

Papa's nostrils flared. "Those damn wops."

Max grabbed Papa's arm, signaling him to come closer. Max whispered into Papa's ear. Papa's face became a mask of fury.

"You two stay home," Papa said. "Minnie, make your brother a cup of tea and a cold compress." He marched out, mumbling, "If those wops aren't dead by the end of the day, they'll wish they were."

~

Mama woke later than usual, grimacing as she rubbed her neck. That didn't, however, stop her from fussing that I wasn't at school.

"Max is sick. I'm taking care of him."

"My Shmerka? What's wrong with him?" She moved to our bedroom door, but I blocked her. She couldn't see him. Not like this.

"No!" The word came out louder than I'd intended. Mama reared back. "I mean, he's sick and you . . ."

"Yes?" Mama waited, unsure whether to be angry with me.

"You . . ." I didn't want to say the words out loud, so I touched her thumb, rubbed the ruby ring. "It's not good for you to be around someone sick."

Mama froze; this was the first I'd acknowledged her pregnancy.

"Mama, I'll nurse him. You rest. I'll bring you tea and toast."

Mama pursed her lips, weighing her options. Finally, she said, "What a blessing you are, my Malka." She kissed me, whispered a prayer, and went back to her bedroom.

During the day, I simmered oxtail soup and took turns checking on my brother and my mother. When Papa returned, he set his hat on the table, hung up his coat, and evaluated the clean kitchen.

"My Minnela. Such a caretaker." He gave me a sweeping smile. "How is our patient doing?"

"Better."

Papa peered into the bedroom as I ladled a bowl of soup for him.

"Sleeping." Papa sat, and I took a seat across from him.

He placed his hand on mine. "Minnie, try not to think about what those boys did. The world is an evil place." I thought he was going to say more, but he took his hand back and spooned up broth.

"Papa?"

"Mm-hmm?"

"What happened to Moishe's gang? That was supposed to be his street."

Papa shrugged. "Things change quickly. One minute you're on top of this world; the next you're at the bottom of the dung heap. Watch out for yourself." He jabbed his spoon toward me. "You are the only person you can rely on. Others will use you, try to take advantage of you. Understand?"

I nodded.

Papa scraped his bowl and wiped his face with the hem of his shirt. After he'd had his coffee, he said, "Let's check on your brother."

In our bedroom, Max propped himself up on his elbow.

"You look better," Papa lied. Max's face was mottled yellow and blue. "I need to go back to work, but I wanted to give you each one of these." After reaching into his pocket, he proffered two dimes. "One for my Minnela. One for my Max. These are for candy or the movies or whatever you'd like. But they are only for you." He winked. "Those boys won't be bothering you anymore. If anyone ever gives you trouble, you come straight to me." He kissed each of us on top of our heads and left the apartment.

Once Papa was gone, I turned to Max. "How did he do it?"

Max gave me a funny look. "That's what he does. He protects. In whatever way he has to."

$$\sim$$

The next day we returned to school, walking first to the shul so Max's friend Leo could accompany us. We didn't want to risk running into those boys alone. We'd left early to avoid Mama so she wouldn't see the marks on Max. We concocted a story for later about a lunchtime boxing match, which would upset Mama, but less so than the truth.

My eyes flitted to every doorway, every alleyway, toward every sound. I held my book bag in front of my waist, sure that everyone could see what had been done to me. I wore my shame like a bright-red cloak, visible to the world.

Waiting for the school bell at the girls' door, Sylvia ran up to me, blabbering. "You have to get a radio. The Singing Comedian was on last night. He was a gas!"

"Hey," I said. "Do I look different today?"

She squinted and looked me up and down. "No. What's different?"

I shook my head. "Just curious."

At lunch, in the schoolyard, kids whispered about Max's bruises, though teachers ignored it; battered children were nothing unusual.

Sylvia and I sat alone at the end of a table. "Your brother's face is pretty bad," she said.

I shrugged.

"Who did that to him?"

I shrugged again.

Sylvia took an unladylike bite of her sandwich. "Well, be careful. Harvey told me about those boys on Second Avenue."

"What about them?"

"Someone took care of them but good last night. Gino and Paolo had their legs broken. And Vinnie—what happened to Vinnie was bad. He'll never be right"—she tapped her forehead—"up here again." She chomped another mouthful. "You didn't know?"

My stomach lurched. "Why would I know?"

"Rumor has it . . ." She thought better of finishing her sentence. I could imagine the rumor. That my father was responsible. Of course, it wasn't a rumor; it was the truth. "Well, I say good riddance. Whoever did it did a mitzvah. They were a terror."

I put my sandwich back in my pail.

"Not hungry?" Sylvia asked.

"Lost my appetite."

I should have felt safe. Protected. My father took care of me. So why did I feel so unsettled?

Chapter Ten

Spring 1924

The more Mama's belly rounded, the darker her mood became. Grayness circled her eyes. She mumbled prayers under her breath. In addition to the ruby ring, she tied a bloodred string around her wrist. I took on more of the chores, and neighbor women brought cakes and soup. I appreciated the distractions. The memories of winter sneaked in when I was too idle.

Papa wouldn't let me quit school, although I argued Mama needed me more than my teacher did.

"Education is important," he said. "Soon the baby is born healthy. Mama'll be back to her old self."

"Pu pu pu." I spit. "Don't tempt the evil eye."

"Yes, my little *Mamelah.*"

~

Every Friday, Mama sent a few pennies to the synagogue, but now she said, "Yitzhak, we need to give more." Even though Papa thought prayer was a form of talking to oneself and the rabbi a charlatan, he gave Mama a nickel a week for the shul.

While Mama wanted to walk to the small shul herself, the trek soon became too arduous, so she sent me.

I hated that tiny synagogue. The somber building was barely more than a storefront, a room where men gathered to say their prayers three times a day. The rabbi and his family lived above. On holidays and Saturday mornings, a lace curtain hung across the back of the room, separating the men from the women. Some of the synagogues on the Lower East Side were elaborate, like the one on Eldridge Street with stained glass and soaring ceilings. There, women peered down from a balcony to watch the men pray.

Our dumpy building served as community center as well as synagogue. Mama stopped by to chat with friends. The members were people from our *guberniya*, our district in Ukraine.

Back home in Bratsyana, I had gone to shul irregularly. Men were required to attend; women were expected to care for the children and the home. Mama had gone when she was able on Shabbos mornings, dragging me with her. I had been young enough, though, that when my fidgeting had grown tiresome, Mama had sent me out to play. I had felt sorry for Max, forced to daven in the crowded men's section, his head bent over a prayer book.

In New York, only a sign distinguished our synagogue as a place of worship. Inside, the musk of men lingered, mixing with the musty smell of books. The men who came weren't the scholars of the Old World, with sidelocks and beards, but the everyday people—the tailors and factory workers, the pushcart operators and street sweepers—the people who dressed like Americans, who looked like Americans, but still sneaked off to pray. The men who put on yarmulkes before stepping into the shul and pulled them off as soon as they emerged.

The synagogue confused me. Papa held nothing but disdain for religion and the frauds who, he claimed, conned their congregants, bilking them of their hard-earned money. But Mama revered the rabbi, a learned man of God. She said religion kept people on the path of justness.

Who to believe?

I hoped to deposit my coin and slip out unnoticed. Of course, that morning Rabbi Umansky sat at his desk in the back. At the sound of my entrance, he glanced up and beamed. Rabbi Umansky was more Bratsyana than New York. His dusty beard reached his chest. His shoulders stooped from a lifetime of hunching over religious tomes. A large skullcap perpetually covered his head. His *peyis*, his curls, dangled in front of his ears, a muddy salt and pepper. "Come, come," he said. I dropped the coin in the box, listening to the plink when it hit the bottom, then slunk to the rabbi.

He reached out his hand. I understood what was expected. I moved close so he could place his palm on my head. He shut his eyes and, in Hebrew, muttered a blessing on my behalf. At fifteen, I was too old to be blessed in such a manner, but what could I do? Leo perched in a corner, a thick book open. He glared at me, as if unhappy his father was gracing others with his benediction, but when I boldly caught his stare, he scowled and returned to his pages.

"So," Rabbi Umansky asked, in Yiddish, "how is your mother?"

"S'okay." I responded in English, scraping my foot on the ground.

"Malka."

I didn't correct him, because one didn't contradict the rabbi. He lifted my chin. His eyes were a vibrant youthful brown, though his face was craggy. "If you need anything—if any of your family needs anything—you come to me. This"—he spread his arms—"is your home. Your people. We are here for you, yes?"

I nodded.

"I'm reciting your mother's name in the *Mi Sheberach*. The prayer for healing."

My jaw clenched. "I know what it is."

He tugged on his sidelock and rocked back on his feet. "Of course you do. You *kinderlach* look so American I forget."

My flush transformed from embarrassment to pleasure.

"You're a good daughter, Malka, taking care of your mother." I was being dismissed, but as I left, he called out, "A *gut* Shabbos to you and your family."

I hoped against hope his blessings might work.

~

Aunt Sara came when she could to help with the chores. She was quiet and docile, not what I had come to expect from those born in New York. Her baking skills were unmatched. Max and I inhaled her treats. Soon, though, it became evident her visits wouldn't continue for much longer as her own belly grew.

Twice a month, on Sundays, Uncle Aaron accompanied Aunt Sara to our apartment. By July, Mama was spending more of her days in bed. Aunt Sara evaluated the kitchen before deciding marketing was the most pressing chore. Unlike other neighborhoods, which closed up tight on Sundays, Orchard Street bustled with life, reopening after the Saturday Sabbath.

Uncle Aaron sat by Mama's bed while Aunt Sara shopped. At the kitchen table, I pretended to read in order to eavesdrop.

"Feige," he said, "I worry about you."

"Sha, sha," she replied. "Don't worry. I've birthed children before."

"No more children after this. You aren't well."

"You sound like the midwife."

"The midwife told you not to have more?"

"Stop! When this child is in my arms, I'll be as well as can be."

"But your last birth . . ." His voice dropped. I slid the chair closer to her room to better hear. "I was terrified."

"I survived, didn't I? Look at my beautiful Malka. You want I shouldn't have my daughter?"

I was a difficult birth?

A gasp sounded from the room.

"Feigela!" Uncle Aaron's alarm scared me. "Are you all right? Do you need a doctor?"

"No, no. Sometimes the baby pinches. Makes it hard to inhale."

"Feigela, no more babies."

I imagined Mama stroking Uncle Aaron's arm, soothing him. "It's a woman's duty to make babies. If the world will ever be redeemed, it will be only through the merit of children."

Uncle Aaron's response was muted, but Mama's came clear. "You will understand when you have children of your own, God willing."

$\sim$

By mid-August, pains kept Mama prostrate. The midwife checked her daily.

"Shouldn't the baby be here by now?" Mama asked.

"The baby comes when the baby comes," the midwife said. To me she said, "At the first signs of labor, find me."

"How will I know?" I twisted the apron. I was now the woman of the house, doing chores and minding Mama. I put cool compresses on her forehead to combat the summer swelter, helped her with the chamber pot when she couldn't rise from bed, brought her cold borscht to keep her nourished.

"You'll know."

Mama's friends dropped in to offer cheer and freshly baked breads. Rabbi Umansky sat by her bed once a week to recite prayers with her. I wasn't able to go out, so Sylvia came by at lunchtimes with gossip and treats from the pushcarts.

At the end of August, Max turned seventeen. Birthdays for American children included sweets and gifts, but that wasn't in Mama and Papa's tradition. We observed Rosh Hashanah, Passover. Dates of significance. Our birthdays, made-up dates, were not of significance.

The night of his self-proclaimed birthday, I bought a cinnamon babka at the bakery. Papa was working, so it was just me and Max,

Mama dozing in bed. I brought Max the cake, sang the birthday song we learned in school, and handed him a wrapped gift.

"Aw, thanks, Min." He untied the string. "*A Passage to India.*"

"The bookseller said it should entertain a dewdropper like you," I teased.

An otherworldly moan from the next room had us bolting to Mama.

"Mama?" She clutched her belly, the moans twisting into a piercing scream. "Mama!" She curled on her side, huddled in a fetal position. "Max, go for the midwife."

He was already halfway out the door.

Max was fast, but even so, time stuttered, spitting out extra minutes. I wiped Mama's forehead and allowed her to squeeze my hand. Her strength surprised me as she crushed my knuckles in her grip.

When the midwife arrived, she ordered me to boil water and tear up rags and for Max to find Papa.

After I gave the midwife her supplies, she banished me from the bedroom. "You're too young to see this."

"I'm fifteen," I protested.

"Too young." She shut the door.

I tried to read the newspaper to distract myself—the front pages still touted the feats of the Americans returning from the Olympics in Paris—but the sounds from the next room were chilling, and I couldn't focus.

At close to nine o'clock, Leo came with a cabbage strudel from his mother and papers for me. "Max told us."

I cursed Max for running to the rabbi when he should've been looking for Papa, though of course Mama would want the rabbi praying for her.

"What are these?" I flipped through the pages.

"Psalms. Papa says you should recite them. He wrote them in English for you."

"Does God speak English?"

He shrugged. "Why not?"

Leo scurried out at the next scream from the bedroom.

With nothing to distract me, I paced, back and forth, back and forth, chanting the Psalms aloud until my throat was raw, and then I chanted more.

At midnight, Max returned, having been unable to locate Papa.

"Sit," he said. "Rest a minute."

"Rest? Can you hear her?" Minutes of silence would pass, a lull between the howls, more animal than human.

"Sit." He led me to a chair and pushed me down. "Eat." He sliced the cabbage strudel and warmed milk on the stove.

I ate mechanically. When I was done, I shoved the plate aside and put my head on the table. I must have been more exhausted than I realized, because at some point I felt myself being lifted and carried to my room. "Shhh," Papa said as I opened my mouth to speak. "I'm here now. Go to bed. I'll take care of everything."

"What if she needs me?"

"Your mother will need you more in the morning. You need to be rested."

~

The next morning, I lingered in bed, trying to shake off the remnants of my dream. The pictures were hazy in the light of day, but in the night they were so vivid, of Mama holding Anshel, singing lullabies to him. What if she chose him instead of us?

Propping myself up, I listened to the sounds. Or rather, to the lack of sounds. The stillness in the air frightened me. No screams, no moans. I ached to jump up, to run to Mama, to see if I had a brother or sister, but my brain slowed me, ever mindful of that whisper that said *What if.* What if . . . I peeled off my blanket and sat up. Rubbing the sleep from my face, I heard a new noise. A mewling. Like a cat. My body understood the noise before my head made sense of it. I tore into the kitchen.

"Sha, hush yourself," the midwife said. Her eyelids drooped, her limbs heavy, the body of a woman deprived of her bed for many nights. She boiled water and set up cups for tea. "We need quiet."

"Where is . . . ?" I peered into the darkened bedroom.

The midwife smiled, though her face sagged. "Go. Take a peek at your new sister. Quietly."

Sister!

Looking in, I blinked to adjust to the low light. Mama wheezed in her sleep. On top of her lay the tiniest of creatures. My new sister. I took in her downy hair, the thinness of her fingers, the nearly translucent squares of fingernails as they rested on Mama's chest. Her back rose and fell with each breath, a wispy sound emerging from her lips. My little sister. I longed to pet her, to nuzzle my nose in her neck, but I didn't dare disturb either of them.

I startled when I noticed Papa, sitting in a chair across from the bed, worry written on his face.

"What's her name?" I asked.

"Your mother wants to name her Gittel. For her grandmother Gita."

"Gittel?" Such an ugly, old-world name.

"You don't like it?"

"She's an American. She needs an American name."

Papa stroked his chin. "An American name."

I thought of those Olympians. "Gertie," I said. Gertrude Ederle had set a world record in swimming. She was the Queen of the Waves. My sister would be a queen of something too.

"Gertie," he said. "I like it. A pretty name for our pretty girl."

The midwife returned and shooed me and Papa out while she tended to Mama. Before I walked out, though, I grabbed our Bible from the top of Mama's dresser. In the kitchen, I retrieved pen and ink from the sideboard. I opened the book and traced the notations written inside the front cover. The words were in Yiddish, so I couldn't make them out. Who had written these? My grandfather? My great-grandfather? Certainly not my mother or Bubbe, since neither of them could read or write. The unreadable words filled me with anguish. Who was I? Not an American. But I wasn't not an American either. I lived in the in-between.

Carefully, I dipped my pen in the inkpot and, in my best penmanship, wrote beneath the Yiddish scrawls, *Gertie Soffer, August 24, 1924.*

My American sister. A product of the New World.

A few hours old, and already she had so much more than I ever would.

Chapter Eleven

Gertie was a sweet thing who grew fast. Once she was six months old, Mama moved her to a crib in our room. I didn't like that crib any more than she did—those jail slats imprisoning her—so when she cried at night, I brought her in bed, covering her fat cheeks with kisses until she fell asleep, her body pressed to mine. Mama scolded me, saying Gertie had to learn to sleep on her own, but I adored the smell of my sister, delighted in the feel of her cool skin, and I ignored Mama's orders to let Gertie cry. Gertie woke, cooing at me. I'd tweak her nose, besotted when she bestowed me with one of her gummy grins.

As I dressed, I held one-sided conversations. "Good morning, Gertie," I'd say. "Isn't this a lovely day? Today I'm turning in a paper on the causes of the great Panic of 1837. Someday you'll need to churn out completely useless facts for teachers."

Max teased me—"Practicing to be a radio announcer?"—but I ignored him. I needed to counteract the Yiddish Gertie heard all day from Mama. Gertie would speak perfect English.

"Malka," Mama would call from the kitchen as she prepared oatmeal for the baby, "change your sister's diaper."

And yet every morning, I'd manage to be running late for school, dashing out the door and yelling, "No time! I'll wake earlier tomorrow. Promise."

I never woke earlier.

Mama cursed at me as I scrambled out of the apartment—"A dog is sometimes more faithful than a child"—but school and homework always gave me an excuse. Mama tried to hide her pride, but she burst with it as Max entered his senior year. Max worked after school in a lawyer's office, to learn what he could. When he came home after a day's work, Mama treated him like a conquering hero.

Most boys his age had left school years before, taking apprenticeships as tailors or blacksmiths or finding work in factories or laundries. Few made it past the eighth grade. "Not my children," Mama often said, appreciative Papa made enough for Max and me to study. "My son will go to college. My daughter will work in an office. No dirty fingernails for my children."

But Mama still chided me. At a dinner in April, Mama lectured me on the importance of tending to house and children. "A young woman must learn how to run a household and raise a family. It's not enough to play with the baby. You need to care for the baby."

"Oh, Feigela," Papa said. "When we sell our land, we'll be rich. We'll hire help to care for babies."

"Land?" I said.

Mama beamed, forgetting her annoyance with me. "Your papa is a smart man." She tapped her forehead. "We're investors. Like Americans."

Max asked, "Where is the land?"

"Florida," Mama said.

Did Mama even know where Florida was? "And this is a good investment?" I asked.

"Do you *ever* open the newspaper, other than to the gossip column?" Max said.

I kicked him under the table. "I read plenty."

Papa stood and riffled through a drawer. He returned to the table with newspaper clippings. "Look at this one." He handed me one from the *Daily News*, with a headline that read, He Made Millions on $250 in Florida Boom. "Here's another." It was a photo of a packed boat with the caption Florida Gold Rush.

"And you agreed to this?" I asked Mama, wondering if this was one of Papa's big ideas. Papa dreamed big, but I didn't trust those dreams. But then, neither did Mama, and she seemed enthusiastic.

"You see the articles. The newspapers wouldn't lie."

"What do you think of this, Max?" I asked.

He shrugged. "Could be a good investment." To Papa he asked, "What'd you buy?"

"Plots in a place called the Everglades. Your mama and I bought a small plot and sold it. We made enough money to buy a bigger plot. The land is swamp—"

"You knowingly bought swamp?" I said. How in the world was that a smart decision?

"Let me finish. The land is swamp, but it's being drained and developed. It's like there's gold in that mud."

Gold? Hadn't I heard that before? "The streets will be paved with gold," Mama had said as we'd traveled by foot from Bratsyana to the train station that would take us to the port.

"Don't worry, Minnela," Papa said, placing his hand on mine. "Someday we'll be rich."

"Be happy," Mama said. "This will bring us joy."

If even Mama and Max liked the idea, then who was I to disagree?

∼

When Gertie was nearly a year old, she had thick rolls beneath her neck and pudgy arms. On a hot August midday, she sat in a high chair, waving a spoon, while I leafed through a *McCall's* magazine.

"Help your sister eat," Mama said.

"I'm reading. No dirty fingernails, remember?"

She picked up the magazine and flipped through it. "I may not be able to read English, but I know this is no literature. Feed your sister."

With a dramatic show, I sighed, stood, and moved to Gertie, trying to angle my body away from her. Gertie was in a food-throwing phase, and I didn't want my new dotted Normandy voile dress to be covered in barley cereal.

Mama tsked at me. "Put on an apron."

"They're so frumpy."

Mama muttered under her breath as she worked on a chicken. I made faces at Gertie, and when she laughed, I *choo choo*ed in a bite. We'd made it halfway through the bowl when a pounding on the apartment door interrupted us. That someone was knocking midday in August wasn't alarming; women of the neighborhood dropped by to sit and sew with Mama, borrow eggs, or have a cup of tea and share news from the old country. But this knock was insistent, a hammering with the side of a fist.

Mama's hand was inside the chicken, emptying its innards for soup. "What are you, a statue? You can see I'm otherwise engaged. Answer the door."

I hesitated. More bangs.

"Malka, go! Before it upsets Gittel!" But of course it was too late, and the toddler wailed, throwing cereal from her high chair.

I yanked open the door but took an involuntary step back when I saw who was on the other side.

A police officer.

"Lookin' for Mr. Soffer." A thick New York accent flattened his vowels. What had my father done? Did the cops know about the bar? Was Papa to be arrested? My throat went dry.

Mama set aside the chicken, wiped her hands on her apron, and came to the door, ignoring Gertie's cries.

"Mr. Soffer here?"

Mama wrung the apron in her fists, the muscles in her forearms straining. Mama understood the simple sentence but couldn't respond, so she said to me in Yiddish, "Tell him your father is at work."

"My father is at work."

"Where's that?" the copper said.

"He owns a soda shop. On Baxter Street." Should I have told him that? If the cop went to Baxter Street, would he discover the bar? Then again, how could I have avoided telling him?

The cop fingered the top of his nightstick, which rode at his waist. "Checked there. Didn't find him. Soda jerk said maybe he was home." If the officer knew where Papa worked, why did he ask?

He took in our small space. I was grateful at how well Mama kept the apartment, making it shine even if the tenement itself was gloomy and grimy. The officer didn't seem in a hurry, so it occurred to me Papa couldn't be in much trouble.

Since Mama was unable to, I asked, "Why do you need my father?"

From his back pocket, he pulled a sheaf of papers. He paged through till he found what he was looking for.

"Kalmen Soffer's been detained at Ellis Island." Mama cocked her head at the mention of Kalmen's name and the words *Ellis Island*. Kalmen was a cousin, not close, on my father's side. The cop continued, "He's sixteen, a likely public charge." He squinted at the page. "Listed your father as his nearest local relative. Your father needs to come and give testimony for the kid."

"I'll find my father and have him take care of this."

"Yeah, fine." He turned and left without a goodbye.

When he was out of sight, I gently shut the door, not wanting to draw his attention. I took deep breaths.

"Tell me everything," Mama said.

Mama's hands were still enmeshed in her apron. After I translated, her lips moved in a familiar way—she was uttering a prayer of thanks.

"Kalmen will be okay," I said, although I had no idea if that was true. Knowing Mama, she was worried about whether there would be kosher food for him at Ellis Island.

"What would become of us?" She sounded frail, insubstantial, not the booming woman I was familiar with. Gertie's sobs subsided, and she plunged her fist into her cereal bowl, then brought a handful to her mouth.

"What are you talking about?"

"If your father is arrested. What would become of us?" she repeated. "I was sure that officer was coming to arrest your father."

The drubbing in my chest seized me. What did Mama know? My words came out haltingly; I was afraid of where we were venturing. "What do you mean?" Mama thought Papa owned a soda shop. Didn't she?

She looked toward the ceiling. I thought she was pleading with God, but then I saw she was trying to keep tears from spilling. "That *farkakte* bar of his."

Mama knew? I bit my bottom lip.

Mama shook her head as if shedding a bad dream. "Malka, go to that bar, and fetch your father. He must hurry to Ellis Island and take care of this mess."

"But . . ."

She returned to her chicken. After a moment, she said, "What, you need an engraved invitation? Your cousin needs help. Find your father."

I moved cautiously. I picked up my hat. Before I turned the doorknob, I asked, "How long have you known?"

"How long have I known?" With a splat, the insides of the chicken came free. "When did I not know?"

"So why do you pretend?"

With an exaggerated sigh, Mama placed the backs of her wrists on her hips. Her face regained its sternness, but her hands trembled. "Malka, what if I did know? Should I approve of what your father does? It's illegal, it's dangerous, and we could be deported. If I knew about the bar, I'd have to insist he not work there. What would he do?"

"Keep working at the bar."

"Where would that leave us? I know what the neighbors think. As long as they think I'm in the dark, I don't have to hear about it. Can you imagine what Mrs. Aaronson would say, if she could? 'Feige, it's a *shanda* what your husband does! Have the rabbi talk to him.' Best everyone thinks they're keeping a secret from me so I can live among our friends. Sometimes it's better to turn a blind eye."

Mama knew. Mama knew and had been clever about it. I was stunned. I was impressed. Mama was more cunning than I gave her credit for. "It doesn't bother you?"

"Of course it bothers me. But this is America. In America, you do what you have to do to get by. Your father takes good care of us." She smiled. "Pays for those ridiculous magazines you like. Now, go, find your father." She wagged a finger. "But this? This is our secret."

"Yes, Mama."

"Come here, my Malkala." I was now taller than Mama, so I had to bend down for her to plant a kiss on my forehead. "Go, my love. Tell your father to retrieve your cousin and to bring him home for dinner. Hurry." She shuddered. "That Ellis Island. It's not an easy place."

I ran, holding down the hem of my dress, but it slid upward, igniting the catcalls of men repairing the road. I passed the headscarved women filling baskets with bruised peaches, arguing over pennies and ounces, fruit flies swarming around carts. The rutted streets puffed up billows of smoky dirt as cars rumbled by. The heat made the air shimmer like water in the washtub after the laundry bluing was poured in.

I slowed down at Baxter Street and straightened my hat. A young couple sat in the soda shop, the burly soda jerk behind the counter. I moved past the storefront, walking down the alley I had followed Papa down three years ago.

The door creaked when I pulled it, opening to the tiny dark hall. Another door faced me. The door behind me closed, shrouding the hall in black. I knocked firmly on the second door, though my knees shook.

A window in the door slid open. All I could see were eyes, sunk deep into a skull.

"I'm looking for Ike. Ike Soffer."

"Dames can't come in on their own."

"I'm his daughter. My mother sent me to fetch him."

The small window shut, and the door opened.

The eyes belonged to a tall man, not quite stocky, but he filled his shirt. His arms were as meaty as beef shanks, and while his eyes were a shade too small for his face, he was not unattractive.

A woman in a tight green dress draped over a man at the counter. Her eyes, painted with kohl, flickered to me, evaluating whether I was competition. When she decided I wasn't, she turned back to the man, whispered something in his ear, and then gave a tinny laugh as her hand dropped to his thigh.

"Hey, baby," a man at the counter in a cheap suit and cheaper fedora said. "Perch yourself here, and I'll buy you a drink."

A man with an apron lounged against the back wall behind the counter. His black hair curled on top of his head in a way that wasn't stylish but was still charming. "No women on their own," he said with a faint Irish lilt.

"Where's Ike?"

The bartender had a horsey face, with sharp features and an abundance of freckles dancing across his nose. He cocked his head toward a back room.

I opened the door to the back room to piles of crates and a small desk. My father sat behind it and another man in front, the two of them bent over a map. The room was cramped, and it smelled of aftershave and rat droppings.

"Get the hell out," Papa said, his head still bent. When I didn't move, he glanced up. He jumped when he saw me. "Minnie! What are you doing here?"

The other man was hard to make out beneath his hat, which was pulled low. Something about him made my skin tingle.

"Minnie?"

I focused. "Your cousin Kalmen is stuck on Ellis Island. You need to fetch him." That was when I noticed the holster. And the gun. I pointed to it. "What's that for?"

"None of your business." Papa sat back down. "Go home. I'll deal with it later."

His tone chilled me, but I wasn't about to tell Mama that Papa wasn't going to retrieve Kalmen. She scared me more than he did. "A cop came to the apartment looking for you. He said he was going to your work to find you, but I told him I'd go. If you don't claim Kalmen today, the cop'll come back for you again." I paused. "At the soda shop." It wasn't exactly what the police officer had said, but it had the desired effect.

Papa's jaw twitched.

"Take care of this," the other man said. "Don't want another flattie on your payroll."

"But the shipment—"

"Send the lug serving drinks. It's an easy pickup."

"Frank? Who'll watch the bar?"

Angling his head toward me, the man said, "She can." He tilted his hat with his forefinger, giving me a full view of his face, with its dimpled chin and frosty hazel eyes framed by eyelashes any woman would envy. He smiled, displaying two slightly crooked front teeth, which added to his charm.

I could? Then I figured, why not? Working at a bar, even a bar as scruffy as Papa's, seemed romantic, like in the picture shows.

"Minnie?" Papa twitched his mustache. "A lady bartender? That's ridiculous, Duke. Besides, she's a child."

"I'm sixteen," I said. "And haven't you heard of a whisper sister?"

Duke ran his gaze down my body. "She'll be good for business," he said.

Work at the bar! Sylvia would be so jealous. She always had the adventures, and now it was my turn.

Papa tugged on his chin.

"The cop, Papa." Was I pushing my luck?

"I don't see you have a choice," Duke said.

He sighed. "Fine. Let's go."

Duke grinned at me. He was handsome in an elegant way, with a sharp nose and droopy eyes that made him appear thoughtful.

Duke stayed in the back room as I followed Papa into the bar, where the man in the cheap suit said, "Baby's back!" He patted the counter next to him. "I'll make whatever pains you go away."

Papa crossed the bar in two strides. He grabbed the man's shirt collar in his fist, lifting him off the ground. "You speak that way to her again, and nothing will make your pain go away." Papa tossed the man out the door as if he were no heavier than a bucket of rotten vegetables.

"Everyone understands?" Papa bellowed.

"I can handle myself, Pa—"

He threw his hand up in a stopping motion. "Thinking you can handle yourself is the first sign you can't." To me, he whispered, "No one needs to know how young you are. Folks at the bar call me Ike."

"Okay . . . Ike." If Mama heard me call Papa by his given name, she'd have slapped me but good.

Gesturing to the man at the door, Papa said, "This is Big Al." The man with the thick arms nodded. "Anyone gives you trouble, he'll take care of it." Papa signaled me to follow him behind the counter. "Frank, you need to run an errand for Duke. Teach Minnie what to do. She'll man the bar till you or I return." Papa surveyed the room, clearly reluctant to leave.

"I can do this . . . Ike." The name tripped on my tongue.

"Teach her quick. Duke is waiting for you." Papa mumbled as he walked away, "A lady bartender."

Frank turned to me. "You ever done this before?"

"Sort of?"

Frank was younger than I had first thought, probably the same age as Max. The freckles emphasized the paleness of his skin, which looked like it had never felt a razor. "Don't worry, kid. It's duck soup."

Behind the bar were glasses—not all of them clean—rags, and bottles with amber and clear liquids.

"Another one, Frank," said a man propped against the bar.

Frank filled his glass. To me, he said, "See where the pattern changes on the glass?" The small glass cup was straight bottomed with a slight flare about halfway up. "That's where you stop pouring." I remembered that from my bourbon with Papa and Riley.

Frank pointed at bottles on the back counter: "That's Paddy's Irish, that's American whiskey, that's Jamaican rum, that's Bacardí rum, that's Canadian Club, that's Seagram's. The beer is obviously in the tap." Obviously? None of this was obvious to me. "We're out of brandy. Straight drinks are twenty-five cents; mixed drinks thirty-five cents."

"Mixed drinks?" My voice squeaked. "I don't know how to mix drinks."

Frank shrugged. "Our mixed drinks aren't more complicated than a gin and tonic or a screwdriver. But you don't have to make them. Tell them we're out of mixers. Straight drinks only."

Big Al called out, "Duke is waitin' for you, Frank."

Frank's expression softened. "It's duck soup." He reached behind to untie his apron, which he passed to me.

I laid my hat on a shelf, swept my hair behind my ears, and tied the apron around my waist, thinking, *Duck soup. Duck soup.* Duke and Frank disappeared out the door, but not before Duke gave me the quickest of winks.

The bar was quiet, and no one needed anything at the moment. I felt foolish standing doing nothing, so I took my rag and shined the glasses. One of the men laughed. "Where are we, the Waldorf?"

My eyes flew to the door when I heard a knock. Big Al let in three men. The bar didn't have stools, so they leaned on the counter.

With a deep breath, I made my way over. "What'll you have?" I tried to sound gruff.

"Well, lookee at you," said the one at the far end. "Much easier on the eyes than Frank."

"Watch it, boys," Big Al said from the door. "Ike told me to keep a special eye on her." This felt excessive given these men were old enough to be my grandfathers.

"I'll keep a special eye on her too," the middle one said, with a waggle of his eyebrows.

In a frosty tone, I repeated, "What'll you have?"

"Okay, princess, we'll play nice," said the man on the left. "A round of Canadian Club on the rocks."

At the bottles, I hesitated. Which was Canadian, and which was Seagram's? I peered at the labels a second too long. "It's the brown stuff, princess," the man I would come to know as Walt said. I reddened as the others laughed. There were multiple bottles of "the brown stuff." I grabbed one at random.

I set out three glasses and opened the bottle. The fumes burned my eyes. I poured to the mark as Frank had shown me. The men waited expectantly. "Twenty-five cents each."

"Where's the ice?" one of them asked. I'd learn his name was Otto. Was that what a "rock" was?

Pretending I knew what I was doing, I said, "I just assumed men like you would drink it neat."

Otto laughed. "Neat drinks are a younger man's game. Ice, please."

"Ice." I searched beneath the counter till I found a sliding-door ice chest. I scooped ice before dropping one, then two cubes in the glass, but as I went to drop in a third, he pulled the glass away so the ice cube plunked on the bar.

"Just two," he said.

I put two in the other glasses.

Holding up his drink, Otto said, "Cheers, princess."

The other two echoed, "Cheers."

I held my breath as they sipped. Either I had gotten the drink right or they couldn't tell the difference. Soon I learned it was usually the latter; the premium alcohol was cut with cheaper booze, and the cheaper booze was diluted with all sorts of additives, so in the end, most of it tasted the same. Only the bottle labels, when they were on the bottles, were different.

I relaxed when they ordered another round. Again, with nothing to do, I tidied the bar.

After a few drinks, the three men departed, but when I wiped the counter, I found a nickel. "Oh, Big Al! They've left money behind. Can you grab them?"

Big Al's nostrils flared as he bit back laughter. "That's your tip."

"My what?"

"Your tip. The customers leave you money for your service."

A nickel, for me? Waitresses got tips, but I didn't realize bartenders did too. "What do I do with it?"

Shaking his head, Big Al responded to a knock by peeking through the sliding window. "What does she do with it?" Letting in two men, he turned back and said, "You stick it in your pocket and save it for a rainy day."

This job was the cat's meow! What an easy way to make money. Throughout the afternoon, more coins appeared on the counter.

While I should have been bored when things slowed, I wasn't. Watching the customers fascinated me, the way they chatted about work, women, sports, as if I weren't there. The ones who grew drunk, slurring words, amused me. One man became so corked he tried to start a fistfight with another customer over his disdain for Mayor Hylan. Big Al chucked them both into the alley. The dim light twinkling on the bottles took on a romantic glow, even in those dismal surroundings.

None of the men minded when I couldn't make a mixed drink, though as the afternoon turned to evening—not that I could tell in any way other than the clock on the wall; the saloon had no windows—a woman entered on the arm of a man, and she was not pleased about drinking straight alcohol.

The evening passed in such ease that I was disappointed when, at close to 9:00 p.m., Riley arrived. "Who the hell are you?" he asked.

"I'm Minnie."

"As I already asked, Who the hell are you." His questions sounded more like statements.

A flush crawled up my neck. "Minnie?" Clearing my throat, I tried again. "We've met. I'm Minnie Soffer."

Riley shook his head, as if he couldn't be bothered with me. Wasn't he supposed to kowtow to me? I was the boss's daughter, for goodness' sake.

"Where's Ike or Frank?"

"Taking care of things. Ike put me in charge."

"I'm here now. So you're out of charge."

"My fath—" I cut myself off. "Ike told me to man the bar until he or Frank returned."

"Listen, little girl." He took a step closer to me. "Your father may own this bar, but I'm second in command. I'm here"—he held his hand high up over his head—"and you're here." He threw a peanut on the floor and stepped on it. His voice lowered to a rasp.

"Everything okay over there?" Big Al asked from the door.

"Everything is berries over here," Riley said, though when his hand grazed my thigh, I jumped back, knocking the shelving behind me, the bottles rattling. "Peanut over here was about to run back home to the kitchen, where she belongs."

Big Al intervened. "Minnie, Riley can handle it from here." He opened the door, so I had little choice but to leave.

I was furious at myself for being meek with Riley. He thought he was second in charge? By all rights that bar would be mine. If anything happened to my father, Max and I would be the ones to inherit it. Not Riley.

As I emerged onto the street, the spell of the gin mill broke. I entered the world of pushcarts, corner crap games, and constant shouting in a multitude of languages.

What was Max making such a fuss about? That bar was harmless. Old men soaking themselves with cheap hooch. What could happen at a blind pig like that? Safer than the streets, with Big Al at the door. Max was *meshuga*.

My pocket jingled with the coins I had earned. What an easy way to make money.

I wouldn't let myself be scared of Riley. I was going to work at the bar again, whether he liked it or not.

Chapter Twelve

Papa, on the other hand, didn't agree.

"I can do a much better job than Riley," I said in English so Mama wouldn't understand.

"Out of the question," Papa said.

"Riley is bad for business. He thinks he's second in command, and he's a punk."

Papa sighed. "He is on both accounts."

"So replace him with me. It's your bar."

"Minnie, this business doesn't work that way. Too dangerous," he said.

"Is that why you carry a gun?"

He squinted one eye. "I don't carry a gun."

"I saw it."

His voice was tight. "I don't carry a gun. I said no, and I meant no." He stormed out of the apartment.

I never asked again.

~

In the fall of 1926, Mama needed me again anyway; her humming returned, and the ruby ring reappeared on her thumb.

I hovered over her. When she reached up to pull down the cast-iron stockpot, I dashed over. "Let me do it."

"Malka, stop your fussing." She pushed me away and grabbed the pot.

"You're always telling me to help. I'm helping."

"Now she helps," Mama said to the ceiling. "Now, when she should be studying." She slapped carrots down on the cutting board. "This is your final year of high school. Then secretarial school. Study!"

"Yes, yes."

"A mother's joy is in her children. Max will be a lawyer. You will be a secretary. Good matches you will make. Beautiful grandchildren you will give me."

She bent to pick up the ten-pound bag of potatoes.

"Please, Mama." I jumped to snatch the bag. "You had such a difficult time with Gertie."

"Sha, sha!" She spit three times. "Are you trying to invite the evil eye? Go." When I didn't move, she waved me off. "Go!"

All I could think about were the warnings not to have another baby.

Mama's joy, though, spilled into our stomachs. For Rosh Hashanah, she baked honey cakes and teiglach, sending me to deliver the treats to friends. For Sukkos, she made kreplach that we ate in the shul's sukkah. At Hanukkah, she lit candles in her grandmother's menorah and fed us latkes drowning in sour cream. Mama told Gertie the story of each holiday, of each celebration, and though Max and I could recite the stories by heart, still we sat close to listen.

"Just think," Mama said, flipping potato pancakes on the stove. The entire building smelled of the cooking oil, latkes frying in every apartment. "Perhaps next year we'll spend the holidays in our own house. When we sell the land, we will buy our own."

Papa's face blanched. He turned away and said, "Mm-hmm." Mama was so lost in her joy she didn't notice.

When I questioned him about it later, he merely said, "Nothing I can't take care of."

By February, Mama was spending more time in bed. Her face was drawn. Her body ached, and at the end of the day, Papa or I would massage her legs.

Passover of 1927 approached. Mama's body was ripe, and simple tasks were taxing. The midwife checked on her frequently, urging her to take it easier.

"Make this your last," the midwife said to Mama. My stomach lurched.

"Oh, hush," Mama replied. "This is what God made us to do."

Passover was Mama's favorite holiday. "The first sign of spring," she'd say as she made her delicious macaroons. To me Passover was a chore to endure. The holiday meant work: Mama scrubbed the house, boiled the dishes and silverware, and cooked for weeks, which meant I had to do the same.

Back home, our seders were leisurely, with Zayde leading the prayers and songs. Even when times were lean, we scrimped in the weeks beforehand so we could enjoy brisket and gefilte fish. All the women of the family gathered to clean and cook together. Our table crowded with relatives and those with nowhere to go, the yeshiva men, the widowers. Us children, woozy from the sips of wine we were permitted, with full bellies and warm from the fire, would drift off at the table as the men's voices roared with the joy of the holiday.

In America, seders were different. At our seder, Papa read through the Haggadah without lingering to ask questions, tell stories, or add in songs. Mama admonished Papa to slow down, but he never did, and her face would sag as "Dayenu" became a hurried recitation instead of the lengthy, robust song.

On Passover, I missed our old life.

Yet this new, speedy seder was the way it was done here. At school, over lunches of matzah and boiled eggs, kids bragged about how short their seders were. "A new record for us," Sylvia said one year. "Forty-five minutes." The newer immigrant children remained silent, not wanting to confess their four-hour dinners.

For this Passover, I took on the preparations. Though I'd helped Mama my entire life, still she called instructions from the bedroom, rising periodically to inspect my efforts. I was falling behind in my schoolwork, missing days of class, and I dreaded the scolding I'd receive when she realized it. But how else could I manage holiday preparations, keep the house, and watch Gertie? The neighbors helped, taking Gertie a few hours at a time, but it wasn't enough. History homework was the least of my concerns.

On the first night of Passover, Mama sat at the table for the beginning of the seder. Her head drooped as Papa read, but after the first taste of matzah, she excused herself back to bed. Under normal circumstances, Papa would have abandoned the rest of the liturgy, but it was a clear sign he was worried when we continued as if she were still sitting with us. Part of me wanted to beg him to slow down, as Mama always did, but instead I drank more than my share of the sweet wine.

Passover ended, and still the baby hadn't come. My birthday, though, had. I was eighteen years old. Max bought me a bottle of toilet water, and Sylvia gave me a lipstick, which I hid from Mama. My final school year was nearly over, but I wouldn't graduate until the fall. I was so far behind in trigonometry I'd have to retake it over the summer. In my other classes, I had to pass my exams to avoid even more summer school.

~

A few weeks later, I lay on my bed reading Oliver Wendell Holmes's "Old Ironsides" for the fourth time, trying to identify the major themes. It wasn't that I couldn't find the themes; it was that the poem was so boring my mind couldn't grasp the words. I read each word out loud so the rhythms echoed in my ears, which was why I didn't hear Mama's moans right away. Not until Gertie cried did I realize something was wrong. After leaping up, I bounded to the kitchen, where Mama was doubled over.

Taking her by the elbow, I led her to her bed. "Is it time?"

She waited for the pain to pass. "It may be."

After settling her on the feather mattress, I called the midwife. However, I was told she was at another birth, at a house with no telephone.

"Mama." I returned to her side. "I need to go for Mrs. Oberman." I stayed as another wave passed through her, her face contorting into that of a stranger's. The sounds she made reminded me of home, of the lowing of cows. I rubbed her forehead, my stroke gentle, though I wanted to hold Mama so tightly the pain would flee her and enter me.

When the spasm subsided, she released my arm. "Hurry." Her desperation filled me with foreboding.

Gertie played with a stack of wooden blocks on the kitchen floor. I'd run faster unencumbered, so I slipped out before she could fuss.

I dashed to the birthing woman's apartment and banged on the door.

"What's this racket?" an old woman said as she peeked out.

"I need the midwife." I panted, the three flights of stairs only adding to my misery.

"She's busy." The woman moved to close the door.

"Please." I stuck my foot in to prevent it from shutting.

The midwife emerged from a back room. When she spotted me, she said, "Malka. Is it time?"

"Yes." I gasped for breath. "It's not good."

She put one hand on her hip and looked toward the bedroom. "She'll be delivering soon. I'll be by immediately after."

I wanted to cry. I wanted to demand, *No, come now!* I wanted to scream, *My mama needs you!* Instead I turned and ran back.

Mama's bed was drenched in sweat. She grasped her stomach, as if that could keep the pain from spilling out. Gertie cried in the kitchen, so I scurried between the two. I brought Mama water, untied her headscarf, wiped her forehead, rubbed her back. I gave Gertie the last piece of kuchen, held her and bounced her, and sang softly in her ear. When

Gertie quieted, I soothed Mama. When Mama could take a breath, I calmed Gertie.

As I tended them, my lips moved automatically, forming the prayers Mama always recited, the ones calling for healing. In the time between spasms, which was shortening, Mama muttered her own.

Why wasn't the midwife here yet? If only Papa would show up. If only Max's class would end early. They could take care of Gertie while I tended to Mama.

Mama's cries grew more severe.

"Malka!" she said between wails. "Where is the midwife?"

"She's coming, Mama."

"Malka," Mama whimpered. "There's blood."

A small red dot on her skirt blossomed into a sea of crimson. Panic surged from my every pore. "Okay, Mama. Let's clean you up." I loosened her skirt's waistband, wondering why I hadn't thought to do that hours ago. Ignoring Gertie's cries, I hurried to the kitchen for warm water and rags, when a knock came at the door.

The midwife.

"Thank God," I said, tears releasing.

The midwife checked on Mama. She came into the kitchen to wash up and order me to boil more water and rip the rags I'd found. "When you're done, take Gertie, and find your father."

I returned to Mama's side. "You're in good hands now. I'm going to find Papa, okay?"

She couldn't speak, so I waited for the swell of pain to pass. "Find him. Quickly."

Before I could leave, Mama grabbed my wrist, with more strength than I'd imagined she had.

"Malka," Mama said, "make me a promise."

"Of course, Mama."

"Whatever happens, don't let them take me to a hospital. Hospitals are where you go to die. I'm not ready to die."

"Mama! How can you say such things! No one is dying!"

"Malka—"

"*Pu pu pu!*" I spit on the floor three times. "*Kein ayin hara*. No talk of death."

"I need to hear you say this, Malka. Say you promise."

"I promise, Mama."

"Put Anshel near me." I moved the family photo from the dresser to her bedside. She said faintly, "My sweet Anshel. Protect me. Protect my baby."

The midwife bustled in with her supplies, so I slipped out, scooping Gertie up. "Come, *bubelah*," I whispered in her ear. "Let's find Papa."

The warm spring breeze brightened Gertie's spirits. "Down," she ordered in Yiddish.

"Down," I repeated in English. "But no, we don't have time for that." Walking with an almost-three-year-old was time consuming; she had to examine every flower, pick up each rock, and follow ants down the sidewalk.

She howled, straining to escape my arms as we reached the bar on Baxter Street.

"Closed," a voice growled as I pounded on the door.

"Big Al, it's urgent! It's Minnie."

The door swung open.

"Where's my father? Where's Ike?" My words stuttered, coming out on top of each other. "I need him now. We need him now. Right now. I need to find him." Tears flowed down my face, and Gertie bawled in my arms.

"He's picking up a shipment. What's wrong?" The gentle tone from such a hulking man disoriented me.

"It's my mama." I couldn't catch my breath. "Where's my father? I need my father. Mama needs my father." I was babbling, frantic.

"Come here." Big Al led me to the bar. Behind it, he uncorked a bottle and poured a glass of brown liquid. He slid it across the counter. "Drink this."

Juggling Gertie on my hip, I gulped it in one swallow, then gagged and sputtered. Gertie stopped crying to laugh at me. "Jesus Christ." The drink was fire in my throat, slipping flames into my stomach. Heat rained through my body, and a metallic taste filled my mouth. It did the job, though. The bourbon halted my hysteria, allowed me to breathe.

"Tell me what's wrong," Big Al said.

"Mama's having the baby." I shifted Gertie. "It's not going well."

Frank came out of the back room with a crate of bottles he set behind the counter.

"Frank," Big Al said, "find Ike. Tell him to get home right away. His wife needs him."

"Tell Papa no hospital. I promised. No hospital."

With one look at my tearstained face, Frank said, "No hospital," and left quickly.

I exhaled. Mama'd given birth plenty of times. Anshel. Max. Me. Gertie. Mama would be fine. The baby would be fine.

"Frank will find him. Go."

"What about the bar?" Would Papa be angry at me for not staying to help with Frank gone? All I could think of was being with Mama.

"So we open a little late." His chin pointed toward Gertie. "Take care of your family."

~

The noises from the apartment reached me in the stairwell. Inhuman sounds. My arms ached from holding Gertie, but I pulled her closer.

I opened the front door to discover Mama's friend Mrs. Brodman at the sink, washing rags. She took one look at me with Gertie and said, "Get her out of here. Now."

"But Mama—"

"Your mama has Mrs. Oberman, and she has me."

"I'll drop Gertie off at—"

A keening wail came from the next room.

Placing her hand on my back, she moved me toward the door. "Both of you. Go."

"But—"

"Go to Toibe's. Your sister needs you. I'll send for you later."

Gertie's tiny fists clung to me, pinching the skin beneath my dress, her howling face buried into my shoulder.

Mrs. Brodman pushed us out the door, then shut it behind us.

With nowhere else to go, I carried Gertie to Mrs. Brodman's daughter's apartment. In grammar school, Toibe and I had been in class together. Like me, she was a few years too old for her grade, but while I had learned English and caught up, Toibe had remained with the younger children until she'd dropped out. She had married and had a son of her own.

Toibe welcomed us in. Gertie toddled to Toibe's son, Herschel, as if she knew the boy, which I supposed she did. Toibe may have been my age, but with her Yiddish, her child, and her Old World sentimentality, she socialized with my mother rather than me. Even her apartment appeared as if it belonged to an older couple, with a credenza brimming with Yiddish books, a sizable menorah taking up shelf space, and Shabbos candlesticks in a place of honor. As a married woman, Toibe covered her hair with a scarf.

"Drink this." Toibe offered me a glass of tea.

I stirred a sugar cube in mindlessly, going round and round and round, until Toibe placed her palm on my hand to still me. "Why don't we pray?" She rose and pulled two books off the shelf. She passed one to me, but when I opened it, I saw pages of Yiddish.

"I can't . . ." Why hadn't I learned to read Yiddish? How happy Mama would be if I could write letters for her and read her *The Forverts*. I promised myself I would start learning that week. As soon as the baby was born, I'd have Max teach me my Yiddish letters. If Max was too busy, I'd bear that dark shul and ask Rebbetzin Umansky, the rabbi's wife, to help me.

Toibe opened her book. "This is the prayer for a woman giving birth." I closed my eyes and listened to her Yiddish words, pleading for *Hashem* to open my mother's womb. To show mercy on her. To allow my mother to give birth.

Her words rained over me, washed through me, cleansed me. Mama was a righteous person, a woman of valor. God wouldn't abandon her. As Toibe recited, I mouthed prayers of my own.

I don't know how long I sat there, deep in prayer. Gertie cried, and Toibe fed the children, but I stayed, my hands clasped, my torso rocking as Yiddish words flowed from my lips. I didn't stop until a knock came at the door.

"You're needed at home," the small boy who lived a floor down from our apartment said.

Toibe handed me Gertie. "Go in good health."

I ran the three blocks, squeezing Gertie. I sprinted up the stairs, and when I reached the top, I wanted to collapse from the weight of my sister, the weight of the exertion, the weight of my fear. I realized I hadn't eaten the entire day, but I wasn't hungry. Just weak.

I plowed into the apartment, my senses alert.

My attention was drawn to a sound, a howling, but it wasn't the howling of Mama.

It was a quieter howling, more constant, not a howl of pain.

A baby.

It was the sound of a baby. Such sweet relief I'd never felt. The baby sounded angry but very much alive.

And yet.

My eyes couldn't reconcile that sound and the scene in front of me. I registered what I saw, but the feelings, the meaning, wouldn't sink in.

I saw Papa, immobile at the kitchen table, staring at the wall, a cigarette burning in his hand, ashes dropping on his pant leg. I saw the midwife, bouncing a baby—my sister Louise—in her arms, attempting to feed her from a milk-soaked rag. And I saw the men from the *chevra kedisha*, the burial society, preparing Mama's body for the funeral.

Part Two

Chapter Thirteen

The morning after Mama's passing, I woke in total darkness in a fog. Gertie clung to me in her sleep, her arm entwined around mine. My chest throbbed, twisted into knots, a burning sensation, as my head caught up: Mama was gone. The grief spread like fire through my limbs, my whole body engulfed in pain.

Wails rose from the Moses basket at the foot of my bed.

Louise.

The midwife had left in the wee hours, after showing me how to feed the baby. I untangled myself from Gertie and peered into the basket. Louise's face was balled up like a fist, her eyes squeezed shut, her cheeks bright red, her tiny tongue pressed to the bottom of her mouth as she howled. This baby. So alone, so vulnerable, so angry. Snatched from the warmth of her mother's womb.

I placed my hand on her chest, startled at the way it rose up and down. I stroked, whispering, "It's okay, Louise. It's okay," even as I realized nothing was okay—and nothing would ever be okay again.

From the next bed, Max asked, his voice cracking, "What do we do, Min? What do we do?"

I stared at this tiny creature, a blanket of heartache embracing me. This girl was mine now. I looked to my brother, his eyes puffy, his skin blotchy. They were all mine. Papa. Max. Gertie. Louise. I was the woman of the house.

I longed to return to bed, pull up the covers, and pretend every-thing was the same. I longed for Max to rise and rub my back and promise me everything would be all right. I longed for Mama.

Louise continued to cry.

"I'll feed her," I said.

In the kitchen, I turned on the light and placed a pot on the stove. As the midwife had shown me, I poured in milk, added water, and stirred in sugar. The formula had to boil for five minutes.

The midwife had tidied up, placing the pots used in the birth in a stack on the counter, a tower threatening to topple. The door to Mama and Papa's room was open. I went to close it, so as not to disturb Papa, but when I peered in, I saw the bed was empty. Did Papa leave because he couldn't bear to be in the room without Mama? Or because he had work to do? I swallowed a knob of bitterness. He should be here. He should be taking care of us.

The sheets had been stripped from the bed and piled in the corner, a bloody tangle of cloth. The mattress was stained with the remains of the birth. I couldn't stomach looking at it. I took hold of one side to pull it from the bed frame. I tried to turn it over, but it was lumpy and uneven, and it fought me. I pushed it and shoved it, but all I did was knock over the picture on the end table. Defeated, I dropped the mattress to the floor and sobbed.

An acrid smell made me jump to my feet. The forgotten milk had boiled over, spewing onto the stovetop. Grabbing the pot handle, I burned myself and leaped back. An angry crimson streak creased my palm.

I ran my reddened hand under cold water. Later it would blister. *Mama,* I silently called to the heavens. *I hurt myself. Come bandage me. Come kiss it and make it better.*

With a dish towel, this time, around the handle, I poured the mess into the sink. A thick brown crust coated the bottom of the pot. From the next room, Louise wailed.

Mama?

No reply.

It was up to me.

Pulling a new pot from the cabinet, I started again.

~

The funeral was that day, but someone had to stay with Gertie and Louise. I ached to be with Mama, to ensure the rites were observed, to make sure she would be at rest. Of course, the rabbi would do that, but I wanted to see it for myself. I couldn't believe she wouldn't be walking in the door at any moment with vegetables for me to chop or sewing for a widower neighbor.

I'd remain with the girls. One look at Papa's drawn cheeks and hollow eyes, and I didn't dare argue. That Max attended was a given. Kaddish needed to be said for Mama, the blessing for the dead, and only men could say it. A son's recitation was especially important, for it elevated the soul of the deceased.

Alone with the children, in a stupor, I made formula, filling jars, placing them in the icebox. No matter how many I made, it was never enough. I'd warm the formula, drip it into Louise's mouth with a medicine dropper, and then make more for the next time she wailed with hunger. For Gertie I cut up salami and sliced bread and attempted to read her a book, but every few pages my mind wandered until Gertie fussed and brought me back to the task at hand.

I rocked Louise over and over, peering into her face, searching for a family resemblance. "Louise," I whispered, wondering who had given her this name. Papa? The midwife? Was she named for someone? This child was a stranger, an exchange I hadn't asked for. If only I could return her and have my mother back.

The burial ground was in Queens, so the journey took over an hour. An army of neighbors followed Papa and Max home, coming to sit shiva—the seven-day period of mourning. The women filled our icebox with soups and casseroles, piled breads on the counter. A team of them entered Mama's room with bleach and scrub brushes. One of them scooped Louise from my arms, and with relief, I lay down. Max paced, reciting Psalms. In so many ways, he was Mama's son.

From my bed, I heard the busyness of women, the running of water, the swishes of a broom, the scratch of furniture being shifted. I drifted in and out of wakefulness, numb, with no knowledge of the passing of time. The house hummed. I was sick, though nothing ailed me. I lay feverish, though my body was cool. Through the night, women cared for my sisters. I fell into tortured sleep, images of home, of Mama, of Anshel, of the two of them tempting me from my dreams.

The next morning, I forced myself from bed. In the front room, a dark cloth covered the mirror, and the cushions had been removed from chairs, for we were told not to gaze at ourselves in our grief and to embrace the discomfort of death. The women bustled, and in my haze, they merged into one, offering bowls of soup or pieces of liver. At their urging, I'd eat a bite or two. For the first three days of shiva, the house was full, Louise in someone's arms and Gertie clean and fed. The women took shifts, caring for us around the clock. Sylvia and Mrs. Goldwasser arrived each morning, but I stayed in bed curled into a tight ball, not wanting to face them. Sylvia had her mother. I didn't have mine.

At the prescribed times, the men came. Mourner's Kaddish was to be recited by the mourners with a minyan—a group of ten Jewish men—at morning, midday, and evening prayers. Women didn't count, weren't supposed to recite the prayer. Only the men mattered, a notion that, when my mind was less clouded, would bother me. Three times a day, Rabbi Umansky came to our house with seven men in tow to say Kaddish with Max and Papa. Papa, as the husband, said it for a month. Max, as the son, the primary mourner, recited it daily for eleven months.

Uncle Aaron came in the evenings. Aunt Sara, pregnant once again, couldn't make the journey, so he came laden with soups, casseroles, breads, and sweets she'd made. Uncle Aaron muttered the prayers and cried to Papa. I avoided him, wouldn't let him corner me, because the sorrow in his eyes was too much; I was afraid it would break me.

For three days, Papa said Kaddish among the men. On the third night, after I'd gone to bed with Gertie curled next to me, Papa and Uncle Aaron exchanged harsh words. I didn't want to hear it, so I put the pillow over my ears.

On the fourth morning, Papa woke me while Max paced in the front room reciting prayers. Max's prayers were endless.

"Minnie." The brittleness in Papa's voice cut me.

I rolled on my side so he wouldn't see my tears, my pillowcase damp beneath me. He sat on my bed.

"Minnie, I have to return to work." He took my shoulders and pulled me back so he could see me.

I wiped my face with the blanket. "Work? But there are three more days of shiva."

"Problems with shipments." That would have been what Uncle Aaron and Papa argued about. Uncle Aaron must have been horrified.

"Make the men at the bar help." Papa's callousness was another thrust of the knife to my chest.

"This is work only I can take care of."

"But shiva—"

"Minnela, I don't like it either. If I don't return, I'll look weak. In my business, looking weak is . . ." He closed his eyes and took a breath. "Well, it's best not to appear weak."

"Mama would have wanted you here."

Pain flashed across Papa's face, though he straightened his back and steeled himself. "Mama is gone. Sitting shiva for three more days won't bring her back."

I gasped.

"Minnie, this world won't wait for shiva. I don't like it, but that's how things work." His shoulders slumped, as if saying that sapped him of his energy. "Besides, we need the money. Tonight . . ." He wouldn't meet my eyes. "Tonight we need to discuss what happens next."

"Happens next?" Who could think of next when I was drowning in now?

"Minnie, I don't know how to keep you in school. I have no one to care for the girls."

"We can hire someone. It's only for a couple of months."

"The money I owe . . ." He rubbed his brow with his handkerchief. "We don't have the money." His voice was small, like Max's back home when he had broken the eggs meant for dinner and we couldn't afford to buy more.

"The land," I said. "The Everglades. Sell it."

He stared at the floor. "There's no land."

"You lied about it?" Fury blended with my ache, a lethal mixture. It was one thing to hide the bar from Mama, but to outright lie to her?

"No. I had the land. But the hurricane."

I fought to keep my voice level. "What are you talking about?"

"In Florida. A hurricane last September. Wiped out the land. Wiped out us. I . . . I'd borrowed more to buy that land." His hands were shaking. "You have to believe me. We were making good money, and this development was a sure thing. I invested all we had, but it didn't cover the cost. So I borrowed another thousand. And it's gone. All of it. Washed out to sea.

"I didn't want your mama to know." Papa looked up, his eyes wet. I'd never seen him teary before. "Didn't want her to know I'd failed her.

"We can live off the bar. But there is no extra." Tears streamed down his face. "I let your mother down. I let this family down." He put his head in his hands. "I'm so sorry, my Minnela. I'm so sorry."

His tears sliced through my anger, reaching deep inside, allowing the heartache to resurface. I hugged him, my tears falling onto his shoulder. He held tight enough that I felt as if I were the adult and he were the child.

"I loved her so much," he mumbled into my shoulder. "How will I live without her?"

We clutched one another for a full minute before he pulled away. I thought he was going to say more, but instead he shook his head and wiped his face. He closed the door quietly behind him as he left.

I'd never felt more alone. I didn't want to have to be the strong one. But I didn't seem to have a choice.

What did school matter anymore anyway?

I stared at the cracks in the ceiling, the spidery webs now trapping me in the confines of the apartment.

I was the mama.

~

The apartment buzzed with motion. After dressing, I slipped into the washroom and tried to rinse some of the stink off me with a cloth. Bathing during shiva was forbidden. When Mama had received word of her own mother's passing—my bubbe—she had mourned in full compliance of Jewish law. For seven days she sat—not on our upholstered chair but on a crate, so as not to be in comfort. She didn't bathe. She didn't put on fresh clothing. She didn't work. While she herself could not say the Mourner's Kaddish, she sent Papa to the synagogue each morning, which surprisingly, he did. After sitting shiva, Mama observed the thirty days, during which she worked but didn't take enjoyments, not that she'd taken so many to begin with. For a full year, she adhered to the mourning rituals, and when the anniversary of her mama's death came—the *yahrzeit*—she sat for the entire day in tears, distraught she couldn't be at the unveiling of the gravestone. Mama's only comfort had been knowing Bubbe would care for Anshel.

So I knew the rules of mourning. I understood what we—me, Max, Papa—must do. With a deep breath, I left the bathroom. I loved Mama devotedly. But this was America. Work had to be done.

The women paused when I entered the kitchen. I took notice for the first time of what was happening around me. These were Mama's friends, the women who lived in the shadows, hair covered, skirts floor-sweeping, their only language Yiddish. They moved like mice in the apartment—quickly, quietly, efficiently.

"Come, sit," said an older woman with a brunette wig that sat slightly askew. Mrs. Kurtz, I dredged from my memory. "You haven't eaten properly in days."

"I'm not hungry."

"Minnie," a woman with a flowered headscarf said, and I realized it was Toibe. "You need to eat. You need your strength." She gently pushed me into a chair. "Here." She placed a bowl of broth in front of me. Everyone in the room spoke Yiddish, and I responded in kind.

The broth was warming, and without thought, I finished the soup.

Toibe was so like Mama. Married. Covered. With child. Approaching problems with prayer. Toibe would never cut her hair short or serve drinks in a bar. Mama wanted more for me. An education. A job. A husband who earned a proper living.

I promised myself I would become that girl. For Mama. Someday. For now I would be a mother—to Gertie and Louise. Later I would be a secretary. I would do things. See what else this country had to offer. That's why we had made the trek across the ocean, wasn't it? It would take longer, but it would happen.

Louise wailed, and I stood to soothe her. For the past four days, Louise's basket had sat in the kitchen, where the women had tended to her.

"Sit," said Mrs. Kurtz.

"I need to take care of my sister."

Picking her up, I cradled her head. Despite the scrunched-up anger, she was striking, with a dusting of downy hair, bushier eyebrows than I'd ever seen on a baby, and lips that puckered with her cries. Her skin was as soft as warm challah, and she smelled of talcum and dried milk. As empty as I was, I could see where Louise might, a little, fill a corner of the hole in my chest.

"Let me feed her," Mrs. Kurtz said.

"I need to learn how. She's my responsibility."

Mrs. Kurtz appraised me. "Yes, yes, she is."

The women were thorough in their lessons. The baby needed so much: bottles, nipples, measuring glasses, enamelware funnel . . . I forced their words to memory: Pierce rubber nipples with a hot sewing needle before boiling—but don't store the nipple in boiled water, because bacteria will grow. Soak wet diapers immediately in cold water. Empty soiled diapers into the toilet, then wash them in boiling water with mild soap.

As I sat feeding my sister, listening to the advice, Rabbi Umansky arrived with seven men. His face wrinkled in confusion. Mourners weren't to leave until shiva was complete, except to attend Shabbat services. Yet Papa was not here.

Mrs. Kurtz approached the rabbi and spoke softly to him. The rabbi raised his eyes to the ceiling, as if apologizing to God for my father's disrespect. One of the men left, then returned in a few minutes with an eighth man, who, with the rabbi and Max, made up ten. They recited the prayers.

Late that night, when I couldn't sleep, I thought of the rabbi's determination to watch over Mama's soul. I didn't quite understand it. "Max," I whispered. "Papa always said Rabbi Umansky was a shyster, but he doesn't seem so bad."

Max, too, was awake, staring at the ceiling. He exhaled slowly. "Papa isn't always right, you know." His fists clenched the blanket as he pulled it high, covering most of his head, as if he were a child. "He should be here."

"He can't," I said.

"I don't understand."

But I did. I supposed I was Papa's daughter.

～

113

On the sixth day of shiva, the door opened to reveal a tall man in a fitted herringbone suit with a bowler on his head. He looked nothing like the neighborhood men. Everyone in the apartment stared.

"I'm Duke," he said. "I work with Ike."

The man from the bar. Max lowered his prayer book, his lips pressed flat.

"Ike?" Mrs. Kurtz said.

"My papa," I said.

"Ah."

"I've come . . ." He shifted from foot to foot. "I've come to pay my respects." To me, he said, "My mother makes delicious *mohntortes*. I asked her to bake one for your family."

"That's lovely of you," Mrs. Kurtz said. "Let me take that." I recognized the tight smile she gave Duke. It said, *I will be polite to your face, but the moment you leave, we will be discussing exactly what you and Yitzhak do for a living.*

He flashed me his crooked grin, but in my misery, it held none of the charm it had last time. "Well," he said, "I should get going." He twisted his hat. "Minnie"—I was surprised he remembered my name—"and . . ." He waited for my brother to supply his name.

When he didn't, I said it for him. "Max."

"Max," Duke said. *"Hamakom ye-nachem etchem be-toch she'ar ave-lay tziyon v'yerushala'yim."*

That he knew the traditional Hebrew words of consolation surprised me.

"May the Lord comfort you together with all mourners of Zion and Jerusalem," he repeated in English.

"Thank you," I said.

He glanced around the room one more time, nodded, and put on his hat, but before leaving he said, "If you need anything . . ." His voice trailed off.

"We will take good care of Minnie, Max, and the girls." Mrs. Kurtz pierced him with a stern gaze. "Thank your mother for the cake." She practically pushed him out the door.

I gave him the slightest of smiles to let him know I appreciated his coming. He touched the brim of his hat and left.

As soon as he was gone, Mrs. Kurtz picked up the cake and threw it in the trash bin.

"What are you doing?" I asked.

"Who knows how kosher that kitchen is. You want to eat *treyf*?"

Later that evening, when everyone was busy with the girls, I sneaked a piece of the cake from the trash. Duke was right. It was delicious.

~

For the final days of shiva, the women surrounded me. At the end of shiva, though, they returned to their homes.

"You call on me when you need me," Mrs. Kurtz said.

"Bring over your sewing," Toibe said. "We can pass the time together."

"Your mother would be proud," said the oldest of the women, stroking my cheek.

After they left the apartment, tears started anew. Mama had wanted to teach me how to care for a child. I could have learned at her side. Instead, strangers had imparted the lessons. I should have listened to her; I could have made her happy.

Gertie tugged at my dress. "Hungry."

I bent over and gathered the toddler in my arms. "Then let's feed you."

I would make Mama happy now.

Chapter Fourteen

I stopped attending school.

Papa still delivered and collected for Mr. Rothstein. Max attended City College on the Upper West Side, a journey of almost an hour. Papa made an effort to join us for dinner, leaving immediately after to return to the bar, so I tried to cook meals worth coming home for. During the day, I piled Louise into a pram and took Gertie by the hand to do the daily shopping. I played games with Gertie. We took trips to the library, where I chose books for the girls. Gertie loved *When We Were Very Young*; every time I read the poem "Market Square," about a boy longing for a little brown rabbit, she'd squeal, "Again!" I checked the book out over and over, even after the librarian raised her eyebrows and said, "We do have other books, you know." I cleaned the house. I fed Louise, changed diapers, bathed her. Louise alone was a full-time job. Gertie made my work go into overtime.

Sylvia stopped by many evenings on her way home from her office job, where she was one of many in a typing pool. But by the time she arrived, it was the witching hour, when Gertie was grumpy and Louise cried ceaselessly. Sylvia would bounce the baby while I teased food into Gertie, but our visits were disappointing. On weekends, when Max was around, I used the freedom to do laundry, clean the apartment, and do the other chores I couldn't do with the two at my feet.

Once a week, I took the girls to Toibe's house. Gertie played with Toibe's son, Louise napped, and Toibe patiently answered my questions about child-rearing.

Just as Rabbi Umansky had done for Mama, he did for us, knocking on our door on Friday mornings, checking if there was anything we needed, bestowing a blessing. When he came, he made a pot of tea, put Louise on his lap, fed Gertie a sweet, and allowed me to sit, albeit with my sewing, attempting to keep up with ripped clothes and growing children.

We didn't chat about religion. We didn't chat about money for the synagogue. We spoke of the children. Of my grief over Mama. When he left, I always found challah bread, a carton of eggs, and a quarter sitting on the counter.

Only once did he bring up anything of a spiritual matter. "I notice," he said, "Max doesn't come to say Kaddish for your mother."

I had little knowledge of what Max did or did not do.

"Saying Kaddish helps a spirit rise. If Max says Kaddish for your mother, her spirit will ascend."

That night, I asked Max about it. He glanced to see if Papa was listening. "I say it. I go every day before class and at lunch at a shul near school."

On his next visit, I reported this to Rabbi Umansky, who smiled broadly, displaying the gap of missing teeth on the left side of his mouth.

I did everything I could to mimic the life Mama had created. We recited the blessings over candles on Friday nights, but I didn't hold a tune as well as she had. I told stories but without the many voices she'd used. I couldn't juggle feeding Louise, baking a casserole, and entertaining Gertie at the same time. My sewing was uneven, my chicken soup salty, and my hugs too often had tears in them. The life I was creating was a poor imitation of Mama's.

The rabbi's visits continued for a few months, until one day Papa arrived as the rabbi was leaving. Papa's hours were erratic; he showed up when he showed up. When he saw the rabbi, his eyes darkened.

"*Gut Shabbos*, Yitzhak," the rabbi said as he walked out of the apartment.

Papa's eyes flew about the kitchen. "What did that man want? Was he asking for donations for the synagogue?"

"No, Papa." I pointed to the counter. "Look, he left this for us."

When Papa saw the food and the money, he pounced. He picked up the quarter, grabbed the challah and eggs, and ran out the door.

I didn't know what was said between him and the rabbi. All I knew was when Papa returned, out of breath, his face flushed, he said, "Don't take charity. Ever! We Soffers take care of ourselves." His voice hissed. "Religion is a racket, and believe me—I know rackets."

The next Friday morning, I nervously eyed the door. I couldn't wait to show the rabbi Louise's first tooth. To tell him he was right: spreading butter on her gums helped relieve her pain. But I also feared what my father might do if the rabbi returned. I wanted him to visit. I wanted him to stay away.

Rabbi Umansky didn't come.

I mourned the loss of my friend.

~

A hot wave in July tested my patience. Not only was I doing the work of Mama, but I found her words coming out of my mouth. "Why can't you let me know if you won't be on time for dinner?" I scolded both Papa and Max one night when they arrived long after the meal had been made. I placed a cup of coffee on the table for each of them. The girls were asleep. "You could give me the courtesy of a call." I held up the receiver of our phone. "Why do we have this if you're not going to use it?"

"The bar gets busy," Papa said. It still felt strange that he could acknowledge the bar at home.

"So call." I threw my hands in the air.

He gave me a sheepish smile.

I turned to Max. "And you? What's your excuse?"

"When do I have time?"

"You were in class till eight at night?"

"I went to the library to study. I lost track of time."

"You lost track of time." I grumbled as I reheated the chicken, which had been moist at 6:00 p.m. but was now drying to rubber. "Papa, use some of your hard-earned money, and buy that boy a wristwatch."

"Yes, Mama." Papa's teasing tone stopped me flat.

"I'm not Mama." How dare he joke. How dare he diminish her memory.

A wail from the next room. Louise.

"Papa, comfort Louise while I plate your food."

"She's fine. Check on her later."

"Do your ears need cleaning? She's crying now."

"And she'll be crying again later."

I considered the past few months. How Papa would tickle Gertie, make treats appear from behind her ear, let her sit on his lap.

He'd never touched Louise. Was that possible? He'd never asked about her, shown an interest in her, cared for her.

"Why do you ignore Louise?"

Papa pulled a cigarette from his jacket pocket.

"I asked you a question."

He struck a match on the table and lit the tip of the cigarette, then took a long draw.

"Louise needs a father," I said.

Papa exhaled a plume of smoke. "And I need your mother." He spoke with an eerie calm.

"Papa!"

"Minnie," Max said. "You're worked up."

"Of course I am!"

Papa casually tapped the ash off his cigarette. "That baby stole your mother from me."

"Mama wanted Louise more than anything." My voice echoed in the small kitchen.

"More than her life?"

Hadn't Mama been warned not to have more children? Hadn't she ignored it because she'd wanted more? "Mama wanted Louise," I repeated.

"Louise is a *mamzer*."

I gasped. Louise was no bastard. She'd had a mother and a father, although now, it appeared she had neither. "Mama would be ashamed to hear you talk like that!"

The slap came from nowhere. My hand flew to my cheek. I stepped back, wide eyed.

"You will not speak to me like that." Papa's iciness made me shiver.

"You need to be a father to Louise." My tone matched his.

"I don't need to do anything."

My cheeks burned. I'd given up my life for these girls. He couldn't do the bare minimum?

How dare he.

Afraid of what I might do next, I pulled off the apron, tossed it onto the counter. "Max, take care of Louise." I walked to the door.

"Where are you going?" Max sounded frightened. "I don't know what to do!"

"You can comfort her, feed her, sing her a song, change her diaper. When I get back, Louise better be sleeping peacefully!"

With that, I was out the door.

~

Once I was on the street, I realized I had nowhere to go. It was late. Toibe would be busy with her own family. Perhaps I could find Sylvia.

How could Papa feel this way?

Approaching Sylvia's building, I hesitated. At 9:00 p.m., knocking on her door would alarm her mother. With disappointment, I realized

I could do nothing, so I turned to leave. I stopped, however, when the front door of the building opened, and Sylvia hopped down the steps.

"Minnie?" she called. "Are you actually out of the house with no crumb snatchers hanging on? Gads, I adore Gertie, but seeing you without her pulling my hair is the bee's knees."

"Where are you headed?"

"To the Back of Ratner's."

"Alone?"

"Of course not, silly." She wore a lovely red sleeveless shift with gold bead trim. "I'm meeting Ray."

"Who's Ray?"

"My current sheik." She appraised me. "What're you doing here?"

"Had to get out of my apartment. Dear lord, when did you replace Curtis?"

"What's tonight?"

"Sunday."

"Then . . ." She counted on her fingers. "Curtis and I ended last Monday. Met Ray the same night. Keep up, would you?" Sylvia's teasing made me feel like the young woman I was. "Let's go. You're coming with me."

"I'm not dressed for it." Spit-up stains decorated my top, a pastel yellow blouse with a Peter Pan collar. My skirt, a simple black one with pleats, fell to midcalf and beautifully showed off the oatmeal Gertie had flung at me at breakfast.

With a laugh deeper than what you'd expect from such a fragile frame, she said, "It'll be dark. No one will be looking at your clothes." She tugged me along. "Let's go."

On the walk to Ratner's, she filled me in on work, her boyfriend, the shopping she'd done, the movies she'd seen. I listened, with nothing to add.

A block from Ratner's, Sylvia stopped. "Before we go in . . ." She dug in her handbag and pulled out a compact, a pencil, and lipstick. "Put these on."

I'd never left the house with makeup on. The lipstick Sylvia had given me was for play only. Mama disapproved of makeup. Of course, Mama wasn't here anymore, and I didn't care what Papa and Max thought, although I was pretty sure they'd never notice.

Sylvia held open the compact. I peered into the tiny mirror as I traced my lips with the pencil. It was a bright red, much darker than I would have expected, but it gave me a Clara Bow pout. I rubbed my lips together, smoothing it out. "I like this color."

"Helena Rubinstein. Red Raspberry." She squinted. "You're lucky. You're so pale. No need to lighten your skin." I was pale because I'd spent the entire summer inside with the girls or under the shade of trees in parks. "But your cheeks." She took the lipstick, rubbed some on her fingers, and applied it to my face. "There. Pat it with powder."

I did as instructed. The color emphasized the roundness of my face. I moved my head from side to side, pleased with my reflection.

Sylvia led me down a back alley, where an older man with thinning hair and a pouchy stomach paced.

"There you are." He oozed impatience as much as he oozed sweat. "You're late." This was Sylvia's guy?

Sylvia laughed. "I'm worth waiting for." She pecked his cheek. "This is my dear friend Minnie. We ran into each other and were having so much fun gabbing I insisted she come. I was sure you wouldn't mind."

"Don't mind at all," he said.

At the end of the alley, Ray flashed a card to a loitering man, who knocked on an inconspicuous door. We were swept into a dark corridor, another man opened a second door, and we continued into a large room, dimly lit, with couches and plush chairs around cozy wooden tables. A few smartly dressed fellas sat on stools at the bar. Dotted around the room were couples and small groups. The women in the joint were dolled up, with heavily plucked eyebrows and skin powdered to pastiness.

This bar looked nothing like Papa's.

"Grab seats," Ray said before making his way to order.

Before Sylvia pulled me to a small wooden table with mismatched chairs, I saw Ray pull out his wallet. I understood his appeal to Sylvia: the leather bulged with cash.

"So what does your sheik do?"

"Finance big shot," she said. "At RCA."

Ray came to the table carrying a bag and two teacups, which he set in front of us. Sylvia winked at me as she picked hers up, so I raised mine. I sipped. Bourbon. Smoother than the one at Papa's bar.

Ray frowned. "You've drank before?"

I think he was disappointed I didn't sputter and spit it out. I smiled and sipped again. "What's in your bag?"

"Bottle of beer." His arm draped casually around Sylvia.

"How was your day?" she asked.

While they playfully bantered, I studied the room, trying to pinpoint the differences between this place and Papa's. Better-dressed people, for starters. No one looked like they'd labored the day away. Stools at the bar. Moody lighting providing sultry ambience. A multitude of small tables—steady ones, at that—allowing for intimacy. A general cleanliness. Tastier hooch.

Two bartenders made drinks—not that drinks were made. They poured alcohol, some clear, some brown. As I gazed at the folks at the bar, I caught the eye of a man staring at me. Even sitting, I could tell he was tall by the way his legs stretched before him. Something about his sculpted face looked familiar. He cocked his head at me, and when he grinned, I saw two teeth, slightly crooked. I raised my chin in greeting. Duke.

Duke turned to the barkeep and signaled with his fingers. The barkeep left the patrons he was serving—to their audible groans—and brought Duke two teacups.

"Daydreaming?" Sylvia asked, bringing me back to them.

"Excuse me?"

"Ray was asking what you do."

"Ah." How to answer that? I didn't want to admit to taking care of children. "Trying to find a decent job." It was an out-and-out lie, but it was easier than the truth. To lighten my tone, I added, "Not all of us are as smart as Sylvia. Snagging that plush job."

Sylvia winked at me.

Someone from behind placed a teacup of bourbon in front of me, saying, "Oh, I'd say you're plenty smart."

Ray jumped up. "Mr. Hess!"

"May I join you?"

"Of course." Ray hurried to find an empty chair. Ray's deference startled me. Who, exactly, was Duke?

"What makes you think I'm so smart?" I asked.

He bent down and whispered so only I could hear, "I don't know another girl who could manage a bar on her own."

Giddiness bubbled in my chest.

"Do you mind?" he asked me when Ray returned with a chair.

I waved. "Be my guest."

"Mr. Hess, to what do we owe this pleasure?" Ray's obsequiousness overflowed like the street gutters in a storm.

"I spied Minnie across the room and wanted to say hello."

"You two know each other?" Ray didn't sound like such a big shot anymore.

Duke's hazel eyes, flecked with gold, didn't leave mine. "I'm a business associate of her father's."

At *business associate*, Ray's ears pricked up.

"Duke, this is Sylvia and Ray." Duke broke his gaze to tip his hat at Sylvia and shake Ray's hand. Ray acted as if he'd met a movie star.

"So," Duke said to me, "how are you?"

His earnestness cut me. "Fine."

"Max getting along okay?"

"He is. Attending classes at City College."

"Oh yeah?"

Ray reassessed me. Duke clearly knew something of my family. Ray must have wondered how powerful my father was. I wondered the same.

"And your sisters?" Duke asked.

I hesitated. Talking about my sisters would only revive my anger. Duke's brow furrowed. "Sorry. Didn't mean to pry."

"Let's talk about you." I stashed my hands in my lap to hide my trembling.

"What would you like to know?"

Ray and Sylvia no longer sat cozily but leaned across the table, fascinated by our conversation.

"Is Duke your real name?"

He chuckled. "If you ask my mama, she'll say it's Mendel. If you ask my papa, he says it's Myron. But I apparently was a demanding baby, so my bubbe called me 'His Highness, the Duke of Brownsville.' Duke stuck."

"That reminds me—you were right: your mother's *mohntorte* is exceptional."

"She'll be pleased to hear that. I'll have to ask her to bake you another. I love waking to the smells of her oven."

"Speaking of waking, what time is it?"

"Too early for you to be asking such silly questions." Sylvia's fascination with Duke was so obvious I thought Ray would be bothered, but he was just as spellbound.

"It's almost midnight," Duke said.

"So late!" Like Cinderella, I needed to leave the ball to return to my drudgery.

"Late? This is when the evening starts." Sylvia—who would drink for another hour, do whatever it was she did with Ray for another hour or so, and sleep six solid hours till she had to hop out of bed to rush to work—could say this.

Resentment simmered, as I knew I would sleep for two hours before Louise wanted a bottle and then for another two hours until

Gertie woke for the day and then the cycle of feeding the family, doing housework, and caring for the girls started over again. Toibe had told me it was time to stop feeding Louise when she woke, but the neighbors complained when she wailed in the dead of night, and I couldn't bear her tears. I ached with exhaustion merely thinking how little I'd sleep. "I'm afraid I have to go."

"You didn't finish your drink," Sylvia said.

I slid it across the table. "You finish it." The bourbon made me woozy, soft around the edges. I was a mother now. I didn't have time for hangovers.

"Let me walk you home," Duke said.

"Oh, no need." I stood. "I don't want to interrupt your good time."

He stood too. "How can I have a good time if you're not here?"

My stomach fluttered. "Well, then. Shall we?" Turning back to the table, I said, "Sylvia, thank you for inviting me along. Ray, thank you for the drink."

"Anytime," Ray said, delighted to be proven the gentleman in front of Duke.

Placing his hand on the small of my back, Duke led me out of the bar, which had grown more crowded. A few men attempted to waylay him into a conversation, but Duke ignored them.

Once we were outside, he dropped his hand. The spot on my back chilled.

"You're a popular person," I said.

His smile was lopsided. "Not me. My boss. Everyone wants access to Rothstein."

"Have you worked for him a long time?"

"I ran numbers for him as a kid. Moved up the ladder."

"Do you like working for him?"

"Well"—he pursed his lips and considered—"it's not a matter of like or dislike. It's what I do."

The walk was only five minutes, but Duke strolled leisurely, prolonging our time together. The two of us alternated peeking at each other from the corners of our eyes.

"How are *you* doing?" he asked.

My voice dried up at his gentle sympathy. I was mortified at the flood of grief unexpectedly washing over me. The heartache always took me by surprise. I'd be fine, changing a diaper or scrubbing dishes, but then an image of Mama would dance into my head, and I'd be floored with the sadness and hopelessness of it all. "I'm . . ." The words didn't form.

"Hey, hey." He took my arm, and we stopped walking. He lifted my chin, and I felt tears running down my cheeks.

He pulled a handkerchief from his pocket and dabbed my face. "I shouldn't have asked." His caress made me tingle.

My display of emotion embarrassed me. Especially in front of a man like Duke. What had Papa said? *Never show your weakness.* Well, my weakness dripped like an ice cream in July.

"Here." He held out the handkerchief.

"I'll wash it for you."

His half grin returned. "Keep it."

We walked in a companionable silence, and a thousand times I thought to say something, but I didn't trust myself. I was overtired, overwrought, and unsure.

When we arrived at my building, the street was surprisingly empty.

"We're here." The tenement was yet another embarrassment, with a huge sign reading COLUMBIA FINANCE stretching from the top floor down to the second floor. I looked up to our place on the fourth floor. Dark. They hadn't even left a light on for me. I curbed more tears.

"I'd like to see you again." He hesitated before adding, "Though I don't think your father would like that."

Fury gripped me. I wanted to see Duke, even if Papa didn't want me to. Hell, maybe *because* Papa didn't want me to.

The truth, though, was I couldn't. I couldn't make a date trusting Papa and Max to be there for Louise and Gertie. I couldn't find the energy after a day with the girls to go out and enjoy myself. Already, tonight, my body was ready to collapse from exhaustion.

My pause was long enough that Duke shifted uncomfortably.

"I wish I could see you again," I said.

"But?" He leaned against the stoop. "Your father?"

I shook my head. "My sisters. There's no one to watch them." Briefly I thought I could ask Toibe—Sylvia wouldn't know what to do with a baby and a toddler—but I couldn't imagine telling her I was going on a date with Duke.

"Well, Gertie and Louise won't be babies forever. Perhaps when they're older."

"When they're older," I agreed.

He placed his hand on my cheek, and I thought he'd pull me in for a kiss. I'd never had one before. I'd dreamed of a man like Duke giving me my first kiss.

But instead of the kiss, he slid his hand down my cheek and cupped my chin. "Ah, Minnie," he murmured. "Sweet dreams."

He turned and sauntered down the street. My stomach tangled into a knot that had nothing to do with the bourbon. There was but one certainty in my world: when the girls were older, Duke would be long gone, and I'd be a lonely old maid.

Chapter Fifteen

December 1927

As late summer turned to fall and fall slid into winter, the monotony of life settled over me. Things improved when Louise slept through the night, then declined when more teeth poked through. Instead of spending my time making bottles, I mashed food. I taught Gertie to dress herself, tie her laces, and wash herself in the basin. I babbled through the day, narrating my every move in English, although I recited all the Hebrew blessings I'd learned from Mama so the girls would know those too. Entire days I cleaned and cooked. With Papa paying back Mr. Rothstein for the bar and his investment loans—at an interest rate of 22 percent—we made economies. I haggled with pushcart operators over the price of carrots. I bought chicken legs instead of whole chickens. I scrubbed, dusted, mopped, scraped, sewed, neatened, laundered, and polished. From time to time Mama's friends stopped by to drop off food and check on us.

By December, I didn't recognize myself. My hair had grown out, my hands were a ragged mess, my nails were brittle, and my skin was dry. My frame had thinned, because who had time to eat? One morning, looking into the mirror, I realized with shock:

I looked like Mama.

Had Mama enjoyed this life? Why hadn't I appreciated all she did? She had been happiest when tending to her children. Why couldn't I feel the same? I was so tired. I was hungry. I was miserable.

How much I had taken for granted. How much I missed Mama.

The tears streamed and didn't stop, not even when Gertie encircled my neck with her pudgy arms and plastered tiny kisses on my cheeks. "No crying," she said in English, her four-year-old voice plunging a knife of guilt into my chest. "I love you, Min."

I wrapped her in my embrace, inhaling her scent, that sweet smell of Lux soap and sugar.

"I love you, Gertie." I held her snugly.

Across the room, eight-month-old Louise sat on a blanket. Her eyes followed us. She rocked forward and, with stilted motions, took her first tentative crawls.

Through my sniveling, I grinned. "Gertie, look!" She turned to where my finger pointed as Louise, with determination, made her way to us.

"Louise crawling!"

Though heaviness weighed in my chest, a lightness trickled through. When Louise made it to us, she climbed into my lap, nestling next to Gertie. I squeezed the two of them tight.

Those two. They were my loves. They were my everything.

For them, I would be Mama.

⁓

Life with a mobile child was complicated. Completing my work with Louise on the move was near impossible. I reminded myself to be patient. In four years, Louise would start kindergarten, and I'd earn my diploma. An office job, nights out, and a first kiss were still in my future.

The second week of March, Max came in from school with a stack of books. He woke before dawn to deliver milk, spent his days waiting tables at the Tip Top Diner, and attended classes at City College at night. Two years of college were required to attend law school, but because he took only a couple of classes a semester, his path to becoming an attorney would take twice as long.

"I'm short on money," I said. "After tomorrow, I won't have enough for groceries."

He spread his books on the table, pulling out a pencil and a notebook. "Don't look at me. I gave you everything I had."

"Maybe you need a better job."

"I'll get a better job. Once I graduate."

"I don't know that we can wait, Max."

"What do you think I can do that'll pay better?"

"You could work at the bar." All those tips left on the counter, tips that could fill our icebox.

"I'm going to pretend you didn't say that. It's an illicit job." He opened a large tome on post–Civil War American history.

"I'll remind you that the *illicit job* is what fills our icebox. The legal investments were what put us in the poorhouse."

"I'm not going to argue this. Get money from Papa." He flipped pages till he found what he was looking for. "I have a test tomorrow."

His eyes puffed, the whites lined with red. Max slept as little as I did. Possibly less. All his salary went directly to me to use on the family. He was doing the best he could.

I pulled a cup from the cabinet and poured coffee from the stovetop percolator. It wasn't as warm as it had been an hour ago, but it would do the job. I spooned in a heap of sugar and a generous dollop of cream. "Here." I placed it before him, along with a plate of cookies I'd baked earlier in the day.

"Thanks."

As I cleaned the dishes from the girls' dinner, it occurred to me I hadn't seen Papa in several days. His disappearance for a few nights wasn't unusual. He often made overnight trips, a quick run to the northern border for a truckload of liquor. Eleven hours there. Sleep in the truck. Get the goods, then eleven hours back. He'd never left us for an entire week.

"Is Papa on a delivery?" I asked. Max shrugged, only half listening. "Max, I'm asking you a question."

"I have no idea where Papa is."

"He hasn't been here since Thursday."

Max scribbled on his notepad.

"Max, it's Wednesday."

"So?"

"He's never away this long."

"He's fine."

I wrung out the dishcloth. "The girls are asleep. Keep an ear out for them. I'm going to see if Papa's at the bar. If we don't find money in a day or two, I won't be able to feed anyone."

Looking down at my housedress, I slipped into the bedroom where Gertie and Louise slept with me—Max had moved his mattress into Papa's room—and pulled out a dress from last year, one I didn't wear because it was too pretty to clean in. It draped loosely, my weight loss apparent. I brushed my hair, which grazed my shoulders, and swiped across my lips the lipstick Sylvia had given me for my last birthday. I rubbed a pinch on my cheeks.

It would have to do.

Fifteen minutes later, I approached the first door of the bar. When I knocked on the second, I said, "It's Minnie. I'm looking for Ike."

The door swung wide.

"Hey, Big Al."

"Minnie."

"You seen Ike?"

"Hasn't been around of late."

"No?" I scanned the room, as if I might find him hiding in a corner. The scene was remarkably like it had been the last time: the darkness, the groups of men, a woman or two. The same man behind the bar.

The only difference was the last time I was here, Mama was alive. Now she wasn't.

"Any ideas where he might be?"

"No. Frank might." He jutted his chin toward the counter.

As I walked to the bar, my feet stuck to the muck on the floor. I stood at the counter, waiting for Frank to finish with a customer. After a minute, he came over.

Frank cocked his head before a grin spread across his face. "Minnie! Almost didn't recognize you."

Self-consciously, I pulled at my dress, trying to hide how it fluttered about my waist. "Have you seen Ike?"

He placed two glasses on the counter and poured a splash of brown liquid in both before sliding one of the cups toward me.

I lifted the glass, noticing the water spots, and sipped, understanding where the term *rotgut* came from. "This is not good bourbon." Having drunk at Ratner's, I had something to compare it to.

Frank shrugged. "We get what we get."

"Where's Ike?"

"Went upstate last week to pick up hooch crossing the border. Should've been back by now. You're not the only one looking for him. His payment was due on Monday, and his distributors have a new shipment for him."

"Where does he go when he's not here?"

"Dunno. Doesn't have a sidepiece, if that's what you're asking."

It had never occurred to me Papa might have a girlfriend. It was not something I cared to ruminate on. I downed the rest of the bourbon, even as it burned. It seethed in my stomach.

"Everything okay?" Frank asked.

"Of course." But it wasn't.

"Hold that thought." He scooted to the other end of the bar, where one of the men waved an empty glass. After taking care of the customer, he returned. "He'll turn up."

"Yes, but before the rent is due?"

"Wait a sec." Frank dipped behind the counter and rose with a stack of bills. Handing it to me, he said, "Hopefully this'll tide you over till he's back."

"I can't take this!"

"You understand this bar belongs to Ike. Everything in here belongs to him." He waved in front of me. "It's his money."

Swallowing the lump in my throat, I stuck the packet in my purse. "I still need to find him."

"I'll put out the word," he said. "In the meantime, if you want, I can keep an eye on things here. Deliver Rothstein's payment and deal with shipments."

"You will, will you?" Riley stood in the door of the office, arms crossed over his chest.

"How long have you been standing there?" I asked.

"Long enough to hear Frank volunteering to steal my job." Riley approached the counter, his slow movements menacing in their certitude. When he reached the counter, he leaned on it, and Frank took a step back. His cologne didn't disguise his body odor. I slid to the right to escape the smell.

"Have you seen Ike?" I asked him.

"Nope. And when your father isn't here, I take over."

Frank's tongue ran across his teeth. He stood silent.

"Anything else?" Riley smirked.

I'd rather Frank took over. I didn't trust Riley. But I didn't think arguing with him would accomplish anything. "Just make sure things are done." I turned on my heel and walked out, clutching my purse close to my chest.

~

The money from the bar stretched for two weeks. But still no Papa.

It's amazing how fast things revert when you don't have money. Amazing how quickly you slide back into poverty after experiencing the tiniest taste of luxury. Not that I would have called it *luxury* at the time, but knowing when we'd eat our next meal was an extravagance we could no longer count on. My belly grumbled, knots lodged in my stomach, anxiety pulsed into throbbing headaches. The telephone company took our phone. We rationed our gas usage. I haggled more at the market. I bought day-old bakery items.

Max stopped eating lunch, to contribute more money for food. The days he worked at the restaurant, he sneaked us leftovers. I claimed not to be hungry so Louise and Gertie could have a bit more. April loomed, which meant rent was due. Max wanted to call Uncle Aaron, but I wouldn't let him. Papa would be furious at the idea of us taking money from anyone, let alone our uncle. Uncle Aaron had three children and a small income.

It wasn't enough. I needed to earn money. No one else could help us.

On a Saturday night, Max sat over his schoolwork, but instead of studying his book, he studied me. "You're so thin."

"It's the fashion." I scrubbed at the sink.

"That's not fashion; that's hunger. I'm going to quit school."

"What?" I turned to him. "Absolutely not."

"We need the money."

"Out of the question. Mama wanted you to be a lawyer. You're going to be a lawyer."

"But—"

"I've already thought about this." I wiped crumbs from the table. "I'm finding a job." I'd agonized over whether to do this. I didn't see any other way to put food in Gertie's and Louise's bellies.

"What about the girls?"

"I've asked around. Mrs. Rivkin will mind them." The thought of someone else watching my sisters made me feel small, like a child who couldn't tie her own shoes, a child who couldn't take care of things on her own.

At first I thought to take a job in a neighborhood store, find a way for Gertie and Louise to stay in the back and entertain themselves. But Gertie and Louise weren't capable of that. And a shop assistant wouldn't pay enough to buy them the new shoes they so desperately needed. Toibe couldn't take them, as she was caring for her husband's mother, but she had asked around to find someone to watch them. Mrs. Rivkin.

"That *alte makhsheyfe*?"

"That *old witch* is all we can afford. Plus she's willing to take her first payment after I've found a job." Mrs. Rivkin lived a few streets away. For a dollar a day, she'd watch both girls. Mrs. Rivkin was half-deaf and minded eight other children, but she was my only option.

"But Mrs. Rivkin. She smells bad." He sounded like a petulant child.

A cry came from the bedroom. I opened the door, but Louise settled herself back to sleep.

I stood in the doorway. Max came beside me.

Asleep, Gertie and Louise were angelic. Louise slept on her side, her chest rising and falling with each fluttery breath. Gertie clutched a stuffed dog as old as I was. Her fingers wove through what little fur was left on the mangy thing. Her eyelashes curled, and her rosy cheeks puffed out.

"They deserve better than Mrs. Rivkin," Max whispered.

"They do. But she's all we've got."

⁓

That weekend, Max tended to the girls to free me to go to Sylvia's. In her living room, Sylvia tamed my hair with a pair of shears. She still had the same job, but Ray had been replaced with Archie.

"My Sylvia should settle down, no?" Mrs. Goldwasser said. "Stop this flitting about. You agree, don't you, Minnie?"

"Of course." I winked at Sylvia, who couldn't decide if she should argue or laugh. "Every girl needs a nice husband to support her."

"Exactly!" Mrs. Goldwasser put her hands on her hip. "And you, Minnie? You have a beau?"

I went to shake my head, but Sylvia grabbed hold of my chin so I couldn't move.

"You want me to slice off an ear?" she asked.

"No, Mrs. Goldwasser, I don't have a beau," I said.

"A sweet girl like you. You need a good man."

"Mother," Sylvia said in a warning tone.

Mrs. Goldwasser gasped. "I'm so sorry, Minnie. I've forgotten your situation." Her eyes welled. "You poor thing. Such a *balabusta*."

"Mother, you're making it worse. Leave us."

Mrs. Goldwasser did just that. If I'd told Mama to leave, my cheek would be burning from the slap.

A few more snips, and Sylvia declared, "Done." She held a mirror for me to admire her work.

It was no barber's cut, but it was better than I could do myself.

"Say, maybe I'll go into the beauty business," she said.

I laughed. It felt good. It had been a while since I'd laughed.

We sprawled on the sofa and gabbed, passing a flask of gin back and forth. When her mother entered the room, the flask slipped beneath a cushion. We grew gigglier as the day wore on until at last I had to get back so Max could leave for work.

For three glorious hours, I was eighteen. But the sun went down, and I returned to be Mama.

Chapter Sixteen

The next day I woke earlier than usual. I dressed in a freshly laundered blouse and a pressed skirt.

At the corner newsstand I bought the *New York Times*. Max said the *Times* had more office jobs; the other papers were better for housekeeping and child minding, neither of which I wanted to do.

Back at the apartment, I put coffee in the percolator, boiled water for Cream of Wheat, and, with a nervous excitement, opened the paper to Help Wanted—Females. While I was unhappy at the idea of a stranger watching my sisters, the adventure of a job filled me with a touch of giddiness. I felt guilty, like I was betraying the girls, but Mrs. Rivkin wouldn't be a stranger for long; the girls would grow to love her.

As I ran my finger down the page, my optimism abated the tiniest bit. With a pencil, I x-ed out the jobs I couldn't apply for: Stenographer and typist, Christian; Stenographer-Typist, one who can play piano, Frank Montgomery School of Dancing; Stenographer, legal experience. Some were cagey, not stating straight out they wouldn't hire me but requiring I reply with my religion. One was hopeful—a stenographer who could speak Jewish—but they wanted a middle-aged woman who was a high school graduate. I was neither. Why did so many want older girls?

I circled those that didn't necessitate high school or a baptism, then packed lunches for Gertie and Louise. Max scanned the page. "Not a lot of opportunities without a diploma," he said, as if not finishing school was my choice. "Try one of those employment agencies." He pointed to the listings. "They have lots of jobs, so you don't have to trek all over town."

"Hurry and earn that law degree so we can move to Park Avenue."

I fed the girls and slipped on their coats. Mrs. Rivkin's apartment was a few blocks away. The dark stairwell in her building reminded me of the first place we had lived when we had arrived in America. Gertie squeezed my skirt. Louise's arms snaked around my neck, clutching my hair. The hallways smelled of cabbage and onions. On the top floor, I knocked, but no one answered. I knocked louder, and when no one responded, I panicked. If I didn't have someone to care for the children, I couldn't find a job. If I couldn't find a job, I couldn't feed my family. I pounded the door, alarming Louise, who buried her head in the crook of my neck.

"Coming, coming," came from inside. Opening the door, Mrs. Rivkin, not even five feet tall, scowled. "Why all the noise?"

"You didn't hear me the first two times."

"I heard, I heard." She gestured for us to enter. "It takes me a while to get there."

A baby crawled in the living room space, and a toddler played with a doll in the corner. "This is Louise." I handed her over, but she clung to my hair, pulling it as I maneuvered her into Mrs. Rivkin's arms. Louise's face closed, a sign she was about to holler. I pushed Gertie toward her, hoping the sight of her sister might prevent a tantrum. "This is Gertie."

It didn't; Gertie bellowed too.

"Noisy ones, aren't they." Mrs. Rivkin's pinched face resembled a prune. "Come on." She prodded Gertie inside.

"Here are their lunches." I held out the basket.

"Minnie, Minnie, Minnie," cried Gertie.

Louise wailed.

"Hurry up. The neighbors don't tolerate screaming *kinder*."

I bent down to Gertie. "You're going to have so much fun with Mrs. Rivkin!" My voice rose an octave. "Keep an eye on Louise, and mind your manners." Pulling her close, I planted a sloppy kiss on her head, then leaned toward Louise in Mrs. Rivkin's grasp to give her one too. Mrs. Rivkin smelled of liver and decay. My eyes moistened. If I were Louise, I'd be sobbing too.

"I'll be back by five."

"Not a minute late, or I charge extra."

As the door closed, I hurried down the stairs, trying to outrun the gloom settling over me.

~

With the paper under my arm, I walked to the Castle Hill Employment Agency. Liberty Street was two blocks north of Wall Street, and the closer I neared the financial district, the more men in suits, imposing buildings, and fancy cars dotted the streets.

At the agency, a woman at the front desk was on the phone. "Comptometer operator. High school. Uh-huh. Brooklyn. Yes, I got that down. Uh-huh." When she hung up, she said, "May I help you?"

"I'm looking for a job."

She pushed a button on an intercom, and when a woman responded, she said, "Applicant here." To me, she said, "Have a seat."

Smoothing my skirt, I sat with my knees together and my ankles crossed, as I'd learned in school. The office behind the receptionist bustled, with women at desks and men in glassed-in offices.

After ten minutes, a broad woman in a manly suit came out. "Miss . . ."

"Soffer."

Her eyes narrowed slightly. "Follow me, Miss Soffer." Whether it was my name or my darker complexion, I could tell she was subtracting the jobs requiring a Christian girl.

"Thank you, Mrs. . . . ," I said, but she didn't fill in a name.

She wound through the desks until we reached the back of the room. She indicated I should sit and passed me a steno pad. "Dear Mr. Star. The receipts of September third totaled eight hundred and seventy-two dollars. We are expecting a shipment to arrive at the warehouse on October the eighth."

I looked at her as if she were mad.

"Take my dictation," she said.

Of course. A stenography test. Embarrassed, I put pencil to pad and transcribed into shorthand every word. I didn't miss one.

"Take it to that machine, and type it up."

I moved to a bank of typewriters. She raised a stopwatch. "Start."

I rolled in a sheet of paper and, reading over my notes, typed. When I stopped, she clicked her watch. "Hmm, forty words a minute. Slow."

My face warmed. I could drill myself on shorthand but not typewriting, as I didn't own a machine. "I'll speed up with practice."

She arched an eyebrow. "We hire girls to work. Not to practice."

I bit my lip, then worried about getting lipstick on my teeth.

"Come to my desk."

Once there, she interrogated me. "High school diploma?"

I shook my head. If I lied and she asked for a school reference, I'd be humiliated and unemployed.

"Office experience?"

"No, ma'am."

"Keypunch?"

I looked at my feet. This was not going well.

"Elliott-Fisher bookkeeping knowledge?"

I shook my head again.

After another few questions, she determined I had no skills but minor typing and stenography. "Well, all is not lost, Miss Soffer."

"No?"

"I do have an opening for a beginning clerk. You appear appropriate, and you are not completely without competence." She flipped through a box of cards on her desk. "Here. They need an office girl and are willing to take beginners."

"I'm a fast learner, I promise."

She raised her brow again. "I wish I could say I hadn't heard that before, but alas . . ." She read the card. "A buying company on Thirty-Second Street. You'll report to Mr. Whitaker. Mostly filing with some shorthand and typing. Pays twelve dollars a week."

"Twelve dollars?"

"Quite reasonable for a girl with no experience nor a high school diploma."

"Is it possible to earn more?"

The woman set down the card. "You could try your luck as a sales-girl. They work on commission, so if you're clever, you can make a great deal. But if you're not clever . . ." She shrugged. "Well, you'll be broke."

"Do you have sales jobs?"

She jolted her head back as if she smelled rotting carp. "No, of course we don't. You apply directly at stores."

I couldn't imagine trying to push perfume on women. But twelve dollars a week? Forty-eight dollars a month. Max earned fifteen dollars a week. Rent was fifty-five a month. Five a week for childcare. After that, we'd have about ten a week for food and gas. I'd need to budget carefully and pray no one got sick and the girls didn't grow too fast. New clothes would be out of the question.

The woman softened her tone. "Take the job. Work for six months. Then you'll have experience. You can return, and I'll find you a better position."

"I appreciate that, Mrs. . . ."

This time she smiled. "Mrs. Swanson."

"Thank you, Mrs. Swanson."

~

With Mrs. Swanson's card, I made my way to the office. This time, I splurged on carfare in order not to lose the entire day.

The squat three-story building hid in the shadow of PS 116. As I watched the schoolchildren playing in the yard, my heart cracked at the thought of Louise and Gertie in that awful apartment. *I'm doing this for them,* I reminded myself.

On the third floor, I knocked and pushed open the office door. The front room was empty.

"Hello?" I said.

"Be right there," a voice called from an interior office. A second later, a lanky man with a mop of blond hair falling into his eyes emerged scowling. His expression changed when he saw me, a carnal smirk crawling across his face. "How may I help you?" He sounded silky smooth. Too smooth.

"I've been sent by the employment agency." I extended the card to him. "I'm Miss Soffer."

Without looking at it, he dropped the card on the desk. "The agency has done well."

"Are you Mr. Whitaker?"

"Indeed, Miss . . . What was it?"

"Miss Soffer."

He leered, until I was so uncomfortable I broke the silence. "Where shall I start?"

He stared long enough I thought he'd never speak, but finally he said, "File these." He indicated the desk, which was piled high with folders and documents and scraps. "The filing cabinets are in there." He jutted his chin toward a small closet, where metal cabinets lined the walls. "You'll catch on to the system."

My face must have betrayed my horror at the mess, because he said, "I had a wonderful secretary for years, but she retired. I have yet to find an adequate replacement."

The front door opened, and a man with a fedora poked his head in. "Clayton, ready to go?"

"Yes. You can handle this, Miss Soffer?"

Feigning confidence, I said, "Of course, Mr. Whitaker."

"Let's go, Clayton."

The door shut behind them, and my shoulders slumped. The mountain of papers was daunting, more so when I realized it spilled onto the floor behind the desk.

The office was small—the front room; Mr. Whitaker's office, which I didn't dare peek into; and the closet. The cramped front room had no windows. The closet was worse, a claustrophobic cell.

For the next four hours, I acquainted myself with the filing system, placing papers in their metal jails. The process was slow—I evaluated each paper to decide where to put it—so by the time Mr. Whitaker returned, I'd made scarcely a dent. He, however, seemed impressed with my industriousness and retreated into his office to do whatever it was he did.

By the end of the day, my stomach rumbled, as I'd skipped lunch. At four thirty, I tapped on the door of Mr. Whitaker's office. "May I be excused for the day?"

Glancing at the clock, he said, "The workday ends at five. Eight thirty to five, with thirty minutes for lunch."

I wrung my hands. "I didn't take lunch."

"True, but you arrived at ten a.m."

The ticking of the clock ricocheted in my ears. "I need to pick up my sisters at five p.m."

"You Jews. Always trying to squeeze out a bit more."

I froze. "Excuse me?"

"Jewing down your hours on the first day. Not a great impression."

I refused to let him see he upset me. "The woman caring for my sisters expects me at five. They're waiting for me."

"I'm sure they'll still be waiting for you at five thirty."

"Is there any way—"

"For you to keep your job? Yes, work until five."

Mrs. Rivkin would be furious; I'd owe more money, and the children would be miserable. I unhappily filed for another thirty minutes. At 5:00 p.m., I dashed looks between Mr. Whitaker and the clock. At 5:03 p.m., he dismissed me, and I ran to the streetcar.

When I arrived, Louise was in tears again. At least, I hoped it was *again* and not *still*. Gertie was a mess, the remnants of her lunch on her dress.

"Five p.m.," Mrs. Rivkin said. "We said five p.m."

"I'm so sorry," I heard myself pleading. "My job doesn't end until five. Would it be possible for them to stay until five thirty?"

"Interferes with dinner preparation. Can't get a thing done with kids at my feet."

"Is there any way?"

She twisted her lips, considering. "For an extra quarter a week."

"A quarter!"

"Interferes with dinner preparation."

"Yes, ma'am. An extra quarter." As if I had a choice.

~

The girls whined, difficult to settle. Louise punished me by throwing her food, and Gertie pouted. Max found all three of us near tears.

"I stopped by Uncle Aaron's today. He gave me ten dollars to tide us over."

"You weren't supposed to tell Uncle Aaron."

"Min, it's okay to ask for help."

"Papa would never approve."

"Well, he's not here, is he?"

Max prepared the girls for bed. They weren't as sullen with him. A pang of jealousy struck when I heard them giggling.

The next morning, the girls all-out rebelled. I fought them into their clothes and practically dragged Gertie to Mrs. Rivkin's, with Louise twisting, trying to dive out of my hold. It was all I could do not to bawl on my way uptown. I walked, determined to save every penny. Even though the day was chilly, I arrived with perspiration stains beneath my arms.

That day, and those that followed, passed slowly. I answered phones, filed papers, and occasionally took dictation and typed letters. The majority of the time, though, was spent avoiding Mr. Whitaker's hands, which found all sorts of occasions to graze my body.

To think this was the job I'd aspired to. A job where I wasn't on my feet. The job Mama had wanted me to have. I'd have laughed if I had any sense of humor left. Oh, I was on my feet. Running from Mr. Whitaker.

At the end of the first week, he held up my paycheck. "This is for you."

"Thank you." I extended my hand, unsure what he expected.

"You need to earn this." He shook the check just out of my reach.

"Isn't that what I do? Filing, typing, and answering phones?"

"You forgot one thing. Your last task."

I left the office in tears. I'd finally had my first kiss. But not the way I had wanted it.

Chapter Seventeen

Exhaustion was a constant companion. Between darting from Mr. Whitaker's hands, avoiding Mrs. Rivkin's crow-like sneers, and caring for the girls, Max, and the apartment, I wanted to crawl into bed and sleep for a week. I wanted Mama to bring me a cup of hot tea to drink through a sugar cube.

At the end of March, the invitations poured in. "What are you doing for the seder?" the women of the neighborhood asked. "Come celebrate with us."

Sitting with others, pretending to be joyful, was just another chore. I couldn't face it. How could I exalt in the freeing of the Hebrews when I was so trapped? Besides, the idea of celebrating Mama's holiday with anyone else was too bleak to consider.

"We have plans, thank you," I said.

Toibe was suspicious. "What, exactly, are your plans?"

"We're going to Uncle Aaron's."

"Good," she said. "It's important to be with family."

Uncle Aaron dropped by Max's work to say, "Come to our house for Passover."

"We're joining Toibe's seder," Max said.

Uncle Aaron beamed. "Good. It's important to be with friends."

Wednesday, April 4, was the first night of the eight-day holiday. After the girls were in bed, Max and I sat at the kitchen table, a box of matzah and a bottle of sweet wine between us.

Mama's presence hovered above, disapproving, but if Mama couldn't be there, it wasn't Passover.

I opened the wine and brought it to my lips, drinking straight from the bottle. I wiped my mouth with the back of my hand and passed the bottle to Max. "*A zissen Pesach,*" I said.

He guzzled almost a quarter of the wine. He started to say something, but his eyes welled, and the words didn't come out. He swigged once more before retreating to his bedroom.

His muffled cries cracked my already brittle brave front.

I finished the wine myself.

A sweet Passover it would not be.

~

The girls grew more sullen as the days passed. One day, changing Louise's diaper, I discovered an unusual bruise.

"What's this?" I asked Gertie.

Gertie was churlish. "Don't know."

"Gertie."

"Don't know," she insisted.

I began to notice more marks and purple spots. Max assured me they were the normal bumps and bruises of kids, but I looked at Mrs. Rivkin with suspicion. Not that I had another option.

Papa'd been gone for too long. Was he safe? I consumed a package of sodium bicarbonate a day to ease the sourness in my stomach. It didn't work.

"What do we do?" I asked Max. "Should we call the police?"

"And say what? 'My father, who owns a gin joint and owes thousands of dollars to mobster Arnold Rothstein, has been missing. Can you find him?' They'll find him all right. And if he doesn't have a bullet in him already, they'll put one in him."

That damn gun. Did Max know about it? "Don't say such things," I said. "He'll be back soon."

Three days later, a knock on the door startled us. It was too late to be Sylvia or any of the neighbor women.

Tentatively I opened the door. It was Duke.

"Minnie." None of the friendliness of last time. "I need to speak with you."

"Max, you remember Duke." I gestured to the kitchen table. "Shall I put on coffee? Or tea?"

"No, thank you." He remained standing but clutched his hat in front of his chest. "We've been looking for your father."

"We have no idea where he is," Max said, but Duke held up his hand.

"We found him. Upstate. In jail."

I buckled into a chair. "You're sure?"

"We're sure."

"What for?" Max asked.

"He was picking up a shipment from Canada. Tricky transaction. Cop ended up dead."

My stomach screamed for bicarbonate.

"Took a bit to find him," Duke continued. "Word was slow to reach us."

"What now?" My throat was as raw as it had been the night Papa had made me smoke the pack of cigarettes.

"We're having him transferred here. A trial will be arranged soon."

"Is that a good thing?"

"You don't want him lingering in the holding cells. Folks can be stuck there for months—even years—before trial. He'll be in the Tombs by week's end. You can see him on Saturday."

"The Tombs?" I thought of Anshel. I thought of Mama. This couldn't be happening.

"City Prison. Called the Tombs."

"Papa's tough," Max said. "He can handle himself."

"That would be an understatement," Duke said.

"What about the bar?" I asked.

"Riley's watching things, making the payments, but I wouldn't be surprised if some of that kale was finding its way into his own pocket. Max should take over."

"I can't," Max said.

"Max is in school. Studying to be a lawyer."

Duke flashed his half grin. "Rothstein can always use another attorney on his team."

I shot Max a look of warning. We'd get nowhere if he shared his feelings about Mr. Rothstein. We needed him on our side.

"You have some time before Rothstein decides what to do with the bar. At least until after the trial."

"Do with the bar? It's Ike's bar," I said. Max threw me a queer look. I'd never used Papa's given name in front of him.

"It is his bar. Until the payments stop. Then it's Rothstein's bar." He slid me an envelope. "From Rothstein. To tide you over."

"What happens next?" I asked.

"We got Ike a lawyer. Courts are backed up, so it could be a while till he stands before a judge. Rothstein'll do the best he can for your father. Ike's been a valuable member of our organization."

Max paled at *organization*.

"Thank you, Duke."

Duke slipped his hat back on. "If you need anything—with the bar, with your father—get in touch. Send word through Frank. It'll reach me."

Once the door shut, I turned to Max. His fists clenched at his side, his legs bowed out, taking up space. "You are not," he said, "I repeat, not to step foot into that bar. You hear me?"

My energy was too sapped to argue. "Good night, Max."

As I lay in bed, I tried to picture Duke, to lose myself in visions of his hazel eyes. But I couldn't hold the image. Instead, all I saw was a gun. A dead cop. And Papa.

In a place called the Tombs.

~

The hundred dollars Duke had given us covered April's rent, groceries, and the gas bill, with a little left over.

On Saturday, after my half day of work, I thickly sliced a rye bread, then smeared the sides with mustard.

"What are you doing?" Max asked.

"What does it look like I'm doing?" I piled the bread high with meat before wrapping it in paper and placing it in a basket. I'd spent much of our grocery budget on Papa's favorite food.

"He doesn't deserve pastrami."

"Shut up, and get dressed."

We were going to visit Papa.

~

After I dropped the girls off with Toibe, Max and I trudged to the Tombs. The walk wasn't even fifteen minutes, but my feet were bricks, each step a chore.

The enormous building dominated the block, the kind of building that inspired terror, that made kids cross the street in fear of being swallowed up. It rose, a dingy gray spired fortress, the windows tiny slits on the expanse of wall.

This was what my father had left Bratsyana for?

We turned a corner, and a sign on a door declared VISITOR'S ENTRANCE.

A line strung down the block. People, mostly women, stood silent, stone faced, as if awaiting their own executions.

We took our place at the end. Max jittered, hopping from foot to foot.

I touched his arm. "Stop."

"I'm cold."

I didn't feel any chill, my anxiety an inferno in my chest.

At last we made it to the door. A guard stood outside with a ledger. "Visiting?"

"Isaac Soffer."

He pursed his lips, checking his book. He wrote something on a slip of paper and handed it to a younger man next to him. The younger man disappeared into the building. "Name?"

"Minnie and Max Soffer."

"One visitor at a time."

I grabbed Max's hand and squeezed. Enter this dungeon on my own? "Do you want to go first?" I hoped he'd say yes.

He shook his head. "You go."

"Number sixteen."

I wanted to ask what the number meant, but the guard was already signaling to the next person. Letting go of Max, I entered a narrow hallway stretching farther than I could see in the dim light. I understood why the guard stood outside. The barrage of noise battered my eardrums. The clamor only grew louder the farther in I walked.

On the right was a gray wall. On the left, steel walls divided tiny areas about the size of horse stalls. In each stall a person sat, yelling through a mesh wire. Numbers emblazoned the stalls. I found sixteen. The compartment, even without metal bars, was claustrophobic. What must it be like for Papa?

Through the mesh screen was another mesh screen about two feet away. I took a seat on the stool and waited. It may have been five minutes, it may have been an hour, but eventually Papa's face appeared behind the wires across the way. My basket sat at my feet. No way to get the food to him.

"Papa," I said, but my voice blended in with the others, so I, too, had to shout. "Papa!"

"Minnela."

I pressed my face to the mesh. The holes allowed for a clear view of Papa. He'd aged in the past month. His body hunched, and his skin was mottled with blue and yellow. A ragged gray beard covered his chin, the beard Mama had expected when we'd arrived at Ellis Island.

"Papa, how are you?" It was a terrible question; I could see how he was.

In Yiddish, he responded, "How do you think I am?"

"What happened to your face?" I followed his lead, replying in Yiddish.

"They think I killed a cop. They don't take kindly to that."

"Did you?"

He ignored my question. "How are you, Max, and Gertie?"

Even though he was at his lowest, I had to add, "And Louise."

"And her."

"I work as a secretary. Max wants to quit school, but I won't let him. Mrs. Rivkin watches the girls. It's not ideal. Duke brought us some money to help out."

"He should be giving you more money than to just 'help out.'" His fingers poked through the wire. "But you're healthy? You're all right?"

"We're all right." Papa didn't need to know about Mr. Whitaker and his wandering hands, about our fear of not making rent, of the bruises on the girls.

"Minnela, you should run the shop."

I shivered. Mama always said when you shivered, it meant someone was walking over your grave. "Run the shop?"

"If you don't, we'll lose it. Rothstein will claim it, or Riley will steal it out from under us."

"Max won't let me go to the shop."

"Since when have you ever listened to anyone?"

Disobeying Papa and Mama had been second nature. But Max was my ally, my confidant. And he was all I had left.

"Max should finish school," Papa continued. "He doesn't have your shrewdness, your spunk."

It was wrong, in this dank cage, but a tinge of pride warmed me. "What about the girls?"

"Can't whoever is watching them now watch them at night?"

"No." I shuddered as I pictured how Mrs. Rivkin would deal with the girls when they woke in the night or when Gertie wet her bed. She wouldn't sing them the right songs or read them the right stories.

"I don't know how to make it work, Papa. What if we sell the shop?"

"Selling a shop like ours . . . not so easy. Plus the interest I owe . . ."

I wished I could reach through the wires, to curl up in Papa's arms as I had when I was younger, to have him tell me everything would be all right. But he couldn't, so I had to do the reassuring.

"You'll be out soon. I'll make sure the guys at the shop have things covered until you're released."

"Be careful."

A bell rang. "Lunchtime," a guard yelled, walking up and down the aisle behind me. "No visitors for thirty minutes."

"Papa!"

"Think about it. Please!"

Behind him, a shadowy figure approached. "Let's go," I heard.

"Papa!"

"Minnela." Was he crying? "I love you."

He'd never said those words before. Love wasn't something we articulated in our family; we simply felt it in everything we did for each other. That he needed to say it made me more frightened than anything else. "I love you too."

But I said it to an empty cell.

The noise died down immediately, the only sounds the shuffling of stools and the rustling of feet as everyone stood to leave. We filed out. Belatedly, I realized I had taken too much time, hadn't allowed Max a turn.

At the exit, I signed my name in the ledger.

"Well?" Max said when I approached him.

I burst into noisy sobs. "Here," I managed, handing him the basket. "Have a pastrami sandwich."

Max embraced me before putting his arm around my shoulder and guiding me away.

Chapter Eighteen

The next day, I asked Max to watch the girls. "I'm going to the market."

Max nodded, head bent over his books. He was too enmeshed in his studies to do more than basic care for the girls, but they'd be bruise-free when I returned, and sometimes that was enough.

I walked down Baxter Street and slipped into the alley. At the bar, Big Al let me in. It was early, so only a couple of men stood with drinks.

"May I talk with you and"—I checked to see who was working—"Riley?"

Big Al double-locked the door, and we walked to the counter.

"Riley?"

"You again?" Riley asked.

"A little respect. This is Ike's daughter." Big Al's tone reminded me of my father when he was laying down the law.

"I know who she is." He returned his attention to the customers.

"Riley." I tried to sound authoritative. "I need to speak with you."

He flexed his biceps, making the muscles jump. "What?"

"My father asked me to check on things." I stood straighter, pretending I had my emotions under control.

"Why?"

His question startled me. "What do you mean *why*? He wants to make sure you're taking care of things. He doesn't want to come back to mayhem."

His face contorted into what I thought was supposed to be a smile. He pulled out a bottle of bourbon and poured himself a glass. "He's not coming back." He tilted the bottle toward me in invitation. I ignored the gesture.

"He'll be back."

Riley shrugged.

"Play nice, Riley." Big Al's eyes narrowed at him.

"The bourbon should only be poured to the line." I knew a thing or two about the bar. His glass was filled three-quarters of the way up.

"That's for lightweights." He downed the entire glass and poured himself another.

"Take it easy, Riley," Big Al warned.

Riley crossed his beefy arms over his chest. "What happens when he's sent to the big house?"

"My father is not going to prison." I wished I'd accepted the shot to ease my jitters, but that would've made me look weak. *You can't look weak in this business.*

"If you say so."

My fists balled at my side. "How about this. Until his trial, you watch the bar. After that, we'll discuss what happens next."

"Who made you the boss?"

Through gritted teeth, I said, "My father. This is his bar, not yours. And if he can't take care of it, I decide what happens. Do you understand?"

Big Al moved closer to me in support. Riley held his hands up as if I'd pointed a gun. He made a big show of saying, "I understand, I understand!"

I wanted to punch that smirk off him.

As Big Al let me out, he said, "Don't worry, Minnie. I'll keep an eye on things."

Papa's *Trust no one* echoed in my head.

I'd need to keep an eye on things myself.

~

The next week, as I fed the girls, Max walked in early.

"Don't you work tonight?" I asked.

"I switched to a later shift so we could talk."

"Sounds ominous." I spooned Cream of Wheat to Louise's mouth. Gertie picked at hers. I'd made it with water, instead of milk, to save money.

"One of my professors mentioned something today."

"Oh?"

"Any convicted felon who is not a citizen can be deported after he serves his jail time."

"What?"

"If Papa's found guilty, he could be shipped back to Ukraine."

"But he's an American."

Max shook his head. "He applied for his papers, but he was arrested before the process was completed. He's not a citizen." He rubbed one of his temples. "Gertie and Louise are Americans because they were born here. But we're not. Children are included on a father's petition for naturalization."

"Can we be deported?"

"It's not likely. But it's possible."

My spoon hovered midair. "What do we do?"

"We apply for citizenship."

"How?" Louise cried because I wasn't feeding her fast enough. "Gertie, stop playing with your food."

"I picked up papers at the Riverside Community House near school." He removed a sheet from his satchel. "My professor helped me fill it out. Go to the Henry Street Settlement House. They can help you."

My mind raced. When would I have time to go? I'd have to figure it out. "So all I do is fill this out?"

"That's only the start." He pushed the paper toward me. "Complete the Facts for Declaration of Intention. Bring it to the clerk at the naturalization office. Unfortunately, they're only open during working hours."

"Great. I'm sure Mr. Whitaker will love that. Can you turn them in for me?"

"You have to go in person. After the papers are filed, you have to wait at least two years to apply for the next set of papers, your petition for naturalization. Then you take a civics test and an English exam. Finally, there's a court hearing."

Not only was I not an American, but it would be forever until I became one.

"I gotta head to work." He rose. "I'm sorry this isn't easier. I'm going to turn in my papers tomorrow morning."

Louise banged on the table with tiny fists. "Here." I scooped cereal, but before I could feed her, she grabbed the spoon with both hands.

"There are fees. A dollar for this set of papers." He grinned. "Hey, in happier news: I'll be home early tomorrow with dinner."

"You're skipping a work shift?" We needed that money.

"I told the cook tomorrow's your birthday. He's gonna slip me something tasty to bring home."

My birthday? I'd completely forgotten. Did birthdays still happen when your life was in chaos?

Max stood and kissed Gertie and Louise on the top of their heads. "You two mind Minnie, okay?"

Gertie stared at her cereal. Louise threw the spoon on the floor.

This was not how I had pictured my life at nineteen.

～

Once the girls settled, I examined the declaration paper. The questions didn't look difficult. I'd miss work to go to the courthouse, but I'd save time filling out the form myself. The settlement house helped new immigrants. I was not a new immigrant. I could read English.

I wrote my name, *Minnie Soffer*, and my occupation, *office clerk*. I guessed at my height and weight. Would the fact that my birthday was made up be a problem? Everything else—place of birth, visible marks, what ship I had sailed on—was straightforward.

The last line gave me pause: *I am now a citizen of and intend to renounce allegiance to the Republic of* _____. While I didn't feel like an American, I was startled to realize I was still a citizen of Ukraine. I'd lived in the United States for eight years. I couldn't picture what my life in Bratsyana might have been had I stayed. If I were deported . . .

The thought was too terrifying to imagine.

I wrote *Ukraine* and decided to risk Mr. Whitaker's wrath. I'd bring my papers to the courthouse in the morning. A birthday present to myself.

The sooner I became an American, the safer I'd feel.

~

After dropping the girls at Mrs. Rivkin's, I walked to the courthouse. A balloon inflated in my chest, making it difficult to breathe. Would Papa go to jail? Be deported? Would I be deported? Who would take care of the girls? My one comfort was that Gertie and Louise, as Americans, would never have these worries.

Outside the enormous building, I paused, imagining the others who had climbed these steps, hungering to be made citizens.

Now, walking up the stairs, I was one of them.

The courthouse buzzed. A woman sat behind a desk that dominated the center of the room.

"Yes," she said.

"I'm here to become a citizen."

"Declaration or petition?"

"Excuse me?"

"First papers? Second papers? Court hearing?"

"First papers."

"Deputy clerk's office, third floor."

On the third floor, a line of people trailed down the hallway.

"Is this where we become citizens?" I asked the last person, a man with a gray ring of hair and stooped shoulders.

"Vat?" His Yiddish accent was thick.

I switched to Yiddish and tried again.

"English, English." He fluttered his hands in annoyance. "You want they think I don't speak English? I understand just fine." He cupped his ear. "My hearing's no good."

For a third time, I said with all the patience I could muster, "Is this where we wait to become citizens?"

"Yes, yes. Wait to fill out papers. Land of the free. All we do is wait."

A crowd snaked in front of us. After forty minutes, I reached the office door, which led to a foyer lined with chairs and yet more people. A metal contraption spit out numbers, so I grabbed one and found an empty seat.

"Twenty-three," a man called into the waiting room.

A couple hopped up and followed him. I was thirty-seven.

Most of the others sat lost in thought, a few with newspapers. I daydreamed of becoming a citizen. When I filed for my second papers, I'd be twenty-one, Louise would be three, and Gertie of school age. We'd celebrate that all the Soffer children were Americans. Maybe go to a baseball game. Or Coney Island. Something truly American.

"Thirty-seven" broke my reverie. I jumped up.

A man led me to a desk in the back room, where a dozen clerks hunched over typewriters, a motley assortment of immigrants before them. He gestured for me to take a seat.

"I'm here to turn in my paperwork to become a citizen."

"You and every other guy in the room." He cranked a blank form and carbon paper into his typewriter and held out his hand.

I passed him my paper. He started typing.

"Happy birthday," he said without looking up.

"Um, speaking of. That birth date may not be correct."

"You're not the only one."

I perched on the edge of the seat. When he'd finished inputting the information, he read what he'd typed and asked, "Do you renounce all allegiance to the government of Ukraine? Do you swear you're not an anarchist, a polygamist, and that it's your intention to become a citizen and reside in the United States permanently?"

My heart pattered. "Yes, yes, yes. I swear."

He pulled out the sheet from the typewriter. "Can you sign your name?"

I nodded.

He pointed to the bottom line.

With my most careful penmanship, I signed *Minnie Soffer*.

He took the paper and signed on the line for the Deputy Clerk of the District Court of the United States. Thomas Grady.

"One dollar."

I pulled a bill from my clutch.

"Here's a copy for you. We keep two. In two years, fill out Form 2214, Preliminary Form for Petition for Naturalization." His words droned monotonously. *How many times a day must he recite these instructions?* "After you turn that in, we search for your certificate of arrival. That takes a few months. You'll be notified by mail to appear in court with two witnesses who are citizens who have known you for at least five years. No near relatives. At the preliminary hearing, we ensure your paperwork is in order, your witnesses say you're of strong moral character, that you speak English, and that you can pass the civics exam. If you do, you'll be sent to the clerk of the naturalization court to file your petition. That'll be four dollars. At that time a notice is posted for ninety days in case anyone has any reason to declare you unfit for citizenship. After ninety days, you'll receive a court date for you and your witnesses to appear for the final examination. If you pass, you'll be sworn in as a citizen."

My head spun with the complexity of it all.

He stood abruptly and walked to the door, glanced at the number counter, and called out, "Fifty-three."

I made my way through the waiting room, which was as crowded, if not more so.

Two years I had to wait.

Two years ago I'd had a mother. A father who'd lived with us. An entire future ahead of me.

Anything could happen in two years.

Chapter Nineteen

I beelined uptown. Mr. Whitaker was indeed furious at my late arrival. "You're lucky you've got nice"—he gazed at my chest, and I hunched, trying to minimize my bosom—"assets." I'd been gone for half a day, but he docked me a full day's pay.

That night, Max brought chicken and potatoes from the diner. We toasted my birthday with kosher wine. Sylvia came over with a chocolate cake. Gertie clapped as I blew out the candles. I'd hoped their cheer would raise my spirits, but I wanted to crawl under the covers and sob.

How important birthdays had once seemed. How important to be an American child. I understood why being an American hadn't mattered to Mama; when you were as busy as we were, who had time to think of frivolities? Surviving each day was all that mattered.

Sylvia gave me a compact and Max a Dorothy L. Sayers mystery novel. He handed me another package neatly wrapped in butcher paper and tied with string. "Uncle Aaron stopped by the diner today. Gave me this to give you."

"Did you tell him about Papa?"

Max shook his head. "He'd worry himself to death."

I tugged the string, and the paper fell open to reveal a handkerchief. It was simple cotton, exquisitely embroidered, a crown of leaves and delicate purple flowers circling an elegantly sewn *M*. A note from Aunt Sara read, "A *freilichen* birthday, my sweet Minnie."

Aunt Sara, with three children. Aunt Sara, who occasionally helped Uncle Aaron at his shoe store. Aunt Sara, who baked the most delectable treats. She still made time to embroider gifts. She made time to think of others. She wasn't constantly on the verge of falling apart.

Why was it so hard for me?

~

I couldn't sleep, so in the predawn hours I retreated to the kitchen. At the table, my head sank into my hands, and the tears slipped out, growing in intensity like a summer storm. Why couldn't I do this? Why couldn't I support us and have time for the children and let Max earn an education? Why was I so miserable?

Part of my role was to be optimistic for the family. To be cheerful and comforting. To smile for Papa when I visited him, to convince him things were going well, that he should fight in court, not plead guilty. To smile for Gertie and Louise when I picked them up, reminding them they were loved. To smile for Max so he wouldn't know Mr. Whitaker was no better than those boys on Second Avenue.

I had no cheer left. No smiles left. My facade was crumbling.

I wanted to wallow. But if I was up, I should start breakfast, sweep, clean the bathroom.

I swiped my arm across my runny nose and sniffled. I didn't want to do any of the chores. At the least I'd write Aunt Sara a thank-you note. Mama used to say that the gift was not as special as the thought. Now that I was the mama, I understood this. That someone had thought of me, the one who barely existed anymore, meant something.

The letter started as a simple thank-you note, praising her embroidery skills and her generosity, as Mama had taught me. But soon the letter drifted where I hadn't intended it to. I wrote about Papa in jail. I wrote about the girls with Mrs. Rivkin. I wrote about Mr. Whitaker. I wrote about how hungry we were sometimes. I stuck the letter in an envelope and yawned.

Writing it released a bit of the weight in my chest. Perhaps I'd sleep now. I returned to bed, where I dozed for a few hours before Louise's fingers found my nostril and woke me up.

The girls had let me sleep, and we were behind in our morning routine.

Briskly I dressed them and packed their baskets with the last crusts of bread. I'd skip lunch. "Hurry!"

Gertie dawdled every morning but always more so on the days we ran behind.

By some miracle, we were out the door. I thought of the letter. I'd write a proper note that evening.

That night, halfway through dinner prep, I recalled the letter. I went to grab it, but it wasn't where I'd left it. "Max, did you see an envelope around here?"

"Your thank-you note to Aunt Sara? I mailed it for you."

My hand stilled. A lurking tingle in the back of my neck spread, a pair of dice shooting craps in my skull.

"Hungry!" Gertie yelled from the bedroom.

I rubbed my forehead. And I kept cooking.

~

The knock I expected came on Shabbos afternoon. Gertie and Louise played quietly on the floor. They didn't cry as much as they had, which was in so many ways worse, as if they'd resigned themselves to how things were.

"Hello, Uncle Aaron," I said before the door was fully open.

"Minnie." He opened his arms, and I fell into them like a child, the softness of his hug making me weep. "Why didn't you tell me?"

I remained in his clasp until, embarrassed, I pulled back and wiped my eyes. "Come in, Uncle Aaron."

As he removed his hat, Uncle Aaron's eyes skated over the apartment. I saw the place through his eyes. A funky odor hung in the air, the smell of unwashed bedding and sweaty bodies. Burnt milk crusted the stovetop. The girls' dresses had schmutz on them. When had I last given them a bath?

Uncle Aaron lifted a basket. "Aunt Sara baked for you."

Gertie scrambled up. "What did you bring?"

I picked up Louise. "Gertie! Your manners! Say hello to Uncle Aaron."

"Hello, Uncle Aaron. What did you bring?"

Before I could reprimand her, Uncle Aaron laughed.

"Aunt Sara baked you schnecken." He pulled a pastry from the basket. "Snails." The buns, wound to resemble shells, brimmed with brown sugar and nuts. My mouth watered.

I placed Louise in the high chair. Gertie climbed up to the table.

Uncle Aaron gave Louise a schnecke, and she devoured it so quickly I wondered if Mrs. Rivkin had given her lunch. I paid extra for her to mind the girls on Shabbos while I worked the half day.

"Take one, Minnie," Uncle Aaron said.

They smelled delectable, but I wanted the girls to have them, so I said, "I'm not hungry," though the rumble in my stomach belied my words.

"Sit." He guided me into a chair. "There's plenty. Milk in there too." He passed me a pastry and pulled tin cups from our cabinet. He filled three of them, then sat across from me. The girls swallowed the milk in fat gulps. "Where's Max?"

"School. Or work. I can't keep track." I bit my snail, the sugar melting on my tongue. I hadn't had anything that delicious since . . . well, since Mama had been baking.

"There are some breads for you too. Some chicken and a kugel."

"Please thank Aunt Sara for her kindness."

"You're family."

I didn't want to cry again, so I said nothing. I took small bites of the schnecke, wanting it to last.

"So tell me. What's it look like for your father?"

167

I glanced at the girls. Gertie was singing to herself as she ate, not paying attention to us, but I switched to Yiddish anyway. Gertie's Yiddish was fading. "Not good." Mr. Rothstein's people had hired a lawyer, who had made a plea bargain with the prosecutor. Papa would plead guilty to the lesser charge of bootlegging, and the murder charge would be lowered to manslaughter, which didn't carry a death penalty. When I had last visited Papa, I'd tried to talk him out of the plea bargain, but he had said it was too risky to go to trial for second-degree murder. Any hopes he might be innocent had faded. "He'll be sentenced on Monday. The seventh."

"And you have a job."

"Yes."

"But not a good job." It was a statement, not a question.

I thought of Mr. Whitaker's not-so-subtle grabs. Of the kisses required to receive my paycheck. Of how happily he docked my pay if I was a minute late to work. "It's a job."

He looked around again. Louise cooed in her seat, and Gertie, done with her treats, ambled back to the floor, where she played with an old doll. "It's hard," he said.

I couldn't speak, because if I did, I'd start sobbing.

"You're doing the best you can."

He picked up his hat from the table, preparing to leave. How I wanted him to stay, to make everything better.

"I need to return. Sara is minding both the store and the children." He spun his hat. "She's expecting again," he said.

"B'sha'ah tovah."

He reached into a pocket and drew out a ten-dollar bill. "I wish I could give you more."

"Thank you," I whispered.

"Sha, sha. Don't thank me. You're family. I'll be back."

Papa'd be furious if he found out, but my need to fill the cupboard was stronger than my fear of his disappointment.

Uncle Aaron stood, but I remained seated. He tousled my hair, gave me a faint smile, and left.

~

On Monday, May 7, 1928, Max and I dressed in our best outfits for the sentencing. It took a lot of pleading and ever-shorter skirts for me to convince Mr. Whitaker to give me the morning off.

The courthouse wasn't the same as the one where I had submitted my papers. This one, a massive edifice at 60 Centre Street, had been completed a year ago. Pillars guarding the front intimidated me. Etched in the cornice were words from George Washington, about justice, the foundation for good government. Justice. As if justice reached the Lower East Side of New York City.

After asking for directions three times, we found the courtroom. For such a new building, the room was dingy, with wood-paneled walls and rows of hard benches. We slid into the second row. My stomach churned. I crept my hand toward Max, who grasped it.

We sat silently as court cases were called. I listened to the discussions, the elaborate rules, the lawyer's double-talk, trying to imagine Max up there. This was what he wanted: to be a lawyer. Protecting the innocent. My heart cracked a little thinking that if Max were up there, he'd be the one putting Papa in prison. Max's back was erect, his legs pressed together, the only sign of nerves the way he squeezed my fingers.

I shivered, the hairs on the back of my neck rising. I scanned the room and saw I was being watched. Duke sat across a thin aisle. He tipped his hat but didn't stand to greet me. I was grateful. I needed to concentrate on my father.

We'd been there a half hour when another body slid next to me. Uncle Aaron. He patted my knee and smiled before grimly facing the front of the room.

Shortly after eleven, Papa walked in from a side door, guards flanking him. His clothes were ragged and dingy, the clothes he must have been wearing the night of his arrest. His lawyer met him at the desk. I willed Papa to turn around, but he focused on the judge.

Things happened fast. The judge was less imposing than I expected, a scrawny man who, though clearly Papa's age, still had childhood acne. I couldn't imagine why he didn't grow a beard to cover it.

"In the case of the State of New York versus Soffer, for the crime of bootlegging, Mr. Soffer, how do you plead?"

My father glanced at his lawyer, who nodded. "I plead guilty, Your Honor."

"In the case of the State of New York versus Soffer, for the crime of murder in the first degree, Mr. Soffer, how do you plead?"

"Your Honor," his lawyer said. "The charge has been modified to aggravated manslaughter in the second degree."

"Is that correct, Counselor?" The judge looked to the other table.

"Yes, Your Honor."

The judge noted something on a paper in front of him. "In the case of the State of New York versus Soffer, for the crime of aggravated manslaughter in the second degree, Mr. Soffer, how do you plead?"

I held my breath.

"I plead guilty, Your Honor."

My stomach dropped. Even though I had known what he would say, part of me had hoped he'd declare his innocence. But I thought of that gun. This plea would keep him from the electric chair.

"For the crime of bootlegging, I sentence Isaac Soffer to eighteen months' imprisonment at Sing Sing Correctional Facilities."

Eighteen months? A glimmer of hope flared in my chest. Eighteen months wasn't long. We'd have Papa back. Life would return to normal. We'd find a lawyer to prevent deportation. Max would study law full time. The girls would have a family again.

But the judge wasn't done.

"For the crime of aggravated manslaughter in the second degree, I sentence you to no less than ten years in jail and no more than fifteen years. Sentences to run concurrently."

A gasp escaped me. Ten years? At the best?

Uncle Aaron's arm wrapped around me, holding me up as if he were afraid I'd pass out. My hand ached, Max clutched it so forcibly.

The gavel banged. "Next up, the State of New York versus Esposito."

We stood as the guard led Papa from the room.

He never looked back.

Chapter Twenty

Ten years. Ten years, if we were lucky.

Once we were outside the courthouse, Max said, "Concurrently is good," though his voice was flat. "It means the sentences run at the same time." I wrapped my arms around myself to ward off the chills.

Ten years.

"Minnie, we need to talk about the girls," Uncle Aaron said.

I nodded, afraid to speak.

"Can you manage this life for ten years?"

"Yes." *No.*

"You're running yourself ragged."

"I've got a good job"—although *good* was a lie—"and Mrs. Rivkin is adequate." Another lie. "We manage."

"I know that's not true," Uncle Aaron said. "And ten years is a long time."

Ten years. I hadn't even lived in America for ten years. My life ten years ago had faded, a hallucination. Ten years from now? Unimaginable.

"I'm doing what Mama would have wanted."

"No, you're not. Your mother loved you as much as she loved those girls. She wanted you to live your life, not hers."

I didn't want to admit I wasn't living Mama's life. With Mama, our clothes were always clean, and homemade *mandelbrot* greeted us after school. She was never too tired to sing or tell us an old Yiddish tale. I tried as I snuggled with the girls in bed, but I'd rarely get past "In a shtetl in a dark corner of Ukraine lived a beautiful maiden" before I drowsed off. I wasn't living my life. I wasn't living Mama's life. Whose life was it?

"Those girls and Max are all I have."

"It shouldn't be that way. Your mother brought you to America to live a better life. Find a husband. Have children of your own."

"I have children of my own. Gertie and Louise." I trembled.

"Minnie"—Uncle Aaron ran his hands up and down my arms to warm me—"you have sisters. When you have children, you'll have a husband who earns money so you can dedicate yourself to your family. So you're not torn in a hundred directions."

"Speak more plainly."

"I explained the situation to my rabbi." His hands stilled on my shoulders. "He had a proposition. An option that would provide the girls a better life. To give you a better life."

"Max, why aren't you saying anything?"

"I think we should hear Uncle Aaron out," he said.

I wanted to slap Max for his betrayal; I dug my fingernails into my palms to stop myself. "There are no options," I said between clenched teeth.

"There are people who can take wonderful care of the girls, who can—"

"No." I bit my cheek hard, and I tasted blood.

"Minnie." Uncle Aaron rubbed his face, fatigued. "Forget what you want. Think what's best for Gertie and Louise. Think about what they need. Your love for them is abundant. That's clear." He took my hands, sensing I was about to run away. "But they need more than love. Children grow fast. They'll need new clothes. More food. Toys. Books. Trips to the park and the library. Someone with the time to teach them their ABC's and how to tie their shoes. Someone to take them to synagogue and help them learn Torah. Children are expensive and require a lot of time." He squeezed gently. "Minnie, you and Max can't give them all of that." He paused, letting the words sink in before saying more quietly, "My rabbi knows a couple who can. No one doubts your love." He looked to the sky. Was he fighting back tears? "Love them enough to let them go."

"I need to be at work." I yanked free of Uncle Aaron, knots of hopelessness and guilt roiling through me.

"Minnie—" Max said, but I cut him off.

"I'm late for work." I bolted, not wanting to listen to any more. Not wanting them to see me drowning in my tears.

~

By the time I picked up Gertie and Louise that evening, I wanted to sink into bed and never rise again.

As the girls picked at their dinner—herring salad and day-old bread from the bakery; the food Uncle Aaron brought hadn't lasted long—I studied them. They looked almost . . . I searched for the word, dismayed when I realized it was *haunted*. Gaunt. Grimacing more than smiling. Their clothes needed mending and a more careful washing. Gertie's hair had oatmeal crusted in it. *How many days ago did we have oatmeal?* I stifled yet more tears. My sweet sisters. I was making a muck of it.

A whine interrupted my brooding. "Minnie, I said more milk!"

I forced a smile. "Of course, my love." I moved to the icebox. "Anything for you."

~

Exhaustion and despair greeted me the next morning, along with Louise's milk-sour breath. She'd been regressing, waking two, three times a night. Toibe warned me the girls needed to sleep in their own beds; otherwise they'd be too dependent, too needy. But I craved that quiet time with them, their bodies nestled against mine. It wasn't them who were needy; it was me.

I spent the day buried in dictation, shifting constantly to remove Mr. Whitaker's hands from my knees. He kept me a few minutes past five, so I flew to pick up the girls. I arrived at Mrs. Rivkin's more tired than I'd thought possible.

When Mrs. Rivkin opened the door, Louise howled in an unusual way.

"What happened?" I took the baby into my arms.

"She fell," Mrs. Rivkin said. "Making a mountain out of a molehill. Only thing that baby needs is a *potch* on the *tuchus*. You need to discipline more."

"Our discipline is fine." Louise's arm hung oddly. "How did she fall?"

"Who knows?" Mrs. Rivkin held the door. "If she keeps being this difficult, I'm going to charge more."

"Mrs. Rivkin—" The door closed in my face.

I sat on the top step for a better look at Louise. I ran my hand down her arm. Bumpy in the wrong places. She cried harder. I wanted to squeeze her close and cry with her, but I feared hurting her more. "My sweet baby," I said to her. To her sister, I asked, "How did she fall?"

Gertie shrugged.

"You can tell me."

Gertie whimpered. "If I tell, tomorrow I get a pinching."

If I hadn't been sitting, I think I would have fallen down the stairs. "A pinching?"

Gertie nodded.

"Who pinches you?"

She looked at me, her eyes wild, full of tears.

"Never mind. I know."

Louise's howls didn't abate. The door to Mrs. Rivkin's apartment cracked open. "Get that caterwauling out of here. Giving me a headache."

I stood, cradling Louise in my arms. "Caterwauling? My sister is hurt. Hurt! Why didn't you call a doctor? What were you doing that she—"

The slamming door cut me off. I fought the urge to pound it, race into the apartment, and shake the old woman until something loosened inside of her, but my priority was Louise.

"We're going to the hospital."

Gertie started to complain, "I'm hungry—" but I accidentally bumped Louise, and her howl rose so loudly that Gertie bit back her words, a worried crease slipping across her brow. My stomach dropped. A three-year-old should never have an expression like that. We moved to America so children didn't ever have to have expressions like that.

The New York Infirmary for Women and Children was a mile away. When we arrived, the place was pandemonium. Hours passed before we were seen. Without fanfare, a nurse declared the arm broken and wrapped it in plaster of paris. "Minimize her activity," she said. When we were leaving, I was handed a bill, which I stuffed deep into a pocket.

At home, Max paced the kitchen. "Where were you?" he asked. "It's nearly ten p.m.!"

Louise was too tired to continue her full-scale sobbing, but her red face and whimpers drew Max's attention to her arm. "What happened to Louise?"

"Put her to bed carefully." I passed Louise to Max. "Gertie, let's feed you dinner."

Gertie shook her head and followed Max into the bedroom. Fully dressed, she lay down and, within seconds, was asleep.

Max set Louise down on her back. She whimpered, a sound that sliced me like a *shohet* slaughtering a chicken, a sound I'd never forget. Max sat with her, rubbing her belly until she drifted off.

Back in the kitchen, Max poured a cup of tea. "Hungry?" He opened the cupboard, but I shook my head. "What happened?"

"Mrs. Rivkin happened. I can't send them back."

Max placed a box of crackers on the table and slid the teacup in front of me.

"What are we going to do, Max?"

"I don't know, Min."

My throat seized, strangling my words, holding my breath hostage. "I can't keep the girls safe." The saltiness streaming down my face slipped between my lips. I pushed the teacup away. "Go." I stood. "Go."

"Go?" Max said, but the way his eyes welled and his color drained, I knew he understood.

"Go call Uncle Aaron."

Max hesitated. *Argue with me,* I begged silently. *Tell me we can keep them safe!* But, with a sob, he left to find a pay phone.

I lay down between Louise and Gertie, wrapping Louise in my arms. Gertie stirred and scooted closer to me. I whispered her favorite poem, "Market Square," into her ear. Without fully waking, she murmured, "No rabbits. "

Gertie, my own little rabbit.

~

In my half sleep, I heard sobs. Louise had rolled over and couldn't push herself onto her back. I picked her up delicately. Her good arm slipped around me, and she burrowed her head in my neck as she fell back asleep.

My chest grew tight. For Gertie and Louise, I would be strong. For Gertie and Louise, I needed to be strong.

The rest of the night, I sat in the bed, holding those two girls, trying to tattoo the shape of my sisters onto my body.

Chapter Twenty-One

The next morning, Max skipped classes. At 10:00 a.m., Uncle Aaron arrived.

"I brought more treats from Aunt Sara," he told Louise and Gertie. His gaze lingered on Louise's arm. "Kichel."

"Cookies in the morning?" I forced lightheartedness. "What a treat!"

I placed a pile of cookies on a plate and handed it to Gertie. "Why don't you play in the bedroom with Louise while Max and I talk to Uncle Aaron?"

Gertie observed me suspiciously. At three and a half, she was old enough to know we should have left for Mrs. Rivkin's, but I said, "Go on," and she took the plate with a huge grin. Max helped Louise into the next room.

When he returned, he shut the bedroom door.

"Minnie," Uncle Aaron started in his soft tone, but I stopped him.

"No sympathy." I couldn't bear it. I sat. Max and Uncle Aaron joined me at the table.

"I wish Sara and I could take them in."

"I know." Even without a fourth baby on the way, it wasn't feasible for them to add two more.

"The rabbi assures me," Uncle Aaron said, "the couple is warm and caring."

I picked up one of the bow-shaped cookies and tore the corner off.

"The rabbi vouches for them. They have a spacious apartment with bedrooms for both girls. He earns good money at his dry-cleaning business. His wife is a wonderful cook and an excellent seamstress. The girls will be well fed, beautifully dressed, and loved. The couple is unable to have children of their own; they are pining for a family."

I rolled the crumbs between my fingers. "The girls are loved. They're well loved right here."

Uncle Aaron placed his hand on top of mine, stilling the crushing of the kichel. "Of course they are well loved. What I should have said is they can pay for doctors. Make sure the damage to Louise's arm isn't permanent."

Lame legs, limp arms, missing limbs: so many accidents befell children on the East Side. What doctor would tend to Louise when I couldn't pay the hospital bill we already had?

"Would I be allowed to visit?"

Uncle Aaron gave the barest shake of his head. "They want to raise the girls as their own. Gertie and Louise are young. They'll grow to think of the couple as . . ." He trailed off but then braced himself. "Their new parents."

His words unleashed a pack of wolves in my chest. "I can't lose them. I can't let them fend for themselves."

"They won't be fending for themselves. They'll have parents. And each other."

Max couldn't hold back his own tears. "They already fend for themselves. What do you think they do at Mrs. Rivkin's? How did Louise break her arm?" His head fell into his hands. "Minnie, we can't protect them like they need protecting."

"I need to meet the couple." I wanted to look at them, see if they were the type of people who would truly love the girls.

"That's not the best idea," Uncle Aaron said, but for once, Max sided with me.

"No," Max said. "We need to see them."

"This is—" Uncle Aaron started.

"Not optional," I said.

He raked his hands through his hair. "All right." He stood. "I'll bring them to pick up the girls. Saturday." From his pocket, he drew twenty dollars. "This is from the rabbi." Before I could protest, he said, "If you don't want to spend it on yourself, spend it on the girls."

I took the money for the girls.

"Minnie, this is the right thing." Uncle Aaron kissed me on the cheek. "I'll see you Saturday."

Max and I sat at the table, the twenty-dollar bill in front of us.

By the time Gertie came in, our tears had stopped, but our cheeks were still wet. "Are we going to Mrs. Rivkin's?"

That woke me from my stupor. "Come here, baby." I opened my arms, and she crawled in. "You don't ever have to go to Mrs. Rivkin's again."

~

Once again, I was standing on the ship to America, the massive green woman rising from the sea, unknowing, uncertain of what was to come.

Another tardiness, Mr. Whitaker had said, and I'd be out of a job. Well, fine. If I had only three days with the girls, I wasn't going to banish them to Mrs. Rivkin's while I avoided his groping hands. If anything remotely good came of this, it was that I'd never have to see his gloating face again. What did it matter if I didn't have a job? What difference if I couldn't make rent? The girls would be safe. Max and I could sleep on the stoop, for all it mattered.

Gertie was near the age I was when Anshel had died. He was frozen in the picture resting by my bed, the one that used to sit on Mama's nightstand. I would be to Gertie what Anshel was to me, those memories so hazy, so vague. And Louise? Louise wouldn't remember me at all.

How many people can you lose and still remain whole? How many tiny rips can your heart take before it shreds into pieces too small to repair? At a wedding, the groom stamps his foot on a glass. The rabbis said it symbolized the destruction of the temple in Jerusalem all those millennia ago. Mama said it represented the fragility of marriage, how what was broken could never be fully repaired, the seams and cracks always visible. What must my heart look like, with chinks and fissures that would never heal?

The girls and I went to the park. We ate hot bagels off the push-carts. We went to the bookstore, where I bought Gertie her own copy of *When We Were Very Young*. I recited "Market Square" so many times I hoped she could never read it without hearing my voice.

With Louise in my arms and Gertie holding my hand, we took in everything we could. I was determined to etch myself into their memories.

Even though I was going through the motions, I didn't truly believe I'd be losing the girls. Yet those nights, I sobbed myself to sleep—in the morning trying to disguise my puffy face, the red lines striping the whites of my eyes.

With some of the money from the rabbi, I purchased Gertie and Louise new dresses.

"They'll have plenty of dresses soon," Max said after the girls had gone to sleep. "They'll be well taken care of."

I bristled. "For as long as I can, I will make sure they are loved and tended to."

I told Max to skip his early classes the next day. Since I'd agreed to the adoption, Max had treated me delicately. I dressed Gertie and Louise in their new dresses. My dress and Max's shirt were laundered and ironed. We arrived at the photographer's studio like a little family.

"Six photos for five dollars," the man said.

"I only need four," I replied. I hoped the girls would treasure the photo as I did the one from Bratsyana.

"Six for five dollars. Send 'em to relatives back home."

Who was left back home?

"Best to have extras." He moved us into position. "You never know."

"Fine, six photos."

The four of us stood in front of the camera. The photographer turned us this way and that, adjusting lights. He angled us so Louise's broken arm wouldn't be visible.

In an hour, we were done.

"When can I pick up the photos?" I asked.

"A week's time."

"No!" Gertie and Louise were leaving on Saturday. "I need them tomorrow."

The photographer snickered. "I develop film on Tuesdays."

"Develop it now." Desperation oozed from my words.

"Rush job costs double."

Ten dollars? That was ridiculous.

"We'll pay it," Max said. "C'mon, Minnie."

Max was right. I didn't have a choice.

"Fine. Ten dollars. I'll be by tomorrow afternoon."

He took the money with a lascivious grin. "They'll be ready at one."

~

Early Friday morning, I stood with the girls outside the small building that had terrified me so many years ago. How harmless it appeared now. I waited until the stream of men exited, removing yarmulkes from their heads as they returned to the secular world. One of them stopped.

"Minnie?"

Max's old friend, the rabbi's son, Leo.

"Minnie, how are you?" Leo's voice was soft. I despised the pity I heard in it. Max must have told him.

"Just fine." I turned my back on him as we walked inside. I didn't care if I was rude. I had more important things to worry about.

At the entrance the *tzedakah* box stood guard. More guilt: I had no coins to drop in.

Rabbi Umansky gathered prayer books. When he heard my steps, he squinted, and then a wide smile spread across his face. "Malka? Is that you?"

"Malka?" Gertie said, but I shushed her.

"Come in, come in. Sit down." He took Louise from my arms. "Her arm she hurt?" He spoke English for the children's benefit.

My failures weighed so heavily upon me. "I left her in the care of another woman while I worked, and she fell."

The rabbi's eyes glided over the three of us, taking in my haggard frame, the lines on my face. "So big she has gotten. You too." He patted Gertie's head. "Children are the world's greatest blessing."

I wiped away tears, afraid of the girls seeing how upset I was. The rabbi walked to the back door that led to the stairs. He called up to his wife.

Returning, he asked, "How are things, Malka?"

I wasn't sure how to speak in front of the girls, but I didn't have to, as the rabbi's wife emerged. The rebbetzin smiled as the rabbi passed her the baby. "Gertie, come have a snack." Carrying Louise, she guided Gertie to their living quarters.

In Yiddish, I said, "Rabbi, I don't know what to do. My father's in jail, and I can't take care of the girls. They are hungry and alone, and I have to work, but there still isn't enough. My uncle wants me to give them up. To strangers. I can't bear the thought."

"Your uncle found someone?"

"Yes." My voice was faint.

"They're Jewish?"

"Yes."

"You trust your uncle?"

"Very much."

"Your mother? She trusted her brother?"

I remembered how much Mama had depended on Uncle Aaron. "Uncle Aaron was the most important person in her life, other than us."

"Do you think your uncle would do anything that would hurt your mother?"

Of course he wouldn't. Of course Uncle Aaron would do only what he thought Mama would want. "No," I said, the word barely more than a sigh.

The rabbi steepled his fingers. He spoke in measured tones. "Hashem sometimes gives us more than we think we can handle."

I pulled a handkerchief from my bag.

"Sometimes, though, He provides a way out. It can be difficult for us to see."

"What do you mean?"

"Giving up Louise and Gertie will be the hardest thing you ever do." That he spoke of it not as a question but as a fact made my stomach burn in hopelessness. "But Hashem has provided a way for Louise and Gertie to flourish. And, perhaps, for you as well."

For ten minutes, I sat and cried. Rabbi Umansky finished tidying to give me time to unleash my grief. When I composed myself, he brought the girls back to me. Rabbi Umansky placed his palm on Louise's head and recited a blessing. He turned to Gertie and did the same.

"May I?" he asked, holding his hand out to me. I stepped closer.

His hand was heavy on my head, and his words floated over me. *"May God make you like Sarah, Rebecca, Rachel, and Leah. May the Holy One bless you and keep you. May the Holy One shine light upon you and be gracious to you. May the Holy One turn toward you and give you peace."* He moved his hand to my chin, raising my face. "I'm here when you need me, Malka."

We left the synagogue for our final day together.

~

Friday flew by too fast. The last thing I did was take them to the soda shop fronting Papa's bar. It hurt to go in, to be near the place that had torn our family apart, but I needed to show them who we were. While we slurped Black and Whites, I told them stories of coming to America. Of Anshel. Of Bubbe and Zayde in Ukraine. Of Papa opening the soda shop. Of Mama's pride.

On Saturday morning, at 10:00 a.m., Uncle Aaron returned with a couple. "This is Earl and Mabel."

The use of first names surprised me, but then I understood. Uncle Aaron didn't want me to be able to find them.

Mabel fidgeted, nervous, which comforted me. Her face was round and her body fleshy. Earl had a thick mustache and elephantine ears.

"Lovely to meet you, Minnie," Earl said.

Mabel tugged at the sides of her dress. "I can't tell you how grateful . . ." Her words trailed off.

Earl took Mabel's hand. "We've so wanted a family." His voice was soft and warm, the kind of voice a child could lose herself in.

"We'll give them everything," Mabel said. "I promise."

Her words were claws, ripping across my chest. But they seemed sincere. They seemed like decent people.

Max went to retrieve Gertie and Louise.

When Gertie saw the strangers, she hid behind my legs.

I wanted to keep her there. I wanted to bury her in my skirts and never let her out. Yet I couldn't feed her in my skirts. I couldn't shelter her. I couldn't provide her with clothes. I couldn't play with her or teach her the ABC's if I also wanted to make enough money to provide a roof over her head and food to eat.

Uncle Aaron squatted to Gertie's eye level. "Gertie, this is your new mama and papa."

My entire body recoiled. I grabbed Gertie. Of course they'd want to be called Mama and Papa.

Gertie's eyes grew to twice their normal size. Mabel opened her arms, and Max handed her Louise. Louise didn't have any reservations, and she curled into Mabel's shoulder.

"Minnie?" Gertie said.

185

"Gertie, my love." The words cut my mouth as if I were chewing rocks. "These people have a warm home with a bedroom just for you. They have fresh bread every night and chickens every Friday. You'll have lots of new dresses."

"I don't want my own room."

"Gertie." Mabel's voice had a musical lilt. "We have dolls and a toy carriage and a whole shelf of fairy-tale books."

Gertie rocked her head violently. "I want Minnie."

"Gertie, you will be happy with them," I said.

Earl reached for her, but Gertie clung to me, grasping my dress so firmly her knuckles turned white.

"No, no, no, no, no," she screamed.

Earl, with Uncle Aaron's help, pried her fingers loose. Earl picked her up, but Gertie angled her body toward me, kicking Earl's side.

"Shh, shh." Earl stroked her hair.

"Gertie, I have something for you. For you and Louise." From the table, I grabbed the photo we had taken on Thursday. "Look! It's us. Keep it close, and remember I'm with you in your heart."

Displeasure crossed Mabel's face. I took a second photo. "For Louise. For when she's older."

Mabel hesitated before holding out her hand. It hadn't occurred to me they wouldn't want photos of us. I prayed Mabel didn't throw it away.

I retrieved a package from the cabinet. "This is for the girls." I passed Mabel *When We Were Very Young*. "Plus a little brown rabbit for each of you." I pulled out two small stuffed animals. "Gertie loves bunnies. Her favorite poem is 'Market Square.'" I placed a bunny in Gertie's hands and then the other in Louise's. "Now you each have a brown rabbit." My voice squeaked. "Your own rabbit to cuddle every night."

Louise hugged hers in her good arm, and Gertie buried her face in her bunny.

"We'd better go," Uncle Aaron said.

"Go?" Gertie asked.

"We're going home," Mabel said.

"This home," she insisted.

"I love you, Gertie. I love you, Louise." I kissed each of them. Mabel smelled floral, of freshly laundered clothes.

Gertie bucked and screamed "No, no, no!" over and over as Mabel and Earl walked down the stairs. The echoes of Gertie's cries rang through the hallways, ripped through my chest.

Max put his arm around my shoulder, drawing me tight against him.

Uncle Aaron lingered. "Will you be all right, Minnie?"

It was as if stray dogs feasted on my heart, consuming it in tiny bites so the pain wouldn't end. I had no words, so I turned and crawled back into bed.

Part Three

Chapter Twenty-Two

The emptiness was vast, tangible, grabbing me around the neck, making it difficult to catch my breath. How could a lack, a nothing, hold so much weight?

Sylvia couldn't cheer me. Toibe couldn't make me eat. Max couldn't force me to leave the apartment.

My bedroom was cavernous without the noises of Gertie and Louise, the rustle of sleep, the shrieks of nightmares, the purrs of pleasant dreams. The silence pounded, throbbing in my ears. My mourning for Mama returned anew without the busyness of the girls to distract me.

The rent was overdue.

"We should move somewhere cheaper, smaller," Max said, but I refused. This apartment held my memories.

We skimped on food and used Max's paycheck to pay some of the rent. The landlord gave us an extension.

The stillness in the apartment was unbearable. I sank into it. Max avoided it, spending more time at school and work.

On the morning of May 15, a knock at the door. Rabbi Umansky.

"Malka." For the first time, I took pleasure in my old name, my connection to Mama, the name she had chosen for me. "How are you?"

I stared mutely until he nodded, using his entire torso, as if praying. "Of course, of course. As well as might be expected."

"Where are my manners?" I cinched the belt on my housecoat tighter. I was wearing one of Mama's. "Come in. Have some tea."

"I'm afraid I can't stay," the rabbi said. "Mr. Kanev's gout is acting up, so I need to teach *cheder*, but I wanted to give you this." From his pocket he withdrew a short, thick candle in a glass jar. "This is a yahrzeit candle. Tonight is the anniversary of your mother's death. You light it at sundown."

"But Mama died on May twenty-eighth."

"In the Gregorian calendar. On the Hebrew calendar, your mother passed on the twenty-sixth of Iyar, which starts at sunset this evening."

He rocked back and forth on his heels, always in motion. "Malka, you need to take care of yourself."

Self-consciously, I patted my hair. I hadn't bathed since the girls left. I ate the bare minimum. It was as if I were sitting shiva anew. "Why?" It came out more bitterly than I'd intended.

He stilled his movement. "Because it's what your mother wanted."

My throat stoppered, as if I'd swallowed a bottle cork.

"Come to the shul, Malka. Let your community take care of you."

I nodded.

"We haven't forgotten her, Malka. Your mother is in our hearts. Her memory is a blessing for all of us." He put his hand on my head and mumbled the prayer I had so despised. Now I wanted nothing more than to be a child, to have my mother come and take care of me. "Be well, Malkala."

I rolled the candle, weighing the heft of it, a chunk of wax designed to blaze for twenty-four hours. Mama had lit them for her parents on the anniversaries of their deaths. Now it was my turn.

That evening, I struck a match, staring at the flame as it slid down the stick, not moving to ignite the candle. When the flame reached my fingers, the burn shocked me. Not because of the pain but because I had felt it. I hadn't thought I was capable of feeling anything.

It didn't seem like the anniversary of her death. It wasn't Louise's birthday, and the two were intricately tied. On May 15 of last year, Mama was alive, sleeping in the next room.

I struck another match and lit the candle. As the burn on my finger subsided, the nothingness deluged me again.

~

The next morning, Max sat at the table, bewitched by the flame. He stood to pour me a cup of coffee, then stirred in sugar and milk.

"I said Kaddish last night," Max said. It was his duty to recite the prayer every year on the yahrzeit. "I'll go back to shul and say it again today."

It's what Mama would have wanted.

The coffee was fresh, coating my tongue. It tasted good. When was the last time something had tasted good?

"Min, you need a job."

"I don't want a job."

"We need to pay rent. Buy food."

The coffee didn't taste as good anymore. "Why?"

"We need to survive."

"What is there to survive for?"

"What about Papa?"

The coffee turned bitter, the acid raging against my stomach. "What about him?"

"Someday he'll be released. Where will he go?" He swirled the glass candle, the melted wax clinging to the sides. "If you don't find a job, I'll have to quit school."

Quit school? What was the point of all this if he quit school? Mama wanted Max to be a lawyer. To even consider his dropping out of school was an affront to her memory. "Fine, I'll get a job."

He slid over last Sunday's paper, as if he'd known I'd agree, which annoyed me.

"Thanks," I said. "I needed something to wipe with." And I headed to the toilet.

~

I didn't wipe with the newspaper. I opened to the Help Wanted—Female section and started circling. I couldn't go back to the employment agency after walking out on Mr. Whitaker, and with no diploma and no reference, I'd have little luck at another agency.

I put on my best dress. With the money Max had left for food marketing, I stopped at the barber's for a trim, the same barber Papa had taken me to all those years ago. Now, though, I wasn't treated like anyone special.

Once I was bobbed, I made the rounds. Many of the jobs were filled. "Why didn't you come on Monday?" I was asked, heads shaking as if searching for a job on Wednesday meant I wasn't serious. The telephone company said my accent was too strong. Yet when I heard a woman with a thick British accent, I raised my eyebrows. The man said, "Okay, you have the wrong kind of accent." At a furniture store, the saleswoman asked where I lived. When I told her, she turned me down. "Why does where I live matter?" I asked.

The saleswoman said, "Your friends are poor. We need salesgirls who can bring in customers." I was offered a job as an office assistant, but when the interviewer grabbed my *tuchus* as I turned, I walked right out the door.

The next day, I accepted a job as a salesclerk at a large clothing store on Fourteenth Street, where I was placed in the corset department and promised a healthy commission. But after three days, I quit. Who bought corsets in 1928?

Rent loomed, so I took a job as a sandwich girl at the Woolworth counter, where I lied and said I was German, as the ad stated white girls only. It took only one mother to come in with two young girls for me to start bawling in the tuna salad. I was fired.

~

The next Sunday, I leafed through the *New York Times* classifieds. Glancing at the date, I saw it was May 27. Tomorrow would be Louise's birthday. Tomorrow would be the one-year anniversary of Mama's death. At least on the American calendar.

"Heading to work," Max said as he left the apartment. "Can you buy groceries?" He didn't wait for an answer before slamming the door.

I couldn't stand to read one more good appearance and address, commission basis, or married preferred, so I figured I'd at least do the shopping. I shook our money tin, and $1.37 in coins fell out. We needed money. Soon.

I'd scarcely enough money for the basics: A loaf of bread from the baker. A bag of potatoes from the produce cart. At the grocery store, a pound of coffee, a quart of milk, a pound of sugar, rolled oats, and a can of peas. Walking to the cashier, I spotted yahrzeit candles on a low shelf. They were the same price as the peas. I put the peas back and bought the candle.

All afternoon, I roamed the streets. This was the last day I would ever be able to think, *A year ago on this day, Mama was alive.* The distance between life with my family and life without was expanding, like a child's balloon on the verge of popping.

The sun set, and I returned to the apartment. I placed the candle on the table. Hebrew dates were difficult to remember, the lunar months shifting from year to year. I didn't want to have to rely on Rabbi Umansky to know when to honor my mother. I would light a candle for Mama every year, but at sundown before May 28. A compromise: a Jewish tradition on an American date.

As I lit the candle, I wondered what Louise would be doing on this, her first birthday. I was certain there'd be a fuss. There was nothing American parents wouldn't do to spoil a child on her birthday. In Bratsyana, birthdays weren't a given, with typhoid and starvation and Cossacks. Birthdays, if they were known, were an excuse to spit on the ground—*pu pu pu*—and say *Kein ayin hara,* warding off the demons who stole children. Why flaunt to the devil that you'd managed to keep your child alive another year?

Earl and Mabel were Americans. They spoke with the crispness of those whose lips had never touched Yiddish. With a start, I realized Louise would never understand the language of her mother, that Gertie would forget entirely her first tongue.

How absurd that for the past eight years I'd done nothing but distance myself from Yiddish, and now I worried Gertie and Louise wouldn't speak it. Someday—so very long from now, I prayed—when we met in the next world, would Gertie and Louise be able to talk to Mama? To Anshel? They would never know our language, remember our stories of Bratsyana, of our family's history.

Or rather, my home. My stories. My history.

The two girls were Americans.

I was . . . what? I belonged nowhere.

The flame mesmerized me. It was both a birthday candle and a death candle. One light that encompassed the entirety of life.

It wasn't the Hebrew anniversary. I wasn't a man. I didn't have ten people. But still, I closed my eyes and recited from memory the Mourner's Kaddish. I said it for Mama, hoping my words would be enough.

~

On Monday, I poured myself a cup of coffee and opened the *Times.* Candy saleslady. Canvasser. Elliott-Fisher operator. Laundress. Nurse. Even if I was offered one of those jobs, they sounded so dismal—smiling for sales, running numbers on a machine, keeping out of reach of a man's wandering hands.

Uncle Aaron's words danced in my brain: *Your mother wanted you to have a better life.*

I wasn't going to have a better life working as a cashier. I wasn't going to rise in the world selling hosiery.

The one time Papa had gone legit—the land deals—he'd lost it all. Only one place had brought him an income, even if it wasn't much.

It was a chance to make money. A chance to be the boss. A job I'd enjoy.

The hell with Max for telling me not to do it.

I slid on a dress, ran a brush through my hair, and applied lipstick in front of the mirror. I stood a little taller as I put on my hat.

The day was crisp, as if the world was airing itself after a musty and murky winter.

In twelve minutes I arrived at the soda shop. Inside, a teen served a mother and her toddler. I forced myself to look, to not give in to the pity.

Your mother wanted you to have a better life.

The toddler glanced up, and through the window, I gave her a half smile before walking around the corner to the plain black door.

I knocked and waited.

The door opened. I took in the bar, the sticky floors, the dismal lighting, the fermented smell.

Turning to Big Al, my hands on my hips, I said, "I'm here. What needs to be done?"

He stood, unblinking. He jutted his chin toward the back room. "You need to place this week's orders. Payments are due today. You're behind on the vig."

Orders? Payments? Vig?

I strode to the back room. Papa had left absolute chaos. *Where should I start?*

I'd have to learn.

It was time to go to work.

197

Chapter Twenty-Three

The first task was understanding the flow of money.

In the back room, I found a ledger tossed on top of crates. Papa's handwriting was almost impossible to read. On the last few pages, Papa's scrawl was replaced with the blocky handwriting and poor spelling of someone who hadn't completed much school. The orders appeared to be for the soda shop, but of course they weren't.

"Big Al," I called out, "do you know how the books are kept?"

"No idea."

I stared at the book so long the numbers blurred. Was *chocolate* code for bourbon? *Vanilla* for gin? Then what was *strawberry*?

"What the hell are you doing?"

Looking up, I saw Riley in the doorway. His expression was unreadable.

"I'm glad you're here, Riley." I turned the ledger around to face him. "Can you explain the accounting system to me?"

"'Accounting system'? This ain't the Bank of Manhattan. Why you lookin' in the books?"

"I'll be taking over while my father is"—I searched for the word—"incapacitated."

"You mispronounced *incarcerated*." His arms folded over his chest, and his words became slower, more deliberate. More sinister. "I told you, I run this place. You have no business in the books. People have gotten hurt for far less."

He oozed hostility. Was he threatening me? Suddenly I was fourteen. Riley was Gino demanding money. Paolo kicking Max. Vinnie fondling my chest.

Those three had gotten the better of us. I wouldn't let Riley do the same. I wasn't going to let a low-life gangster run me out of my father's bar. "This is Ike's bar. I'm Ike's daughter. He told me to run this place." I stood, hands on the desk, trying to make myself look bigger.

"I've been taking care of this bar since your father was pinched." Riley's biceps tightened, the wiry blue veins of his arm popping.

"Now I'm here. I'm the boss."

"I'm not taking orders from a broad. He owes me."

"He owes you nothing. You got paid. You just work here. For me."

Riley's arms dropped, fists curling. "That so?"

"That's so." My voice surprised me. It wasn't my voice. It was menacing. Fierce. I liked it. "Are you the one who took out the loans? Are you the one who built this bar?" Anger propelled me. "Should we ask Mr. Rothstein?" Rothstein had nothing to do with this, but I thought Duke might back me should it come to that.

Riley laughed. "Do you think *Mr.* Rothstein cares?"

But I must have hit a nerve, because he retreated to the bar as customers trickled in.

~

An hour later, I gave up on the ledgers. I'd have to wait for Frank to explain them to me. Yet I couldn't go home. I had to make my presence known. I'd serve drinks.

Riley leaned on the bar at the other end, chatting with a stout man who drank his gin in large gulps. When Riley refilled his glass, he filled it too high.

"Riley, you're pouring away the profits."

He shrugged. "What do I care? You seem to think this is *your* bar."

Yids want to use my street, they need to pay for the right. Sliding behind the counter, I kept my hands low so he couldn't see how I dug my nails into my palms. "Pass me an apron."

Slowly his head turned toward me. "So it's not just the back end you want? You want to take this over too? Gonna steal my tips?" *Yids always have money.*

"I'll do what I like." In my periphery, I saw lemons on the shelf below the counter, a paring knife next to them.

"Maybe I'll do what I like." Riley leered. *I'll check the girl.* He took a step closer.

But he wasn't Vinnie. And I wasn't that girl.

I moved in front of the fruit, reaching behind my body to take hold of the knife.

The few men at the bar watched with fascination, some leaning forward to see better, as if they were at a baseball game.

Big Al called, "Enough, Riley!"

"I've got this." I was flinty and unforgiving.

"I've had it with you." Riley cracked his fingers one by one. "You think you can run this bar?"

"I can, and I will." Electricity sparked in my chest. I was strong. "This is my bar."

"Fuck you."

No one had ever directed those words toward me. "Well, fuck you too." The words tripped, alien on my tongue. I'd never used such language before. But then I'd never taken over a bar before.

He stilled. He grinned, but it was a cold grin, the grin of someone who was plotting. "Go back home, little girl. No one wants you here."

What would Papa do?

"Riley." The words came out flat, cold. "You're fired."

"Excuse me?" He took a step forward.

"You are fired." I enunciated, each word crisp.

"You can't fucking fire me." Another step toward me. I squeezed the knife handle.

"Just did." My vision was blurred by my rage. "Get out."

Big Al moved behind me, unsure whether to intervene. I ignored him.

Riley stood close. I smelled sauerkraut on his breath. *You can do this,* I told myself. *You are your father's daughter.*

Without warning my hand shot out from behind my back. I whipped the knife up, bringing it to Riley's face, sinking the tip into Riley's temple.

"What the fuck!" He jerked backward, but I moved with him. He hit the back wall, rattling bottles.

"Minnie," Big Al said. "Enough."

"Step back, Big Al."

A knock on the door. "Open the door, Big Al."

He hesitated, unsure what to do.

"Don't keep the customers waiting." My knife hadn't moved from Riley's face.

Big Al obeyed, opening the door. At least someone listened to me. The three older men from last time entered, but Big Al stuck out his arm to keep them from approaching the bar.

"Riley"—I dug the tip deeper into his skin—"I won't tell you again. You're fired."

His Adam's apple bounced. "I dare you."

Riley's face shimmered in front of me, till all I saw was Vinnie. Vinnie deserved this. Riley deserved this. I wasn't going to keep letting men hurt me. This was for Max. This was for me.

Pressing the knife deeper, I drew it down the side of his face, the dull blade making a ragged slash.

"Jesus!" His hand flew to his cheek, blood spurting through his fingers.

"Minnie!" Big Al yelled.

I took a step away from Riley. "Leave."

"Let me clean his wound first," Big Al said.

Shaking my head, I said again, more loudly, "Leave."

The wound bled fast, dampening his shirt, spilling on the floor. He was immobile, staring at me in shock. Well, he'd dared me.

Without taking his eyes off mine, Riley edged around me to make for the door. His steps were slow, deliberate. At the door, he sneered. "You will regret this."

When the door slammed behind him, I exhaled, unaware I'd been holding my breath. I hoped Papa had kept his protection payments up to date.

One of the men at the bar applauded, and the others joined in.

"Give me a moment," I said.

I slipped into the office, closed the door, and leaned against it. The palpitations in my chest throbbed so hard I feared my heart might stop. It scared me, how naturally that had come to me. I didn't feel frightened. I didn't feel remorse. I felt powerful.

A knock on the door. "Minnie?" It was Big Al.

I let him in.

Big Al entered. "That was foolish. You could have gotten yourself killed."

"But I didn't."

"My sole job is to protect the bar. You need to let me handle it."

"Riley needed to learn some respect."

Big Al stared at me for a moment before shaking his head. "We'll put that on your gravestone." He returned to his post at the door.

My breath was ragged, so I stayed put until I could breathe easily. On a stack of crates was a half-full bottle of the brown stuff. I poured myself a glass and downed it in one swallow.

Once calmed, I returned to the bar. "So, fellas. What are you drinking?"

"That was quite a show, princess," said the taller of the three older men.

"Learn how to make drinks?" asked another.

"Not yet, but give me time."

"Time?" the first one said. "Does that mean you're sticking around?"

"Gentlemen." I put three glasses on the bar. "I'm here to stay."

"Did you hear that?" The second one slapped the other two on their shoulders. "'Gentlemen.' She might class this place up."

In another life, that might have made me smile. But I wasn't ready to smile yet.

As I poured their drinks, a thought settled: *I just might make this bar work.*

Under my breath, though, I muttered, "*Kein ayin hara. Kein ayin hara. Kein ayin hara.*"

Chapter Twenty-Four

When Frank arrived, he bobbed his head in greeting, as if he'd expected me.

"Riley's out," I said.

Frank raised his eyebrows. "For the night or for good?"

"For good." I lowered my voice. "Hey. Noticed a teen in the front store. What happened to the burly guy?"

"Too expensive."

The idea of putting a price on safety made me queasy.

"Do you know how to read the ledgers?"

"Not really. I pour the drinks."

If Frank didn't know the books, I was in a serious jam.

After a few hours behind the bar, I retreated to the back room. It was a dump. A rancid odor hung in the air. Boxes of bottles everywhere. Newspapers strewed about. Piles of papers with numbers.

I wanted to tidy, but I didn't have the energy. Now that I had time to think, now that my adrenaline wasn't firing through me, my certainty from earlier evaporated. How could I run this bar? I had no idea what I was doing.

My head throbbed.

"Payment due." Duke stood in the doorway, hat low on his forehead, a toothpick sticking out the side of his mouth. A tiny quiver of heat fluttered through me, though it drowned in the anxiety telling me I couldn't run a bar. "You're not Riley."

"Nice of you to notice." I prayed he hadn't seen me moping. I opened the ledger again and scanned the columns as if I understood them. "How much do we owe?"

"Where's Riley?" He poked his head out of the office, as if he might find Riley lurking behind the bar.

"Riley wasn't happy with the new management. He's gone. I'm taking over."

"I'm guessing he didn't leave on good terms."

"He left on the only terms I gave him."

Duke shifted the toothpick to the other side. "Watch out. He's got friends."

My stomach burned. Must have been a delayed reaction to the bourbon. "I should worry?"

Duke shrugged. "You pay for protection. But you still need to be careful." He raised his eyebrows. "You okay?"

"I'm fine. Let's get to business." I gestured for him to sit.

"You know the liquor business?"

"As much as anyone does when they first start."

"Not sure that's true." He turned the chair around and straddled it, tossing his hat on the desk. "This is a dangerous business. People get hurt."

Hurt? I thought of all the hurts. I'd left Bratsyana. My name had been forcibly changed. A boy had touched me where I didn't want to be touched. I thought of Max lying in bed with swollen eyes. I thought of Mama dead, Papa in jail. Days without food. Mr. Whitaker's unwanted advances. Louise's broken arm and the bruises dotting Gertie. I thought of the holes those two girls had ripped in my chest. What was left to hurt?

"Duke, I appreciate your concern. Now, kindly tell me how the payments to Mr. Rothstein work."

Duke chewed the inside of his cheek. The silence grew, but I refused to be the one to break it. Finally he sighed. "Ike always said you were the one who got all the goods."

I'd be lying if I said Papa's opinion of me didn't make me swell with pleasure.

"First off," Duke continued, "it's Rothstein. Skip the *mister*." He turned the book to face him. "Whatta ya need?"

"Do you understand the ledger?" I looked weak asking for help, but I didn't have a choice. If I didn't figure out the system, understand how to run the bar, then I'd lose the place. "Tell me the basics I need to know."

Duke scanned the columns. "Everyone has his own system. But I can make guesses. This looks like the alcohol orders. Judging by the amounts, *chocolate* is probably bourbon, and *vanilla* gin."

I pulled a piece of paper from a drawer and wrote "Chocolate is," but my pen skidded off the page as the sheet was yanked away. "Hey!"

"What are you doing?"

"Taking notes?" I didn't mean for it to come out as a question.

He tore the page into tiny pieces. "No notes. There's a reason this is in code. Nothing in writing. Rothstein insists on no books. Everything is done up here." He tapped the side of his head.

As a kid I'd struggled to memorize multiplication tables. This, though, was more important than grammar school math, so I forced myself to commit his every word to memory.

"Both your loan and protection payments go through me. Loan payment goes to Rothstein. Protection covers Tammany Hall, police, gangs. Doesn't mean you don't need to pay off individual flatfoots, but if you're arrested, you'll be sprung fast."

"How?"

"Not important."

"Big Al mentioned a vig?"

"Vigorish. That's the interest you're paying."

For the next hour, Duke detailed what I owed, who to pay off and how, the liquor to order, and the overhead to pay.

When it was time to pay up, I must have looked confused.

"Cashbox in bottom left drawer," Duke said.

I handed Duke a princely sum—two hundred and twenty-five dollars—for the loan and protection.

"Good luck, kid," he said. "Can I give you advice?"

"Indeed."

"Watch your back." With that he popped on his hat and exited, leaving a sweet, musky scent in his wake.

I shuddered, though the room was toasty.

~

Running the bar was not going to be easy. But compared to telling Max I was working at the bar, it was a game of tiddlywinks.

When I walked in at 3:30 a.m., Max was asleep over an open book, drool staining the pages. I tried to close the door quietly, but he woke.

"Where the hell have you been?" He wiped his face with the back of his hand.

With his hair flattened on one side and the imprint of the edge of the book on his forehead, Max made me ache for the little boy who had stood next to me on the ship as we'd gazed at New York in awe.

I know you don't want me to, but I'm running the bar, was what I thought. *The bar is our family's legacy. It'll be okay. I can take care of it. I can keep you out of it.*

Yet those words didn't come. I willed myself to tell Max. He'd be disappointed. Angry. But that was nothing new. We'd had a life of disappointments.

"Minnie? I asked you a question."

"I found a job."

"A job? All night?"

"I'm a nighttime telephone operator." Where that had come from, I had no idea. Must have lodged in my head from all the classifieds I'd read. Papa had his soda shop; I'd have my telephone company.

"Nighttime?" Max dabbed his book with the corner of his shirt, trying to wipe off his slobber.

"It pays more than daytime."

"How much?"

The books were such a mess I wasn't sure what I could take. "Eighteen dollars a week." That sounded reasonable.

"A nighttime operator," Max said. "Let's hope this one lasts."

With that, my goodwill fled, so I retreated to the bedroom, where I fell into an exhausted sleep.

I slept until noon, then woke to an empty apartment. I lay in bed, replaying the night before. Lying to Max crushed me. Lying to Max was the final betrayal. Max and I had always been on the same side, the same team. Me and Max against the world.

Not anymore.

With the bar, I was on my own.

Papa kept the bar keys in the top drawer of his dresser. I returned to the bar at 2:00 p.m., letting myself in. The room was simple, dismal. Plywood topped the counter, badly stained from the condensation of cold drinks. The footrail at the bottom was also light wood, scuffed by the oxfords and work boots of patrons. Three rickety tables were scattered about the room, surrounded by wood-backed chairs, many of which were missing slats, furniture clearly purchased from a junk dealer. The speakeasy at Ratner's was filled with ambient light and intimate tables. Papa's bar—my bar—was more utilitarian, to put it kindly. Did it even have a name? I'd always thought of it as the bar on Baxter Street.

Perhaps things could change.

First, though, I needed to tackle the office. It was dank and smelled of stale smoke and something rotten. I searched the makeshift shelves and opened drawers until I found the source: a green, furry sandwich, with unidentifiable meat inside. I placed a sheet of newspaper on top. Holding my breath, I used the paper to pick up the living science experiment and threw it in the trash in the alley. Old newspapers piled on the desk. Sheets of paper with what looked like horse bets. Crumbs everywhere, which explained the mouse droppings on the floor.

I attacked the room with a broom and mop. Could have used a shovel to scoop out all the garbage.

An hour before opening, Big Al entered.

"You came back," he said.

"Told you I would."

"So you did." He took his place at the door. Fifteen minutes later, Frank came in and prepped the bar.

The hours flew by when I was in that back room. It turned out I didn't dislike doing office work; I disliked doing office work for other people.

The bar was costly. We paid $2,500 annually—all up front—to rent the basement room, typical for illegal establishments. Rothstein had lent us money for the first year's rent, plus money for the initial liquor purchases. Plus Rothstein had covered Papa's investments. We still owed about $6,000. Papa had borrowed $10,000 for the bar and then another $1,000 for the land. He'd paid almost half; however, with the interest—or rather the vig—$11,000 was really $13,420. We paid the loan in weekly installments of $125. Protection was $100 a week. Checks to the local Democratic club. Outrageous Christmas gifts to politicians and cops. Donations to the police fund. Then the booze itself. The cost fluctuated, but generally, rye was $48 a case. Gin $22. A case of wine was $20, but that could last a month. For liqueurs, we purchased the base at drugstores and added alcohol to it ourselves. Beer was relatively cheap, but we didn't make much off it. Bottles were reused. I returned the empties, which were refilled and sold back to me the next week.

Salaries came to $41 a week, even after subtracting Riley's take. The soda shop, which sat empty most of the winter, lost money.

The bar cost almost $800 a week to run.

The amount took my breath away. Was it possible to make that much? Papa had said the bar had kept us afloat when he'd lost everything. I'd have to keep it floating. I wanted to pay off that debt and quickly. I didn't want to be beholden to anyone.

There was no making heads or tails of the balances, so I drew a line across the last page, turned to a fresh one, and started from scratch.

Chapter Twenty-Five

The next week, my real education began. In the early hours, Frank taught me to make basic drinks. I learned the difference between vodka and gin and which bottle held rum and which rye. I took sips of each, grimacing at the bitterness, but I could indeed note a slight distinction between the liquors.

Frank was amiable and handsome, in an Irish kind of way. I wasn't sure I could trust him—*trust no one* echoed in my head—but I didn't have much choice, given I knew nothing and he knew everything.

On Monday, when Duke returned for payment and the liquor order, I had a list of questions.

"Would you look at that." He slid into the chair. "Didn't realize this desk had a surface." He ran his hands across its top, as if admiring a fine horse. He placed his hat in front of him.

I realized the room had no hooks. In a small notebook, I wrote *Buy coatrack*. "My father has many attributes, but clearly organization is not one of them."

Duke chuckled. "How are you enjoying the life of a whisper sister?"

"Not bad." A bit of a lie, as I thought of Riley. Yet the bar would definitely bring home more than the eighteen dollars a week I'd told Max. And it had the potential to bring in even more than that. I was sure of it.

"I hear you've learned to take care of yourself," Duke said.

"Excuse me?"

"That gash on Riley's cheek didn't get there by itself."

"Hmm." Was he impressed or horrified?

He tilted his chair back. "Perhaps you're tougher than I thought."

"Perhaps. So I have more questions."

"Shoot."

"Why was my father doing all those extra jobs?" I gestured to the ledger. "Bar does okay."

"He got himself in a bit of a hole with some investment he made."

I realized Papa had been trying to recoup the land losses. So Mama wouldn't know the money was gone.

Duke continued. "Kale he borrowed pulled a Houdini. That's why he was upstate when he had his little problem."

Little problem was a mild way of saying "Killing a cop, ten-year jail sentence."

"Okay," I continued. "I'd like to get out of debt. The bar needs to bring in more money. What expenses can be trimmed?"

"You don't have a lot of leeway. You could buy cheaper booze."

"There's booze cheaper than what we serve?" The stuff we served was garbage, based on my one outing to the Back of Ratner's. "No, keep the booze as is."

"Sorry." He shrugged. "It's an expensive business."

"How do I make this place more profitable?"

"Raise prices. Sell more drinks." He flashed me his crooked grin.

"Is that how it works?" I said, my tone dry. "What do I do to sell more? To make this place nicer?"

"Pink curtains and lace tablecloths?"

"I'm not trying to scare the current customers away. I want to appeal to a broader crowd."

"It's difficult to distinguish yourself among the thousands upon thousands of speakeasies in New York City. The snazzier places are uptown." He rubbed his chin. "Neighborhood guys come here. Drink beer. Not much kale to be made there. The office workers, they're the ones you make cabbage on. They'll drink cocktails. Easier to water down. Plus you can charge more."

I jotted down everything he said, substituting the code words for the alcohol names. I was pleased I remembered them all. When he stopped speaking, I glanced up. He smirked. "You're quite the student, aren't you?"

"Never been called that before." I tapped the pen on my chin. "Cocktails, hmm." I tilted my head. "Can you teach me to mix cocktails? More than Frank's gin and tonics?"

"I drink cocktails; I don't make them."

"I need to taste some. To see what I can do. Where should I go?"

"Traipsing New York's speakeasies on your own? How you getting in?"

I hadn't thought of that. Even getting into the bar on Baxter Street required knowing Big Al, and women on their own were turned away. I flashed my most winning smile. "You'll take me."

"Asking me on a date?"

Heat climbed from my belly to my cheeks. "This is business." I willed my face to cool. "The more I sell, the more liquor I buy from you."

"True." He rose, picking up his hat. "So we're going for Rothstein's sake?"

"Yes." I stood to see him out. "For Rothstein's sake."

"Because he surely needs your order of an extra case of gin each week."

"It's gonna make him rich."

"I'll pick you up. Thursday. Eight o'clock."

"I'll be here," I said, already thinking about what I would wear.

～

Later that evening, Frank poked his head back. "Need you out here."

When I emerged, Frank asked when I'd hire a new bartender.

"I'll take care of it. Until then, I'll work the bar." I'd have to ask Duke how to find one. I couldn't exactly put an ad in the paper. The three older men—Otto, Ben, and Walt—stood at their perch. "What'll you have, boys?"

"Same as always, princess. Canadian on the rocks."

I reached under the counter and grabbed a bottle. I gave Frank a quick peek, and he gave a minuscule nod. I was learning. I poured to the line on the cup and plunked two ice cubes in each glass.

"Here you go, boys," I said. "Tonight drinks are a quarter. Prices are going up next week."

"What?" Walt said. "For this rotgut?"

"You don't like our rotgut, drink somewhere else."

"Going up to what?" Otto held his drink to the light, gazing as if it might be the last drink he'd have.

"You'll find out next week. Now"—I turned to a group of factory workers who approached the bar—"what'll you have?" A charge buzzed through me. Looking at the dilapidated bar, I thought of all it could be. Of all I wanted it to be.

This ramshackle, decrepit blind pig, this basement bar on the back side of Baxter Street.

I was going to make it mine.

Chapter Twenty-Six

On Thursday night, I headed to the apartment at 6:00 p.m. I'd left a note for Sylvia with her mother. I hoped she had gotten it.

When I arrived, she was sitting on the top stair, a dress draped over her forearm. "Minnie." She jumped up to hug me. The dress pressed against my back. "Ain't you a sight for sore eyes."

I unlocked the front door. "C'mon in."

"So what's the dress for?"

"I'm going to a speakeasy."

"A speakeasy! Aren't you ritzy. With who?"

I took the dress and held it up. It would do. "Duke."

"Duke?" She sat down, propping her arms on the table so she could rest her chin on her fists. "From the Back of Ratner's Duke?"

"One and the same." I moved into my bedroom to dress, leaving the door cracked so we could talk.

"How did this come about?"

Sylvia didn't know yet about the bar. I worried she'd try to talk me out of working there, fret about my safety. I also worried about Sylvia's mouth. That girl would give anyone an earful. I couldn't risk it getting back to Max. "He asked." A fib. I'd asked.

I strutted into the kitchen. "Whatta ya think?"

The dress was black crepe, sleeveless, with a drop waist. A pink flowered clasp at the side provided a splash of color. Tiny crystals made the fabric sparkle. The deep V-neck revealed more than I was used to, but it was stylish and sophisticated.

She whistled. "Well aren't you the cat's meow?" She fumbled in her purse. "Sit."

"I have to go," I said, but she stopped me.

"Not with that plain face." From her bag came lipstick, kohl, cake mascara. She pointed to the chair.

Dutifully, I sat. Sylvia spent fifteen minutes lining and powdering and patting and painting. Leaning back, she evaluated her work. "Now you're ready to go."

I looked in the mirror by the door. "Horsefeathers!" I said. "How'd you do that?" Rimmed with black, my eyes had grown larger. The cupid's bow on my lips invited kisses. The gentle blush on my cheeks put a sheen of life on my drawn face.

She dug into her purse once more. "Finishing touch." She held out a dangly pearl necklace.

"I can't take this," I said.

"Sure you can. It's fake."

I slid the strand over my neck. It danced provocatively in my décolletage.

She handed me the lipstick and, before I could refuse, said, "You'll need it for retouches. After he kisses you." Walking out of the apartment, she said, "Go find your beau. And I'm going to want all the details."

After another admiring glance in the mirror, I returned to the bar.

~

The outfit had the reaction I'd hoped for. When I walked in, conversation stopped. A man at the bar tipped up his hat with his index finger and hooted.

"Look at you, dolled up," Otto said.

Frank tilted his head. "Aren't you a sheba."

"It's just a dress." Behind the counter, I put on an apron, covering my cleavage. The chatter resumed. A scruffy man approached the bar. "What'll you have?"

Thursday nights were busy, patrons swamping the bar. I didn't notice Duke until he stood in front of me.

"What're you drinking?" A grin tickled my face.

His eyes captured mine. My insides flipped. "Nothing here. I'm going to show you what a real drink tastes like. Ready to go?"

A twinge of guilt at leaving Frank on his own cut through me, but I pushed it aside.

"Frank," I called down the bar, trying to sound like a boss. "Handle things on your own."

"On a Thursday night?" Frank caught Duke's eye, and something must have passed between them, because Frank turned and mumbled, "Fine," as if he were a moody toddler. I glanced back at Duke, but he was all smiles.

Pulling off my apron, I said, "Let me grab my hat and purse."

When I stepped out from behind the bar, Duke raised his eyebrows and said, "My, my," and I made a mental note that as soon as I had enough money, I was going to buy Sylvia an expensive present.

On the street, Duke hailed a taxi, held the door for me, and gave the driver an address on Lexington Avenue. "Ready to learn about speakeasies?"

"Absolutely. Where're we going?"

"We'll make a few stops tonight."

His body was close. I shifted, trying to scoot nearer without being obvious. When the driver turned sharply, I fell into Duke with perhaps a bit more force than necessary.

"Whoa," he said, righting me, but when I sat back, my leg remained pressed against his. My body hummed. I thought back to those boys on Second Avenue, to Mr. Whitaker cornering me in the office; their touches had repulsed me. But I was craving Duke's. It confused me. My mother's admonishments to keep my legs shut suddenly made sense. My body tingled in ways it never had before.

We exited the taxi in a neighborhood of brownstones. A couple of boys scampered to us, yelling, "Mister, Mister! Go down these steps," but Duke said, "Beat it."

One of the kids mumbled, "Cheapskate." Duke looked to retaliate, his face shifting to annoyance, but then he rearranged his expression to its familiar impishness.

"You have to watch out for the crumb snatchers," he said. "They direct people to your place but harass them for tips. A better-quality establishment has someone chase them away."

"So this isn't a better-quality place?"

"It's the Cellar Speakeasy. A neighborhood joint."

We walked down the steps to a door. If Duke hadn't led me straight there, I'd have passed by it, never knowing it existed. Duke knocked, someone peered out, and we were permitted entry.

A man rushed up to welcome us. "Duke, always a pleasure to see you." He greeted Duke much like that barber had greeted my father. "Let's find you a table," he said, which seemed excessive given the room was half-empty and plenty of wooden tables sat open.

The bar was masculine. Classier than the bar on Baxter Street, but not by much. I was overdressed for this place and a touch disappointed he hadn't taken me somewhere fancier. The room was brightly lit, more so than one would expect, although the light didn't quite reach the four pool tables lined up in the back. On one wall was a photograph of Theodore Roosevelt in an ornate golden frame, and on another, an over-size American flag. A machine for salted peanuts stood in the corner.

A waiter took our orders. "An ale for me, and an old-fashioned for the lady," Duke said. To me, he said, "Try an old-fashioned at every bar to see how different they can be."

I'd never had a cocktail before. The man returned with our drinks. I sipped mine.

"What do you think?"

The cocktail coated my tongue, hid the taste of the bourbon. What my father had said about drinking bourbon straight now made sense. "So sweet. Like drinking syrup." I drank more. "Are you sure there's bourbon in here?"

"This place is run by three brothers, in it more for the camaraderie than the business. The oldest is a softy, always lending folks money. Keeps a shaving kit beneath the bar for the guys who don't want to go home."

"That's quite a service."

"The Gallaghers are decent people."

After another sip, I said, "Not sure this is the drink for me."

"May I?" Duke asked. I handed him the glass. "Not a great old-fashioned. Watered down."

"Isn't whiskey usually watered down?"

"Yes, though some places stretch the bourbon even further. There are ways to dilute alcohol without making it watery."

"I've much to learn."

"There's another place a few blocks away. Are you all right walking?"

"Yep." I'd seen enough sloppy drunks at the bar to be worried how a night of boozing might affect me. I was happy to not finish that drink.

As we headed out, I realized Duke hadn't paid. But no one chased after him. In fact, the bartender watched us leave with something like relief on his face.

From the Cellar Speakeasy, we strolled to a brownstone in the Sixties, off Fifth Avenue, where stone lions guarded the doors instead of gossiping yentas.

Beside a list of names were rows of buttons. Duke pressed the one next to A. Samuels. An apartment with a locked front door. I couldn't think of one building in my neighborhood with a door that barred entrance. Who would ever choose to go into those crumbling tenements if they didn't have to? After a click, Duke pushed the door open.

We entered a hallway glowing from silver sconces. Carpet stretched up the stairs, and from the way my feet sank into it, I could tell it wasn't from the Sears catalog.

On the third floor, a squat man stood outside a mahogany door carved with flowers and dominated by a brass knocker. His suit must have been custom made, the way it hugged his lumpy body. His hair was slicked back, and he held a cigar like a woman flaunting freshly painted nails.

"Duke," he said, transferring his cigar to his other hand and reaching out to shake. "Welcome back."

"Adam," Duke said, "meet Minnie. Minnie, this is Adam."

"Lovely to make your acquaintance." I winced at my inability to hide my Yiddish accent, which grated, like the screech of tires on Shabbos.

"Please, come in."

I swallowed my wonder and stood straighter, hoping to give the impression I'd seen a million places like this. Inside, though, I was in awe. The apartment came straight from the picture shows. The living room boasted lush, hunter green floor-to-ceiling drapes on windows the size of doorways. Velvet sofas, leather easy chairs, glass-topped tables, reading lamps with silk shades scattered about the room. A buffet on the back wall displayed newspapers and magazines, and a man in the corner lounged with the paper, as if he were in his own home. The place had more of the hushed ambience of a library than a gin joint.

"Does Adam live here?" I whispered.

"He does."

Next to this place, my apartment was a shtetl hut. I delicately draped myself on a couch, stroking the nap of the soft fabric. I hoped Duke might perch next to me, but he sat catty-corner on a chair. He ordered drinks from a man who approached us.

"I think this must be what heaven looks like." I'd never sat on a couch so comfortable.

He laughed. "The drinks here pack a punch. But don't worry if you have too much—Adam keeps his medicine closet fully stocked with everything you need to avoid a hangover."

A man returned with two drinks on a tray. "Speaking of hangovers," Duke said. He raised a glass to mine. *"L'chaim."*

Turns out I did like old-fashioneds. This drink was nothing like the last one. Smooth. Less saccharine. A deep smoky flavor. This drink settled in my bones, making them looser, more fluid. "This is a stunning drink."

"Adam attracts more of a Wall Street crowd. Folks who can afford better liquor."

"So how does that work? Who gets the better liquor, and how?" I wanted this to be a date, but I reminded myself it was business.

"Most of the alcohol comes through Canada or Florida."

"Florida?"

"Brought in from the Bahamas. Goes to a distillery in Brooklyn that repackages it. In the process, it's diluted. The more diluted, the cheaper the drink. Obviously the less cut the booze is, the better it tastes. But you need a serious budget for the uncut stuff." He held his glass out. "Try this. His specialty."

I sipped. "Wow!" I took another sip, swirling it on my tongue. "That is both delicious and deadly."

Duke's fingers brushed mine as I passed his drink back. "Planter's Punch. Made with Gold Bar Jamaica Rum. The quality of the ingredients affects the quality of the drink."

These drinks were magic. I understood why they were outlawed. If this delight were legal, folks would spend their entire lives floating on a cloud of contentment. It was becoming infinitely clearer that the stuff we served at my bar was coffin varnish.

"Ready for another?"

I was surprised to find my glass empty. I knew I shouldn't drink more, but it was delectable. "And how." Duke pushed a small black button on the side table, and in a minute the waiter reappeared to take our order.

"So what do you do for Rothstein besides collect payments from me?" I asked, my voice slippery. The alcohol worked its way around my tongue.

"Those aren't the kind of questions you ask in this business."

The waiter returned with our drinks. The second was as exquisite as the first.

Emboldened by the alcohol, I batted my eyelashes. "I'm simply making small talk."

"It's not so small." He chuckled. "I run distribution for a few wards on the Lower East Side."

"Quite a job. How old are you?"

"Twenty-three."

I wanted to keep him talking, to listen to his plummy voice all night. "Where's your family from?"

"The drink making you forgetful?" he teased. "Brownsville."

"No, I mean before that."

He shrugged. "Somewhere in Russia."

"You don't know?"

"Nah. My mother was born here, and my father won't talk about the old country."

"He doesn't want the family stories passed along?"

"Guess not."

Maybe passing on stories wasn't as important as I thought. Maybe it didn't matter if Gertie and Louise didn't know their history. *No,* I told myself, *don't do this.* In my short time at my bar, I'd seen my share of sad drunks. I would not be one.

"Ready for our next stop?"

"Okay," I said, though I was disappointed to leave this one. Sitting in Adam's living room, I could imagine a life like this, as if I were an Upper East Side woman, with a doorman and a kitchen with a maid and no rodents.

As we trod down the stairs, my head was pleasantly buoyant, but my body was strangely disconnected, my feet uncoordinated with the rest of me. I stumbled, and Duke grasped my arm.

"Let me help you." His voice was as creamy as that drink.

He placed my hand in the crook of his arm to steady me. Outside, I shivered. Duke asked, "Are you cold?" which was ridiculous given the warmth of the evening, but I said, "A little," so he set his coat upon my shoulders.

He hailed a cab. After helping me in, he gave the driver an address and scooted to the other side.

What would it take to make my place as keen as Adam's? Could I earn enough to move to an apartment like his? "Does Rothstein own the distilleries?"

"Again with the questions." His tone was light, but it held a warning.

"I'm curious how it works."

He twisted his lips, but then his face softened. "Some things," he whispered into my ear, "are best left unasked." His warm breath on my neck made me quiver.

I turned toward him. His face was inches from me. Ever so slightly, I lifted my chin, but it was enough. His lips touched mine. *This,* I thought. *This is what a kiss is supposed to be.*

"This is a bad idea," he murmured, lightly landing kisses behind my ear.

"Why?"

"Mixing business and pleasure."

I drew him in for another kiss. "But this business is a pleasure."

"Not always, I'm afraid."

Before he could kiss me again, the cab pulled over. The driver said, "One Hundred and Forty-Second Street and Lenox Avenue."

My attention had been focused on Duke, so I hadn't noticed where we'd driven. Harlem. I'd never been so far north. On the building in front of us, a mammoth glowing sign illuminated the whole block.

"The Cotton Club!" I opened the door, ready to burst.

"Slow down." Duke paid the driver, amused by my enthusiasm.

"I've heard so much about it." Sylvia'd been pining to go there. She'd be jealous when I told her.

He grabbed my hand and led me past a small crowd on the sidewalk. At the front door, Duke asked for Clarence, and we were escorted into the nightclub, across the dance floor, to another door.

The man knocked, and a window in the door opened.

"Looking for Clarence," Duke repeated. We were granted entrance.

The room was bright, but not overly so, with tables jammed closely together, tiny lamps atop them. Once again I had an old-fashioned. This one wasn't as watery as the one at the Cellar Speakeasy, but it didn't have the quality of Adam's.

"Thoughts?" Duke sat next to me.

"It's satisfying," I said. "Strong, but not as flavorful."

"This place caters to a larger crowd. They need to make drinks quickly and in quantity."

The patrons were swanky, the women in gowns with sparkles and lace. The drink went down effortlessly. My toes tapped, my nose tingled, and when the waiter returned, I ordered another, all worries about drinking too much wafting away. Duke talked of his childhood in Brownsville. A few times when the conversation steered to my family, I asked a question or made a comment about the bar. The evening was too gay to discuss my family.

"I like the music," I said.

"Would you like to dance?"

"And how!" I lifted my hand for him to draw me up. In the next room a band played, the drum lettered with "Duke Ellington and the Cotton Club Orchestra." The bourbon and the drumbeat and the soothing sounds of the singer turned my muscles into puddles, my head floaty. Duke's arms wrapped around my waist; mine wound around his neck.

I wasn't sure of the steps, but I mimicked what I remembered from the movies. His body sizzled next to mine. I ached for Duke to touch me, to cover me with his lips. The explanation about men and women Sylvia had given me flashed through my mind. That's what I craved.

The hair at the nape of his neck curled in the heat of the room. I toyed with it, twirling the strands. I rested my head on his chest, feeling the wiry cords of muscles beneath his shirt. When the song ended, we stayed put, waiting for the next.

How many dances did we have? Hard to say, as the night meandered, and when the band stopped, we went into the back room for another drink.

At some point, Duke glanced at his watch. I asked the time.

"Five a.m.," he said.

"Oh! My brother will be worried." The crowd had petered out.

"Then your chariot awaits." He bowed and extended his arm.

The streets had lost their glow. Workers scurried on their way to or from jobs. At night, the Cotton Club's entrance swarmed with white folks; now the neighborhood was dominated by the colored. Odd to think of the party raging inside while regular life plodded on outside.

Once we were in the cab, the buzz of the drinks mingled with the quiet jabs of an impending headache. My stomach sloshed. Duke carelessly threw his arm over my shoulder. As much as I wanted to curl into him, to kiss him as I had on our way to the Cotton Club, my body no longer felt appealing. In the harsh light of day, kissing seemed vulgar.

In the dawn, Duke's imperfections were visible: A faint scar on his forehead. A prominent brow. A slightly hooked nose.

And then he turned and bestowed that smile on me, and I couldn't find a single flaw.

"Feeling all right?" he asked.

"I've felt better."

"I can imagine." Leaning forward, he said, "Driver, make a stop on Grand and Norfolk."

"I'm at Grand and Allen," I said as the cab tilted precariously. Or at least my stomach felt like the cab tilted precariously.

"Quick stop," he said.

Looking outside made me dizzy, so I closed my eyes. I must have dozed off, because when the car stopped, I jolted awake. Duke was saying something to the driver as I nervously put my hand to my face, praying I hadn't drooled.

Duke gave me a wink and hopped out. "Wait here."

We were back in the neighborhood, in front of Kalish's Drugstore. Duke knocked on the door, which was unlocked for him. He returned with a small bag. To the driver, he said, "Grand and Allen."

"Kalish's is open?"

"In about an hour. Kalish was putting away inventory. Here." He pulled out a bottle and opened it for me. "Drink." It was Bromo-Seltzer. I managed a swallow, immediately bringing up a burp, which I forced down.

"And this." He gave me a bottle of Listerine.

The humiliation. "That bad?"

Duke kissed me lightly. "I'm rather fond of the taste of bourbon on your lips," he said. "But if you're worried about your brother, take a swig of that before breathing in his vicinity."

In a matter of minutes, we were at my building.

Duke jumped out to help me.

"Thank you, Duke," I said. "What a lovely evening."

He lifted my hand to his lips and lingered for a moment. "Good night, my whisper sister."

I laughed, but it echoed poorly in my head. "Good morning, Duke."

He hopped back into the cab. When he was well out of sight, I swigged the Listerine, swished it around my mouth, and then spit it on the sidewalk. I did it two more times for good measure. The bottle was too large for my small purse, so I left it on the stoop and ran upstairs.

Before my key turned in the lock, the front door flew open.

"It's nearly seven in the morning," Max said, his eyes wild. "Where the hell have you been? Don't you get off work at four?"

The sound of his voice pounded in my head, but I smiled and tried to ignore it. "Max, you're not my mother."

His eyes skated up and down my body. "You wore that to work?"

"What I wear to work is none of your concern." I pushed past him. With relief, I saw the percolator on the stove. I poured myself a cup of coffee. It came out thick. Opening the icebox, I saw it was empty. "No milk?"

"Have you been to the store?" He looked like Mama scolding me. "Because if you haven't been, then, no, there's no milk."

I spooned too much sugar into the cup, trying to make the brew tolerable. When I sipped, it burned my tongue.

"Explain that dress," he said.

"If you must know, I had a date before work. I didn't have time to come back here and change first, so I wore it to work. When you're on the night shift, no one sees you. I'm permitted to dress as I please." Lies flew out so readily it alarmed me.

"A date? With whom?"

"The brother of one of my coworkers."

"What's his name?"

"Charlie." The words tumbled carelessly. Perhaps I was my father's daughter in more ways than I'd imagined.

"Who are his parents? Is he Jewish?"

"Max! Enough. I'm exhausted. I'm going to bed."

"If you went out before work, why were you late this morning?"

"Because Charlie's sister wanted to grab a bite so she could hear about the date."

"What does he do?"

The coffee was atrocious, but it certainly covered any lingering smell of bourbon on my breath. "Max, I had a date. Then I worked for nine hours. Then I went for a coffee. I'm dead tired. We'll discuss another time."

He stood there, fists on his hips. "I suppose."

"Good night, Max."

I thought my guilt over the lies would keep me up, but I was asleep in seconds.

Chapter Twenty-Seven

When I awoke the next afternoon, Jack Dempsey threw punches in my skull. I stumbled to the bathroom for whatever medicines we had. Dressing hurt: raising my arms to slide on a dress, the sound of cotton fabric scraping my skin. My belly sloshed, both desperate for food and revolted by it.

Outside the sun singed my pupils, forcing me to walk with my eyelids half-shut. My body craved darkness, but I had an errand to run before work.

At a bookshop, a bell jangled as I opened the door, annoying Dempsey, his jabs more bruising.

"May I help you?" asked an elderly man with a yarmulke on his head.

The tiny room's shelves overflowed with books, with stacks on the floor as well. "I'm looking for a cocktail book."

The man slid his glasses down his nose. "Excuse me?"

"A book explaining how to make cocktails. Ingredients. Instructions."

"Miss, drinking cocktails in this country is an illegal act."

"Selling or buying alcohol is illegal. Drinking cocktails is lawful."

He pushed his glasses back up. "This is a literary bookstore. I do not carry such books. Good day."

"Where do I find such books?"

He sighed. "One of the less discerning bookstores, perhaps. Try Booksellers' Row."

"Booksellers' Row?"

"Not much of a reader, are you? Fourth Avenue. South of Union Square."

"Thank you," I said, then continued to the bar.

~

Customers already sat at the counter.

"Afternoon, gentlemen." Bags drooped beneath Frank's eyes. I realized the night alone at the bar must have been grueling.

"Was last night busy?" I asked.

"Earl from Platt Iron Works is marrying this weekend. The entire crew bought him whiskeys till closing. Big Al had to carry more than one of them out."

"Oy vey."

I crouched below the counter to evaluate if I needed stock from the back room.

Frank squatted next to me. "Minnie? Be careful with Duke. He's . . ."

"Yes?"

"Well, be careful."

"I can take care of myself." Though as I said it, I remembered Papa's words: *Thinking you can take care of yourself is the first sign you can't.* But after seeing those swell bars, I thought I could do this. I could make Papa's bar a true success.

I retreated to the back to grab more gin, but when I came out, I surveyed the room, seeing it in a new light. The place was dingy, the dark walls bare. A layer of stickiness carpeted the wood floor, suctioning shoes as people walked. Tables skewed haphazardly, matchbooks stuck under legs in a futile attempt to level them. Men stood at the bar. Even on a Friday night, the crowd was decidedly male working class. If we added panache, maybe we'd attract those who spent more on their drinks.

Beneath the bar, I placed a notepad to tally what people drank to help me decide what to charge.

In the postmidnight hours, a young couple stumbled in.

"Brandy Alexander," the woman said. She was dressed in the latest fashion, but the Lower East Side version, the cheaper knockoffs one purchased at Mays or Ohrbach's. They'd probably come from a show at the Yiddish theater or the movies. Why couldn't we attract more people like this?

"Where d'ya think you are? The Stork Club? We don't do Brandy Alexanders." Frank splayed his hands on the counter. "You want a fancy drink? I can make you a martini, a Manhattan, or a gin and tonic. Want to get wild? How about a screwdriver?"

The woman's annoyance seeped from her. "Just red wine for me."

Her date said, "I'll have a martini."

Frank prepared both, and the two moved to one of the tables. As the woman sipped, her face blanched. She held it out for her date to try, and he made a face as well. The two didn't order second drinks.

"Why don't we do Brandy Alexanders?" I asked.

"Requires cream," Frank said. "We keep only the basics. Nothing fancy."

Mixed drinks, as I had learned the previous night, could save money. Cheap mixers hid the taste of the lower-quality alcohol, so I could dilute it more. Yet we could charge more for those fancy cocktails with less alcohol.

"Pass me the wine."

Frank poured a glass for me. I sipped it, forcing myself not to spit it out. "Ugh. Vile."

Frank shrugged. "That's what we get. Talk to Duke if you want a better class of wine."

Until I yelled last call at 2:45 a.m., the bar remained busy. At 3:15, I took off my apron and hurried out; I couldn't be late two nights in a row.

~

I wrote Papa regularly, but I didn't dare tell him about the bar. Papa would write me back about it, Max would see it, and that would be the end of it. Instead I sent meaningless missives, asking questions, my worry for him leaking onto the page. Papa wrote back his first month at Sing Sing.

His handwriting in the letter was as difficult to decipher as it was in the ledgers. "I can barely read this," I complained.

"He's writing in English," Max said. "His third language. His third alphabet. It'd be easier to read if he wrote in Yiddish or Russian. But of course you can't read either."

Embarrassed, I squinted to make out the words.

> *Dear Minnie,*
> *I received your letters. Thank you. I am happy to hear that Max continues his studies. What do you do now?*
> *They cut my hair. Remember when you cut your hair? Looked like a mangy dog. So long ago. A different time. My haircut isn't much better. We can go to the barber together when I get out.*
> *I can write one letter a month. You can send me a box of eatables every other month. Money too. I know you don't have much, but money is useful here. If you ever have any extra, I'd appreciate it.*
> *Do you know what's happening at the shop? A reminder: there's money to make there.*
> *Don't worry about me. I'm tough. Just like you.*
> *Love,*
> *Papa*

Max, of course, read it. "Don't you dare check in on the shop." He wagged his finger like Mama used to. "Do you understand?"

I understood. Didn't mean I had to obey him.

I took the letter into the bedroom to read it again.

Papa didn't mention what it was like in prison. Didn't mention his cellmates or the guards. Didn't tell me how he was.

I could only assume the worst.

The least I could do was make the bar more profitable. The least I could do was send Papa money.

~

On Saturday morning, Max and I emerged from our bedrooms at the same time. We looked at each other, then both raced to the bathroom.

"I'm first," I said, slamming the door behind me.

"Don't take forever!"

I washed up, brushed my hair and teeth, applied lipstick and mascara, and sprayed toilet water behind my ears before returning to the kitchen.

"How is it you take so long in there yet come out looking exactly the same?" Max grumbled. He scooped Maxwell House into the percolator. "Coffee?"

"No time. Gotta run errands."

Max grunted.

I made my way to Union Square. Walking up Fourth Avenue, I was surprised by the number of bookstores. I was a reader—the old man was wrong—but who had the luxury of buying books? I read them for free from the library.

I popped in the first store, but a gray-haired man sat behind the counter. I retreated, not wanting to face his judgment.

I peered into each shop until I wandered into the Corner Bookstore, where a younger man arranged books on a high shelf and an older man stood at the cash register.

"Excuse me," I said. The younger man glanced down from his step stool. "I'm looking for a recipe book."

"You've come to the right place." His deep voice boomed. "We specialize in cookbooks. Is there a particular kind you are looking for?"

"Cocktails."

The man's eyebrows furrowed. "A cocktail recipe book?"

My face heated. "Yes, a cocktail recipe book." I mimicked his tone.

"Now, I don't—" he started, but he was interrupted by the older man, who emerged from behind the counter.

"We have what you need." He took me by the arm and led me toward the back.

"Now, Father," the young man started, but the older man again interrupted him.

"Nathan, I'll help her. Continue shelving." To me, he whispered, "The young set today. They don't understand what it was like in the good old days."

I laughed. Nathan was at least ten years my senior.

The man ran his finger over the shelf. "Ah, here we go," he said. "For the home cook, I recommend *Wet Drinks for Dry People*." He chuckled. "I especially recommend it because we don't have an extensive selection of cookbooks of this sort."

Opening it, I read the subtitle: "*A Book of Drinks Based on Ordinary Home Supplies.*"

I flipped through, spotting concoctions I'd never heard of. A Dream Cooler. A Gin Daisy. A Pansy Cocktail. "Perfect." I hesitated. "Do you also have . . ."

"Yes?"

I tilted my head as if it were no big deal. "What about a book that doesn't necessarily use home supplies."

"Let me check the back. I think we recently received what you want."

He slipped into a back room. I picked up *Everybody's Cookbook* and considered purchasing it to surprise Max with a real dinner. The older man returned, and I set the book back. It's not like I had the time for gourmet meals.

"This should do you." He handed me a black book with a picture of a martini glass on the front, *Cocktails by "Jimmy" late of Ciro's* splayed across. Inside was an alphabetical listing of 251 drinks.

"I'll take both."

When I arrived at the bar, I headed straight to my desk, opened one of the books, and studied the drink recipes as I'd never studied before.

I'd try a new one each night. Something tasty that would hide the roughness of the booze. I nixed the first two drinks in the guide—the Alexander and the Angel Tip—because they required cream. The third, the Apricot Cocktail, seemed promising—"a favorite among the ladies," according to the author.

"I'll be right back," I yelled as I rushed out to buy ingredients.

"It's Saturday," Frank said. "Going to be busy."

"Fifteen minutes!"

I sprinted to the corner market to purchase five cans of apricot juice and a dozen eggs.

Back at the bar, I slipped on my apron and put the cans on the counter.

"What's that?" Frank asked.

"It's for our drink special."

"You're special now?" asked Otto. He stood alone at the end of the bar, nursing a Canadian Club, waiting for Ben and Walt.

"I've always been special." I pierced the top of a can with a paring knife. In a shaker, I poured an ounce of gin, followed by an ounce of apricot juice. I squeezed in lemon. "Grab me a bowl, Frank."

Frank placed a small one in front of me. I cracked an egg on the edge of it and, with a flourish, dipped the two pieces of shell, allowing the yolk to flow from side to side until all the egg white dripped into the bowl. Otto whistled. "Where'd you learn to do that?"

"My mother." For the first time, mention of her didn't send me spiraling. *See, Mama, I was paying attention.* I tossed the yolk and shells in the trash, thinking I'd have to find a recipe that used those yolks. I dropped a spoonful of the whites into the shaker. Added ice. Shook.

Frank watched with amusement. I strained it into three glasses filled with cubes. In the faint light, the drink shone a radiant orange crowned with a dollop of foam.

"Pretty enough," Otto said.

"Indeed." I passed a glass to Frank and to Otto. *"L'chaim."*

We took little sips. The juice definitely disguised the bitterness of the gin.

"Not bad," Otto said.

"Rather sweet for me. But," Frank conceded, "it's tasty. If we had female customers, they'd like it."

I didn't say it out loud, but that was the point. "Apricot Cocktail. Our drink special of the night. Fifty cents for straight drinks. Seventy-five cents for the special."

"Seventy-five cents? Highfalutin of you," Otto said.

"Tell your friends," I said.

Otto shook his head. "Highway robbery."

I grinned when he ordered one anyway.

∼

On Monday morning, as soon as I arrived at the bar, I opened the cock-tail book. I didn't like cooking—too much hard work for something devoured in seconds—but a cocktail was different. It took seconds to whip up, and if it was made well, a customer would savor it and order another. I pored over the recipes, trying to understand what combinations worked well and why some things weren't paired together.

I was so engrossed I didn't hear Duke knock when he came for the orders.

"Catching up on some *Moby-Dick*?"

I wanted to jump into his arms, but I only said, "*Jimmy of Ciro's* says I should use cracked ice to make my cocktails."

"You gonna crack it yourself?" He took his place across from me.

"Why not?"

He chuckled. "Okay, what do you guys need?"

With a stab of disappointment at his businesslike demeanor, I put in my order. But when we were done, he didn't stand.

"So." His stare suddenly made me shy. "About last Thursday . . ."

I caught myself picking at a fingernail.

His hand captured mine. "Should we do it again?" His thumb rubbed the back of my hand. "To help your business, of course," he said, with mock seriousness.

"For the business. Of course." I entwined my fingers with his. "Yes, I think we should. But," I hastened to add, "not on a busy night. Not until I've hired another bartender."

"Tonight?"

I hesitated. "Tomorrow night?"

"Other plans?" He raised his eyebrows.

"Monday nights I spend with my brother. It's the only night we're both free."

"A family girl. Tomorrow night, then. Dinner."

The words *family girl* tasted raw in my mouth. What would he say when he learned I was the kind of family girl who gave up her family?

The Gertie-and-Louise-shaped crevice in my chest enlarged. I allowed myself a minute to wallow, to imagine what they were doing on a Monday afternoon. Playing in the park? Visiting the library? Marketing with Mabel?

Enough, I thought. *Work.* My cocktail book, though, wasn't as exciting as it had been only a half hour before.

~

We'd sold out of the specials each night. On Tuesday, when I left for my date with Duke, Frank was knee-deep making Bowmans, a mixture of rum and orange juice.

"Hungry?" Duke asked as we headed out.

"Starved," I said, though my stomach was a jumble of nerves being with him; I wasn't sure how I'd be able to eat.

Duke led me to Moskowitz's Roumanian on Second and Fourteenth. Women with heavily made-up faces wore furs, despite the June heat. Men were dressed in tailored suits. Crisp linen covered the tables, and the menus were printed.

Once seated, Duke offered to order for me. Around the room, couples and small groups laughed and chatted and ate.

"After the dinner hour, there's a show." A small stage perched on one side of the room. "Singers. Vaudeville. Sometimes Moskowitz himself will play his cimbalom."

The waiter sidled up. Duke ordered dishes as he pointed at the menu. He shook the waiter's hand, which I thought odd until the waiter returned with a basket of bread, a bowl of pickles, and two glasses of what looked to be ginger ale. I took a sip. It wasn't ginger ale.

"So last night's special a success?" Duke asked.

"A Mary Pickford. Yep."

"What's in it?"

"Rum, pineapple juice, and grenadine."

"Sounds girly. You don't get many of those."

I raised my glass. "Yet."

"Hmm." He lifted his. "Here's to *yet.*"

"So is this business or pleasure?" I sipped to hide my embarrassment at my forwardness. Sylvia assured me, in 1928, it was every woman's right to be forward.

Duke's hand slid to mine. "Why don't we make tonight pleasure."

I tilted my head down but raised my eyes, hoping to appear coquettish.

The waiter arrived laden with plates of steak and potatoes. It had been a while since I'd had a hot meal made by someone else. The casseroles from concerned neighbors, which reheated to almost edible, had ceased. I dived in.

"Not afraid to eat, I see," Duke said.

"Good food is good food." I tried to be delicate as I devoured my steak.

He laughed.

I hadn't been sure what we'd talk about, but the conversation flowed. We discussed if the weather would allow Amelia Earhart's flight to take off the next day, which led to Commander Byrd's preparation for flights to the South Pole. We debated whether we'd ever ride in an airplane and ultimately agreed we would, if given the opportunity.

As I polished off my steak, Duke asked, "Do you only eat kosher food?"

I shrugged. "Is this kosher?"

"It is. I wasn't sure if you ate *treyf*."

I was touched by his consideration. "Never thought about it. I've only eaten kosher because that's what we had in the house. You?"

"I eat *treyf*. Honestly, though, kosher food tastes better." He sipped his drink, our second. "I bet your mother was a wonderful cook."

"We couldn't get enough of her treats."

The *we* was a mistake. He cocked his head. "Who minds your sisters when you're not home?"

It couldn't have hurt more if he'd physically slapped me, the unexpected reminder of my sisters. "My sisters?" I ate another bite to stall. "My sisters," I repeated. My eyes grew hot and watery.

"Hey, hey." Duke stroked my arm. "I'm sorry I asked. It's okay. You don't have to talk about them."

I nodded, afraid to speak.

"Let me tell you about the time I broke my mother's porcelain candlestick and I blamed it on a golem." He leaned back. "I was about six, I think."

As he told his story, I regained my composure.

He didn't bring up my family again.

After dinner, we stayed for the entertainment, but I had no idea what we saw because once his hand reached over to mine, everything else dimmed.

At the end of the night, he walked me to my apartment. He glanced to the fourth floor, a questioning gaze.

I was relieved I couldn't ask him up. I craved his nearness, but it frightened me. "I live with my brother."

"Of course." He closed the distance between us and kissed me. It was as delicious as I'd remembered.

When I made it upstairs, my body tingled, and for the first time in a long time, I fell asleep not thinking about Gertie and Louise.

Chapter Twenty-Eight

My drink specials were hitting on all eight. Ben, Walt, and Otto wouldn't even ask what was in them; they drank everything I mixed and, God help me, gave honest opinions. On the counter, I placed an easel with a chalkboard, on which I wrote the night's special.

Many nights Duke showed up late for my drinks, lingering to chat. He'd have the special—heavy on the booze, just the way he liked it— and I'd have a straight bourbon. Duke propped himself at the bar at a spot farthest from the door. I'd flirt with him, twirling a lock of hair, until a customer pulled me away. On Tuesdays, we'd have a proper date, dinner, drinks, sometimes a show, always ending with a necking session in a park or movie theater. He made it clear he wanted to be alone with me, but I appreciated his patience, and he never pushed. I'd float instead of walk to work on Wednesdays.

The cocktail specials, though, weren't enough to bring in new—or, rather, monied—customers. I needed to do more. I needed help. I knew just the person.

On a Sunday morning in August, I raised my fist to knock on Sylvia's door. I hadn't spoken to her in over a month. The hours of our jobs prevented us from meeting. I prayed she wouldn't be angry I hadn't told her about the bar before. I also prayed she'd be able to keep her mouth shut.

I lightly rapped, half hoping she wouldn't be home.

The door flew open.

"It's about time!" Sylvia enveloped me in her clasp. "It's been forever. Max tell you I stopped by? He told me you're working nights. You showed up at the right time. My mother about burst an artery when I told her Roland and I split up."

"Wanna go for a walk?"

"Do I!" To the back of the apartment, she yelled, "Going out, Ma!"

"Wait," I said as we headed down the stairs. "Roland? What happened to Archie?"

She snorted. "Archie? He's been gone for an age."

"I can't keep up."

As we reached the front stoop, a steaminess smacked into us, the heat baking the already fetid odor of the sewers.

"So you're a telephone operator?" She didn't wait for an answer. "Oh! Have you had another date with Duke? Is he your beau?"

"I think so? Hey, listen, Sylvia. I need to talk to you about my job."

"I'd rather hear about Duke."

"Promise you won't say anything to anybody. Especially to Max. This is important. Promise?"

"You're not a phone operator?"

"Promise?"

"I promise, I promise."

"This is serious. I mean it." I tugged Sylvia closer so I could speak directly in her ear. "I lied to Max. He forbade me from working at Papa's bar."

"Bar!" She stopped walking.

"Hush!"

"Sorry," she said. "Bar?"

"Indeed." I continued walking, and she hurried to catch up.

"Is that where we're going?"

"Indeed," I repeated.

"The bar. I don't know whether to be impressed or worried. Is it safe?"

"This is New York. What's safe?"

"Still," she said. "Bars are dangerous. What if you're arrested? How do you take care of drunk men?"

"I have a bouncer. Big Al."

"A bar." She said it as if it were a new word, something she was trying out on her tongue. "Okay, I'll go with impressed. Tell me."

I reported on visiting speakeasies with Duke. When I got to my trip to the Cotton Club, she barraged me with questions. I rambled the entire way, and in no time we stood in the alleyway.

"Here?" Sylvia glanced around, confused. "Where is it?"

"Right here." I led her to the basement door.

"Wow. Your father's okay with you running it?"

"He wanted me to take over the shop." I rustled in my clutch to find the key.

When the lock clicked open, I paused. "Listen." I faced her. "This is not a fancy speakeasy. This is an out-and-out blind pig. A gin joint. A place where the *alter kockers* and *shikkers* come to drink."

"Duly warned. Are the *alter kockers* and *shikkers* here now?"

"Not till four." We entered the dark hallway, and I unlocked the second door. With a deep breath, I pushed it open and flicked on a light.

"Hmm." Sylvia took a few steps on the gummy floor, then checked the bottom of her shoe with distaste. "It's . . . interesting." Without people, the place looked more dismal than usual.

Moving behind the bar, I said, "I'll make you a drink."

"You bartend?"

I fluttered my eyebrows up and down. "But of course. Want the special?"

"And how!" She leaned on the counter and then, realizing it was sticky, leaned back. She tried to discreetly rub her elbows to remove whatever was on them.

I mixed her an Ink Street. Whiskey, orange and lemon juices, and, even though the recipe didn't call for it, a cherry on top. I slid it over.

She took a sip. "Wow! If this ain't the butterfly's boots." She inhaled her drink.

"I need your help."

"Spill the beans." She held the cherry stem between her fingers as she plucked the fruit with her teeth. "Can I have another? Don't make me drink alone."

I mixed two more drinks, outlining my plan. "I want to make this bar nice. Swanky. Somewhere you would want to come. Stools and tables that don't wobble. Comfy chairs. New barware. What else?"

Sylvia puckered her lips and evaluated the room. "Cleaning this joint would help a lot."

I set the drinks in front of us.

"Better lighting."

"I thought darker was better."

"Ambience. Remember the Back of Ratner's? It was mysterious dark. Not . . ." She wrinkled her nose. "Seedy dark." She hid her sheepish grin with a swallow of her drink. "Sorry. And stick a light bulb in that hallway so you don't give folks the heebie-jeebies when they enter."

"What else?"

She ran her hand over the pine counter. "A sleeker bar? Shelving for the backbar." The backbar currently consisted of a plank of wood on the wall with a mirror above it. "Something on the walls?"

"Like what?"

"Pictures? Or at least a decent paint job?"

A painter. An electrician. A carpenter. So much money.

Sylvia placed her hand over mine. "You've got the goods as a bartender. A little here, a little there, and you'll have yourself a swell joint." She patted me. "Promise. Now drink your drink while you make me one more."

$\sim$

Sylvia and I plotted until she was too pie-eyed to be coherent. Sylvia's picture of what the bar could be had my eyes shining with cocktails and diamonds. But when I sat down to run the numbers, those jewels turned to coal. The amount needed was daunting.

On Monday, when Duke came by for payments and orders, I steeled myself for what I was about to ask.

"I was wondering . . ." I picked at my fingernails. "How much more money can I borrow?"

Duke furrowed his brow. "Why d'you want more?"

"To spruce up the bar."

"Huh."

"If I'm going to attract a better clientele, I have to polish it up. That requires money." My toes bounced. "I'm going to have *the* place on the Lower East Side."

He chuckled. "Well, then, I suppose some sprucing is in order. What'll you need?"

"I'm so glad you asked." I slid him a piece of paper.

He tipped his chair back and put his feet on my desk as he read my list. "Tables and chairs that don't wobble, barstools, better lighting, cocktail glasses, wineglasses, highball glasses—" He looked up. "Ya got a lot of glasses on here."

"Keep reading."

His eyebrows rose. "A mahogany bar? A hot plate? An icebox? A second bathroom? This is a lot, Minnie. You sure you need all this?"

"It's the bare minimum to spiff this place up. A more attractive bar brings in customers who spend more. The hot plate allows us to make coffee and warm drinks. The icebox doesn't need to be big, just has to hold milk and cream and the like for cocktails."

"This is more than a 'spruce.' You know how much this is gonna cost?"

"Sort of?" From the middle drawer, I hauled out the *Sears, Roebuck and Co. Catalogue*, with folded-down pages. I flipped through, stopping where I'd circled items. "A three-burner gas hot plate is four dollars and ninety cents. A small icebox, twenty-six dollars and sixty-five cents. A fourteen-piece pitcher and tumbler—"

"I get it, I get it." Duke held up his hands in surrender. "How much jack you need?"

"I'm not sure. I know the general price for goods but not services. How much to hire a painter? An electrician? A carpenter to build a bar?"

"Skip Sears. Use a restaurant-and-hotel supplier. The service items can be had for two, maybe three grand. Schwartz over at American Store Fixtures on Bowery can build you a bar. That'll set you back. Eighteen-foot bar, mahogany? Cheapest'll be twelve hundred. Whitewood about four hundred. The bathroom is serious cabbage. Can't you use the one you got?"

"Ladies are not going to share a toilet with men. Besides, I checked. Bathroom fixtures aren't that expensive."

He laughed. "No, they're not. But the plumbing is. Okay, electricians, painters, plumbers—about a buck and a half, maybe two dollars an hour, not counting cost of materials."

"An hour?"

"Folks charge more for places that, shall we say, aren't completely aboveboard. You need, mmm, about nine or ten grand."

The neck of my blouse tightened. I ran my finger around the collar, trying to breathe easier. In my calculations, seven thousand would have done me good. But I hadn't figured all the extras to convince suppliers and tradesmen to work with us. "Ten thousand?"

Duke's eyes crinkled. "Not what you were expecting?"

"No, no." I clenched my fists in my lap. "That's what I was thinking."

"Doable. Interest rate's thirty-two percent."

"What? Papa's was lower."

"Ike used the money to buy liquor from us. This money isn't being funneled back."

So $10,000 was actually $13,200. "Would that increase my weekly payments?"

"We can extend the loan at the current payment until you make enough to pay more."

"So you agree! I will make more."

"I'm not saying that." He stroked his chin. "You're sure you about this?"

Could I improve the place enough to make the money worth borrowing? This would be my debt. Not Papa's. I'd be on the hook, and walking away from the bar wouldn't be an option.

But I wanted to make this bar a place I could be proud of. I wanted to make it my own. Plus more income could free us. Max could go to school full time. I could hire a better lawyer to see if Papa could be released early. I could give more money to the shul. And maybe, just maybe, I could earn enough to bring Gertie and Louise home. "I'm sure."

Duke stood, put on his hat. "I'll let you know what Rothstein says."

When he closed the door, I sank my head into my hands. I knew I was doing the right thing, but still. It was a lot of money.

～

In two days I had the money. Cash. I hadn't expected that. "You think I'd write you a bank check?" Duke asked.

That afternoon I stared at the money. I'd never dreamed of so much. If I'd had champagne, I'd've popped it. Time to class the place up.

～

First thing I did was institute cleaning. "This," I said to Frank, "is a mop. We will be using it to clean the floors. Nightly."

Frank crossed his arms over his chest. "Cleaning?"

"There's a decade of grime on this floor."

"We never mop."

"We do now." I held up my hand before Frank balked. "I'll do the initial scrub. And I've hired a junior barkeep. You'll have to clean, but he can do the bulk of it."

"Humph."

"Wesley starts tonight. Show him the ropes."

Both Wesley and I attacked the floor before opening. It took a few days till I could see the color of the wood, a luscious pale brown.

Walt came in one afternoon, stuck his nose up, and sniffed. "What's that strange smell?"

I arched my eyebrows. "Cleanliness."

"Smells funny," Walt grumbled.

I hired an electrician for when I'd picked out fixtures and a painter for when the electrical work was done. Sylvia accompanied me to a restaurant supplier to choose barstools, tables, and chairs, though her tastes were more expensive than mine. "If you want women to feel comfortable, you need the padded chairs." In eight weeks the furniture would arrive, so I had to hurry and pick my paint colors. The money slipped away fast, and so far I had nothing to show for it except a bigger debt and a staggering amount to do.

Chapter Twenty-Nine

On Mondays, I cooked a proper dinner for me and Max. We chatted about baseball, the picture shows, Max's studies. We didn't talk about Papa. We didn't talk about Gertie and Louise. We didn't talk about my supposed job as a telephone operator.

I was confident in my ability to fool Max.

I shouldn't have been.

On an unusually busy Wednesday night, a patron approached the counter as I was checking supplies beneath it. The mid-August temperatures drove folks indoors to the cool basement in search of an icy drink. "What'll you have?" I called from below.

No response.

"I haven't got all night." I popped up. "What'll—" My words crumbled. In front of me stood Max.

His entire body shook. His face deflated and his shoulders slouched as he gripped his elbows. "I can't ignore this anymore."

"Ignore?"

"I thought if I pretended you worked as a telephone operator, things could stay the same."

Pretend. I thought of Mama pretending not to know about the bar. "You knew?"

"What kind of *schlub* do you think I am? I can't smell the cigarettes on you? The booze on your breath? What kind of telephone operator dresses like that?"

"I'm sorry," I whispered.

"I can't sleep with the worry." He examined the bottles behind me. "I guess I came here with the tiniest of hopes I was wrong, that I was a *schlub* and you were working as a telephone operator."

"Listen, Max—"

He retreated before I finished my sentence, leaving without a glance back.

~

I walked in at 3:45 a.m. Max sat at the table, waiting.

"Max, I'm sorry—"

His hand shot up to silence me. "There's nothing to say."

"I need—"

"Stop. You know how I feel."

Anger nudged at my guilt. "How you feel? How about how I feel?"

"That bar is dangerous. Look what it did to Papa. Those bars are illegal, and they destroy people. If you're arrested, you could be deported. Deported!" His voice cracked. "Why, Minnie?" His eyes were streaked with red; his hair stood on end.

The idea of deportation, of leaving Max completely on his own, reminded me that the only thing we truly had was each other. My outrage slipped away when I realized he was afraid of losing me. I sat next to Max, placing my hand on his shoulder.

"I'm sorry this frightens you." I squeezed, hoping it would be reassuring. "But jobs for someone like me are truly dismal. I could be a salesgirl, where if I'm lucky, I might earn a meager commission. Or a secretary, constantly dodging her boss's advances. Perhaps a factory worker, hunched over a machine, my hands curled into pincers. That's not a good life. That's not what we came to America for."

"Take a sensible job. Go to school at night. You don't need to do this."

"I don't *need* to do this. I *want* to do this." I stood to put on tea water. "Besides, I couldn't leave now if I wanted to. And," I reminded him, "I don't want to."

"Give me one reason why not."

"Debt."

"The hell with the debt. That's Papa's problem. Walk away from it. Let Rothstein have the bar."

"No." I pulled out two teacups. If I acted reasonable, perhaps he'd see me for the adult I was. "My debt."

"What?"

"My debt. I borrowed more money."

When the silence stretched, I turned to look at him. He sat petrified.

"I'm going to improve the place. There's money to be made in speakeasies. You'll be able to go to school full time."

"Do not try to pin this on me. I am not the reason you are risking your life at this bar." He closed his eyes. "How can you be so reckless? Give the money back."

The water boiled. "I've already spent a chunk of it." I poured it into a teapot to let it steep.

A muscle in his temple spasmed.

"Max—"

"God dammit, Minnie!" He slammed his fist on the table. I flinched.

"Max!" How could he be so upset? "If Papa had stuck to the bar, he'd still be here. It was losing all that money—in legitimate investments— that forced him to continue working as an errand boy. It's all a crapshoot. But I'm rolling sevens."

"How can you be so fucking stupid?"

Stunned, I said, "How can you be so fucking naive?" I immediately regretted my words.

Max's mouth opened and closed, as if he were swallowing his words. He then stood and stormed out, slamming the door.

I pulled it open and ran into the hallway. "Max!"

The door next to mine opened. In Yiddish, Mrs. Shukat cursed at me, telling me it was 4:00 a.m. From the floor below, more swears. Where would Max go at 4:00 a.m.?

Defeated, I climbed into bed, where I stared at the ceiling, not sleeping.

Why couldn't he see I was doing all this for us? Why couldn't he see the bar made me happy?

When I got home after work the next day, Max wasn't there. I walked into his bedroom. His belongings were gone. On his dresser lay a booklet, *How to Become an American Citizen*, with the corner of page twenty-three folded down. A sentence was circled heavily in dark lead: *Some courts refuse citizenship to the applicant who has violated the Volstead Act—the national prohibition laws*. Beside it, he'd scrawled, "Is it worth it?"

Yes, I thought. *Yes, it is.*

And yet, I shivered, the room suddenly turning cold.

What if Max were right?

But it was too late either way. I owed too much to walk away.

~

Though Max and I had rarely crossed paths when we'd lived together, the apartment withered with the knowledge he wouldn't return. The echoes of my family inhabited the walls, haunting me. Even after all those months, when the baby next door cried at night, I reached for Louise. Sometimes I thought I heard Gertie calling out to me. There were mornings when my sorrow pinned me to my bed. I'd pick up the photo of the four of us, tracing the images of the girls as if I was caressing their delicate skin.

It was a fantasy, but I dreamed of earning enough money to get the girls back.

The bar had a telephone, so every Sunday morning, I called Uncle Aaron. Max must have told him what I was doing, because Uncle Aaron never inquired about my job, although he asked questions such as "Are you safe? Do you need help?" I'd assure him I was and I didn't. Occasionally I asked after the girls, but he'd either say my name plaintively or nothing at all. More than once he told me he didn't know where they lived, but I didn't believe him. At the end of every call, he invited me to Shabbos dinner. At the end of every call, I declined. I couldn't face him. I couldn't face his happy family.

A two-bedroom apartment for one person was extravagant, and I'd save money if I had a smaller place. But I refused to move. Max. Papa. Gertie. Louise. They needed a place to return. A way to find me.

Even so, I dreaded being in that cell of a tenement. If the back room of the bar was larger, I'd have put a bed in it.

I wrote to Papa, telling him about the bar.

One afternoon on my way out, I noticed an envelope in the bank of mailboxes at the base of the building's stairs. Papa's monthly letter. I stuck it in my purse.

In the quiet of the closed bar, I slit open the envelope.

> *Dear Minnie,*
>
> *Thank you for the money. I can't tell you how helpful it is. It allows me to buy smokes and food. I know you want to know about my life—it's kind of you to ask in your letters—but it's not something to write home about. Trust me, I sleep with one eye open.*
>
> *I'm sorry to hear Max moved out but I'm happy you're running the shop. Take care of it and it will take care of you. But you need to be careful. Your boss's associates can be vicious. The micks and the wops will suck you dry. It's not the best shop for a young woman to run, but I have faith you can take care of yourself.*

Folks get friendly at a bar, but remember, they're not your friends.
You can do this. You're my daughter.
Love,
Papa

I sat straighter. He had faith in me.
I would do this.
I didn't have a choice.

Chapter Thirty

On August 24, the ache in my chest woke me. I wanted to sink into the mattress, let it swallow me whole.

August 24, 1928. Gertie's fourth birthday.

Yesterday was Max's birthday, but that was a made-up date for an immigrant.

But August 24. A real birthday for a real American.

I forced myself out of bed and stumbled to the bar.

I couldn't focus, didn't want to be there.

I wanted to see my girls. I *needed* to see my girls.

Both Frank and Wesley would bartend, so I slipped out. I rounded the corner and ducked into the soda store's phone booth. How many Earls could live in New York? I hefted the phone book on the shelf, but when I flipped through, scanning the pages, the futility sank in. So many people in Manhattan. So many names.

One more thought: I riffled through the directory till I found the diner where Max worked. I ripped out the page and shoved it in my purse.

When I stepped out, I saw Mama sweeping the floor, Gertie toddling around the chairs, Papa heaving cartons of ice cream into the cooler, Max reading at a table.

"Soda, Minnie?" the counterboy asked. My family evaporated.

"No thanks, Hank."

Uncle Aaron lived on the Upper West Side. His rabbi must have lived on the Upper West Side. Therefore, it would make sense Earl and Mabel lived on the Upper West Side.

I would go to the Upper West Side.

Walking to the station, I passed a dry goods store. A doll with a frilly dress, bobbed hair, and chubby arms and legs perched in the window. A sign beneath read, WE HAVE FLOSSIE FLIRT.

Almost without thought, I left the shop with a Flossie Flirt. It was ridiculously expensive—almost three dollars—but I didn't care. I cradled the doll as I made my way to the IRT.

The subway was bleak, nothing but blackness rushing by. Last year on Gertie's birthday, I'd celebrated her. We were here, on the IRT. The darkness of Mama's death loomed over the day, but I was going to give Gertie a special afternoon no matter how much it hurt. We'd packed a picnic basket, filled with Gertie's favorite treats, and a toy boat to float in the Central Park fountain. On the subway, three-month-old Louise curled into my chest, her first finger in her mouth, while Gertie climbed up and down on the seats, exclaiming "Whoa!" every time the train lurched, exaggerating the movements with her three-year-old body. I pretended not to hear the *tsk*s of the frumpy woman across from us. Emerging from the station was difficult: tamping down my longing for Mama, holding Gertie's hand, juggling the picnic basket, and managing Louise's buggy on the stairs. What little did I know then of difficult.

The subway screeched to a halt. My cheeks burned hot when I realized I'd been rocking the doll as if she were Louise. As I exited, I flinched at the brightness of daylight. The dark underground suited me better.

Where to look? With intense focus, I walked the streets, examining the face of every child. Too old. Too young. Too blond. Mothers frowned, pulling their children tighter as I stared at the young girls. More than once, I plowed into someone and mumbled apologies without raising my head. Where might Mabel take Gertie? I checked the libraries, Riverside Park, the ice cream shops, the playgrounds. No Gertie. No Louise.

For three hours I roamed the streets, murmuring prayers to help me find them.

By late afternoon, the doll under my arm was moist from my sweat, my legs tired from walking, my heart throbbing with loneliness.

I sat on the nearest stoop. I wanted to put my head in my hands and cry, but then I wouldn't be able to study the children passing.

This was ridiculous. How many people lived in Manhattan? One million? Two? The odds of running into Gertie and Louise were miniscule.

The fountain in Central Park! Why hadn't I thought of that? Would Gertie ask to return?

It neared five o'clock. Mothers scurried home to prepare dinners, wash the children, ready the house for the Sabbath. Did Mabel bake her own challah? Were her candlesticks a family heirloom, passed down from her parents? Maybe Mabel was icing a cake for the birthday girl.

These thoughts, of the girls cared for and loved, should have consoled me. But they only sank me deeper into my melancholy.

I rose, brushing the grime off the back of my dress.

Only one person would understand.

From my purse, I pulled the phone book page, consulted the address. It wasn't far. Still I walked like an automaton, continuing to search the face of every girl.

In a few blocks, I stood outside the Tip Top Diner. Inside bustled with activity, solo men with dinners before them, students huddled over books, couples on dates.

Through the window, I spotted Max. He wore an apron as he scurried from table to table, picking up plates, taking orders, delivering food. The idea of Max rejecting me again stopped me from entering. I willed him to look up, to meet my gaze. *If he notices me, it'll be a sign. If he notices me, I'll go in.*

For twenty minutes I watched. His eyes never lifted.

If I stood there any longer, I'd combust, my sorrow exploding within me, shattering me like the glass under a groom's foot.

Flossie Flirt still rested beneath my arm. I smoothed her dress and fluffed her hair. I sat her on the ground, leaning her against the outside wall of the diner. I crouched in front of her, kissed my fingers, and placed them atop her head.

Standing, I ignored the odd glances of passersby. Leaving the doll behind, I returned to the IRT.

I made my way back to the bar, because I had nowhere else to go.

Chapter Thirty-One

Papa in Sing Sing. Max at his boardinghouse. Gertie and Louise with a new family.

I was on my own.

I hadn't told Duke about Max moving out. The idea of Duke and me alone . . . well, I didn't know what to think. It frightened me. It tempted me.

Sylvia, though, had no such compunctions. Shortly after Max left, she came to my place early on a Sunday, waking me. "Can I use your apartment Friday night?"

"My apartment?" I pulled my housecoat tighter and put a kettle on the stove.

"Leland and I want time alone." She perched backward on the kitchen chair.

"Leland?"

"My beau. Don't you listen to me?"

Her beaus flew by faster than Lindbergh. I couldn't keep up. "What are you going to do?"

She raised her eyebrows. "What do you think I'm going to do?"

"Aren't you worried about"—I lowered to a whisper, though we were alone—"getting knocked up?"

"Nah. I douche after with Lysol."

"Douche?"

"Yeah, prevents pregnancy." She cocked her head. "You know how to douche, right?"

"If you haven't told me, then who would've?"

"Horsefeathers! Forget the coffee. Where's the bourbon? Let's learn how not to get pregnant."

From the cabinet I grabbed a bottle and two glasses. It was before noon, but I poured us each two fingers of Old McBrayer. Before Sylvia finished expounding on douches—before she even got to prophylactics and pessaries—I filled our glasses to the rim. The conversation required it.

~

Don't open your legs until you're married. But marriage was far off. A bar to run. Papa to support. Debts to repay. Someday I'd stay home and be a wife and mother, but that time wasn't now.

I sent Papa a letter weekly, telling him about the shop, about the new "sodas" I created. Once a month he wrote back, thanking me for the money, making suggestions for new sodas, trying to reassure me it would all work out, that we'd be a family again. In every letter he wrote how proud he was of me. But I never felt worthy of his praise.

The apartment was blackness, a blanket suffocating me; the bar was light—ironic, given it lived in a humid, murky basement. Walking in loosened the knots in my chest. I floated, an airiness raising me above all the miseries of the world.

I wanted Duke. But I wanted my bar more than I wanted to be a wife.

"Shame is for the Old World," Sylvia said. "Flappers do as they please."

Well, then, so would I.

~

On Monday, I placed my orders with Duke, paid my obligations, and blurted out, "Max moved out."

Duke drew in a breath. "Oh?"

"To a boardinghouse. Closer to City College."

He pursed his lips, doing a poor job of suppressing his grin. "Good for Max."

"Yes," I said. "Good for Max."

~

The next night, Duke picked me up from the bar for our usual date. We hopped in a cab, a new frisson of electricity sparking between us. At the French Speakeasy, I drank La Bohèmes until my head hummed and my legs turned to rubber.

"So," Duke said. "El Fey next? Or . . ." The heat of his breath tingled. I ran my palm up his leg. The muscles in his thigh tightened beneath my touch.

"Or," I said.

"You sure?"

My hand slid farther up. "I'm sure."

The taxi ride was a blur of hands and lips. We stumbled up the stairs, laughing. At my door I shoved the key in the lock but couldn't turn it. Duke took it from me and unlocked the door.

In an embrace, we sidestepped to my bedroom. Together we flopped onto the bed, everything dreamlike.

Clothes peeled off. Flesh on flesh. My body bucked in unfamiliar ways; I needed to feel him.

His lips moved down my stomach in the most alarming and delicious way.

My rapid-fire breathing made me lightheaded. "Be careful. No pregnancy."

He slid back up so his mouth reached mine. He pulled away, and I chilled without his warmth. From his jacket pocket, he grabbed something, which he rolled over his most private of parts.

As he entered me, a sharp pain stabbed my lower belly. The experience was uncomfortable, as Sylvia had warned. It was awkward and burning, and I fought back tears as he writhed on top of me. Yet the pain lessened, a hint of pleasure easing in, and when he was done, I was curious to try again. When we did, in the wee hours of the morning, I saw promise in this mysterious act.

Daylight creaked through the tiny window. I fell asleep tucked in the crook of his arm.

~

For once, I was glad the apartment didn't have much light. Waking up naked, a man in bed, a rawness between my legs. What had I done? A wave of pleasure and remorse passed through me. *I'm sorry, Mama.*

Duke slept, one of his arms splayed out.

What was I supposed to do? Get up? Wake him? Make him breakfast and coffee?

Next to me were the family photos—the one of my family in Bratsyana and the one of my family in America. I turned them away from us so they couldn't see.

"What are those?"

"I didn't realize you were awake," I said. "Pictures."

"May I?" He sat, his naked torso on display as he leaned on the wall behind us.

It was blasphemous, sharing my family with the man who'd defiled me.

Stop, I chided myself. *Flappers do as they please.*

I showed him the photo with Mama and Papa.

"Cripes. That's Ike?" The gaunt bearded man with the large skullcap looked nothing like the bootlegger Duke knew.

"That's Papa."

"What an imp you were." He studied the photo. "Your mama was lovely. Who's this?" He pointed to Anshel.

"My oldest brother. He died when I was four."

"Your parents didn't have an easy time." He returned the photo and held out his hand for the other.

I reluctantly passed it over. Would he despise a woman who relinquished her family?

"Ike was pleased as punch when"—he pointed—"what's her name?"

"Gertie."

"When Gertie was born."

I couldn't conjure the memory.

"The little one?" he said.

"Louise." Forcing the words over the lump in my throat took all my effort.

"Louise." He passed back the photo. "You never told me. Where are the girls?" He stroked my shoulder.

I fussed with the pictures on the side table to avoid Duke's gaze. "I gave them away. I couldn't take care of them anymore."

Duke pulled me close.

I leaned into him, his powerful arms wrapping around me.

Lying on his bare chest made me feel safe. Protected.

"It's okay," he whispered. "You did what you had to do." He kissed my forehead. "We all do what we have to do."

I nestled against him, still sad but also relieved.

I'd only done what I'd had to do.

Chapter Thirty-Two

On a Monday morning, I arrived at the ungodly hour of 6:00 a.m. Duke had found an electrician with cheap rates, but he could come only before his afternoon construction job. I'd chosen lights, which he'd bring. They were utilitarian, but I could afford them, and they'd illuminate the bar. I was nervous to see the state of the place in full light.

At 6:03 a.m., I let in the electrician, who was followed by Duke.

"Look at you, up before the fishmonger!" I said. "Or are you still awake from last night?"

"I brought you a little present." He propped open the door and hollered, "In here, boys."

Two men carried in large crates.

"Aw, liquor! You shouldn't have," I teased.

"Wise guy, are ya?" He disappeared into the back room and came out with the crowbar I used on the alcohol crates. He pried the lids from the boxes and removed piles of straw.

Were those diamonds glittering from the crate? Duke pulled something up, and I gasped. No, not diamonds. Something even better: a lighting fixture. Crystals draped from three filigreed gold tiers, shimmering down, a shower of sparkle. A wedding cake chandelier was more than I could have dreamed of. "It's stunning."

"I thought it might fancy the place up."

"I—I don't know what to say." No one had ever given me a gift like that. Something so beautiful, so extravagant, so exactly what I wanted.

"Check out the other crate."

I failed to contain my eagerness as I pulled straw out. "Oh!" Nestled inside were ten sconces. I picked one up. The mounting plate's filigree matched the chandelier. The slip shades opened at the top, with delicate ribbing.

The electrician shook his head. "You're acting like he gave you gold."

"This is so much better." I clutched a sconce to my chest.

Duke bent down to kiss me. "I'll be by later for your order."

"Where do you want what?" the electrician said.

After pointing where the lights should go, I retreated to the office. Giddy or not, I needed to plot out my cocktails for the week.

A few minutes before 2:00 p.m., the electrician knocked on my door. "All set. Doorbell installed. Lights up."

"Lead me out," I said, closing my eyes. "Tell me when."

His sigh let me know I was being childish, but I didn't care. He took me by the elbow and led me to the center of the room. "Open 'em."

I cracked my eyelids. Light fluttered in. The glimmer of the chandelier and the sconces was hotsy totsy, elegant. Yes, they illuminated the griminess of the bar. But I was only getting started.

My reverie was interrupted by Big Al's entrance. "Jesus!" He threw an arm over his face. "Who let in the sun?"

"Whatta you think?"

Big Al lowered his arm. "Classes the place up."

"A gift from Duke."

He squinted. "A pricey present."

I shrugged. "Guess he has money."

Big Al snorted. "Unlikely. He probably lifted them from some worksite."

I didn't want to think about it. I paid the electrician and plotted what I'd do next.

Walt was the first of his crew to arrive. He scowled as he ambled to the bar.

"You don't like it?" I asked.

"It's frilly. You gettin' persnickety? Going to kick us out when this place gets ritzy?"

"Never. My bar will always be your bar."

"Humph. Serve me my drink, wench."

I laughed. "One special, coming up."

~

The next thing to arrive were barstools. When I set them up, I placed signs on the back of three chairs at the end: **OTTO'S STOOL**, **WALT'S STOOL**, **BEN'S STOOL**.

They whooped when they came in. "Now this is an improvement I can get behind," Walt said.

"Or rather sit upon," Otto said.

"This is an improvement I can sit upon," Walt repeated.

~

With the stools and the lights, paint was too plain for such a classy place. Sylvia and I paged through sample books at Mutual Wallpaper on Ludlow Street.

"Ooh, this one is stunning." Radiant-pink cherry blossoms sprouted from soft-green trees.

"Too girlie," I said.

"This one is gorgeous." Between beige diamonds floated delicate bouquets of flowers.

"Give it up, Sylvia. No florals."

The owner, Mr. Goldberg, emerged from the back periodically. "Find something you like?"

"Almost." I waved at him without raising my head.

"What about this?" Sylvia pointed at a bloodred stain of a sample.

"It's a bar, not a brothel. Who knew picking out wallpaper was so difficult? Maybe I should stick to paint."

"Paint's boring."

I turned yet another page. "Hmm." On a gilt background, gold ivy vines striped vertically. Between the columns were diamonds filled with tiny fleurs-de-lis. "This one just might work."

Sylvia took the book from me. "Yes. Classy. Works for men and women."

I arranged for the paper hanger to come the same day as the carpenter. The bar would have to close for three days for the remodel. The loss of three days of income physically pained me, but I had to trust my instinct that this would earn more in the long run.

~

On Sunday, September 16, the plumber started work on the bathrooms. His clanging pierced my skull and drove me from the bar. On Monday, the carpenter and his men installed my bar. I'd chosen oak, with a mahogany stain.

"Is that piece straight?" I asked. "Is the bar the right height? Show me where the shelves will go."

"Lady," one of the workers eventually said, "we'll work a lot faster if you stop asking questions."

Chastised, I went into the back room, only to emerge a few minutes later. I couldn't resist watching the transformation.

It felt like days, but by early night, they were done.

"Wipe the bar nightly," the carpenter said, "with linseed oil."

The last piece was cosmetic. On Tuesday, the paper hanger arrived. My questions to him were ignored. He either didn't speak English or was smart enough to pretend he didn't.

After I paid the paper hanger—the money from my loan disappeared faster than Otto drinking one of my specials—I stood in the center of the room and basked. The bar was beautiful. The radiance of the wallpaper bounced light from the chandelier, bathing the room with a golden hue. The counter was majestic. Shelves graced the backbar. Above it an ornate mirror was displayed.

Time to clean the place, removing the dust and splatters. I swept and mopped and waxed the floor. I wished I could have refinished it, but doing so would have meant closing for a week as the stain dried. I set the barstools at the counter. My tables and chairs had arrived, so I arranged the furniture to give each table space, allowing for a modicum of privacy for my customers.

At 1:00 a.m., my arms ached, so I tore myself away to get some sleep. Yet the next morning, I was back at 7:00 a.m. Was it as beautiful as I remembered? Opening the door, I sighed when I saw that it was. From the back room, I pulled out boxes of new drink ware, which I stashed beneath the counter. The prettiest liquor bottles went on the backbar and the rest in the well. Cream and milk into the icebox. When my ice was delivered, I dumped it in a larger chest.

The bar was everything I'd wanted. Now to get people to come.

~

Frank and Wesley were impressed until I handed them black vests and told them to wear them over white shirts. While they prepped the bar, I slipped out to Sylvia's.

"So?" she said.

"It's done. Wanna come?"

"And how!"

A few minutes before opening, we walked in, and Sylvia whistled low. "This is better than the Back of Ratner's."

"You should work here," I said. A beautiful woman behind the bar could only make men spend more. "You'd get free drinks every night."

"You're such a pushover I get free drinks anyway. I can't, though. Ma would have kittens if I came home at three a.m. every night. Besides, when would I have time to play around?" She waggled her eyebrows, making me laugh.

"Suit yourself. Let me mix you the special."

Sylvia climbed on a stool. "Comfortable."

I whipped up my drink of the day, an Orange Blossom.

"Minnie, this might be a bit of heaven on the Lower East Side."

"Now the final part of the plan. Let's fill the place with a profitable crowd." In the empty bar, my voice carried. "Sylvia, tell the girls in your office to drink here. They can come without an escort."

"What?" Big Al's entire body tensed.

"You heard me. Ladies can come without an escort."

"That's not how it's done," Big Al said.

"It is now." Unescorted women were verboten at bars, where they could be mistaken for prostitutes or, worse, be prostitutes. But a lot of office girls who didn't have beaus still wanted to have a good time with friends. Once the girls showed up, the men would follow.

To Sylvia, I said, "Tell them to say, 'The whisper sister sent me.'"

"I'll have this place so full you'll miss the quiet days."

I raised my bourbon. "Cheers."

Sylvia tapped her glass to mine, a soft tinkle. "To Minnie's Speakeasy."

Minnie's Speakeasy. I liked that.

Chapter Thirty-Three

Sylvia was as good as her word. Within a week, the first young women trickled in. Big Al grumbled every time he heard "The whisper sister sent me." The women oohed and aahed. A girl with a splotchy face, badly covered with powder, said, "I can't believe there's a place like this on the Lower East Side!" Word of mouth spread. Not only did more girls come, but boys who wanted to meet girls came too. We attracted a few goons as well, but I didn't worry about them because everyone knew I was Duke's girl.

We lost some regulars, the ones who came at opening and left at closing, pickling themselves to forget their mundane lives. With the more-expensive drinks and the swanky surroundings, the rummies moved a couple of blocks over where sawdust hid the floor and booze wasn't "froufrou," as I was told.

Because of the increased traffic, I hired a grizzled guy, Petey, to sit outside when the weather was amenable or in the hallway when it wasn't to act as gatekeeper. More people, unfortunately, meant more unruly drunks. Big Al even had to keep watch over me: One night a boy trying to impress his date poured his bourbon on the bar and lit it on fire. I hopped over that counter so fast with my paring knife that Big Al had to fly across the room to prevent me from slicing that boy.

For two months, my life wasn't as bleak. For two months, I was even—dare I say it?—content. I loved that bar. I earned a profit, enough to send Papa more money. Sylvia came almost daily. Otto, Walt, and

Ben became a trio of protective grandfathers. I grew chummier with Frank, Wesley, and Big Al. Many nights, Duke came to sample the special and lingered, then accompanied me to my place.

I still didn't like to be in my apartment. I returned only to sleep or to be with Duke. Duke didn't fill the holes my family had left, but they weren't quite as cavernous when he was with me.

~

Late every Friday morning, on my way to the bar, I passed by the synagogue to leave *tzedakah*. My donations grew with the bar's success—five dollars, ten dollars. I wanted to pay back the rabbi's kindness, to make up for my sins. Occasionally I'd see Leo, who asked about Max, or Rabbi Umansky, who questioned me about my life. I stammered vague answers, afraid of them discovering I worked at the bar.

Toibe and I rarely crossed paths. I didn't market often—all I needed was milk, sugar, and coffee—buying my meals from pushcarts and appetizing stores. When I did run into her, with her bewigged hair and floor-dusting skirts, I'd slink away, sure she judged me for breaking up my family. When I didn't quickly escape, she spoke pleasantly, though she eyed my dresses, my dangling necklaces, my makeup.

It was best to keep to the bar.

~

At the end of October, as I mixed a Grapefruit Blossom, Duke breezed in and set a box in front of me. "Trick or treat."

"Which one is it?" After the rum, I scooped ice into the shaker. I shook the drink over my shoulder with a subtle hip sway. When the shaker chilled my palms, I strained the liquid, allowing it to cascade into the glass.

"You tell me." His cheeks dimpled. I passed the drink to a woman with curly bangs and swept her coins from the counter before turning back to Duke.

He slid the box to me.

I sliced the string and opened the top. Two stacks of crystal ashtrays nestled inside.

"They're . . . lovely?"

"I know. You have ashtrays. But are they like these?"

I took one out. The hefty ashtray sparkled in the dim light. An elegant gold rim added a touch of class. Something was on it. I pulled the ashtray closer to my face. Engraved in the gold, in a delicate script, was *Minnie's*.

"Oh!" I was at a loss for words. I ran my finger over the lettering. "These are . . . I mean . . . oh, Duke!"

"So you like them?"

"They make me want to take up smoking."

Duke chuckled.

I gathered up my old ashtrays—to the protest of one man who said, "I was using that!"—and distributed the new ones down the bar. One, though, I held back. I took it to my apartment, to remind me there was a place for me and a man who believed in me.

~

My peace shattered in November. One punch after another.

The first knock came on the first of the month. The bar buzzed, the drinks flowing swiftly from shaker to coupe. When I wasn't flirting with Duke at the back, I tended to take the front end of the bar, nearest the door, primarily because that's where Otto, Walt, and Ben sat, and I enjoyed our banter. I was mixing a Knickerbocker when a man with a low-slung hat slid onto a barstool.

"Be right with you," I said.

"No hurry, little girl." The voice chilled me.

Riley.

"How'd you get in here?"

"Guess your security isn't so secure." The scar on his face was ragged. It had healed, but clearly without a doctor's help. My handiwork. It made me feel strong.

"What do you want, Riley?"

"Besides my bar back?"

"Look at the ashtrays." I held one up. "Can you read? It says Minnie's. I'm Minnie."

A man, taller than Duke, stood behind Riley. His prepossessing looks, the tuft of dark curls that spilled from the edges of his fedora, and his languorous eyes belied his fierce unsmiling mien. He was icily handsome, which made him more frightening.

"Ashtrays can be replaced," Riley said. He picked one up, twirling it in his hands, spilling ashes all over the counter. I grabbed it back.

"You are not welcome here." I glanced at the door as Big Al was eyeing a group of women entering. He still didn't approve of them. "Big Al," I called.

Big Al approached, and when he saw who sat in front of me, he said, "How'd you get in here?"

Riley sneered. "Wasn't hard."

Big Al grabbed the men's shoulders. "Out."

"No need to get handsy." Riley wriggled from his grasp. "We're paying customers. Just wanted to see what you done to the place. And to try your famous drinks." I glared at him. "Two specials?" He put his hand over his heart. "No trouble. Promise."

Big Al and I exchanged glances. It wouldn't hurt to make peace with Riley.

"One drink, and then you're out." I'd never made cocktails so fast. "That's a buck fifty."

He took a sip. "That's a lot of dough for a drink so light on booze. You must be making a pretty penny here." He eyed the improvements. "Comfy stools." He said to his buddy, "We'll have to keep those when we take the place back."

So much for making nice.

"Get the hell out," I said, grabbing the glasses from them.

"Let's go," Big Al said.

"We're leaving." He held his hand up in surrender. "You know, you owe me, Minnie." His finger grazed his scar. "You will be paying me back."

I fought down a shiver.

The two walked unhurried toward the door, Big Al following close behind them, escorting them to the street.

When he returned, I asked, "How the hell did they get in here?"

"I'll find out," Big Al said.

But it was Duke who brought our soda jerk, Bennie, into the bar a few hours later, his nose crushed, blood spurting from his mouth. Even with a blackened eye, the terror streaming from it was palpable. Duke held the boy's shirt collar, as if grabbing the scruff of his neck.

Duke, the vein in his neck pulsating, pushed the boy from behind. "Go on." His tone was unrecognizable, gritty, throaty.

"Sorry." His voice squeaked. The boy was barely past puberty. I wanted to take the poor boy and wash his wounds, make him a bowl of soup.

Duke shoved him harder, enough that when the boy winced, I realized a few ribs were probably broken too. "Didn't your mother teach you manners? Tell her what you're sorry for." Duke's iciness, his savageness, shocked me.

"Duke, stop. He's a kid."

Duke applied yet more pressure to the boy's back. "A few bucks, apparently, and this guy will sneak someone in through the soda shop." The boy choked back a sob.

Bennie was an amiable kid I'd hired for the soda shop. I didn't even know he knew about the bar.

"Duke! Leave him alone!"

"He's a fink, Minnie." He pushed Bennie again.

"You're what, Bennie, sixteen?"

"Fifteen." His eyes didn't leave the ground.

"He's a child," I said. "He knows from nothing. He's learned his lesson. Haven't you, Bennie?"

"That's it? You're letting him off? He *betrayed* you." His words hissed. He made a subtle move I couldn't see, but whatever he did made Bennie howl with pain. I saw Max, lying on the ground, beaten, sobbing, trying to protect me. Did Duke think he was taking care of me?

"Bennie, go home to your mother."

"Yes, ma'am."

"Let him go, Duke. He's a stupid kid. Nothing happened that Big Al couldn't handle." Duke hesitated. "Let him go." I heard my mother's voice emerge from my mouth. It startled me.

Duke released him but not before kneeing him in the back. Despite his pain, Bennie beelined for the front door. Big Al opened it, and Bennie dashed out.

Bennie, injured, running, reminded me of Max escaping the Italians in that alleyway. Bennie was a year younger than Max had been. Too young to be learning these lessons.

This man, Duke, was a stranger, no better than Gino. This was the side of Duke I'd been warned about. The side that made him so good at his job.

Did he expect me to thank him? I wanted him to go. Get out of the bar. I couldn't look at him.

Luckily, he merely kissed me on the forehead. "See you at your place later."

~

"What was that today?" I asked Duke as I mixed him a cocktail in my apartment. I fought to keep my voice even, nonjudgmental. Images of Bennie intertwined with my images of Max. The dark-purple bruising. The oozing eyes. The broken skin. I couldn't reconcile what I'd seen with the Duke I knew.

"Whaddya mean?" His feet were propped on the table as he leaned back in his chair.

"At the bar. With Bennie." I opened a drawer to remove a long cocktail spoon. My movements were automatic. I made the drink by rote, too shaken for my mind to alight on the task.

"He was a fink. Next time he crosses one of us, I won't be so gentle." Duke's arms crossed tightly across his chest, as if trying to contain his fury at the boy.

The spoon clinked on the glass as I stirred. "He's so young." I kept my eyes on the drink. "It was so . . ." I couldn't find the words. *So horrific? So terrifying? So cruel?*

Duke stood, his hands falling to my shoulders. "I think the drink is mixed." His voice was light. As if nothing had happened. "Minnie, this is part of running a bar. You knew it wouldn't always be easy. Bennie gets away with it, he thinks it's easy money. Signals to Riley you're weak. Opens you up to more trouble." He rubbed my arms, and I let go of the spoon. "If you think about it, we helped Bennie. He won't do anything like that again. We turned him to the straight and narrow."

It was a pretty justification. I knew what had happened was wrong. I knew I should be watchful of Duke.

But it was easier to think we'd saved Bennie. That we were still good people.

~

Two days later, the second punch arrived.

Sunday, November 4, 1928. A normal night. Duke and I ate blintzes at Rapoport's Dairy Restaurant. We returned to my apartment. We made love and fell asleep in each other's arms.

In the wee hours of the night, a banging on the door startled us.

"What the hell?" Duke said.

The pounding was forceful. "Give me a sec," I yelled, throwing on a dress.

"Duke here?" came the muffled voice.

Duke slipped on his pants as I opened the door.

Two men I didn't recognize stood on the other side.

"Looking for Duke." Their hats were pulled low, their eyes hidden, but the one who spoke had a wide jaw he shifted from side to side.

"What's up?" Duke buttoned his shirt.

"Rothstein's been shot."

"What?" Duke grabbed his jacket and hat. "Where? When? Who?"

I didn't hear the answers as the three men rushed from the apartment and down the stairs.

I lingered in the doorway, my arms crossed over my chest, chilled by Duke's sudden departure. My reverie broke when I felt eyes upon me. Looking over, I saw Mrs. Shukat from next door staring and shaking her head.

"*A shandeh un a charpeh*," she said. A shame and a disgrace.

My face burned with both embarrassment and anger. But I refused to let her see that, so I said firmly "*A gute nakht*"—a good night—and closed the door.

~

I tossed the rest of the night. Rothstein was shot. Later, I'd be embarrassed I hadn't given one thought to the man inflicted with a gunshot wound. My immediate concerns were for myself. What did this mean for the bar? For my debt? Where would I source liquor? Would the terms change? Could I afford this? What did this mean for Duke?

Stopping at the newsstand the next morning, I purchased a *New York Times*. Splashed on the front page: Rothstein, Gambler, Mysteriously Shot; Refuses to Talk.

At the bar, the normal hoods were scarce, and for everyone else, it was business as usual, although the boys and I were alert, poised for trouble.

On Tuesday, November 6, Rothstein still graced the front page, reported as close to death. Yet by the time he passed that night, he'd been relegated to page twenty-eight, as the presidential and governor's races dominated the front section.

I didn't see Duke for days.

I was confused and upset and scared, and the person I wanted most to comfort me was involved in the very things confusing and upsetting and scaring me.

In the mornings, I lay alone in bed. The emptiness of the apartment returned, a yawning hole pulling me in.

Max had been right; I'd been reckless. And yet, with all that had happened, the bar was the only thing I had left in the world. The only thing that was mine.

I couldn't lose that too.

Chapter Thirty-Four

Duke fumed as he downed his fourth cocktail. "Another." He shook his glass at me.

"Maybe slow down?"

"Another," he repeated. "And more booze this time." He dangled his cocktail glass at me. "Lansky's taking the East Side."

"Yes, you've mentioned that." I hesitated, not knowing if it would help or hurt, but I went ahead. "Lansky's not so bad."

Duke stiffened. "Excuse me?"

I told him the story about my one-week job in the gambling racket. Duke didn't crack a smile, so I changed topics. "Does this change anything for the bar?" I asked.

"Shouldn't. Same business, new chief." I set another drink in front of him. "Can't trust him, though. Lansky's got a thing for those fucking guineas."

"Hey, this is a classy bar. Watch your language."

A few stools down, a bloated man guzzling beer said, "You got a problem with the Italians? With Lansky?" Next to him, a hollow-cheeked man scowled at Duke.

"He hasn't got a problem." I laid my hand on Duke's in hopes he'd back off.

He didn't. "The dagos are conniving—"

"Duke!"

The two men stood. Big Al moved into position, poised for a fight.

"No trouble here," I said. "This is a friendly place."

"We're not feeling very friendly," the hollow-cheeked man said.

"How 'bout a round on the house? My friend's had a bit to drink."

Duke drilled me with a livid glare. "That's—"

"Duke, let's continue this conversation at my apartment." I stroked his cheek. "Later."

Duke looked from me to the two men to Big Al and back to me. His pupils expanded, and his face flushed crimson. He pounded his fist on the bar. I jumped. "Duke!"

He grabbed his hat, jammed it on his head, and stormed out.

My mouth went dry, and a sudden bout of dizziness made the room shimmer. But I recovered. "So, couple of beers?"

The two men hovered but returned to their stools and accepted a drink.

With icy hands, I poured them each a beer.

~

I went to the apartment on the earlier side, hoping Duke would show up. I had no way of finding him. Who knew where he went when he wasn't with me?

I sat at the kitchen table, staring into the distance, toward Mama and Papa's bedroom. When Max had moved out, I'd shut the door. The room was off limits, waiting for my family to be reunited. Was I to lose Duke too?

It was three nights later when Duke came over.

"Come in. Let me mix you a drink." I winced at my mawkish tone.

He paused in the doorway, inspecting the room as if I might be hiding something. He glowered at me. "You didn't have my back."

I took him by the arm and led him to a chair, pushing gently to make him sit. "I always have your back."

"You didn't the other night."

"I wanted to protect you." I kneaded his shoulders in the spots he liked.

"You mean protect your bar."

I continued massaging, hoping this would pass.

He put his hand on mine, stilling me. "I'm not in the mood. Make me that drink."

"You got it."

Our lovemaking that night was feverish and raw. After we were spent, he held me as if afraid I would leave.

~

On the last Friday in November, I crept into Rabbi Umansky's shul as usual to slip a ten-dollar bill in the *tzedakah* box. The rabbi was waiting for me.

"Malka," he said from a corner of the synagogue. "I'm glad you're here. Saved me a trip to your apartment."

"Rabbi." I itched to leave. "Everything all right?"

"Yes, yes." He came to me. "How are you, Malka?"

"I'm good." I remembered to whom I was speaking, so I added, "*Baruch Hashem.*" *See, Mama! I haven't forgotten what you taught me.*

"We haven't seen your brother in a while."

"He's staying closer to school. Work, classes, studying: commuting was too much."

"Smart, smart." His torso rocked back and forth. "Here." From a shelf, he plucked a small carton from a pile of boxes. Hanukkah candles. "The first candle lighting is this coming Shabbat. Friday night, December seventh."

"Early this year."

He smiled broadly. "Same time as every year. The twenty-fifth of Kislev."

I chuckled. "Thank you, Rabbi." How could Papa have ever doubted Rabbi Umansky's intentions? I wanted to give the rabbi more *tzedakah*. Make his life a little easier.

"*Ah freilichen Hanukkah* to you and Max."

"A happy Hanukkah to you, too, Rabbi."

~

Late afternoon the next Friday, I took the IRT uptown. It had been four months since I'd been up there. Four months since I'd watched Max through the window.

Exiting at 116th Street, I was greeted by a world both the same and different from the Lower East Side. I was more aware of my surroundings this time and spotted at least three doors that would lead to gin mills.

I plodded to the diner, where Max should be working the dinner shift. Even though it was pointless, I couldn't help searching for Gertie and Louise, except this time I did it with no enthusiasm, no hope.

I stood outside the restaurant as I had last time. If Max turned me away, I didn't think I'd recover. This was a bad idea. But I wasn't going back without trying.

With a deep breath, I opened the door. The smell of fried meat assaulted me. The place was not yet crowded, so I took a seat at a booth. He hadn't noticed my entrance, so I observed him bustling, refilling napkin holders, taking orders. Seeing Max after four months was jarring. He was such a . . . well, a man. He had the dark stubble of one who couldn't keep his beard at bay. He had Papa's sure-footed gait, but his profile favored Mama's. I thought of Anshel. Would he and Max have resembled each other? What would Anshel be doing if he'd made it to America?

A paper menu stood between the salt and pepper shakers. I picked it up, more to have something to do than because I was hungry.

"What can I get you?" a voice said above me. Max hunched over his notepad.

"You'll get better tips if you smile at your customers," I said.

His head jolted up. "Minnie!" A grin spread across his face before he remembered he was angry. "What are you doing here?"

I pointed to the other side of the table. "Can you sit?"

Max glanced over his shoulder. "Cook gets furious when he thinks I'm goofing off." His brow furrowed. "Is something wrong? Something with Papa?"

"I came for you. For this." From my cloth bag, I pulled out the candles Rabbi Umansky had given me as well as Mama's menorah. Last year we'd lit it with the girls. The year before with my mother. This year, there was only us. "Hanukkah starts at sundown."

Wordlessly, we both gazed outside. It was about a quarter to five, and already the sun was hidden behind the horizon, rays of color fighting to remain aboveground. Sunset. Hanukkah had begun.

"Pick up!" called a voice across the room. Max scurried to bring a plate to a booth. After grabbing a cup, he came back to me. He filled it from the coffeepot he'd picked up. I took it gratefully.

"Is there somewhere we can light this?"

Pursing his lips, Max said, "Not really," so I set the menorah on the table. I stuck the shammash candle in the center and one candle in the rightmost branch for the first night of Hanukkah. After lighting the shammash, we recited the blessings—softly, so others couldn't hear us—the ones we remembered because Mama had said them every year, for the eight nights of the holiday. When we were done, I lifted the shammash and used it to light the other candle.

"Happy Hanukkah, Max."

"Happy Hanukkah, Minnie."

What were Gertie and Louise doing for the holiday? Did they have warm latkes and bright gelt? American Jews celebrated more extravagantly, with presents and celebrations. I bet Gertie and Louise received gifts and chocolate.

We watched the flames reflected in the diner window. Our own faces stared back at us, a lovely glow, an aura, but the spell was broken when the counterman yelled, "Hey, what's that? No candles in here! Get rid of that thing!" and three more groups came in, taking seats.

Leaning over, I blew out the candles, something Mama never would have done, but then Mama didn't have to return to a job. I put the menorah and candles back in my bag.

"I've got to grab those tables," Max said, but he didn't immediately move. "I'm glad you came."

As he turned, I grabbed his wrist. "I miss you. Come over. Sunday. I'll make latkes." My voice trembled.

"Enough with your girlfriend! Back to work, Max, if you wanna keep your job!"

"Sunday," he said.

He hurried off. Before I left, I tucked a ten-dollar bill under the saltshaker.

Chapter Thirty-Five

The holidays passed, and we welcomed in 1929. Life with Lansky in charge remained the same for me. I placed orders with Duke. Alcohol arrived every Wednesday. Protection and loan payments didn't change.

But the best part? Max and I came to a truce. An uneasy truce, but a truce nonetheless.

"I've been to Uncle Aaron's a few times," he said when he came for latkes. "Watching them, so lighthearted . . . it's lonely. You and me, Minnie. We're all that's left of the Soffer family."

Max fell into the habit of coming on Sunday afternoons. I'd make him an early dinner—usually my breakfast—and he'd read the paper or study as we sat in companionable silence.

Once a month, on Saturday mornings, we'd meet at shul. I'd rarely gone when Mama was alive, but Max had attended regularly. Mama would be proud to see us here now. For her I tagged along.

Max davened in the front of the shul, and I prayed in the women's section behind the curtain. Rabbi Umansky's eyes shone whenever he saw us enter. How could one man hold so many people in his heart? As he prayed for those who were sick, who were struggling, I wished I could help. Rabbi Umansky spent all the shul's money on his congregation, providing for others as he'd provided for me after Mama had passed.

The rabbi had caught me dropping twenties in the *tzedakah* box and scolded me. "It's good to help the shul," he said. "But a young girl like yourself needs to save. If you don't save the penny, you'll not have the dollar." But I wanted to do more now.

~

The bar's crowd had been growing, but on a Thursday in April, it exploded. A new posh group started ringing the bell. Frank, Wesley, and I mixed drinks nonstop. People stood because we didn't have enough seats.

On Sunday, I was too exhausted to cook. I dropped a loaf of black bread and herring on the table for dinner.

"I'm sorry, Max. I'm beat. The—" I almost forgot myself. Mentioning the bar was verboten. "Things have been busy."

"I'm not surprised." He tossed the *New Yorker* on the table. "Read that."

"Too tired."

"Read that."

With an exaggerated sigh, I picked up the magazine, which had been opened to page thirty. The column: Speakeasy Nights. The column was semiregular, and I read it whenever Max left an issue behind. I scanned the article without enthusiasm. The Palm Beach Speakeasy in midtown. The clientele. The owner. Nothing I cared about. But then I did a double take. Suddenly I wasn't so tired. I sat up and took in every word.

> If you can find Minnie's Speakeasy, hidden on a side alley, and make it past the burly doorman, you'll find an oasis of what passes for class on the Lower East Side. The decor is less garish than you'd expect in this part of town, with modest, yet tasteful fixtures and uncommonly extravagant cocktails, which can be had for the bargain of 75¢.

The proprietor, a whisper sister named, obviously, Minnie, is a lithe creature with shades of the *Yiddishe Momme*: a vaguely guttural accent and a habit of inquiring with deep concern after her regulars, most of whom she knows by name. Over the course of the evening she can be heard saying, "Ralph, baby's colic better? Eddie. Eddie! *Tuchus* off the bar or the bum's rush! Thelma, forget the *schmendrik* and have another Green Fizz." Minnie's in constant motion, conjuring her elixirs, polishing the glasses, filling the peanut bowls. The gangly Irish bartender, Frank, at the other end, moves at a languid pace, spending extra time with the bearcats who appreciate his boyish good looks.

Minnie's specials change weekly, and the original concoctions, which wouldn't be out of place at the Puncheon Club, are sweet delectations, rarely cloying.

When the doors open at four o'clock, the neighborhood crowd shuffles in, the ones you'd expect to see in a Lower East Side bar. Three gray-haired artifacts sit at the end, still squabbling over the Long Count.

Around seven o'clock a new crowd enters, one with a more refined demeanor, albeit with a proletariat comportment. Ladies are welcome, with or without a male escort. Any quiff who manages to talk her way inside is immediately bounced when noticed by the indoor goon.

No music, no food, a shame for those who want to linger, but telling by the screeching of the shebas and the ogling leers of the sheiks, no one seems to mind.

"Horsefeathers!" I clasped the magazine to my chest. "My cocktails are delectable!" I wrinkled my brow. "Is my accent really guttural?"

"Minnie, this is not good," Max said.

"What's not?"

"This article. You shouldn't draw attention to yourself. To that . . ." He sighed heavily. "To that bar."

"It's a speakeasy, not a bar. Can't you read?" My body didn't feel as tired anymore. "Look, on one hand it's not great. The cops will have a field day with the payoffs. But if we bring in as much money as we have these past few days, we'll be able to afford the cops plus save even more money." The more I perked up, the more despondent he looked. "Hey. Let me take you out for dinner."

Max shook his head. "I need to get back. I have an exam tomorrow."

He'd study better in the apartment because it was quieter than his boardinghouse, but I suspected he was avoiding an argument.

"Can I keep this?" I held up the magazine.

"Minnie . . ." His voice was quiet, which cut more than if he'd yelled at me. "You're in too deep."

He walked out, leaving the magazine behind. I carefully removed the page. On my way to work, I'd buy a frame and hang it in my office.

~

On Monday, I hunkered over my desk, trying to invent a swankier drink to delight the new customers. I'd practically memorized the article. I delighted in all of it. Well, except for *Yiddishe Momme*. *Yiddishe Momme* stung. My mama had been a *Yiddishe* Mama. If I were one, I'd still have my sisters. I chose to focus on *lithe*, *tasteful*, and *class*.

"So much for a low profile." Duke stood in the doorway.

"Isn't it just the cat's meow? Do you think the uptown crowd prefers gin, rum, or rye drinks?"

Duke perched across from me. "You realize you're inviting more cops?"

"I didn't invite anything. I had no idea a journalist was here."

"Your protection is going up."

"My protection? I figured I'd be paying off the flatties. But protection?"

"You make more money, you pay more protection. You think the Cotton Club only pays a hundred scratch? Twenty a week more."

"Can't you do anything about that?" Given what I'd been earning, it wasn't going to make a real difference, but I worried once payments started rising, they'd keep rising.

"Outta my hands."

The price of making a buck, I guessed. "Fine. Let's talk booze. The ladies can't get enough of my cocktails, but too many men want their drinks straight. I could charge a pretty penny for the high-end stuff."

"That's a big expense, Minnie."

"Aren't you supposed to encourage me to spend more?"

"You're already paying more." The previous month the Jones Act had passed, making bootlegging a felony instead of a misdemeanor. If caught, bootleggers could get five years in jail and a ten-thousand-dollar fine. Plenty had decided it wasn't worth it, so the ones who had stuck around had raised their prices. Significantly.

"So I'll pay even more."

He rubbed his chin. "You currently pay fifty dollars for a case of rye. Old Durham is a hundred. If you can even find Johnnie Walker, it's fifteen."

I perked up.

"A bottle," he said.

I deflated.

"Booth's Old Tom Gin'll run you eighty a case. Same for Bacardí Carta Blanca."

"So at eighty dollars a case, that's about six and half a bottle. One bottle yields about sixteen drinks. So let's call it . . ." I grabbed a piece of paper to do the math. "About forty-two cents a drink. If I charge a dollar for high-end—"

"A dollar? On the Lower East Side? Sooner or later the uptown folks will do their slumming at the next new place."

"A dollar . . ." I scribbled. "Which means I'd make seven sixty-eight a bottle, which would be"—my pencil flew across the paper—"a profit of ninety-two dollars and sixteen cents per case."

"Someone paid attention in math class."

"I'd still use the lower-end booze in the cocktails."

"I can get you five thousand counterfeit labels for a hundred bucks. Slap 'em on your bottles."

My head shot up. "Cheat my customers?"

He laughed. "I've seen you watering down drinks when the guys are too blotto to tell the difference."

"That's not cheating. That's good business." I returned to my numbers. "I can make this work."

"You're spending a lot of dough."

"I've got it."

"New glad rags. Money to Ike. I'll bet dollars to doughnuts you're slipping cabbage to Max. How many drinks on the house you serve those geezers?"

I twirled the pencil. "No idea what you're talking about."

"I'm talking about the huge wreath you sent when—what's his name? The one with the goiter?"

"Gerald?"

"Yeah, Gerald. You spent a wad on that funeral wreath."

"Gerald'd been coming here since before my time. Was I supposed to ignore his death?"

"Yeah. Was a big expense."

I bristled. "I can afford it." And I could. Minnie's wasn't making what the uptown speakeasies made, but I had a few hundred dollars a week to spend as I liked. Most of it I stashed in a hatbox on a top shelf in my bedroom, saving it for the day when Papa got out of jail. In the meantime, though, I allowed myself to splurge a bit, going to Bonwit Teller with Sylvia to buy us each a pair of Corticelli Silk stockings and bottles of Chanel No. 5. Max refused my cash, but when I gifted him a suit suitable for a budding lawyer, he accepted it. I placed as much money as I thought I could get away with in the shul *tzedakah* box. Raises for my workers. And Duke hadn't complained when I'd presented him with a gold watch from Tiffany & Co. "C'mon, Duke. Treat me like any other bar owner."

He sighed. "Fine. What do you want?"

I grinned. "All of it."

Chapter Thirty-Six

Amazing how many cops "stumbled upon" my bar. I stashed extra cash to pay them off. And it wasn't just the money. If I poured out all the free booze those coppers drank, I could sail myself right over to France.

I bought a phonograph and stacks of popular records from the Sears catalog. Changing the records fell to Wesley. He excelled at sensing when the crowded needed a sprightly "I Wanna Be Loved by You" or a somber "My Melancholy Baby."

One evening, Eddie, a regular, decided to be a smart aleck. "It's your song, Minnie," he said, handing Wesley a record. Wesley set the needle, and strains of music drifted through the room.

I furrowed my brow. I knew that song. What was it? The tune unsettled me. My nostrils flared as I recognized the lyrics. "My Yiddishe Mama."

Was this how they saw me? As an old-world *balabusta*?

More than that, though, the song brought to mind Mama, a woman who cared for nothing but her family, a woman who sacrificed so her children could thrive. It brought to mind a home with a family.

Family. Something I no longer had. All I had were failures. My sisters. Gone.

A balloon inflated in my chest. My eyes blurred. I wouldn't fall apart. Not here.

I pounded my fist on the bar with a bang. "No!"

The chatter stopped. Everyone turned to me. I shoved Wesley out of the way as I hurled myself toward the phonograph. A scratching noise pierced the room as I skidded the needle off the record. I snatched up the disk and snapped it in half.

"Got something against Sophie Tucker?" Wesley said.

"You don't play any records I haven't approved!" I pointed my finger around the room. "I am no *Yiddishe Momme*!" Heads bobbed in startled agreement. Eddie shrank back.

My heart pounded. I leaned on the counter and inhaled slowly. After I calmed, I was chagrined by my childish outburst.

I breathed deeply and plastered on a smile. "All right." I stood straight. "Nothing to see here." No one moved. "Next round on me." A murmur spread. "Eddie," I called to the man cowering in the corner. "All your drinks are on me tonight."

Eddie mopped his brow with his handkerchief. "Thanks, Min. Sorry about that."

I held up my hand. "Enough said. I'm mixing you a Thorndike."

As I combined the orange juice, vermouth, and gin, the song burrowed into me, clawing my brain, skittering in my chest.

No one ever called me a *Yiddishe Momme* again.

~

When I next saw Duke, he said, "What happened at the bar?"

"What are you talking about?"

"People are jawing. You do something to Eddie?"

I waved, too embarrassed to tell him. "Nothing worth mentioning." I changed the subject. "The new booze is great. Now I need better wine."

"Wine is trickier. Can't dilute it like liquor. Need a California or French guy to supply, and with the Jones Act, my wine connections turned skittish."

"Surely for enough money, classier wine can be bought. I serve *dreck*."

He crossed his arms. "Doctor it up. Add sugar."

"It doesn't need sugar. It needs flavor." I steepled my fingers and leaned on the desk. "I had an idea. My shul is small. Perhaps my rabbi could source my wine. He gets money for the shul; I get better wine. Everyone benefits."

Duke's legs stretched out, his feet on the corner of my desk. It peeved me his shoes were on my papers, but it wasn't worth an argument. Especially when I wanted something.

His eyes narrowed. "How does Lansky benefit? I provide you with the wine Lansky provides me. Nothing more I can do. Nothing more *you* can do. Tough luck for your rabbi."

I sighed. "Lansky's a Jew. How could he hold a grudge about rabbi-sourced wine? I'm a small-time operation to him."

"No telling how Lansky will react." He softened. "You're sweet to want to help your rabbi. You can always donate more."

I bristled at *sweet*. "The shul needs a better income than my *tzedakah* can give."

"I'll put you down for the usual three cases?" he asked.

I leaned back in my chair, folding my arms over my chest. "Fine."

"Don't be like that. Drinks later?"

I nodded, straightening the pages he'd mussed, trying not to show my annoyance.

~

On Friday, I hurried to the shul as afternoon prayers ended. As they recited the final Mourner's Kaddish, I placed a ten in the *tzedakah* box and waited outside.

The men dribbled out. I stood against the wall, scanning the men exiting until Leo emerged. Max's friend. The rabbi's son. I wasn't about to involve the rabbi in this. I couldn't let Rabbi Umansky learn what I did for work. But the rabbi's son? Different story.

With a twinge of guilt, knowing how Max abhorred my work, I called out, "Leo!"

He turned, surprised. "Minnie."

"Do you have time to talk?"

"Not really. I need to be back at the restaurant. Everything okay with Max?"

"He's fine. May I walk with you?"

He brushed his arm out comically. "After you."

Food stains splotched his shirt, the purple of beets running down his sleeve. Leo stood only an inch or so taller than me. The hair at his temples showed signs of receding. His whiskey-brown eyes, though, shone bright, and his smile was generous.

"How'd you end up at a restaurant? I figured you as Joe College."

"Needed to work. Cooking appeals to me." He took my arm to pull me out of the way of a mother with a buggy. Releasing me, he asked, "You wanted to discuss my career plans?"

Now that I was here, I was nervous. I started and stopped. "I wanted to ask . . . I mean, I was wondering . . ."

His lips twitched. "Why, Minnie. Are you asking me on a date?"

"No!" The word flew out, sharper than I'd intended. When I saw his wounded look, I backpedaled. "That's not what I meant."

"Too good for the rabbi's son? Most mothers would kill to have a rabbi's son for their daughters."

"I don't have a mother." The words fell out without thought. I felt bad for both of us. I was mucking this up.

"I was only teasing," he said, though his ego had clearly been bruised. "What did you want to talk to me about?"

"Let me buy you a knish."

"I work in a restaurant, Minnie. They feed me."

"Then let me buy myself a knish." We stopped at a pushcart. I passed over a few coins in exchange for a steaming disk of potatoes covered with dough. I bit into it and let the heat warm the back of my throat. "I want to help the synagogue. I know your father wants to make improvements, bolster the widows-and-orphans fund. I know a way for the synagogue to make money."

Leo continued walking. "He doesn't want to do it."

"Huh?" I moved quickly to keep up. "Do what?"

"What you're suggesting."

"I haven't suggested anything yet."

Leo stopped suddenly, causing me to run into him. He took a step back. "You want him to buy wine for your bar."

I gasped. "You know about the bar?"

His brow furrowed. "I know about the bar? The whole community knows about the bar. You think it's a secret?"

"That damn *New Yorker* article!"

"What *New Yorker* article?"

Swallowing hard, I asked, "The rabbi? He knows?"

"You're not so different from your father, are you? Think if you're religious, you must be stupid."

"No. I have more respect for your father than I do for anyone else."

"He doesn't want to be involved in the bar."

"How can you be sure?"

Leo resumed striding to work. "Because I suggested it. Years ago, I suggested he talk to your father. When he said he wished he could purchase new Torah scrolls for the shul, I suggested it. When he needed money for the burial of Tzvi Menk, I suggested it. When he noticed the ceiling tiles were falling, I suggested it. But he didn't trust your father. He didn't want to be in business with him."

"It's not my father anymore. It's me."

"I know. And when I broached that with him, he grew furious. Didn't want you involved. I explained you were already involved, that his working with you wasn't what was going to lead you into illicit activities, but he refused to hear it."

Rabbi Umansky knew. The knish sat like a lump in my belly. "This would benefit both of us."

He threw his hands in the air. "You think I like working at Schwebel's? With the money we'd make, I'd open my own place."

"You want your own restaurant?"

"I have ambitions."

"Not going to become a rabbi?" I'd assumed the son of a rabbi became a rabbi.

"Who are you, my mother?"

We arrived. "Why would your father have to know?"

"How's that?"

"The Menorah Wine Company sells to rabbis. Your last name is Umansky. You live above the synagogue. Who's to say you're not the rabbi?"

He looked at me as if trying to evaluate who I was—who I had become. "It would break my father's heart."

I nodded. If there was one thing I understood, it was family. Just because I'd let mine down didn't mean he should too.

Chapter Thirty-Seven

When things were going well, I dared to tempt fate and think, *Life isn't all bad.* I had a handsome boyfriend. A thriving business. A brother on his way to becoming a lawyer. A bar that filled me with pride. A decent income. Maybe, just maybe, things would turn out okay in this *Goldene Medina* of America. Maybe the streets were paved with gold after all.

I forgot to spit *pu pu pu.* I forgot to say *Kein ayin hara.*

Because of course, it all came crashing down.

Not just on me. The entire country. In one day. In one fell swoop.

Black Tuesday. October 29, 1929.

The effect wasn't obvious at first. Some of my regulars had difficulty paying their tabs. Ben started to depend on Otto and Walt to cover his drinks. I floated a few more on the house than I had in better days. People drank more, but they drank the cheap stuff. I couldn't keep enough beer on tap. The bar, which used to fill around 7:00 p.m., had folks waiting for us when we opened at four.

Big Al was busier than usual. When money was short, tempers were even shorter. More sloppy drunks. More guys picking fights. More women sneaking in to sell their wares.

By necessity, I lowered my prices. Everyone did. I stopped buying Bacardí White and the high-end ryes. The uptown clientele that had descended after the *New Yorker* article stayed uptown now, but the bar still hummed with locals.

Lower prices cut into my profits. Fancy dresses and expensive lipsticks would have to wait.

Duke chastised me for all the drinks on the house, but the pain in those men's eyes . . . I wanted to help dull it. I understood what it was to hurt. As night fell, they staggered home to families or slipped off to evening shifts at factories. Some regulars drifted away, new drinkers taking their places. The women still came, but with weariness etched on their faces. The lighthearted flapper gave way to the somber working girl, still in pretty dresses, but pretty dresses from last year.

Changes had to be made to keep the bar afloat.

"Duke, what am I going to do?"

"Cheaper booze. Disguise the flavor in your cocktails."

I didn't have a choice.

~

The rolling over of a decade: 1929 turned into 1930. On Friday, January 17, Max made a rare visit to the bar before we opened.

In the back office, I poured us each a glass of bourbon.

"To a decade in America," he said, raising his glass.

"To a decade in America," I echoed. We sipped our drinks in silence. Ten years ago that day, we had disembarked from the ship, brimming with trepidation and optimism. In ten years we'd acquired and lost two sisters. Our mother was gone. Our father in prison. What had we gained?

When we drained our glasses, Max left for work, and I took my place behind the bar.

A few minutes before four, Frank waved Big Al over. He filled three glasses. "A toast," he said. "Today's an anniversary of sorts."

I reddened. Had Max told him?

Frank raised his bourbon. Big Al and I followed suit. "Here's to surviving ten years of the great experiment."

"Great experiment?" I said.

"Ten years ago today, the Eighteenth Amendment took effect. Happy birthday, Prohibition!"

Ah, yes. I lifted my glass to clink with Big Al and Frank.

Big Al guzzled his in a single swallow. "Thank God for Prohibition. Can you imagine what this country would be like if it were full of drunks?"

"I can't think of anything more awful," I said, tossing down my drink.

~

On a Thursday in February, I checked the shipment. "Only eight cases of bourbon? I ordered ten."

"Shortages this week," Duke said. "G-men cracked down on one of our distilleries."

"Between unemployment and the government, we're being strangled."

"Tell me about it." Duke was chafing at changes in the back end with Lansky, but I kept out of it. The less I knew, the better.

At the bar, I uncorked one of the bottles and sniffed. I winced. The liquor was a pale gold, more reminiscent of what came out of the body than what went in it. My special needed to hide the medicinal smell of this garbage.

Surveying my mixers, I chose pineapple juice and mint. I stirred them with the rotgut and sampled the drink. Nope, still nasty.

I played around with different options—apricot juice, bitters, Coke, grenadine—before going with a variation on a Ward Eight, with whiskey; lemon, orange, and pineapple juices; and grenadine. It was palatable.

I brought the chalkboard into my office to write the special on it. I named it the Ward Off. To the customers, I'd say "ward off evil." In my mind, it was "ward off terrible booze." I couldn't remember where I'd put the chalk. What was this fuzziness? As a seasoned drinker, I required a lot of liquor to become tipsy. I'd consumed about a glass of bourbon while concocting my brew. My skull pounded. I rested my head in my hands, as if holding on would stop the swelling throb. When my stomach churned, something clicked. First, I dashed to the bathroom, barely making it as my drinks returned the hard way. Second, I rushed to the bar to grab the case of bourbon sitting on the floor, but my limbs were too weak to lift it.

"Big Al." It came out as a croak. The intensity of the pain stunned me. "Big Al," I repeated louder.

"What's wrong?"

"Take this into the office."

"Hey," Wesley said. "We need that."

"Now!" I didn't normally bark orders at Big Al, so he lifted the case. I followed him to the back room.

"What's going on?"

"The bourbon. It's bad."

"Wood alcohol?" Big Al moved as if to examine me, but of course he had no idea how to do so.

"Must be." To fatten their wallets, bootleggers cut the booze with wood alcohol, an extremely poisonous substance. "What'll it do to me?"

"Wait." He charged into the bar and returned with my "medicinal" bottle of Old Rip Van Winkle, the one I hid under the counter for myself. "Drink this." He poured a generous glassful.

"That's the last thing I want."

"You need it. Wood alcohol is methanol. Ethanol offsets it."

"How do you know this?" I took the glass.

"How do you not?"

I forced the bourbon down, grimacing.

"How much did you drink?"

"A glass?"

Big Al scrutinized me. "You should be okay. Go to the hospital, though, just in case."

"No!" I thought of Mama's words: *A hospital is where you go to die.* I thought of bringing Louise to the hospital for her broken arm, a trip that precipitated the girls' departure. I would not go to the hospital. "I'll be fine. We can't trust any of the alcohol from that last shipment. Bring it in the back."

Big Al waited a beat, perhaps debating if he should argue about the hospital.

"I'll talk to Duke about making this right," I said.

"If you're not going to the hospital, you're at least going home to bed."

"I'm not leaving the bar on a Thursday," I said, though my words slurred. I was loath to give in to the pain and leave.

Big Al poked out and returned with Frank, who was arriving for the evening. "Wesley is here. Frank'll walk you home."

I stood unsteadily. "I'll walk myself." Then I buckled over the desk as a lightning bolt shot through my skull.

"I got you." Frank took me by the arm. "We'll sort this out tomorrow."

Frank half carried me to my apartment. I didn't even care when my neighbor flung a look of disgust; Mrs. Shukat must have thought I had a new lover. Frank settled me into bed, found aspirin powder in the cabinet, and forced it down my throat. He set four glasses of water next to me. "Drink all of them. Get this stuff out of your system." He stuck a large soup pot next to the bed, which I immediately put to use, once again voiding my stomach. "Good girl. You'll be fine."

He left, and I fell into the most excruciating sleep I'd ever experienced.

~

Banging reverberated in my body, coming from around me, within me. When I heard Duke calling, "Minnie!" I realized some of the pounding was at the front door.

Disoriented, I stumbled from bed and let Duke in. I didn't speak, simply returned to my bedroom, though the smell rising from the pot sickened me. I rinsed it in the kitchen sink, stifling back gags.

Duke barraged me with questions. "Are you all right? How do you feel? Which drink did this to you? Do I need to take you to the hospital?" He nipped about like a nervous terrier.

I held up my hand to silence him, then crawled into bed. I felt better than I had earlier, but not great. My stomach burned and churned. The hammering in my head muted to a dull thump.

"Here." He handed me a knish. "Your stomach must be empty."

I was unsure I could eat, but once I'd taken a nibble, I realized I was ravenous. I devoured it in three bites.

Duke's half smile crawled across his face. "That's what I thought." He lifted a bag. "I brought more."

"Thanks," I managed to say as I took the bag and grabbed another, then shoved it into my mouth.

Kicking off his shoes, Duke sat next to me, stroking my hair as I ate. "I'm so sorry, Minnie. I had no idea."

"I know," I said between bites.

"The guy who sold me those bottles will pay." The steely glint in his eyes frightened me, and I thought of Bennie. I had no doubt the liquor supplier would come to a bad end.

"He probably didn't know."

"Someone knew. Someone will pay."

The knish became a lump in my throat. I didn't interfere in Duke's business, but I didn't want to be responsible for someone getting hurt.

"I'm fine."

He held me tighter. "No one touches you, Minnie. I'm here to protect you."

It hurt too much to think about protection and what Duke might do, so I rolled to my side, slinging my arm over his torso, and fell asleep.

$\sim$

303

The next afternoon, Duke brought us another shipment—I wondered what poor guy wasn't getting his delivery. Before customers arrived, Big Al and I disposed of the bad booze.

"A shame we have to destroy it," I said. "I wish there was a way to test the quality of alcohol."

"But there isn't."

I picked up the bottle I'd opened, the one that had poisoned me, and placed it on the top shelf.

"Saving that?" Big Al asked.

"It's a reminder." The liquor looked like any other bottle of liquor. "Things are not as harmless as they may seem."

We brought the rest of the bottles into the alley and smashed them one by one, letting the poisonous alcohol flow into the street, our own River Styx leading the way to my bar.

Chapter Thirty-Eight

A couple of weeks before my twenty-first birthday, temperatures hovered in the midfifties. On my way to work, with the sun infusing me with the promise of spring, I swung by the Henry Street Settlement House. I bounded to the front desk, where I asked the woman for Form 2214.

"Got it right here." She opened a file drawer. "Do you need help filling it out?"

"No, thank you."

"Mazel tov!"

Form 2214.

Form for Petition for Naturalization.

~

At the bar, I announced, "I'm going into the office to fill out my petition for naturalization, so no one disturb me."

"Attagirl," Walt said.

From his stool, Big Al asked, "Aren't those things complicated?"

"How hard is it to fill in the blanks?" I looked it over. "You think I don't know my name? When I arrived?"

"Dunno. Frank, didn't your father have a problem?" Otto asked.

I waved him off. "I got it."

In the back room, I laid the paper on the desk. I bit the end of the pen as I studied the questions. Nothing difficult.

My full, true, and correct name was Miss Minnie Soffer.

My present residence was New York City.

One question balled me up. Present occupation? After some thought, I wrote *countergirl*. It was the truth. I just wasn't specifying what kind of counter.

The rest of the questions were simple. I'd gone to the drugstore to check my weight so I could fill it in. I wasn't married. Born in Bratsyana, Ukraine.

At the bottom I had to list two witnesses of good moral character. Couldn't ask Duke for obvious reasons. Max was a near relative. Toibe would have been the perfect choice, except I'd avoided her for so long I wasn't comfortable asking now. I'd chosen Sylvia. Max had spoken to his friend Leo, which made me nervous. Leo knew what I did for a living, but he'd agreed.

The line Max had circled in that book haunted me: *Some courts refuse citizenship to the applicant who has violated the Volstead Act—the national prohibition laws.*

I wouldn't feel safe until I held my certificate of naturalization.

~

In August, I received word of my preliminary hearing.

For three weeks, I skipped more than walked. Every morning, I pored over *Civics for New Americans*. Frank and Wesley quizzed me while I mixed drinks.

"What is the presiding officer of the Senate called, and how is he chosen?" Wesley asked as I shook a Bee's Knees.

"President of the Senate, and the vice president of the United States is always president of the Senate."

While cutting more limes, Frank asked, "Who was the tenth president?"

"John Tyler."

As I measured bourbon into a glass, Otto asked, "What's the Eighteenth Amendment?"

"Funny man," I said. "The Eighteenth Amendment declares the production, transport, and sale of intoxicating liquors is illegal."

"Doesn't say anything about drinking 'em, though." Otto downed his. "Another! If you want to steer clear of bein' a felon, you can give it to me for free."

"Aren't you a regular Buster Keaton." I poured him another. "Sixty cents."

"I thought it was fifty."

"Fifty for my friends. Sixty for wise guys."

~

On the date of the hearing, Sylvia and Leo waited with me at the naturalization office.

"How should we celebrate?" Sylvia asked.

"Ice cream," Leo said.

"I was thinking something a little more grown-up."

"What's more American than ice cream?"

"I'm not a citizen yet." My anxiety mounted with the thought. "Not even after today. The waiting period. The final hearing. A few more months, at least."

Sitting on a wooden bench, I tapped my foot.

"Stop." Sylvia placed her hand on my leg. "That thing is going to run away from you."

"Soffer," a man called from behind a glass window.

"Present!" I hopped up.

"Present," Sylvia said under her breath. "Where are we, grammar school?"

"Shh." We followed the man to a room full of desks and took our seats.

He opened a file. "I couldn't find your certificate of arrival. You came over on the name Minnie Soffer?"

"Malka Soffer."

He made a note. "Should've had that on your 2213. I'll find the certificate. First papers and Form 2214."

I gave him my papers.

He glanced at them but then did a double take, examining more carefully. I fidgeted in my seat.

"You have an error here."

"My name?" I bunched my skirt in my fist.

"That's not the problem." He pointed. "You wrote here you renounce allegiance to Ukraine."

"Yes?"

"That's incorrect."

"I was born in Bratsyana, which is in Ukraine."

"Ukraine is part of Russia. You need to renounce allegiance to the present government of Russia."

"I can fix that."

He shook his head. "This is a serious error."

"I understand. I'll change it. I'll renounce allegiance to Russia." I tittered. "I'll renounce allegiance to any country you like. I want to be a citizen of the United States."

"You need to start again."

"Fill out another Form 2214? Apply for a new court date?" That would take another three months. My eyes welled, and I bit my lip.

"No." He passed me my papers. "With Form 2213. Declaration of Intent."

"What?" Leo said at the same time that Sylvia said, "That's ridiculous!"

"I don't make the rules," he said.

"Why didn't the clerk tell me when I turned in my first form?"

"Those monkeys aren't paid to think. They only copy what you write."

I wanted to protest but knew only sobs would emerge.

"Isn't there something we can do?" Leo asked. "We can vouch for her. She'll make an upstanding citizen."

"The only thing you can do is to get her a new 2213 form."

Sylvia moved to sit on the edge of his desk. "Is there nothing we can do?"

"Miss, I'm not sure what you're implying, but nothing can be done."

"But. But . . ." I could only sputter.

"Come on." Leo took my arm and helped me stand.

"But . . ." My eyes darted around the room, searching for someone to rescue me.

"C'mon, sweetie." Sylvia took my other arm.

They led me to the apartment, where I crawled into bed and refused to come out for the rest of the day.

~

The next day I went to the settlement house for a new declaration form. When the woman at the desk asked, "Do you need help filling it out?" I said, "Yes."

As we completed the document, she emphasized the importance of writing the current name of the country of origin, as borders often changed.

I didn't tell her I already knew.

Chapter Thirty-Nine

As 1930 passed, we expected the downturn to reverse, for the market to right itself, for businesses to return to prosperity. We expected the gaiety of the 1920s to come back stronger.

But it didn't.

On a Saturday night, late in the summer, Big Al approached. "Guy at the door says he knows you. Looks suspicious."

When I saw who it was, I said, "He's okay."

Big Al's hesitation was understandable. Men wearing yarmulkes were not our normal clientele. "Big Al," I said, "this is Leo. He's welcome anytime."

Leo, in a droopy suit, rubbed his yarmulke in a circle around the crown of his head, as if it were a talisman. "Quite the security you have." Despite the outfit, Leo stood with confidence and a quiet dignity. He was no Duke, but he was handsome in a neighborhood kind of way.

"We've got to be careful. A lot of Feds are Jews, you know."

"I look that Jewish?"

I laughed. "The yarmulke is a giveaway."

He reddened. He pulled it off and shoved it in a pocket. "Came straight from evening Shabbos services. I don't even notice when it's on."

"You're welcome to wear it."

Leo appraised the bar. I followed his gaze, pride creeping at the results of my hard work: the candlelit tables, couples sitting close to each other, sounds of Ruth Etting singing "Because My Baby Don't Mean Maybe Now" on the phonograph. Frank raised a bottle high as he mixed one of my concoctions. The chandeliers flickered light patterns on the floor.

"Think I'll keep it off here," he said.

I led him to a stool. "Will you let me make you one of my specials?"

"I've only ever had beer or wine on Shabbat."

"I'll start you slowly. How about a Mary Pickford?"

"The actress?"

"The drink." With my usual flourish, I streamed rum into a coupe, then splashed in pineapple juice and a dash of grenadine. "This'll help you get used to the hard stuff." I stirred, and the ice clinked.

"Does one need to get used to the hard stuff?"

"Depends on the hard stuff." I slid the drink to him. "Voilà."

"Aren't you drinking?"

I flashed a flirtatious smile. "Thought you'd never ask." I poured myself a healthy dose of bourbon.

"Straight?"

"Best way once you have a taste for it."

"Cheers."

"*L'chaim*," I responded.

He took a tentative swallow. His head reared back. "Whoa." He rubbed his head again, as if the yarmulke were still there. A nervous tic, perhaps.

"Whoa, good, or whoa, bad?"

"Whoa, packs a punch. But tasty. Compliments to the barkeep."

I curtsied, then sipped mine. "Mmm."

"Isn't that doctored *dreck*?"

"Not this. I reserve this for myself and my special friends. Old Rip Van Winkle, an honest-to-goodness legit distillery."

"Oh?"

"For medicinal purposes only, of course."

"Of course." He smiled.

It's wasn't only the rabbis and priests who could obtain alcohol. The Volstead Act had all sorts of loopholes. Six distilleries in the United States produced bourbon for doctors to prescribe. Luckily, for a premium, some doctors were willing to write a prescription for heartburn or insect bites. "Would you like to try it?" My lipstick stained one side of the glass, a shadow of a kiss.

He held the glass and sniffed. He winced while taking the tiniest of swallows. "Yikes. You drink that for fun?"

I laughed and leaned on the bar. "For so much fun." I moved from flirtatious to provocative, then realized what I was doing. This was Leo. Max's friend. The rabbi's son, for God's sake. I stood and put a bit of distance between us. Leo ran a finger around his collar.

He cleared his throat and took a larger swallow of his cocktail.

"So." I licked my lips and drank my bourbon. "What brings you here?"

"The shul is having trouble making rent."

"Oh?"

"Tateh worries incessantly about his congregants. He can't help them like he used to."

"Asking for more *tzedakah*?" I topped off my glass and held the bottle toward him to see if he wanted another drink.

He shook his head. "Asking you to go into business with me."

I put both elbows on the counter. "What did you have in mind?"

"Someone once reminded me my last name is Umansky too."

"It is indeed." A grin crawled across my face.

"I'll buy you wine. A significant cut, though, goes to the shul."

"What will you tell your father about the money?"

"I'll tell my father it's from the food I'm supplying you with," Leo said. "Food is harmless. He won't mind that."

"Will he buy that?"

"He will because it will be true. It's my one condition."

"Oh?"

"You serve my food. Ten percent of profit to the bar; the rest to me."

"How would you cook here?" The bar wasn't equipped to serve food. But I did like the idea.

"I wouldn't. Get an electric oven. I'll deliver things you can reheat. Knishes. Pretzels. And things eaten cold. Sandwiches. Pickles."

"Not exactly Marlborough House fare."

"This crowd doesn't seem like the type to go for Marlborough House food. I make the kind of food these guys can afford."

"I see your point."

From behind Leo a voice said, "Point about what?" I had been so focused on Leo I hadn't noticed Duke entering the bar.

I grinned and pulled out a glass to start making his cocktail. "Duke, meet Leo. Leo, my boyfriend, Duke. Duke, drink coming up. Heavy on the alcohol, just the way you like it."

Leo held out his hand, but Duke stared a moment, then nodded dismissively. Leo pulled his hand back and rubbed his chin.

"Leo'll be supplying food." No need to mention the wine. I'd tell Duke once it was a done deal.

"Oh?" He peered at Leo, assessing him as a rival.

"It's what the *New Yorker* said we needed."

"How do you know him?" He jerked his head in Leo's direction.

"Leo and I have known each other forever. He's the rabbi's son. A close friend of Max."

Leo fidgeted under the heat of Duke's glare. "Best be heading back," Leo said. "Glad we worked this out."

"Absolutely."

"Nice meeting you, Duke. Good night, Minnie."

After Leo left, Duke glowered. "I don't like him."

"You don't need to like him." I rubbed Duke's arm. "You only need to like me."

∼

The next week, about an hour before opening, Leo carried in a box of potato knishes and sandwiches: chopped egg and pickle; sardine; and cream cheese, olive, and nuts. "The price list." He passed me a sheet of paper.

"I believe it's called a *menu*."

"Reheat the knishes as they're ordered." He popped one in the small oven I'd purchased. After a few minutes, the room filled with the scent of fresh pastry. "Try it."

I bit into it, then spit it right out. "Hot!" When I could feel my tongue again, I took a tentative nibble. "Hmm." Then another. And another. In seconds the knish disappeared. "Why is your knish so much more delicious than the ones on the pushcart?"

He smirked. "I'll never tell. Bread on the sandwiches is homemade too."

That evening, when the bar filled, I stuck a knish in the oven. As the smell wafted through the room, everyone clamored to buy one. Leo's food sold out before nine o'clock. Leo delivered every day except Saturday, and when I mildly suggested Saturdays would be a popular night for food, he scowled. "It's one thing to ask me for wine. It's another thing to ask me to violate the Sabbath."

About a month later, I sat in the office when I was startled by a knock on the door. "Who is it?"

"Leo." He was hours early.

"Come in."

"Can you grab the door?"

When I opened it, he entered holding an unmarked crate.

"Pretzels?" I asked, hoping it wasn't.

"*Shana tova*, Minnie," he said. Rosh Hashanah had been the week before.

"Is it a good year, Leo?"

"It is indeed." He scanned the office until he found the crowbar. He pried the crate open.

It was a crate of wine.

A beautiful crate of wine.

"I am officially a client of the Menorah Wine Company." Leo lifted out a bottle. "Which sells only to rabbis."

I rolled the bottle in my hand, admiring the delicate script on the white label, MALAGA WINE, SPAIN, and beneath that, KOSHER WINE.

"Is it kosher?"

"Not a whiff."

I laughed, gazing at the bottle with pure adoration. "What loveliness."

"You don't get out much, do you." He inclined his head toward the door. "Got two more crates. Be right back."

While Leo carried the boxes in, I slipped behind the bar for a corkscrew.

I uncorked the bottle, held it beneath my nose, and inhaled. I smelled grapes. Not chemicals. Not rubbing alcohol. Just fermented grapes. I filled two glasses and gave one to Leo.

"Bottoms up," I said.

"Careful. This is fortified wine. Higher alcohol content."

I sipped, savoring it. The liquid coated my mouth. Sweet, but not cloying. An oaky aftertaste. Luscious.

"So that's what wine is supposed to taste like." Leo looked at his glass with appreciation. "What do you think?"

"Leo." I held out my hand. "I think we're in the wine business."

Chapter Forty

A few nights later, I broached the subject with Duke of obtaining wine through the shul.

"That's not how it works, Minnie. You know that."

"Duke." I did my best to sound soothing. "It's only wine."

"But not my wine."

"What does it matter? Ninety-nine percent of my booze comes from you."

"Lansky demands a hundred percent loyalty."

"It's from a rabbi." Or close enough to a rabbi. "A heaven-sent gift. What if I went to Lansky myself? Explain things? I can still give him a cut."

"*You* never go to Lansky. That's *my* job." His face remained impassive. "I'll take care of it. You think this is fun and games, but it's serious business." He grabbed his hat and stood. "Sometimes I think you're just a little girl playing grown-up."

My fists clenched beneath the desk. How dare he? I'd been running this bar for over two years. I'd proven time and again this was serious business to me.

We didn't discuss the matter again. Duke kept the liquor flowing, and Leo the wine. Leo avoided Duke. Neither of us said anything, but Leo and I both understood the less Duke saw of Leo, the better.

∼

1930 passed into 1931, and nothing changed—at least nothing for the good. The continuing economic downturn made us antsy. Folks were tense; bar fights broke out more often. I floated extra drinks and sandwiches on the house, wrapping a few up to be taken home to customers' families. I remembered hunger. It crushed me to think of undernourished children. So many places reduced wages, but I couldn't do that to the guys at the bar, so I took less, increasingly dependent on my hatbox savings.

Money went fast. I discovered a slow leak in the pipes and not only needed new plumbing, but I had to replace rotting wood. Then Frank's mom got tuberculosis, so I helped pay to send her to a sanitarium. We could have made more money staying open till 4:00 or 5:00 a.m., but as it was, by the time we closed at 3:00 a.m., I was out of gas. If I could, I'd close earlier. When Duke dropped by and invited me to a night on the town, I was rarely in the mood for more than a broiling at Moskowitz and Lupowitz.

Of course, Duke's mood wasn't much better. The demand for booze was higher than ever, but people wanted cheap liquor, which reduced Duke's cut.

And then there was Lansky. From what I could gather—from Duke, from the gossip at the bar—Duke had shorted the liquor distributor. "An honest mistake," he swore—and Lansky now watched him with a close eye. Duke chafed under Lansky's policing. "Who died and made him king?"

I bit my tongue to keep from replying, "Arnold Rothstein." Instead, every time he whined about Lansky, I poured him another drink.

～

On a Wednesday in June, Duke accompanied his deliverymen. I checked off the inventory on a clipboard. My meticulousness irked Duke. "Don't you trust me?"

"Business is business. Gotta make sure the books balance."

"For what? To pay your taxes?"

He was more on edge than usual. "What's going on, Duke?"

He pinched the top of his nose. "Headache." He sat.

"Do you want headache powder?" I set down the clipboard and moved behind him to rub his shoulders.

"That's not going to fix what ails me."

"Lansky?"

"Lansky. Someone needs to fog that palooka."

My head swung to see if the delivery goons had heard him. Saying the boss should be killed was an excellent way to get yourself offed.

"Don't worry." Duke patted me and jumped up. "Your papers say we're good?" He was trying to tease, but his tone was off.

I ran my finger down the clipboard. "All good."

With a tilt of his hat, Duke was gone.

~

It wasn't all good. As was my habit now, I opened a bottle from each crate and took a sip. One sip an hour, so if something was off, I'd know which one it was. The rum was too sweet, the bourbon too sour, and the gin tasted fine, but dammit, within a half hour, my stomach started to churn.

"For God's sake," I yelled. Big Al came running. "The gin is bad."

"Destroy it?"

"Unless you want to use it to clean the rust from a car." I wanted to return it to Duke, demand my money back, but that was not how this business worked.

We could stretch what gin we had for a couple of days. I featured drink specials with bourbon and rum.

Duke showed on Saturday night, deep furrows between his brows. "Well, hello, pretty lady." His words slurred. To supplement his coffers, Lansky had branched out to narcotics, which was big business, Depression or not. I hoped Duke wasn't sampling the wares.

"Be with you in a sec." When finished with a customer, I mixed Duke my special, using my signature moves: exaggerated shaking with a swivel of my hips, holding the shaker high above the glass so the liquid cascaded, and promising, "This will put you on the roof." Duke loved the theater of it. Sliding the drink in front of him, I asked, "Can we talk business before pleasure?"

"Must we?"

He looked so tired and worn down I almost said *Nah*, but I glanced in the well, where my stock of gin was perilously low. "I'm afraid we must."

With a deep sigh, he walked to the office. "Frank, take over," I called as I pulled off my apron.

When I entered the back room, Duke was already sprawled in the chair. I shut the door and took a seat.

"That last batch of gin you brought me was poison." I spoke mildly, not wanting to set him off.

Yet instead of looking apologetic, a shadow of annoyance passed over Duke's face. "It happens these days."

"'It happens these days'? What happened to 'No one touches Minnie'?"

"Did you get sick?"

Was I loopier from the gin than I thought? Where was his rage from the last time? "Did I get sick?"

"Did you?"

"Well, no." Anger seeped into my confusion. "But if anyone in the bar did, I'd be responsible."

"Not you, the distributor."

"Someone could die, and we're going to argue who's to blame?" His indifference fueled my outrage, my gentleness long gone. "Forget that. Let's bring it back to dollar signs, which you seem more concerned about." Duke's body went rigid, and his feet, which were propped on my desk, swung to the ground. "If I serve bad booze, no one's coming to my bar."

"You do serve bad booze. You're just better than most at disguising it."

"Let me rephrase: poison booze."

"When someone comes to a basement dive on the Lower East Side, he knows the risks involved."

My back arched, and my chin jutted out. "Dive?" Insulting the bar was insulting me.

A touch contrite, he said, "Not a dive. A speakeasy." He put his hands on the desk to push himself up. "I don't want to have this conversation now."

"When should we have it, Duke? I'm almost out of gin."

"I'll get you another case tomorrow." He crossed his arms over his chest. "Are we done?"

"Why are you so angry?"

"First you bring in an outside distributor for your wine. Now you're upset about the booze?"

I threw up my hands. "Duke, this is not unreasonable. I need assurances I'm not going to get more poison. I need assurances I'll get a better quality of booze."

"You want assurances? Run the damn soda shop. There are no assurances in this business."

"Duke." I reached out to stroke his arm, to calm him, but he shook me off.

"If I'd wanted grief tonight, I'd've gone home to my mother." He stormed out, and I followed.

He shoved on his hat in a way that signaled his displeasure and strode out from the bar. I froze. What had just happened?

When I realized patrons were staring, I rubbed my lips to smooth my lipstick, flashed a smile, and returned to the bar. "How're the specials tonight?" The crowd murmured their satisfaction.

Papa had written me; Duke had warned me: don't mix business and pleasure.

I was beginning to see the merit in that statement.

Chapter Forty-One

The next Sunday, early in the day, I was at the office, my head in a cocktail book, when a bottle appeared before me. Old Lancaster. I looked up.

Duke.

He smiled his old half grin. "The pure stuff. For you."

I eyed him warily. "Hello, Duke."

"Aw, Min. Don't be sore. I'd had a rough day."

I softened. "Things worse with Lansky?"

He pursed his lips. "Let's not talk about it."

"Sorry."

"You got your new gin?"

"Yes." If he expected a thanks, he'd be disappointed. I refused to fawn over him for doing the bare minimum of his job.

"It's good?" he asked.

"Define *good*."

"Don't be bent over this."

I set down my book. "How should I feel? This bar is the only thing I have, and I'm being pitted between it and the man I—" My words halted. I'd almost said *The man I love*. But I'd never said it before, and if I was going to, it wasn't going to be like this. Did I love him? The word wanted to bubble to the surface, to be declared, but something held me back.

"The man you what?" His eyebrows rose in a teasing manner.

"The man I enjoy spending time with."

He chuckled. "Just so you know, I enjoy spending time with you too." His hazel eyes sparkled. "What say tonight we have a night on the town? Like we used to."

I wasn't in the mood to forgive so quickly.

"C'mon, Min. We'll go dancing."

"I'll be too tired to dance."

He stroked my cheek. "I'll take you to one of the uptown places."

His touch lit a fire in my belly. "A swanky one?"

"Only the swankiest for you."

~

Duke returned to the bar close to midnight. I ducked into the office to reapply lipstick and fluff my hair. Duke popped in behind me.

"I'll be a second." I preened into my compact mirror.

"It's pretty brisk out," he said.

"It's June. The evening weather is in the fifties."

"You could get chilled."

I put my lipstick down and my hands on my hips. "Duke Hess, if you're trying to weasel out of—" My words dropped when I turned and saw his lopsided grin. He was holding a large rectangular box. "What's that?"

"Open it and see."

I lifted the top, peeled back a layer of pink tissue, and gasped.

"Do you like it?"

My fingers sank into the fabric of a lush fur coat. I pulled it out, marveling at the luxury of it. "For me?"

"Well, I don't think muskrat flatters me."

The coat was a calf-length dream of tawny creaminess with a bolster collar that could be worn up or down. I rubbed the fur against my cheek, not quite believing how soft it was.

"You gonna try it on?" He came behind me and held it open so I could slip in my arms. It draped on me like a warm hug.

"Oh, Duke!"

"You like it?"

"I don't even have words. What's the occasion?"

He kissed my forehead. "I want you to know how much I, what was it? Oh, yes. 'Enjoy spending time with you.'"

The heat spreading through me wasn't just from the warmth of the coat. He cared for me. I liked the way that sounded. "I feel like Lady Astor."

"But much prettier."

I strutted as we walked out. Otto whistled low. One of the women at the bar said, "Well, ain't you the Queen of Sheba! Those are some serious glad rags."

"I'll see you peasants later." I waved my hand as if I were royalty.

"Where you going?" the woman asked.

"Why, I don't know. Where are we going?"

"Now if we tell, everyone will want to go." Duke winked at me.

"We can't have that, can we?" Laughter trailed us out the door.

We hopped in a cab, and Duke directed the driver to Harlem. In the back seat, we necked like we had when we'd first gone out, three years ago. I ran my hands down my own arms almost as much as I ran them down his. My new coat was too warm, but I wasn't going to let that stop me from reveling in it.

The taxi stopped at 131st Street and Seventh Avenue, where a red awning reached over the sidewalk. "Shall we, Min?" Duke jumped to my side of the cab to open the door.

I took his arm, and he led me into Connie's Inn. The cover was exorbitant: $2.50 a person. At the coat check, I didn't want to relinquish my jacket, but I reluctantly handed it over.

We walked into a room bathed in a rainbow of light. Stained glass shimmered on the dance floor. The space was cozier than the Cotton

Club; it didn't look like more than a few hundred folks could fit. The place wasn't yet crowded, so we were able to snag a table.

"Two Manhattans," Duke said to a Negro waiter.

The patrons of the club were white; Negro men served as waiters. My neighborhood housed immigrants from all corners; however, none were as dark skinned as the people in Harlem. These Negros were Americans—born right here in this country—and yet not Americans, because they couldn't go wherever they wanted or do whatever they pleased. If they were born here and not full citizens, what did it mean for me, a Jew from Bratsyana?

At 12:45 a.m., the revue began. The Hot Chocolates came onstage. Leona Williams sang with a voice of honey, and Baby Cox hoofed in a number called "Say It with Your Feet." When the show ended, my throat was raw from hooting. The house orchestra struck up, and Duke asked me to dance.

With his arms around me, I softened into his shoulder, running my fingers through the hair at the nape of his neck. As we swayed to the music, he hummed in my ear, his breath sending shivers of anticipation through me.

"Should we get out of here?" I whispered.

"I thought you'd never ask." He paid our tab—an astounding fourteen dollars.

At the coat check, I handed the girl my ticket as a man called out, "Duke?"

Duke's hand dropped mine like it was hot coal. He stepped away, putting distance between us.

"Herman." Duke practically bowed. "What an unexpected pleasure."

Duke spoke with a deference I'd never heard before.

The man, Herman, looked from Duke to me and back to Duke. "Who's that?" Herman was of medium height with a soft round face, doughy cheeks, and lips so thin they disappeared when his mouth closed.

"Who's who?" Duke's brow creased. His eyes fell on me. "Oh." His voice tinged with surprise. "This is Minnie. Just ran into her." He moved farther away from me. "She runs a bar on the Lower East Side."

I swallowed hard. What was going on? Clearly Duke didn't want this man to know we were together. Was he protecting me? Or himself? Herman studied me.

"Your coat, ma'am." The girl handed over my fur.

"Your little bar must be doing well," Herman said.

"Can't complain."

"Not many folks can afford a coat like that in this economy."

I shifted. "As I said, can't complain."

"You here alone?" Herman asked.

"Here with my girlfriend Sylvia, but when her boyfriend arrived, I got the bum's rush."

"Why don't we chat, Duke?"

"I'll show her to a taxi. Not the safest out there," Duke said.

"I'll wait for you."

Duke placed his hand on the small of my back and ushered me out.

"What was that about?" I asked as Duke waved down a cab.

"Herman Fiedler. An associate."

"Never heard of him. What's he got to do with you?"

"Long story."

"I've got time," I said as a taxi slowed next to me.

"I don't." He opened the door, nervously glancing back to the club. "Look, I promise to explain." Again he looked behind him. "He's waiting for me."

A crease formed in the center of his brow. "Fine." I climbed into the taxi.

Duke leaned through the window of the front seat, passed the driver a five, and gave him my address. The cab pulled away before I could say goodbye.

〜

Sleep evaded me. What was Duke up to?

I arrived at the bar early on Monday, sagging with fatigue. To pass the time, I threw myself into cleaning, scrubbing the mirrors with vinegar, taking a mop to the floor.

"Expecting the King of England?" Big Al said when he showed up.

"Place is disgusting," I grumbled. "Why can't anyone keep the bar clean?"

"What's your beef?"

I propped myself on the mop handle. "What do you hear about Duke? What's his deal with Fiedler?"

Big Al abruptly busied himself collecting last night's trash. "I don't hear nothing about Duke."

"Big Al." I set aside the mop.

"People like to talk. No one ever gets it right."

"So what, exactly, are they getting wrong about him?"

Big Al grabbed a box of empties to put in the back room. I blocked him. "Tell me."

"Nothing good comes from gossip."

"Except your ability to keep a job."

He shook his head. Then he said, "Rumor has it he's steppin' out with Golde Fiedler."

I must have misheard. "Golde? I was talking about a Herman Fiedler."

"Father and daughter."

"Stepping out?" That couldn't be true. "Are you sure?" Just last night he'd told me he cared for me. I *knew* he cared for me.

"No, I'm not sure. That's why it's called *gossip* rather than *fact*."

"Who are they?" A gnawing worry nipped at me.

"Herman Fiedler is one of Owney Madden's goons."

I blinked rapidly at the name *Owney Madden*. Owney Madden, who ran the Cotton Club. Owney Madden, who was called "the Killer." Owney Madden, who did not get along with Lansky. Those nips of worry turned into stabs. Duke *cared* for me! Duke cared for *me*. But no matter how many times I told myself that, I also knew he hated Lansky. Did he hate Lansky more than he cared for me? "What's Duke doing with Madden?"

"Not sure."

"Does Lansky know?"

Big Al shrugged. "Probably. Might be biding his time, waiting for something to happen."

"I'm sure he's not sleeping with Golde." I grabbed the mop again so I'd have something to do with my hands. I was no longer feeling so sure.

Big Al shrugged again. "Do you know where Duke goes when he ain't here?"

I bit my lip. No matter how much I crumbled on the inside, I had to appear tough.

"Golde," Big Al continued, "is a way to cozy up to her father. Her father will do anything she asks."

I didn't want to believe Big Al. My brain said, *Duke'd never do that to you!* But why were my hands shaking? Why did I feel like I might throw up? Why did my head fill with cotton?

I wasn't an idiot. I knew Duke did things I didn't want to know about. But I thought that was limited to how he handled his racket. Not how he handled his women.

I wanted to doubt Big Al. But I didn't.

The tears wouldn't hold back, so I dropped the mop and ran to the door. "I'll be back."

The minute the bar door closed behind me, the tears rushed out like water from a hydrant. I kept my head down so no one would see, except my body heaved in an obvious way.

I dashed to my apartment, taking the stairs by two. I don't know how long I sat on my kitchen floor, sobbing. I yanked on my hair, wanting to feel physical pain. I balled my hands into fists and pounded them on my thighs. I screamed.

I didn't stop until there was a knock on the door. "Malka?" Mrs. Shukat from next door said. "Are you all right? Should I get the police?"

"Thank you, Mrs. Shukat." My voice was hoarse. "I'm fine."

I wasn't fine.

But I had to pretend I was. I washed my face and layered on makeup to hide the evidence of my sobs.

Don't appear weak.

My breath returned to normal. From the chair where I'd put it last night, I grabbed the jacket, then ran back to the bar.

In the back room, the box from last night still sat on my desk, the box for the fur coat that had seemed so sumptuous and romantic the night before. Now it made me feel cheap. Like another woman in his stable. The gift wasn't from love; it was from guilt. I folded the jacket back into the box. I caressed the fur, trying to remember how special I'd felt, but that memory had already been replaced by another woman.

I covered the box and scrawled a note just as Frank arrived.

"Frank, can you place the liquor order today?"

"No problem," he said.

"Make sure Duke sees I left him something in the back room."

"Got it, boss."

As I left the bar, my mind roiled. Duke had never said he was dating only me, but we'd been seeing each other for three years. Three years. We never made promises. We never talked about a future. He never took me to meet his family. Yet I assumed, someday, we'd settle down.

On Delancey Street, I ducked into the Loew's. The movie, *Indiscreet*, was halfway through. Fitting, I thought. I stared at the screen, not seeing it, picturing Duke with another woman. His hands on someone else's breasts, his kisses down someone else's neck, someone else's body beneath his. Was Duke only stringing her along for business? To chummy up to Madden? Did that make it better or worse?

By the time I left the theater, the main show had played three times, and I'd heard Hoover discuss the tariff bill on the newsreel more than anyone could have wanted.

When I got back to the bar, it was late. Frank and Wesley poured drinks for the usual crowd as I headed into my office. The note I'd written sat on my desk.

Beneath my scrawl—*Perhaps this would look better on Golde than it does on me*—was a terse response: *Don't be like this.*

But the box was gone.

Chapter Forty-Two

I moved through the week like I was swimming in sludge. When questioned by Otto, I told him what had happened, and within three hours, everyone knew. I didn't care, but I couldn't stand that everyone treated me delicately. I didn't want maudlin; I wanted for it to never have happened. I avoided the bar during that week when I thought Duke might be around.

But at 6:00 a.m. on Saturday, a banging on the apartment door jolted me awake.

"Minnie! Minnie, God dammit. Open up, before I break the damn door."

I wanted to ignore him, but his pounding had already woken the baby down the hall, the child's wails emanating through the thin walls. I threw on a robe and yanked the door open. "Keep it down." My words hissed. "You're waking the dead."

His body pitched into the room.

"Jesus, you reek!" The sour stench of booze and vomit emanated from his pores. In all the time I'd spent with Duke, I'd never seen him drunk. He was blotto. He crumpled into a chair.

"Minnie, I need you."

"I hear you need Golde Fiedler." *Tell me it's not true. Tell me I'm the only one.*

"Minnie, you're my baby."

"You're a two-timing tomcat." *Tell me! All will be forgiven.*

"Don't be like that."

"Are you sleeping with Golde Fiedler?" *Does he hear how my voice trembles?*

"That's business." He snatched at my hand but missed it. "You're pleasure."

My tremble subsided. I hardened. I stepped out of reach. "I'm pleasure?" *A whore is pleasure. I am not.*

"You're more than pleasure." He grasped for me again and fell out of the chair. "Minnie, I have feelings for you." He climbed back into it. How much had he drunk? Had he sampled his own narcotic wares?

"Feelings?"

"I love you, baby."

How I would have adored hearing those words only weeks ago. But now they were tainted. While a part of me wanted to declare my love, my rational side stayed firmly in charge. "Do you plan to introduce me to your family? To marry me?"

He swayed in the seat. "Can a guy get a cuppa coffee?"

He looked so pathetic, and from the way his head dropped into his hands, I suspected the room spun. I put water in the coffeepot, not for him but to prevent myself from having to clean up his puke.

"Drop Golde." I stood facing the sink so I wouldn't have to look in his eyes.

"I can't."

"You can't, or you won't?"

"I need Madden. Lansky isn't giving me room to breathe. I keep Golde happy, her father helps me. Look at me, Min." I turned. He covered his mouth with his fist. I worried he was about to upchuck. "I don't like it any better than you do. But Herman Fiedler is not someone to anger."

"Neither am I." I crossed my arms, my fingers digging into my skin hard enough I'd have marks later that day. "I won't be your other woman."

"You'll always be number one." He stood, wavered, and grabbed for my waist. I stiffened.

How had it come to this? "You have to choose, Duke. Me or her."

"I can't choose."

My throat constricted, as if I'd swallowed the wrong way. Breathing was difficult. *Don't show any weakness.* I choked out my words. "Get out, Duke. We're done."

"Come on, Min—don't be like this."

"Get out." He needed to leave. He needed to be out of my sight.

"What about my coffee?"

"Here." I snatched my clutch from the shelf. I pulled out a nickel and tossed it at him. "Buy yourself a cup of joe."

The plink of the coin dropping reverberated. Duke's face pinched. He pushed back his shoulders, expanding his chest. He didn't seem quite as drunk anymore. "You'll regret this, Minnie."

"Someone once told me, 'Don't mix business with pleasure.' I'd prefer to do neither with you." I scooted around him and opened the door.

"You're making a mistake."

"Goodbye, Duke." I pushed him, and he stumbled out of the apartment. I locked the door behind him and held my breath. *Please make him go away.* After a moment, his footsteps retreated down the stairs.

I leaned against the door, tears I didn't realize I'd been holding streaming down my face. I stayed there, crying, until the coffeepot percolated.

I wiped my face and poured myself a cup.

My hand shook, and coffee sloshed on the floor. I wanted to call for someone to clean it up. *Mama, I've made a mess. Gertie, can you bring me a rag? Duke, stop laughing, and give me a hand. Max, where did you put the dish towels?*

But there was no one. I had no one.

~

The apartment once again filled with heartache. My loneliness took root, growing offshoots that reached the ceiling, spreading through the room, wrapping around my neck, making it difficult for me to breathe.

I needed to talk to someone. I had no one who could understand. Except, maybe . . .

On Sunday, dressed in my three-piece wool crepe shirt, the most conservative outfit I owned, I boarded the BMT, headed to Queens.

This was my first time leaving Manhattan. Since the trip to America, I hadn't crossed a body of water, and while the East River was considerably shorter than the Atlantic, it felt monumental.

I was going to see my mother.

~

It took well over an hour for me to find the cemetery, and then once in the cemetery, despite the map the caretaker had shown me, it took another thirty minutes to find her grave.

The crying began before I even found her.

Finally, I located her. Her tombstone was made of marble, perched on a manicured lot. Nothing like the fieldstone of Zayde's and Anshel's graves. I put my hand on it, feeling the smoothness of the top, the indention of the engraved words. FEIGE SOFFER, BELOVED WIFE AND MOTHER. Hebrew letters I couldn't read were inscribed beneath. I waited to feel her presence, for her to speak to me. I closed my eyes and breathed deeply. *Come, Mama. I need you.* The only thing that touched me was the bitter air.

With my skirt, it wasn't easy to sit, but I managed, with my legs crossed in front of me as if I were a child.

"Mama," I said out loud. "It's been bad." I pulled at the grass.

I proceeded to tell her everything. Papa's arrest. Running the bar. Max leaving me. My sorrows flooded from me, cascading into her grave. I confessed my indiscretions with Duke. I told her what Louise was like, her favorite foods, how once she crawled, she never let Gertie move more than a step away from her. I mimicked Gertie's speech, the adorable way she pointed in her ABC book and screeched *ephant* instead of *elephant*. How her own name became *Gurie*. How she stood in a chair at the table to stir cookie batter, flour flying everywhere, just as I had with Mama when I was a child. I recited Gertie's favorite poem for her.

Then I choked out my greatest sin: giving the girls away.

"Mama. The girls were being hurt. They were hungry. Uncle Aaron said we should. The rabbi said we should. I'm sorry. I'm sorry. I'm sorry," I babbled, the words and my tears overlapping, my body heaving, shaking as if in deep prayer.

"I'm so unhappy. I don't know what to do. I need your blessing, Mama." I struggled to catch my breath. "I need your approval. I need a sign that you forgive me. Please, Mama. Please."

For an hour, I pleaded to her, begged her, beseeched her. What was I expecting? A bolt of lightning? A sudden rainbow? For a bush to erupt in flames? My body shrank into a tight ball, and all I wanted was to sink into the ground, to be with Mama again.

It was hours before my sobs died down.

Evening turned the sky dusky. I sat up, allowing myself time to compose. I was a mess. Grass covered my skirt, my throat closed, my body drained of the will to move. I could only imagine what I looked like: nose inflamed, eyes bright red, puffy cheeks. With my drenched handkerchief, I tried to wipe my face, but it was futile.

With a deep sigh, I stood, brushing off my clothing.

I needed to find a rock to place on her gravestone, but none appeared on the groomed lawn. Panic rose in my chest as I got on my hands and knees to search. I was desperate. How could there be no stones? Why hadn't I chosen one to bring with me, from the many found in the city parks? Only small pieces of gravel lay on the ground.

I fought the urge to steal a rock from another grave, but Mama would have been horrified. I'd have to make do with gravel. Not an auspicious ending to my visit.

As I made my way back to the city, I had to wonder. *Was that my sign?*

~

Frank took over the liquor orders. We consulted in the morning, and I left when it was time for Duke to arrive.

The restaurant where Leo cooked suffered in the downturn, and his hours were cut. He spent afternoons in the bar, making sandwiches to order. I instructed him, though, to make himself scarce—and fast—if Duke came by. No need to further stoke Duke's fury.

While I avoided Duke at work, I couldn't avoid him in my mind. Thoughts of him filled me, tormenting me. My body craved his. I ached for his warmth next to me in bed. I longed to be in his arms on a dance floor or making him one of my specials. He slipped into the hole where Gertie, Louise, and Mama resided. I hadn't thought there was any more room in there, but the cavern appeared to be bottomless.

The worst part was I understood his betrayal. Weren't we all doing what we had to? Whatever it took to survive?

I'd pushed aside my own brother to run this bar. How could I blame Duke for taking care of himself?

And yet I did.

~

Sunday afternoons, when Max came for dinner, he'd listen to me sob, doing a terrible job of hiding how relieved he was. "This is for the best, Min. You shouldn't be involved with a goon."

But my whole life was filled with goons.

~

By the beginning of December, I'd had it. "Frank, we can't work with Duke any longer."

"Do you have a choice?"

"Probably not. But if he's weaseling his way into Madden's crowd, we need to keep our distance."

"Oh, is that why?" Frank crossed his arms over his chest and raised his eyebrows.

I ignored his—correct—insinuation. "It would be a shame if someone told Lansky that Duke was moving on."

A gruff voice from the other side of the bar said, "What makes you think Lansky don't already know? Duke don't seem to be having any problems with it."

Dammit! I knew better than to talk in front of customers. But I was careless, still so hazy from the breakup that I was slipping up.

"Aw, Chubs," I said to the jowly man who wore a deadpan expression. "I'm just running my mouth. Nothing's changing." Fear threaded icily through my limbs. "Let me get you another drink. On me."

"What about me?" His buddy, Squint, a lumpish man with an impish face, held out his glass.

"Of course." I pulled out my good bourbon and gave them each a generous pour.

"Not bad," Chubs said.

Not bad, my ass. That was pure bourbon, the finest anywhere.

"How much do you like it?" I asked.

"I like it enough that I didn't hear nothin'."

With a quick nod, I headed back to my office.

Something had to be done and soon. I didn't trust Duke. And I didn't trust Chubs to keep his mouth shut.

The new year loomed: 1932. I wanted a fresh start. A new beginning. One without Duke in it.

Chapter Forty-Three

New Year's Eve. 1932. Two years of that damn Depression, and the end still wasn't in sight. Streamers and balloons festooned the bar, paper noisemakers scattered about. I chose three festive drink specials: the Millionaire, the Whiz-Bang, and the Tuxedo. I doctored apple cider with hooch to make a poor man's champagne, since no one could afford the real stuff anymore.

The bar was hopping. I pushed back tables to make room for dancing. Sylvia arrived with her boyfriend du jour, and the regular gaggle of girls turned up. Otto, Ben, and Walt grumbled over God knows what, until one of Sylvia's friends asked Walt to dance. He turned tongue-tied, but he acquiesced. Turned out he was a hoofer. Two other girls dragged Otto and Ben onto the dance floor, and I didn't think those three had ever had a better time.

Big Al allowed entrance to those we knew and turned away the unfamiliar. Too much booze combined with too many heartbreaks made folks mercurial on a holiday. Regulars filled the bar. Frank and Wesley poured drinks at breakneck speed, one continuous stream flowing from a tap. Leo came in late, bringing platters of cookies he'd baked, a gift for our loyal customers. The cookies disappeared in minutes. Leo tried all three specials, unusual for the man who usually nursed one for the night. Even Max came, figuring the cops had better things to do than raid a small-time speakeasy on New Year's Eve. He brought a girl he'd met at the diner, a delicate thing from the teaching college. Adina had a tinkly laugh and iridescent green eyes that didn't leave Max.

The only thing missing was Duke.

And I missed him.

Sylvia didn't understand because she operated on a merry-go-round of men. "All you gotta do is find someone new. You forget the old guy the second you see the new one."

Duke wasn't so easy to quit.

As much as I hated it, I was waiting for Duke to come to his senses, dump Golde, return to me, to realize I was more important than working for Madden.

But that didn't happen.

So my own drinks were doubles. I plastered on a smile and served the crowd, and when the hour neared midnight, we counted down to 1932. When others found sweethearts to kiss at the turn of the year, I turned my back to the room, not wanting to see the happiness on all those faces.

~

January 1. I'd stumbled to bed at 4:00 a.m., exhaustion rooted in my chest. My feet and calves seethed from hours of standing. My head clouded, filled with the cigarette smoke that had endlessly swirled, whispers of a hangover gnawing me. My entire body burned for sleep. But the bar didn't care how I felt. We hadn't bothered to clean last night—we were too drunk and tired—so I dragged myself in early to put the place to rights.

"What time did you get here?" Big Al asked when he arrived at two o'clock and saw how spotless the bar looked. "Wouldn't kill you to stay home a day."

But the thing was, it might. The memories suffocated me—memories of what had been and what would no longer be. I might be bleary. I might be headachy. I might sleepwalk through a shift, but the bar was where I wanted to be.

About half an hour later, I was writing my list of specials in the back room when a clap of thunder startled me. Was it raining? I rubbed the bridge of my nose, trying to understand something, a thought not quite coming to the surface. I needed more sleep. By the time it hit me—I couldn't hear the weather in my cellar room—the door to my office flew open so hard it slammed against the back wall, making the crates in the room shiver.

"What the—" I stood, my chair stumbling backward. I didn't finish my sentence as a compact, beefy man reeled back his arm and punched me in the stomach.

He lunged for me, but I ducked beneath his arms and ran into the bar. A second man was behind the counter with a crowbar. I couldn't see much of their faces under their hats. The one behind the bar was tall, black curls dripping from his hat. The iron bashed through the back shelves, every bottle tumbling to the floor, shattering in a rain of glass.

The sound transported me to the old country, to huddling in the cellar at home as men in khaki-gray jackets and furajka caps stole food from our kitchens, smashed plates on our dirt floor, ripped the curtains from the walls. Bubbe squeezed me tightly, my face pressed against her bosom, her hand hurting me as she held it over my mouth so I couldn't make noise.

I refused to be that terrified little girl again.

I charged toward the man with the crowbar, but my legs flew out from under me as an arm grabbed me from behind, then tossed me to the ground. Kicks to my side immobilized me as I curled to protect my stomach. Trying to escape the blows, I rolled over, yet I stilled when I saw Big Al. He lay on the floor, blood puddling beneath him. The clap of thunder. It wasn't an act of God. It was an act of Smith & Wesson. "Big Al!"

His eyes fluttered.

I stretched toward him, but before I reached him, I was lifted, as if I were a rag doll, and hurled across the room. As I landed, I heard a crack, and my body convulsed.

The compact man hauled crates from the office. "This, little girl."

Little girl. I knew that voice.

He dropped a box at my feet, twelve bottles exploding, red wine streaming out, a river with a broken dam. The tall guy retrieved another crate and handed it to the first. It crashed down. "Is not." Another crate dashed upon the floor. "Properly sourced." He seized the final crate. "Wine."

The tall guy said, "Wait." He pulled out a few bottles, then stashed them in a bag. He threw another at the mirror behind the bar, wine and glass shooting like fireworks as the mirror exploded.

I couldn't move. I couldn't breathe. The pain in my side radiated outward, reaching into every joint, every muscle, every limb. Never had I been so aware of each and every organ, each and every body part.

"Your wine comes from Lansky." The beefy guy leaned so close I could feel his breath on my face. "Only Lansky."

He sneered and, with his index finger, pushed up the brim of his hat. The ferrety eyes, the slash on his cheek, his sneer. My fear turned to fury.

"Riley."

"Told you you'd regret it."

"Do we bump her?" the other asked. He was the goon who had accompanied Riley to the bar that day, the one who had been eerily handsome. Now his face contorted with a chilling combination of viciousness and pleasure. He enjoyed his work.

"Orders to keep her alive," Riley said.

"As if we obey orders," he replied with a chuckle as he delivered a swift strike to my side.

Riley hovered over me. He stroked his scar. "I believe a bit of payback is called for, little girl."

Without realizing I had the energy to do it, I kicked upward with as much power as I could muster, making contact with his groin. He fell to his knees, one hand shooting to his private parts. He gasped, "Why you—" but I couldn't hear what he said because the ringing in my ears, as the fist of his partner hit the side of my face, made the words unintelligible.

The walls of the bar shimmered. Spots danced behind my eyelids.

"You motherfucking—" I began, but nothing else came out as a bottle slammed down on my skull.

Part Four

Chapter Forty-Four

Darkness and pain enveloped me, an unholy pain. Nothing existed outside the pain.

As my eyelids fluttered, slivers of light eked through, making the torture in my head scream with rage. Sounds amplified, a cacophony of agony.

"Shut it all up." My words slurred, my tongue thick.

"Minnie? Can you hear me?"

The voice was an echo from far away. Max shimmered into view, a mirage.

"Max." Did I speak out loud?

"Nurse," he called. "She's awake!"

Was I, though?

"Max," I said again, before drifting back into blackness.

～

The next time I awoke, the noises around me were dulled, as if filtered through wads of cotton. I shook my head to clear it, but spasms of pain shot through my brain. I must have moaned, because a woman in white rushed to my bedside.

"You're awake." The sound was muffled.

"Max?" My mouth was dry, as if I'd been on a drinking binge.

"Your brother?" She held my wrist and fell silent as she counted beats. She dropped my arm and lifted my eyelids, shining a light that made me wince. "Visiting ended hours ago." Something pulled on my face. A bandage came off, soaked in red. "You've had quite the parade of visitors. A motley assortment. Your brother, of course. And a lot of other men."

"What men?" Had Riley come to finish what he'd started?

"Three, shall we say, characters? Older men. And a younger man with one of those skullcaps. An Irish guy. One woman. About your age." Otto, Walt, and Ben. Leo. Frank. Sylvia.

No shades covered the windows. Lights glinted from buildings below us, bright in the pitch dark of night. "What time is it?"

"Near midnight. My shift's almost over."

I turned my head, and fingers of fire stretched through my neck. I groaned. A bed to the left held a woman lying inside a cloth triangle with square mesh cutouts. It hung suspended from wooden poles, with a tube running to a hulking tank. The nurse saw my gaze. "That's an oxygen tent."

"Why does she need it?"

The nurse ignored the question. "You had quite a throbbing. You'll be hurting for a while." I expected a nurse to be demure, but she didn't mince words. "Who beat you senseless?"

"No one. Fell down the stairs."

She clucked her tongue. "Fellas who brought you in said more or less the same thing." She taped gauze to my face. "Men aren't worth it. Rotten creatures."

Ah, she assumed a husband or boyfriend did this to me. "Just the stairs."

She raised the top of the bed to bring me to a seated position. "Open your mouth." She dropped in two tablets and brought a glass of water to my lips. "Swallow." The pills were stones scratching at my throat. "Those will help with the pain and let you sleep."

"I've done nothing but sleep for . . . How long have I been here?"

"This is your third night. It's Monday, almost Tuesday morning. And being unconscious is not the same as sleeping."

"I'll never sleep with all the noise in here."

"Mm-hmm," she said.

I wanted to reply, but nothing came out as my eyelids fell shut.

~

The sounds during the day were sharper: the clatter of bedpans, the clip-clop of nurses, the wails of patients. The ward was filled with beds. Five rows. Wooden dividers separated rows of four beds—two on each side divided by an aisle spacious enough to accommodate stretchers. Tall windows surrounded the room, filling it with light.

"I knew you'd wake as soon as I stepped out for a smoke."

I blinked until I focused on the owner of the voice. Frank. He sat in the chair by my bed, the smell of tobacco emanating from him.

"I don't care if you smoke."

He indicated the bed next to mine. "You don't, but she does."

The sign by it warned against smoking and flammables.

"The second I pulled out a matchbook, the nurse hustled me out. Apparently oxygen and smoking don't mix. Who knew? I breathe the stuff every day, and it's never interfered with my cigarettes." He grinned, no doubt hoping to lighten the mood.

He hadn't.

He chewed on his lower lip. "Can you remember what happened?"

Could I? I searched my memory, trying to picture it. "It was . . . raining?" Why couldn't I remember?

"No," Frank said, "it was a clear morning."

Why did I think rain? Because of the thunder. Because of the . . .

"Big Al!" Though the pain was intense, I bolted into a seated position. Frank hurriedly cranked up the bed so the mattress met my back. "Big Al was shot!"

"Shh, shh." Frank sat back down and took my hand. It was an odd gesture—we never touched—and I wanted to find it comforting but instead found it cloying. "Big Al is here. He's in critical condition. Alive."

"Oh God." A phrase of Mama's floated through my mind. *Vai vind iz meine yoren.* Woe is me and my years. "Oh God." This time I shouted. I tried to get out of bed, tried to move, throwing off the covers, swinging my legs.

"What are you doing?" Frank jumped up and pinned me down.

Images of Big Al came unbidden. Lying on the floor. The blood pooling beside him.

"I need to go to Big Al." A cord was strung to a needle in my arm. I yanked at it.

"Minnie, stop!" Frank held my shoulders tight. "Nurse! Nurse!"

Nurses bustled over as I screamed, "Let me go!"

"I got this," one of the nurses said.

A needle stabbed me. Spots danced in front of my eyes. The walls undulated. Then blackness.

~

The next time I awoke, Max sat by me. My eyes were crusty, but when I moved to rub them, I couldn't. "What the—" My arms were bound to the metal sides of the bed.

"Minnie." Relief oozed from him.

"What is this?" I shook my hands, which were restrained with a cloth binding.

"You gave the nurses a hard time."

"I have to see Big Al." It was my fault Big Al was here. I had to see him with my own eyes, had to make sure he was still breathing.

"You're not well enough. He's not well enough."

"Get these things off me."

"So you can make a run for it? No."

"God dammit, Max Soffer, get these things—"

A clearing of a throat interrupted me. A tall man in a white coat approached my bed. "Miss Soffer," he said. "I'm Dr. Harris."

"Can you take these off me, Dr. Harris?"

"Can you be trusted to stay put?"

I attempted to flash him a winning smile, but it hurt my cheeks. I was sure it came out a crooked clown's grin. "Of course."

He raised his eyebrows. "I'm not sure I believe you, but we can give it a try." He signaled a nurse to untie me. "If these need to go back on, they don't come off until you leave."

"Which will be when?"

"Another day or two. We suspected internal bleeding. We think it's stopped, but we want to be certain. Most of your other wounds simply need time. There's nothing we can do about the broken ribs. The bruises will heal on their own, but you'll have to be careful about cleaning the cut on your face so it doesn't become infected."

Cut on my face? Everything hurt so much; no individual pain rose to the surface.

"That man didn't take any mercy on you." He peered at me over the top of a clipboard. "Are you sure you don't want to report anything to the police?"

"Nothing to report. I fell down a flight of stairs."

"Those flights of stairs are a menace to society. I can't tell you how many people are in this hospital thanks to those stairs."

"She needs to be more careful," Max said. He wasn't talking about stairs.

"Uh-huh. Well, rest, and we'll work on getting you home."

"Thanks, Doc," I said, thinking, *I have no home to return to.*

～

On Thursday morning, Uncle Aaron stopped by. What could I say to Uncle Aaron? I was so ashamed of the disgrace I had brought to the family name that when the nurse told me he was coming in, I pretended to be asleep.

He sat by me, stroking my hair, mumbling prayers for so long I did fall asleep. When I awoke, he was gone, a plate of Aunt Sara's cookies by my bedside. I placed one in my mouth, but it hurt too much to chew.

So much pain. But I was thinking more clearly.

That wasn't necessarily a good thing.

I stared at the ceiling, listening to the whir of the oxygen tank next to me, trying to focus on the voices around me, hoping they'd shut out the memories.

Big Al on the floor, the crimson liquid surrounding him, the crimson liquid that filled my vision, my nose, my lungs, drowning me. The leer of Riley peering out from beneath the brim of his hat. The sound of the crowbar as it swept through the bottles.

I curled into a ball, eyes squeezed shut, hands over ears to block out the shattering glass, the crunching wood, the thud of flesh upon the floor, the crack of shots. I thought of Vinnie under the El, of Gino and Paolo demanding our nickels, of Max lying on the ground as boots rained upon him. I thought of Anshel in a grave I would never visit, that no one would visit, because who was left to remember him? I thought of the yelling between Mama and Papa and the deep unhappiness that had draped Mama when she had lost the babies. I thought of Papa in jail, the hair on his face making him look like the Jew he'd been a lifetime ago, the one he had tried to escape becoming by sailing to America, the place where he'd traded open skies for a tiny cell crawling with rats.

This was my life? This was how far I'd come?

For the first time, I was grateful Gertie and Louise were safe. Grateful they had escaped this life. My two American-born sisters leading their American lives with American parents. None of this would touch them. Max had a way out; he would become a lawyer.

But what about me? What was my way out? The bar had been the one place truly mine.

And Riley had stolen it from me.

～

Friday morning, the doctor discharged me. "You need rest. But there's nothing more we can do for you. Might as well recuperate at home for free than pay for a hospital bed. Clean the wound on your face three times a day. Starting next week, let it breathe before rebandaging. As for your broken ribs, make sure to take deep breaths as often as possible—the biggest risk is an infection in the lungs." He jutted his chin toward the bed next to me, the woman in the tent. "You don't want to end up in one of those. Aspirin for pain."

After the doctor left, the nurse helped me remove the white hospital gown. She had a pile of clothes.

"Is that what I wore when I came in?" I didn't want to face evidence of that night.

"We had to cut the dress off you." She maneuvered the garment over my head, taking great care at keeping a sheet over me for modesty, making sure not to graze the bandage on my face. "Your brother brought you fresh clothes."

"Is he here?"

She shook her head.

The dress was a loose shift, for which I was relieved, because the thought of clothing binding my sides was agonizing.

I could hardly stand.

"Lean on me," the nurse said. With my weight on her, I shuffled across the floor. I prickled with tears; I was alone.

We made our way—slowly, slowly. The nurse said, "Your father is waiting in the hall to take you home."

Ice surged through my veins. "My father? That's impossible. My father is—"

I didn't finish the sentence. The nurse, misunderstanding, turned a bright pink as she stammered, "Oh, I'm so sorry. I assumed—" She thought my father was dead. I didn't correct her. "Well, then, an elderly gentleman is here to assist you."

My confusion dissolved when I saw Rabbi Umansky in the doorway. He rushed to help me. I was surprised how ably he moved. He took my other arm, though I didn't lean too heavily on his frail body. It was more comfort than support.

"Malka, Malka, Malka. What have they done?"

Tears of relief streamed down my face. The nurse hurried to dab them. "None of that. You don't want to wet your bandage."

The rabbi led me down the hall to a chair. "Let's wait here. Leo will be up in a moment."

"Leo's here?"

"He's taking care of the hospital bill."

"Leo's paying the hospital bill?"

"Malka, Leo is not paying the bill. The community is paying the bill. This is where *tzedakah* goes. This is what we do."

"But why me? I don't go to synagogue. I don't pray. I'm barely a Jew."

"Never say that." His voice was cutting. "You are a Jew. Whether you pray or not, you have a Jewish *neshama*, a Jewish soul." His tone softened. "You are one of us, Malka. You will always be one of us."

I thought of my father's demands not to accept charity. How everyone wanted something from you. How you had to make your own way in the world.

Except, this felt nice. Rabbi Umansky had never asked anything of me. Would I be beholden to him? And if I was, would that be so bad?

"Thank you," I whispered, as if afraid my father would overhear.

Bandage be damned. I let my head fall to the rabbi's shoulder as tears fell. Gently, the rabbi patted my back. We sat in silence until Leo found us.

Leo wrapped an arm around my shoulders, and I leaned on him. His arm felt safe, and I wanted to stay there, protected. The rabbi stood at my other side, arms out, ready to catch me, not that he was strong enough to do so. As we made our way to the main hall, I stopped.

"Can you go on?" the rabbi asked.

"Yes," I said, though I wasn't sure. "I need to check on Big Al."

The rabbi looked confused.

"He was with me the night of . . ."

Leo walked to the desk and consulted with a nurse. He called, "What's Big Al's last name?"

From the depths of my brain came "Reed."

The nurse flipped through a ledger.

Leo said, "He's on the third floor. You sure you're up for this?"

"I have to see him."

~

We took the elevator to his floor.

Rabbi Umansky and Leo led me to the men's ward, which, even in daylight, was dark. This room was smaller, with fewer beds. A nurse sat by the door.

"I need to see Al Reed."

She shook her head. "I'm afraid it's not visiting hours."

"Please," I said.

"Is there any way . . . ?" the rabbi asked. "She's been through so much."

The nurse's gaze lingered on my face. "Not for long."

She led me to a bed by the window. Big Al lay there, swathed in gauze. "Will he be okay?" I whispered, not wanting to disturb the quiet.

She picked up the chart by his bed. "They operated to remove the bullet, but it was in such a location it was deemed safer to leave it in. It nicked his liver. He's not out of the woods yet."

"Can he hear me?"

"Unsure," she said. "I'll give you a minute."

She scooted to the door. I sat in the chair by the bed, stifling a groan; the upright position aggravated my ribs. Big Al's skin was sallow. The giant of a man lay shriveled and small. I pulled back the covers to find his hand.

"Big Al, it's me, Minnie. This is my fault. I'm so sorry." The tears came again. I resigned myself to a life of crying. "You have to get better. You're my rock, my friend. How can I do it without you?" I held his hand tighter. "Please, Big Al, please. I'm so sorry." I repeated this over and over, until the nurse startled me.

"Time to leave."

I didn't let go of his hand.

"Miss." The nurse gripped my shoulders, pulling me up. "You need to go." She was gentle but firm.

She led me to the door, where once again, Leo and the rabbi took me by the arms and guided me out.

Chapter Forty-Five

Normally, I ran up the four flights of stairs to my apartment in a minute. Less if I was feeling jaunty. After the hospital, climbing the stairs was a twenty-minute odyssey. When I entered the apartment, I stopped in shock.

"How on earth?" The stove shone, the floors gleamed, and in the middle of the table was a tin cup overflowing with chrysanthemums.

"Let's get you settled." Someone had taken one of the mattresses from my bedroom and propped it on a pallet in the front room, so it resembled a lounge on the floor. The men led me to it, angling the pallet so I was in a seated position. "We thought it'd be easier to be closer to the kitchen and the washroom during the day." Next to the makeshift lounge was a stack of books.

"Who did all this?" I hadn't lived in an apartment this clean since Mama died.

"Toibe and some of the women of the neighborhood. Your friend Sylvia brought you the books. Someone will be by tomorrow to help with dinner. In the meantime, there is bread and herring if you're hungry now."

Damn these tears!

Rabbi Umansky hovered, until Leo made a show of looking at his wristwatch. "Tateh, isn't it time for afternoon minyan?"

"Oh, yes, it is." With goodbyes and promises to check on me, the rabbi left.

"He means well, but he can be a little oppressive at times." Leo fixed me a plate, which he set beside the bed. "Anything else I can bring you?"

"No," I said but then added, "Yes." I swung my feet to the side. "Can you help me to the mirror?"

"Maybe you should wait a few days."

I held out my hand in response. He shuffled me to the mirror by the front door.

The woman in the mirror was a stranger. My face was swollen, not black and blue but a mottled yellow green. The puffiness of my skin made my eyes tiny. A large bandage hid half my face.

Leo waited for a reaction, but I had none to give. For once, my exterior matched my interior.

I unpeeled the tape holding down the gauze.

"You're supposed to keep that covered."

"I'm also supposed to clean it," I said.

An angry red slash, crisscrossed with black stitches, emerged from under the bandage. The edges of the wound curled up, as if wanting to escape the sutures. I brought my finger to the top of the cut, drawing down, tracing it, when Leo caught my wrist.

"Your hands have germs," he said. "You don't want to infect the wound."

We both looked at my reflection.

"You're still a beautiful woman," Leo said. His face held a tenderness I'd never seen before. Suddenly the room closed in, the smallness of the space tightening my chest.

"I should rest," I said.

Leo helped me back to bed. As he pulled the blankets over me, I noted his scent, a light sweat, tinged with the smells of cooking, a hint of onion, a touch of cabbage. The smells were not unpleasant.

At the door, he turned toward me. "I'll come back tomorrow to check on you."

Without touching the food, I drifted into sleep.

~

When I awoke the next morning, the sun was up. Everything hurt.

I took in my apartment, unfamiliar in its scrubbed state. I remembered asking Aunt Sara why I had to wash the floor when it would only become dirty again. Maybe there was something to living in a clean place.

My stomach grumbled. The plate Leo had fixed was still next to me. I devoured the black bread and herring, tearing it into little pieces so I could chew it more easily.

I surveyed the room, trying to decide where to start. I wanted to get up, use the bathroom, practice walking. My wound needed washing. But the thought of doing anything exhausted me. The thought of doing nothing exhausted me. When I lay there, staring at the ceiling, pictures played: The sound of thunder that wasn't thunder, and Big Al in a pool of blood. Riley's sneer as he crashed a bottle of wine on me. The danger I had put everyone in. Duke's angry glare the last time I had seen him.

"Orders to keep her alive," Riley had said. So it wasn't just Riley's revenge. Who had given him those orders? Would Lansky be in such a rage as to destroy my bar over three cases of wine a week? I didn't think so.

But I knew someone else who might. Not necessarily because of wine. But because of me.

Duke.

It was too much to take in. I had to shut my mind off. Turning to the stack of books, I picked up the one on top. *The Secret of the Old Clock*, by Carolyn Keene. Underneath were *The Murder at the Vicarage*, by Agatha Christie; *The Maltese Falcon*, by Dashiell Hammett; and *The French Powder Mystery*, by Ellery Queen. Sylvia's mother adored mysteries. Sylvia must have raided Mrs. Goldwasser's shelf.

I read awhile, taking breaks to inhale deeply. My bladder made moving imperative. I needed to return to the business of life. I needed to recover so I could visit Big Al. I needed to recover so I could stop worrying Max. I needed to recover so I could get back to the bar and earn enough to pay back Rabbi Umansky.

Yet I was uneasy: I'd gotten cocky.

And I'd paid for it.

～

After two weeks trapped in the apartment, I needed to have my stitches removed. It was a relief because it would give me a chance to visit Big Al. When Frank dropped by, he told me the latest on Big Al, but I needed to see him for myself.

Despite my insistence I could go alone, Max and Uncle Aaron accompanied me.

Uncle Aaron never mentioned the attack, and I was grateful. What was there to discuss? He'd visited twice to deliver baked goods and check on me.

I pretended descending the stairs was easy, though each step was excruciating. Outside, freezing wind pummeled my face. My wound itched like crazy; the dry air made it worse. At night I wore socks on my hands to prevent myself from scratching in my sleep. The scar would be bad even if I didn't rip it open.

Max hovered like a Jewish mother. After he asked, yet again, "Are you okay?" I fought to keep from exploding.

Not bothering to conceal impatience, I said, "I'm the same as I was the last ten times you asked." His arm remained firmly around my shoulders as Uncle Aaron hailed a taxi.

Each bump of the cab rattled my broken ribs.

The car turned off First Avenue. The hospital loomed. The massive building rose twelve stories, not including the solarium on top. In the heart of winter, Stuyvesant Square was barren, with naked trees and people scurrying, not wanting to linger in the bitterness.

Max and Uncle Aaron guided me to the doctor. Removing the stitches took only minutes. When we were done, Max and Uncle Aaron prepared to lead me out.

"I'm not going home yet," I said.

Max ran his hand through his hair. "Now what?"

"I need to see Big Al."

"I need to head back uptown," Uncle Aaron said.

"I can handle myself," I said.

"Don't worry, Uncle Aaron. I'll take care of her," Max said.

Uncle Aaron plucked a few bills from his wallet. "For a taxi home."

"I can pay for it," I said.

Uncle Aaron bent a little to look me in the eyes. "I don't care if you can pay for it. I'm family. Let me do it." He embraced me, careful not to squeeze. It comforted me.

Max propped me up more than necessary as we walked down the hall. The stink of bleach, feces, rotting flesh wafted in the hallways.

When we reached Big Al's ward, I said, "I can walk the last five steps on my own."

Reluctantly he let go. "I'm right here. Holler if you need me." He pulled a book from his back pocket and leaned against a wall.

I braced myself for what I'd find. Mama's fear of hospitals coursed through my veins, even though the doctors of Beth Israel had mended me. *Hospitals are where people go to die.* I pushed away the thought, the one that tormented me: Would Mama have lived if we'd brought her to one?

Big Al slept, but his cheeks were less wan than last time. His black hair dusted the tops of his ears, and scruff covered his chin. The staff must shave the men, but Big Al was due for another.

He'd lost weight; he was still twice my size, yet he appeared fragile.

I sat by his bed, wishing I'd thought to bring a gift or flowers for his nightstand. Men in various states of distress lay in the ward. Some rested peacefully; others moaned. A few had their beds inclined as they ate or chatted with visitors.

"I'd hate to see the other guy." Big Al didn't sound strong, but happily, he didn't sound like a dying man.

I turned back to him. "You're awake." Relief flooded through me as the old twinkle in his eye returned.

"Can't lose me that easily."

Whether it was my prayers, modern medicine, or old-fashioned good luck, Big Al was alive. For the first time since the attack, a spark of hope lit within me. "I was terrified."

"I know."

I curled my fingers around his. "I've thought of nothing but that day, of what happened. Al, I'm so sorry."

His brow creased. "What for?"

I lowered my voice. "For getting you into that mess. For firing Riley. For slicing Riley. For wanting to bring in better wine and a new distributor. For challenging Duke. I brought this on us. I'm the reason you're here."

"My job was to protect the bar. I failed."

"I failed. My job was to run the bar. Not get us killed."

"I blame myself."

I sighed. "We can argue all day. I guess we both failed."

Big Al chuckled. "Fine. Two failures."

My hand held his as if I'd drown if I let go.

"Do you . . ." I drifted off, unsure if I wanted the answer. "Do you know what happened?"

"They came in through the front shop, which is how they got a jump on me."

"The soda shop? Wouldn't you have heard them?"

"They didn't break the lock. The door must have been unlocked."

"How?"

"The bar was full of people. Anyone could have slipped in and unlocked it when I was busy at the door and you were tending bar. Could have been unlocked for days, and we wouldn't have noticed. Others have gotten in before . . ."

"Riley was one of the thugs."

"Yeah."

I bit my lip. "Riley always said he'd get even."

Big Al ran his tongue over his lips, considering. "He did."

"You don't think he masterminded it, do you?"

"It's unlikely he'd do his own dirty work. If he's gonna nick the place, he'd have someone else zap it. For deniability. Someone else probably pulled the strings."

"Lansky?" The hope in my voice embarrassed me.

"Could be. But we're a little small time for him. That was a lot of carnage for a minor offense." Big Al stared at me hard. "I don't think it was him."

I didn't think so either. So Big Al also thought it was Duke. I tried to sound even keeled. "So when are you breaking out of this joint?"

"Doc said another week or so. I'll be back in the bar by March." He smiled. I looked at our hands, intertwined on the sheet above his leg. "The bar is salvageable, isn't it?"

"Haven't seen it yet. When Frank visited, he said it's up and running. He replaced the shelves, and he and Wesley cleaned the place."

"You going back?"

"I don't know."

"No one would blame you."

I thought of the smashing glass. The sound of gunfire. The crack of my body meeting the floor. My whole body trembled.

"Minnie, it's okay," Big Al said. "The bar's a dangerous place."

"Oh, Big Al. The world is a dangerous place. The bar is where people go to forget the danger." Although the scar on my face and the bullet in his side belied that statement.

I squeezed his hand, taking comfort in its warmth.

Chapter Forty-Six

Every morning, Toibe put food in my fridge, made coffee, and changed my bandage.

"I thought you disapproved of me," I said as she knelt next to my bed to peel the soiled gauze from my face.

"I disapprove of your work." She soaked a clean rag in hydrogen peroxide and dabbed at my cheek. "I never disapproved of you."

I winced at the sting.

Toibe looked so old-world, with a wig hiding her hair and clothes covering most of her body. She wore no makeup. She was plump, a *balabusta*. Yet she moved with ease and had children born in this country. Her father had naturalized as a citizen when she was a child, so Toibe was a citizen too. Where did she fit in?

I tilted my head, but she grabbed my chin to steady it so she could continue her ministrations. "Do you consider yourself an American?" I asked.

"What a ridiculous question."

"But do you?"

"Of course I'm an American."

"But we're not like other Americans."

She tore a new strip of bandage. "Which other Americans? The ones with the Irish accents? The ones eating those noodles with *treyf*-filled sauce? The ones constantly crossing themselves? What makes the others more American than us?"

"I'm not an American."

She sat back on her heels. "Minnie, you may not have the piece of paper, but you run a speakeasy. You dress like a flapper. You have boyfriends."

I blushed. I hadn't realized how much she knew about my life.

"I hear tell you make a serious cocktail. You fight thugs in bars." She leaned forward to affix the bandage. "If you get any more American, you're going to get yourself killed."

~

Visitors dropped by, different ones every day. Rabbi Umansky. Uncle Aaron. Sylvia. Even Otto. I was antsy to leave the apartment, but merely walking to the washroom was painful, so I was stuck.

Between his last class and his evening shift at the diner, Max made me dinner while I read mysteries from my stack. When I finished them, Toibe fetched me books from the library. I didn't however, specify the public library, and the ones she brought were from the synagogue's collection: Sholem Aleichem's *Tevye the Dairyman*, a collection of Hasidic parables, and *The Magician*, by I. L. Peretz. I didn't have the heart to remind Toibe that while I spoke Yiddish, I couldn't read it.

"What books are these?" I asked Leo.

"You don't read Yiddish?"

"No. My parents couldn't afford to educate me at home."

"Why do you do that?"

"Do what?"

"Call Bratsyana *home*. You've lived here longer than you lived there."

The thought startled me. I was almost twenty-three. I'd been in New York for twelve years. Longer than I'd lived back home. Or rather, back in Bratsyana. Was New York home?

Leo fell into the habit of coming at lunchtime, bringing me his knishes and sandwiches. As I ate, he read the Yiddish books aloud. The cadence of his tone soothed me, transported me back to childhood.

When Leo left, I paged through the books, the scribbles meaningless to me. I mourned once again my rootlessness. I wasn't a Ukrainian. I wasn't an American. Despite what Rabbi Umansky said, I didn't feel like much of a Jew. I wasn't suited for an office job. I wasn't anyone's girlfriend. I wasn't anyone's wife. I wasn't anyone's daughter anymore. I didn't even know what place was "home."

Where did I belong, if not at the bar?

~

On a Friday morning, Frank brewed a pot of coffee and rambled about the antics of our customers. "Everyone asks about you." He poured me a cup. "Want to know when you're coming back. Otto grumbles the glasses aren't as clean when you're not there."

"I'm sure they aren't." I sipped my coffee. "What are you doing about specials?"

"Making old ones." Frank spooned heaps of sugar into his cup. "Leo's back. His food's as popular as ever." Leo had taken time off to nurse me, but I'd encouraged him to return. We both needed the money.

"Liquor orders okay?"

"No problems."

My finger circled the rim of my cup. "Who's handling 'em these days?"

Frank stirred his coffee. "Duke."

"Does he show any remorse for ordering me roughed up?"

Frank's gaze remained on his cup. So everyone thought it had been Duke.

I remembered something Mama had said to Papa during one of their fights: *When a thief kisses you, count your teeth.*

We sat in silence for a few moments.

Then Frank asked, "Are you coming back to the bar?"

"That's the question."

He glanced at his watch. "Gotta buy fruit for today's specials. If you decide not to return, I'd understand." He drained his coffee in one gulp. "That said, the place hasn't felt the same since you've been gone."

I wanted to smile. But I couldn't.

∼

That night, at the kitchen table, a bottle of bourbon, a short glass, and Mama's Shabbos candlesticks sat before me. I filled the cup to the rim, lit the candles, and recited the blessing. I closed my eyes. *Mama, speak to me.*

Only silence.

The idea of returning to the bar kept me up at night. Loud noises from the street made me jump. My skin crawled at the thought of about being alone in the bar.

Yet I missed it.

Which would hurt more? Returning to the bar and ending up in the hospital again or, worse, deported? Not going to the bar and eking out a living as a shopgirl?

I loved the bar.

I was afraid of the bar.

I downed the bourbon in one shot. Grimacing, I poured another. I hadn't drunk anything stronger than coffee since New Year's Eve. The liquor both burned and comforted.

Duke was responsible.

He didn't need me anymore, so he had thrown me out.

He had Golde now.

He had chosen business over pleasure.

He had chosen someone else, and he'd wanted to destroy me in the process.

I thought I'd feel more hurt. But what rose to the surface was anger. Fiery anger. Scorching anger. On the credenza sat the ashtray, the one he'd had engraved with *Minnie's*. I brought it to the table, rubbing the lettering.

I worked my way through the bottle, my anger intensifying.

My muscles tensed.

He had hurt me. He had hurt Big Al.

I wanted to do something. To lash out. To show him he couldn't fuck with me. But I knew it would only start a cycle of revenge, each of us going after the other.

The bar was mine.

How dare he try to take that away from me?

Should I do as Max wanted? Get my secretarial degree and take my chances with the Mr. Whitakers of the world?

Spots danced before my eyes. I thought I'd burst out of my skin I was so furious.

My anger at Duke consumed me, bleeding toward others.

Toward Rothstein, who made my father rot in jail.

Toward Lansky, for not keeping a rein on Duke.

Toward Uncle Aaron, who convinced me to give away my sisters.

Toward my father, for putting us in this position in the first place.

Toward my mother, for agreeing to bring us to this god-awful country.

Toward Max, for wanting to control my life.

Toward whatever God might be up in the heavens, for creating this *balagan* of a world, this mess of a world, to begin with.

My body tensed in fury. Truly there was only one person to blame. Myself. For everything.

I grabbed the ashtray and, as hard as I could, threw it against the wall, shattering it, leaving a fist-size dent in the plaster.

To hell with them. That bar was my legacy. That bar was mine. That bar wasn't going to be taken from me.

Chapter Forty-Seven

On Sunday, I made the effort to prepare dinner for Max. I needed to show him I'd recuperated. And I had. Mostly. My sides still ached, and I tired quickly, but he didn't need to know that.

He stepped in the apartment and yelled, "What are you doing?" He tossed his books on the table and hurried to my side.

"Cooking."

"You shouldn't be doing that. You went to the market?"

"Leo shopped for me."

"You should be resting."

"I've been resting for the past five weeks. How much more rest do I need?" I bent to pull a chicken from the oven, but he leaped in front of me to do it. "Max, I can handle this!"

"I don't like it." He placed the chicken on the counter and grabbed a knife.

"Well, I have something you won't like even more." I wrung my hands in a dish towel.

The knife halted midair. "Yes?"

"I'm going back to work. Tomorrow. At the bar."

He stared at me, then whacked at the chicken.

"Careful! Don't shred the meat." The knife smacked down again. "Did you hear what I said?"

"I heard you." He twisted off the leg.

"Nothing to say?"

He stabbed the knife into the breast. "Oh, I have a lot to say. Are you going to listen?"

"No."

He pulled a plate from the cabinet and flung it hard on the counter. I was surprised it didn't shatter. He tossed the leg on it and continued hacking.

I stood there. He'd have more to say.

But he was silent.

He dismembered the chicken until the carcass lay bare. The knife clattered as he grasped the counter with both hands. "Why are you doing this to me?" He blinked hard.

"To you?"

"You're all I have left."

I'd expected anger, not sorrow. "This isn't about you. You have your law career. I don't have anything."

"You could have so many things if you tried."

"It's my bar, Max. It's what I want."

"It's Papa's bar."

I shook my head. "I transformed that bar. I make the drinks. I do the books. I make the payments on the loans I took out. That bar is mine."

He pushed himself back and walked over to me. He clutched me, surprising me, grasping me in a tight hug, so tight my ribs throbbed, but I wasn't going to stop him.

"Be careful," he whispered. "I can't lose you."

We clung to one another, all we had left in the world.

~

February 8. I was a different person than I'd been on January 1. Smarter. More determined. And yet more frightened. At noon, Leo arrived at the apartment.

"I can walk the stairs myself." I pinned my hat. Even though I'd altered my dresses, the fabric hung loosely at my waist. The swelling and mottled coloring on my face was gone, but I looked gaunt.

"I'm sure you can," he said. "But I'd never hear the end of it from my father if you took a tumble."

The crown of my hat, as was the style, tipped back, showing my face. I'd given a great deal of thought as to how to handle my scar. The wound still looked ferocious. Cover it with powder? Keep it bandaged? Wear wide-brimmed hats to shadow my face?

I'd decided to do nothing. My scar was a badge, proof I wouldn't be taken down that easily.

My scar would remain visible to the world.

Looking in the mirror, I adjusted my hat. Leo's eyes caught mine in the reflection. "You look lovely."

In a firm voice, I said, "Let's go."

Leo took my arm. I leaned into him, reassured by his strength.

For the first three flights of stairs, I humored him, but with only one to go, I said, "I need to do this on my own."

He released me but stayed close as I gripped the handrail. It wasn't too bad. The pain was manageable.

"I've got this." We strode into the crisp air.

I'd been out only to go to the hospital. This was different. This was freedom.

Leo flitted at my side, a nervous mother with a toddler, ready to pounce at the slightest stumble. But I threw my shoulders back and held my head high. A few people shot me curious looks—my fresh wound on display—but this was New York, the Lower East Side, and deformities were nothing new, so most ignored me.

On our walk, I broached a topic that had been chafing me. "Leo?"

"Yes?" He stepped closer, probably imagining I was going to complain of pain.

I waved him away. "What does your father think happened?"

"A robbery."

"And . . . ?"

"Robberies happen to everyone. Legal, illegal. That he understands. He'll worry, but in a regular way." The crime rate had increased since the start of the Depression. It was a plausible story. Leo hesitated. "Was the attack because of the wine?"

"No."

"How can you be sure?"

"This was personal. I assure you."

When Leo didn't respond, I stopped. "You are not to blame. Understood?"

"Understood," he said, but his feet shuffled, and his brow creased.

I stroked his cheek, and he looked into my eyes. "I promise," I said. "It wasn't you." We stood there, my hand on his face. For a moment, I thought to lean in, to kiss him softly.

But instead, I pulled my hand down and turned to continue walking.

We made decent time to the bar; I was healing. As we approached the door, I said, "I've got it from here."

"Lemme come in. I can't report back I left you at the door."

Leo tried to open the door for me, but I pushed him away. This was my moment. My return. The lock clicked. The door swung wide. I held my breath. The bar was empty of customers. I waited to be flooded with memories, but they were slow to nip. The mirror over the backbar had been removed. I conjured an image of a bottle smashing into it. Holes in the wallpaper were crudely patched.

Frank and Wesley had done a serviceable job cleaning. A chair or two were missing—not that anyone but me would notice—and the floor had been swept and washed. I peered closely. No bloodstains that I could detect.

A man popped up from behind the bar. "Minnie?"

I gripped Leo's arm, my body tensing. "Who are you?" It came out harsh, a bark.

"Sorry, wiping up spilled water." He extended his hand. "Vernon Miller. Frank hired me. Big Al's replacement."

I dropped Leo's arm, embarrassed by how frightened I had been.

"Right, Vernon." I shook his hand, taking in the beefy, barrel-chested man. His massive arms and muscular frame were at odds with his soft emerald eyes and full lips. Frank had told me about the new hire. I was more jittery than I had thought.

"Okay, Leo. Made it here in one piece."

"I can help. Carry things. Make sure you're set up."

I turned Leo toward the door. "Tell your father you've done good. I'm fine. When you come back with the food, I'll mix you a drink. In the meantime, I've work to do."

"Call me if you need anything. Seriously, anything."

"I got it, I got it." I shoved him playfully. "Now go."

Before walking into the back room, I tested the door to the soda shop. A new barrel bolt, screwed high on the doorjamb, was latched tight.

Next I checked the shipments and smiled when I saw how carefully Frank had kept the books while I was gone. He may have thought my recordkeeping tedious, but he'd maintained it. A quick scan showed everything in order. Then I looked again more closely. I felt giddy.

Three more payments, and my debts were paid off.

But I wouldn't celebrate until then.

Time to get to work. I tapped my pen against my chin. What would be that night's special? I grinned when it came to me.

A "Don't Mess with Me Martini."

∼

Word of my return spread. I hadn't been back long when there was a scuffle outside the office.

"Doesn't want to see you," I heard, followed by the noise of a body hitting the wall.

I ran out to find Duke pinning Frank against the backbar, Vernon bearing down on Duke.

"Let him go," I yelled.

Duke smirked, released Frank, and tilted up the brim of his hat. "You have quite the bodyguards. Seems you don't want to talk to me."

"I don't. Frank will take care of the orders."

"But I want to talk to you." His eyes fixed on my scar. I thought I saw a flicker of emotion. He sat on a stool, looking like he intended to stay.

I didn't feel like I had a choice, if I wanted him to leave. "You have five minutes." I retreated to the back room before Vernon or Frank could protest.

Duke followed, closing the door behind him.

"Leave it open."

"Don't trust me?" His smirk grew. "I'd never do anything to hurt you."

The door stayed closed. I sat in my chair and waited for him to take a seat. My body trembled at our close quarters. I didn't know which was stronger: my fear or my fury. He came to my side of the desk and perched on a corner. I was trapped.

"Minnie." His fingers traced my scar. I jolted back, but he moved with me. "I'm so sorry."

I held my breath.

"You don't believe me?" His hand slid down my cheek to my chin. "It wasn't me. It was Lansky. I told you not to source your wine elsewhere."

Of course I didn't believe him. I exhaled, trying to remain calm.

"Minnie, let's stop with the nonsense. I miss you. I think you miss me. We're a strong team."

I pushed him off me and stood, hugging the wall to reach the door. I thrust a piece of paper at him. "Here. My liquor order." I reached into the cashbox for his payment. "Here." I shoved it at him.

He counted the bills. I fumed. He didn't trust me any more than I trusted him. "Three more weeks till the debt is gone," I said.

Duke's brow wrinkled. "Oh?"

"Oh," I said.

"I don't think so. You have six more months of payments."

"No, three weeks."

"Not according to our accounts."

Before I could argue more, he stood, nodded, and left, slamming the door behind him.

What was he up to?

Chapter Forty-Eight

I needed Duke out of my life. I needed him far away.

I paid my debts. I paid my protection.

Lansky wasn't protecting me.

It was a gamble, but it was a gamble I had to take if I ever wanted to live without fear of Duke.

It was time to meet with Lansky.

~

Rumor had it Lansky breakfasted in a private room at Ratner's. That's where I'd go.

Wanting to appear as the respectable businesswoman I was, I dressed in a polka-dot button-up blouse with a fitted waist, a navy silk tie, and a wool skirt that reached midshin. My hat and suede gloves were new, pulling the outfit together.

Under my arm I tucked my ledger with the years of income and expenses, still coded as supplies for the soda shop.

Ratner's was a ten-minute walk. I entered through the front door to the deli, underneath the huge sign taking up the width of the building.

I breathed deeply to steady my nerves as I headed toward the back.

White cloths covered the tables, and mirrors on the wall made the room look larger than it was. A waiter in a white jacket and bow tie stopped me. "May I help you?"

"I'm here to see Lansky."

"I'm afraid Mr. Lansky isn't here."

The door to the private room was behind him. "I'll check for myself." I pushed past the waiter, who grabbed me by the shoulder.

The room was noisy, drowning out our conversation.

"Mr. Lansky isn't here."

Behind me, the door opened.

"Henry," a man passing by said to the waiter.

"Mr. Luciano," Henry said. "Excellent to have you again."

Charlie Luciano? "Mr. Luciano, I need to see Lansky. I'm certain he's here, but this man is insisting he's not."

"Miss, you'd better—"

"It's okay, Henry." Luciano glanced my way. "I'm sure she can't do any harm. You're not carrying, are you?"

"The only thing I'm carrying is my ledger."

He laughed, though he signaled a man by the back door to frisk me. He was all-business, staying away from delicate areas.

"C'mon," Luciano said.

He opened the door, revealing four men at a table, plates piled high with toast and lox next to bowls of cream cheese. I recognized Lansky immediately. His features were sharper, his clothing finer, but he still looked like the guy who had given me a shot working craps.

"Meyer, this lady's got business with you."

Lansky's eyes raked my body. He lingered at my scar. When he saw the ledger I gripped, he smiled. "You know, 'the Accountant' is just a nickname."

The men laughed.

A heat rose in my cheeks. "I'm aware."

"Then, by all means, tell me why you're here." Lansky sat with an ease in this world I'd never felt, draped over his chair, arms spread out, as if he owned the place. Which in some ways, I guess he did. I was sure he never had any doubts as to whether he was an American.

I shifted. "I'm here about . . . um, well." A lump knotted in my throat.

"What's your name?" he asked.

"Minnie Soffer."

"Soffer? Ike's kid. The one who wanted a job."

"You remember that?"

He tapped his forehead. "Photographic memory. I remember everything. Where you from?"

"Minnie's Speakeasy on Baxter Street."

His eyes crinkled in amusement. "No. Who are your people? Your *landsmanshaften?*"

"Oh." My face burned. "Bratsyana. Ukraine."

"You know I'm from Grodno."

I nodded, though I knew no such thing. If I listened carefully, the vague hints of a Yiddish accent tinged his speech, but the American was so strong that if I hadn't been paying attention, I'd've missed it.

"When did you arrive in America?" Lansky was handsome, with a thick head of slicked-back hair and mahogany eyes.

"1920." And then, because he'd appreciate the irony of it, I added, "January seventeenth." The day Prohibition began.

"Oh ho!" The men laughed more. "You brought us a bit of luck." Prohibition was popular with the element that profited from it. "Heard you work at your father's bar."

My back straightened. "I work at my bar."

Lansky's eyebrows shot up. "Do you?" He picked up a cigarette pack and offered it to me. I shook my head. "I take it you have some issue?"

"Yes, I do."

Lansky rubbed the end of his cigarette and put it in the corner of his mouth. "Care to elaborate?"

My stomach churned. This was what I was here for. "I'm having problems with my supplier. Duke Hess."

The glances the men gave each other were unreadable. One of the men whispered into Lansky's ear. Lazily Lansky lifted his lighter and flicked open a flame, cupping the tip of the cigarette even though we were indoors. His gaze never left mine.

"What are your problems?"

"For starters, this." I pointed to the scar on my cheek. "Don't I pay protection to avoid this?"

"It's unfortunate, but sometimes men go rogue."

"Why wasn't it stopped?"

"We don't get involved in matters of the heart."

My skin prickled. "He said it was because I sourced my wine from my rabbi."

"That's good," Lansky said. "Important to support your shul."

So Lansky'd never cared about the wine.

"I've been getting bad booze." We were two people, discussing business. I refused to let my voice quaver.

"Not much we can do about that. Our sources are strapped in these times of difficulty." He inhaled on his cigarette.

"He also says I still owe, but by my records, I've nearly paid in full."

He blew out a stream of smoke. "I guess I am an accountant today. Let me see." I passed him my ledger.

He gave a low whistle. "Maybe we should call you the Accountant. Never seen books this thorough."

"Except yours, of course." I winced. It was a fine line between flattery and obsequious, and I didn't want to cross it.

"I don't keep books. It's bad business to have evidence. Everything's in my head."

Chastened, I studied my feet.

He flipped through the pages. "Ice cream. Nice. Which are your payments to us?"

"Rent is my loan. Insurance is my protection."

"Carlo, this is your territory, no?"

A ruddy man at the other end of the table hurried to stand behind Lansky.

"These numbers look right to you?"

Carlo ran his finger down the page. From his pocket, he pulled a notebook. To me he said, "I ain't got Lansky's memory."

He compared his notebook to my ledger. "Don't add up."

"My calculations are accurate."

"Not your math. Your payments. Don't match what we received."

"Oh?" A chill ran through my body.

"Says here you paid a hundred twenty-five a week for your debt. We only got a hundred."

Confused, I looked from Lansky to Carlo and back again.

"It happens," Lansky said. "Money doesn't always make it all the way to the office. Men get greedy."

The wheels in my brain chugged before it clicked. "Duke was skimming money from me."

"Bingo," Carlo said.

"My payments were one hundred a month for the loan?"

"Yep."

"Always?"

He examined my ledger again. "Always."

That son of a bitch. From the beginning, even as he slept with me, he was stealing from me. More and more, my anger at Duke solidified into hatred. Although *hatred* wasn't a strong enough word. There were no words to describe my loathing for him.

Carlo handed my book back. I gripped it so hard my knuckles turned white.

"I want a new distributor."

"Can be arranged," Lansky said.

"Duke comes today."

Lansky chuckled. "Can't be arranged that fast." He puffed on his cigarette.

"Next week?"

378

Lansky looked to Carlo, who nodded.

"Anything else I can help you with?"

"That's it." It was as if royalty had granted my favor, as if I should curtsy. Instead, I said, "Thank you."

Lansky waved his hand. Cigarette smoke billowed above him.

I couldn't wait to tell that bastard his gravy train was about to derail.

Chapter Forty-Nine

I hurried back to the bar, arriving well before everyone else. I went straight into my office, trying to make sense of everything.

Duke had stolen from me. He had stolen from me and then ordered the attack on my bar.

Which was the worse betrayal?

We had been spending our nights with our bodies entwined, his mouth on my skin, my fingers entangled in his hair, and he had been stealing my money.

He'd stolen from my father as well. What could those extra twenty-five dollars a week have meant for us? Would it have been enough to keep my father from taking the extra work that led to his jail sentence? Those twenty-five dollars could have changed our lives.

I don't know how long I sat there staring into space. When Frank opened the door, I startled. "Minnie? You okay?"

"What?"

"Did you hear me?"

I shook my head.

"The special. What is it?"

"Not sure yet."

"Straighten things out with Lansky?"

I looked blankly at Frank. Did I straighten things out with Lansky? "Yes. Yes, I did."

~

I sidled up to Vernon. "Packing heat?" Since the attack, I made sure someone in the bar was armed at all times.

"Expecting trouble?"

"Possibly."

"We'll be on alert. Me, Mr. Smith, and Mr. Wesson." He opened his jacket, revealing the gun in the holster.

I sliced lemons and limes, mixed a fresh batch of simple syrup, juiced citrus. I replaced the half-full bottles in the well. I refilled the jar of cherries. I pulled mint off the stems. My jitters made me sloppy, though, and I moved clumsily, slashing my ring finger. I sucked on it until Frank noticed and brought me a Band-Aid.

Duke meandered in around noon. "Minnie."

"Duke."

Frank hovered, ready to pounce.

"Back room," Duke said.

"We're fine here."

He snorted. "Payment." It was a demand, not a question.

From my pocket, I retrieved the envelope and slid it over, not wanting to touch him.

He opened it and counted. He clenched his jaw. "It's short."

"It's the exact amount I owe, which—surprisingly—is twenty-five dollars less than what you've been collecting."

He shifted, and his hands slipped into his pockets. Did he have a gun? I was grateful he couldn't see the sweat running between my breasts. "Who told you that?"

"Lansky."

"You weren't supposed to go to Lansky."

"You weren't supposed to be skimming money off your girlfriend. I'll pay what I owe."

"That's not how this works, Minnie."

"It is now." My shaking hand rested near my paring knife. "And this is your last day taking my orders."

He sucked in his cheeks. "We need to chat."

"We are."

He jerked his head toward my office. "In private."

"Whatever you have to say can be said in front of Frank and Vernon."

"I don't think so."

"I'm not stupid."

"No one said you were. But I have something you want to see. A bit of insurance I've been carrying around." He bared his teeth. "You know bad things can happen to little girls."

"I can take care of myself."

"I wasn't talking about you." He reached into his jacket. I tensed, ready to drop to the floor should he have a gun. But instead, he pulled out a slip of paper. "A present. For you."

My entire body froze, droplets of perspiration turning to ice.

It was a photo.

Of Gertie and Louise.

Four years was a lifetime to a child. Gertie had Papa's unmistakable mischievous grin. Louise was a double of Anshel. Louise rounded the way a child should, her arms sausages and her cheeks pudgy. She clung to Earl. Gertie, at seven, was a young lady, fashionable in a plaid dress with a Peter Pan collar. She held Mabel's hand, gazing up at her with adoration. They clustered in a backyard, a picnic in evidence in front of them.

They were beautiful.

They were happy.

The flood of emotions threatened to fell me—the heartache, the relief, the mourning, the love, the optimism—but I couldn't show any of that to Duke.

"In the back." His calm terrified me. I'd sacrificed everything to make sure my sisters were safe. I would do anything to keep them from coming to harm.

I jutted my chin toward Vernon.

"Jacket," Vernon said.

Duke opened his arms into a T shape, and Vernon frisked him, pulling a small gun from Duke's pocket.

"After you, Minnie," Duke said.

I walked into the office, my body moving mechanically, as if my feet were glaciers. I was cold. So cold. I sat at my desk as he took a seat. How different this was from those times I'd eagerly welcomed him, awaiting his kisses, his caresses. Now, he was a stranger. Now I saw the sharpness of his features, the menace in his face.

"So?"

"So," he said.

I held out the picture, my fingers burning as if with frostbite. "Who are these girls?"

"No, no, no." His nostrils flared. "We're not playing that game."

The tips of my ears tingled. I was freezing from within.

"Gertie and Louise, right?" he continued. "Living with Earl and Mabel Alterman? A charming family. Way up on the West Side."

My mind didn't know where to settle. The cold permeated every part of my body, and yet something hot burned in my chest. Was I coming down with a fever?

"Now, about that payment."

I nodded, not trusting my voice.

"You know, Minnie." He leaned back, all smiles now, smiles laced with malice. "We can make this work."

Again I nodded.

"Tell Lansky I'll continue working with you. And when I move to Madden, you'll join me."

I stifled a whimper. After all I'd done to keep the girls safe, after all I'd given up, I'd once again put them in jeopardy. I couldn't let that happen.

"I can't hear you."

"Yes."

"And the money?"

I forced myself to stand. "At the bar." I held out my hand. "After you."

He pushed his hat farther back and walked out.

My body moved in slow motion. I'd say it was a split-second decision, except no thought was involved. My hand, of its own volition, grabbed the bottle on the top shelf. The bottle that had made me so sick. The bottle that reminded me to trust nothing. Trust no one. I returned to the bar.

He would not touch my sisters. No matter what I had to do to ensure that.

"Have a seat," I said, but he remained standing. I stashed the bottle in front of the others in the well.

"What's going on?" Frank moved close.

"It's fine, Frank." I looked to Duke. "We've come to an understanding."

Duke touched the brim of his hat and dipped his head in salute.

"Frank, can you grab twenty-five dollars from the register?"

"Twenty-five?" Duke asked.

"That's what I owe."

"Let's make it a hundred, why don't we."

I stared, numb. "A hundred."

When Frank went to the till, I hissed at Duke, "And nothing befalls them. Not a hangnail, not a splinter."

"As long as I'm paid, not a hair on their heads."

Frank passed me the money, trying to read my expressionless face. I handed the money to Duke. When our hands brushed, the fire that swept through me was one of danger, not heat. He counted the bills.

Then, as if nothing were amiss, I said, "A drink to seal the deal?"

He grinned and took a seat. "I've missed your drinks. What's the special?"

"The Whisper Sister." From the well, I picked up a bottle. *The* bottle. The label read Sam Thompson Pure Rye Whiskey. The label lied. I poured a few ounces into a shaker, twice the alcohol I'd normally serve. Before I set down the bottle, he grabbed my arm. My heart sped up so fast I couldn't hear the phonograph over the sound of throbbing in my chest.

"You've always been stingy with the pour."

I added another ounce.

Frank, Wesley, and Vernon gaped at us but, thankfully, kept silent. Three dashes of Bénédictine and a splash of cognac. I cracked an egg, the yolk dancing from shell to shell as the white streamed into the shaker. After scooping in ice, I closed the lid and shook it vigorously so the honey dissipated and the liquor chilled. The colder the booze, the harder it was to discern the bitterness of the alcohol. I set a strainer over a cocktail glass and tipped the drink in. The egg white floated on top, a creamy coda. I twisted in a lemon peel before sliding the poisonous concoction across the oak counter to his outstretched hand.

From my special bottle of Old Forester—the real stuff—I poured myself a glass. Always straight bourbon for me.

He closed his fist around the glass, flashing me that half smile. For a moment, I thought to knock it out of his hand, to blame clumsiness and mix him a proper one.

But I didn't.

"To our understanding," he said.

"To our understanding." Never had words tasted so sour.

In two swallows he downed it. "Nice tang. Though maybe more honey."

I stood frozen before realizing he meant for me to make him another. I thought back to when I'd drunk that rye. I'd had about a third of the amount. The dizziness. The headaches. The nausea. Of course, I was half the size of Duke. I had no idea what it would do to him, if it was enough or if he'd come back in a raging ill fury.

I prayed it was enough.

I mixed another one. I watched him as I poured the rye so he could indicate when he wanted me to stop. I passed him the drink. The floor swayed beneath my feet. I was once again standing on the ship, entering uncharted new land. I placed a hand on the bar to brace myself.

He downed the second. When he finished, he stood abruptly. "I'll see you next Monday." He retrieved his gun from Vernon. Vernon opened the door, and Duke marched out as if he owned the entire East Side.

As soon as he left, my legs crumpled, and I listed forward.

"What the hell was that about?" Frank said.

I swallowed the rest of my drink, hoping it would stop the tremors. I poured myself a second, then took the bottle of poisoned rye and smashed it in the sink.

"Minnie!" Frank said. "What's going on?"

My head swam; my stomach seethed. How could I be seasick on dry land? I ran to the bathroom and retched, only liquid emerging, as I'd consumed nothing else that day. I rested my skull on the toilet, remembering when I'd sat on the bathroom floor after the Italian boys had roughed us up. I'd thought then things couldn't be worse.

Things were worse.

At the sink, I swished water using my hand as a cup. I splashed my face and returned to the bar.

"Take over for today?"

"What just happened?" Frank asked.

"I need to rest." I walked out of the bar, leaving the men with their mouths gaping.

I was pretty sure Duke wouldn't be showing up next Monday. Or any Monday.

But if I was wrong, then this would be the last night of peace I'd ever have.

Chapter Fifty

I meant to go back to the apartment, straight to bed, pretend the outside world didn't exist. But that's not where my feet took me.

I headed north. I'd say I didn't know where I was going, but I walked with purpose, my legs defying my brain. A few blocks from the bar, I dipped into a drugstore, entered the phone booth. I flipped through the *A*s in the phone book.

Alterman, Duke had said. My fingers moved as if through water, slippery on the pages.

ALTERMAN, EARL LAUNDRY 121 W 116

No home address.

I walked to Franklin Street and Seventh, descended the steps, paid my nickel, and waited for the IRT.

The car shouldn't have been so filled at midday. More than one man in less-than-clean clothes seemed to be perched for the day. These men had histories. Mothers and fathers. Maybe wives. Kids. They might be Brooklyn Dodgers fans or enjoy listening to Rudy Vallée or eat date-nut cream cheese sandwiches every day for lunch. Each man sitting there had ideas and dreams and hopes and despairs.

Histories.

Duke had a history.

Did I end it?

~

I exited at 116th Street.

A block and a half away, I found it. A sign read **HAND LAUNDRY**. Piles of packages, presumably wrapped shirts, were stacked high in the window. Someone moved behind a counter, folding, perhaps.

I stood and watched.

What on God's earth did I think I was going to do? March in there and demand to see Gertie and Louise? I toyed with the bottom button on my shirt. I could ask about the girls. Find out how they were.

Would that satisfy me? Or would I appear crazy and frighten Earl?

No, I had nothing I wanted to say to Earl and Mabel.

But I had lots I wanted to tell Gertie and Louise.

I didn't want to disturb the girls. I only wanted to see they were okay. I *needed* to see they were okay. Turning away from the store, I walked till I found a woman with young children.

"Excuse me," I said. "Which street is the grammar school on?"

"Hundred 'n' Twenty-First. Near Eighth."

I headed in that direction.

～

The grammar school was a boxy building, not unlike the one I'd attended as a child. The brick exterior rose three floors. It was about 2:00 p.m., another hour till the end of the school day, so I sat on the stoop of an apartment across the street. And waited.

People flowed to and from the elevated at the corner of Eighth Avenue. A beat cop strolled my way. Pins and needles prickled my legs. Had I been caught? Had Duke died and the officer come to arrest me? Of course that was ridiculous. No one knew where I was. The cop ambled, without purpose, and when he came to question me, I realized it was out of flirtation not concern.

"Miss, waiting for someone?" His Irish brogue was thick. He rested his elbow on the short column at the bottom of the stoop.

"My charge," I said. When I faced him, his eyes darted to my scar. "My new boss told me not to be late picking up her daughter from school. I'm scared of losing my job, so I came early."

"I appreciate someone who takes her job seriously." He lifted the brim of his cap to better evaluate me.

I've done nothing wrong, I told myself. All I did was mix him a drink. Using his own liquor.

"Can't lose it," I said. "Not enough of them out there." *Go away, cop!*

His finger pointed at my face. "What happened to your cheek?"

"Clumsiness on the stairs."

"Not so bad," he said. "Got a beau?"

"A sweetheart of one. We're saving to marry." That did the trick, for the cop tilted his cap and ambled away.

I'd had a beau. Once.

And then I'd poisoned him.

Snap out of it. I didn't know anything. Last I'd seen him, Duke had walked out of my bar on his own two legs. He'd looked hearty and hale and off to ruin some other poor schmuck's life.

I closed my eyes. I wouldn't cry. I couldn't cry. Not now.

So I waited.

~

At 3:15 p.m., the sound of the school bell shattered the air. I leaped up, crossed the street, and stood by the door marked **GIRLS**. I was afraid to blink, afraid I'd miss her.

A rush of girls teemed out, chattering and laughing and screeching as they dashed, eager for the freedom of a New York afternoon.

My eyes skated over each girl. I worried I wouldn't recognize her. Dozens flooded past, my head bobbing as I searched the face of each one. Too blond. Too chubby. Too young. Too old.

And then. There she was. Those brown ringlets, the thick lashes, the way the edge of her lip curled. Her dress wasn't fashionable, but it was flattering. She had an uneven and dirty ribbon in her hair, but I imagined it had been tied that morning with loving care.

She looked healthy. She looked happy. *Move out of the way,* I ordered myself. *Don't let her see you.*

And yet I was frozen.

A friend had her by the arm, and they giggled as they practically jumped down the steps to the sidewalk.

"Gertie." My hand flew to my mouth. *Damn, damn, damn.* Her name had slipped out, barely more than a sigh. *Run away. Let her be.* She looked so much like Papa. So much like me. I started to spin away, when I caught the look on her face.

It was too late. She'd heard me.

Her eyes lifted and widened. She took the tiniest step back.

"Gertie," I said. Her name felt like a prayer. "Do you remember me?"

She slowly nodded just once.

"Who am I?"

"Minnie." The word came out like a secret. She remembered me.

I wanted to grab her and bury her in my embrace. I wanted to smell the sweetness of her skin, her hair. But a smidgen of sense fought its way through. I clasped my hands behind my back to keep from reaching out, from caressing her cheek, from stroking her hair.

"Who's Gertie?" the friend said.

Gertie stared at my scar.

"Just a little accident. Doesn't hurt." I knelt to be eye to eye with the seven-year-old. "How are you, Gertie?"

She remained silent, but her friend said, "Lady, you bumping gums. Why you keep calling her Gertie?"

"I'm fine." I strained to make out Gertie's whisper.

I had so many questions, but the anxiety in her face, my fear of upsetting her, held me back, so I merely asked, "Are you happy?"

Again she nodded.

"Betty!" I heard the cry, the terror. "Betty, come here this instant!"

Gertie's face jolted toward the voice. They had changed her name? To Betty?

"It's okay, Gertie. I only wanted to make sure you're being cared for."

"Betty!"

Across the avenue Mabel frantically searched for help. She gripped Louise by the hand, but when she caught my gaze, she swept Louise into her arms, holding her tightly as if afraid I might steal her.

"Your name isn't Gertie anymore?"

She shook her head.

The questions roiled through me, all the things I wanted to know about her life. *What's your life like? What's your favorite subject? Can you read? What's Louise like? Is she a sweet little girl? Do you still have the brown rabbit? Do you still like to hear "Market Square" over and over?*

But I saw the terror. I stood. Forcing a smile that made my wound throb, I said, "Go. You're being called. Go to your . . ." I couldn't fill in the word, couldn't say *mother.*

Cars traversed the street, making it difficult for Mabel to cross. Gertie looked at Mabel and then back at me.

"It's okay, Gertie," I said.

She turned, cried, "Mama!" and ran to Mabel, dodging cars. The word *Mama* pierced me.

"Be careful, Betty!" When Gertie arrived on the other side, she threw herself onto Mabel, wrapping her arms around Mabel's hips.

Mabel lowered herself, still holding Louise, as she enveloped Gertie. Mabel glared at me over Gertie's head. I wanted to yell apologies across the road, to promise I wouldn't see them again. But she wouldn't hear me, and it took too much from me to say it.

Mabel stood, grabbed Gertie, juggled Louise, and rushed away as fast as she could, encumbered by the two girls.

My feet froze on the spot as the three disappeared in the distance. Betty? They changed her name? Gertie had been named for her great-grandmother Gittel. Would Gittel still be honored?

Betty. Betty Alterman.

I should have felt relief. She was doing well—healthy and fed, educated, clothed nicely. She had friends and a girlish giggle. Yet darkness descended, a despair for the family I'd lost.

I thought of the photo of the four of us—Max, me, Gertie, and Louise—the photo I'd spent my last dollars on.

Her copy of the photo, I realized, lay somewhere in the bottom of a trash dump.

Gertie and Louise.

They were gone.

Forever.

At least to me.

Chapter Fifty-One

I walked toward the subway yet didn't go down the stairs. My feet wouldn't stop.

It was hard to breathe. Needed fresh air.

The fog in my brain expanded, clouding my thoughts. Gertie and Louise were no longer Gertie and Louise. What was Louise called now? I didn't know them anymore. The thought weighed in my chest. This was what Mama had wanted—for Gertie and Louise to be healthy, well fed, attending school—but all that reverberated in my head was *You failed. You failed.*

And yet I'd also saved them. Duke would not be their problem.

Without even noticing, I walked the entire six miles.

The next morning, my neck ached from tossing in bed. Thoughts of Gertie, Louise, and my family were pushed aside.

I was terrified.

Not that I had killed Duke.

But that I hadn't.

~

I headed to the bar before noon. I held my breath when I opened the door. I didn't exhale until I saw it was just as I'd left it.

I checked the soda-shop door. Bolted. At the office, I stepped to the side to push open the door, cringing, as if I expected shots to be fired. Nothing.

I peered in. Empty. I scoured every inch of the bar and the soda shop as if I were searching for monsters hiding in the closets at bedtime. Only the monsters I hunted were real.

The place was vacant. Time to do the inventory I hadn't done the day before.

It was back to business as usual.

Or so I hoped.

~

By 3:00 p.m., Vernon was at the door, and Frank and Wesley were behind the bar, preparing to open.

I turned on the radio to avoid conversation. I shaved lime peels and squeezed grapefruit for the Florida cocktail.

"Everything okay, Min?" Frank asked.

"Why wouldn't it be?"

"Because you met with Duke yesterday. Because you disappeared for the rest of the day. Because you jump every time a truck clangs outside."

"Dry up. I'm fine."

"You're not fine."

"Just a headache," I said, to which he muttered, "Says you."

Once the juices were prepped, the olive jars filled, and the lemon and lime garnishes sliced, I stepped back for an overview. These minutes before the bar opened were peaceful. I savored the orderliness of my counter. The cups gleamed, the bottles were full, and the towels were washed and neatly stacked. In a matter of an hour, the place would be in disarray as we kept everyone drunk and happy.

At 4:00 p.m. sharp, Vernon unlocked the door.

The bar filled with our usuals. *Act normal,* I told myself. *Everything is the same.* I made small talk with Otto. I commiserated about jobs with those down on their luck. I chatted about the policemen arrested for taking graft. Leo came with his knishes and to makes sandwiches for our hungry customers. I polished glasses. I mixed drinks. Yet I couldn't stop watching the door. Couldn't stop cringing at every knock.

As the afternoon progressed, I realized the headache wasn't a lie. I rubbed my forehead and searched my office for aspirin.

At close to 8:00 p.m., the first visitors came.

Two guys, who must have said the right things to Vernon, entered.

I recognized one of them.

Lansky.

"It's been a while since I drank on the Lower East Side." He took in the chandeliers, the wallpaper, the bar. "If I'd known how swanky you'd made the joint, I'd drink down here more often."

The seats at the counter were filled, but he said to one of the guys sitting, "May I?"

The man jumped up. "Of course, Mr. Lansky."

Apparently everyone recognized him.

"So, Lansky." I fought the nausea building in my throat. The second guy stood behind him, more bodyguard than colleague. "To what do I owe the pleasure?" The whole bar hushed. Frank froze midpour. Leo dropped the knife he was using to slice pickles. Wesley turned off the phonograph.

"Did you hear the news?" He picked up the chalkboard, examining it.

"News?"

"What's this? The Florida?" The only sound was Lansky's voice. The bar was as quiet as a morgue.

"One of my specials."

"I'll try it."

In a shaker, I poured a pony of rum. From pitchers on the back counter, I added orange and grapefruit juices. I kept my back to the crowd so Lansky couldn't see how my hand quivered when I poured the honey syrup and allspice dram. Turning back, I scooped in ice and shook the drink. I tried to force the rictus grin off my face, to ease into something more natural, but my mouth wouldn't budge.

"You had news?" I tried nonchalance.

Lansky examined one of the ashtrays. "Nice touch." He stroked where my name was engraved. He pulled out a cigarette. Frank hopped over to light it.

I poured the drink into a squat glass, added a lime peel, and placed the drink in front of him. He raised the glass to his lips, but before sipping, the corner of his mouth turned up in a smirk. "This isn't going to kill me, is it?"

My hand flew to my heart. "What?" It pounded, throbbing at twice its normal beat. "Kill you?"

Lansky knew. Bile rose in my throat.

Put the music back on, Wesley. Frank, mix some drinks. Leo, tell a joke!
I needed something to create a distraction. Anything.

No one moved.

"I hear some bad alcohol's going around," Lansky said.

"I assure you," I said, "I know precisely what's in my drinks."

He raised his eyebrows.

Straining to keep my hand from shaking, I took the glass from him and sipped. "Delicious. As all my specials are." I slid it back to him.

He laughed. "That's what I thought." He tried it. "My missus would enjoy this."

"Your news, Lansky?"

"Impatient, aren't you?"

"Should we go into my office?"

"Nah. Nothing everyone won't know about soon enough." He waved the hand with his cigarette toward the folks sitting around.

I'm not afraid of Lansky. I'm not afraid of Lansky. It wasn't working. "So?"

"Right." He set his drink down. "Duke kicked it last night."

"Kicked it?"

"What?" Frank's voice squeaked. I'd never seen Frank cowed. Leo paid close attention.

"Duke," Lansky said. "He's dead."

"How?"

"His mother said he was loaded when he got home. Suspected bad booze. Complained of headaches and poor vision. Gone by morning. Sounds like wood alcohol."

"Where did it happen?" My heartbeat echoed through the room, taunting me with its raucous betrayal. I held the edge of the bar to steady myself.

Lansky didn't stop staring at me. "That's the question now, isn't it?" The smirk hadn't left his face. "He did his rounds yesterday. Could've been anywhere."

"What happens now?"

Glancing down, Lansky looked at my hands. The knuckles were white. I pulled them back, busied them with a bar cloth, scrubbing the already spotless counter.

Lansky pursed his lips. "Now you get that new distributor you wanted." He flicked his thumb toward the guy behind him. "That's Joe. He'll be taking your orders from now on."

"He knows how much I pay?"

He chuckled. "He knows." He evaluated me. "Duke was that much of a thorn in your side?"

"Excuse me?" *Smile naturally. You don't know what he's talking about.*

"Nah, don't worry about it. Duke was a thorn in everyone's side."

Otto chimed in. "Is anyone looking for revenge?"

I'd wondered the same thing myself. I heard the gunshot that hit Big Al. I felt my body thrown across the room. I tasted blood in my mouth.

"These kinds of accidents happen." Lansky's smirk changed subtly into a grimace. "I trust, however, accidents like this won't happen again."

Relief. Pure relief. "I don't see how it could. At least not here. We're extremely careful about what we serve." My face defrosted, my smile thawing.

"I'm sure you are." Lansky finished his drink. "Watch out for Fiedler. Word is his daughter cast a kitten when she heard the news. When we meet again, Minnie, I hope it's under more pleasant circumstances."

"Thank you, Lansky."

As soon as Lansky was gone, I melted, leaning on the counter for support. Frank turned to me. "What the hell, Minnie?"

"What the hell to you, too, Frank."

~

Was I in the clear? I moved by rote. I smiled, I made drinks, I sang along to the records Wesley played. I did the things I always did, but I was a shell of myself.

In late evening, Sylvia came.

"I heard about Duke," she said.

"Good lord, how'd it reach you?"

"Thelma heard it from Eddie, who got it from Wesley."

News in our little shtetl traveled faster than lice in a schoolroom.

I mixed her a Florida as she babbled. "You okay? Think it was an accident? Anyone who'd want to rub him out? Are you in danger?"

"I'll get through this."

To my surprise, she shot behind the bar, threw her arms around me, and embraced me in a tight hug. "I'm so worried about you!"

A banging on the interior door interrupted us. "Police! Open up!"

Vernon slid the bolt to the front store. "Everyone out through the soda shop!"

Frank shooed customers toward the door.

People flew out, one or two first downing their drinks. Leo didn't move.

"You have to go. Think of your father."

"My father will live. I'm not leaving."

I was too harried to argue, so I moved to push Wesley out the door. "Frank, Vernon, outta here. You guys too"—Walt, Ben, and Otto sat in their usual seats. "Go!"

"Cops won't arrest us."

"We're in this together," Frank said. Vernon planted his legs, crossed his arms over his chest.

The intensity of the pounding increased. "Open up before we break the door."

"Glad Petey's doing his job," I mumbled, wondering where our outdoor bouncer was.

I nodded to Vernon. Sylvia stepped closer to me, grabbing my hand beneath the counter.

Three uniformed officers came in, ones not on my payroll. Behind them marched a horsefaced woman with buckteeth in a fur jacket unbuttoned to reveal a trim figure. She wasn't unattractive, but she was no beauty either. The jacket looked familiar. Like a jacket that had been gifted to me once upon a time. The woman pointed in the direction of me and Sylvia. "One of them must be her." She glared. "Arrest her. Hell, arrest them both. They're probably both murderers."

"Lady, how many times can I say it? No one's talking murder."

"Dammit, arrest them!"

So this was Golde. Duke really had given her the fur he'd bought me. I'd half a mind to tell her that her gift was used.

The officers approached us. A squat one asked, "Which one of you is Minnie?"

"I am," I said.

"Don't be ridiculous," Sylvia said. "You don't need to cover for me." To the cop, she said, "I'm Minnie."

The cop rubbed a hand over his face. "Which one of you is Minnie?"

Sylvia moved in front of me, pushing me back. "I am."

I opened my mouth to protest, but before the words emerged, Sylvia elbowed me in the stomach. In the lowest whisper I could manage, I said to Sylvia, "What are you doing?"

"Hush," she whispered back.

"Ask them about Duke!" Golde's high-pitched screech grated.

The squat cop raised his eyes, as if pleading for help from above. With a sigh, he nodded to the lanky officer, who took over the questioning. "Did Duke Hess come to the bar yesterday?"

"Came early to take an order," Frank said. "Didn't stay."

"Talkin' to her." The lanky cop jutted his chin toward Sylvia.

"She wasn't here," Frank said.

"No?" The cop rested his hand on his nightstick.

I squeezed my hands, digging the nails into my palms. "I—"

"Definitely not," Otto said, glaring as he cut me off.

"You're awfully sure," the cop said.

"Mondays are her day off," Otto said. "Which is why we come on Tuesdays."

"She makes the best—" Ben halted, remembering to whom he was speaking. "The best Milk Fizz. Other guy never puts in enough honey."

"I'm here every day to cook," Leo said. "She definitely wasn't here."

"Milk Fizz, huh?" The cop peered at the bottles on the back of the bar. "So where were you yesterday?"

What was everyone doing? "Listen, I don't know—"

"Keep out of this, Sylvia," Sylvia said.

"But—"

"Sylvia Soffer, shut the hell up!" I'd never heard such vehemence in Sylvia's voice before. "I can handle myself."

"We know where she was yesterday! She was poisoning Duke! Why is this taking so long?" Golde strutted to Sylvia. "You think I don't know who killed Duke?" Her finger, with a sharp bright-red nail, poked Sylvia's chest.

"I have no idea what you are talking about," Sylvia said, her voice steely.

Golde moved closer. "He was my fiancé"—she held up her left hand, which sported a small diamond ring—"and you stole him from me!" She shrieked while wrapping her hands around Sylvia's neck.

"Hey, hey!" one of the cops yelled.

My body reacted before my head caught up. "Let her go," I yelled, grabbing Golde from behind. I ignored the shadow of an ache in my ribs. I ripped Golde off Sylvia, putting more muscle into it than was necessary. Throwing her to the ground, all I saw was fury. I knelt on her so she couldn't get up. "Stole him from *you*? Who do you think you are? He's using you to get to your father!"

The lanky cop pulled me off her, and the silent third officer pulled Golde up and held her in his grasp.

Sylvia rubbed her neck, shaken. I was pretty sure she was asking herself what she'd gotten herself into. Why was Sylvia doing this?

Golde glowered. She attempted to wriggle away from the cop's grasp, but he held her firmly.

"Get her out of here." The squat cop seemed to be in charge.

"No! Arrest her now! I want to see it with my own eyes!" Golde's voice reverberated as a cop dragged her out of the bar.

The lanky cop said, "Fiedler wants an arrest."

The cop sighed. "All right, young lady, you're coming with us. You're under arrest for violation of the Volstead Act."

My breath escaped me, my throat closing as if I were the one who'd been strangled. Violation of the Volstead Act. That's why Sylvia had claimed to be me. She'd understood faster than I had what the cops had come for. They'd said it themselves: They didn't care Duke was dead; there was no evidence of murder. They had only the word of some hellcat they clearly didn't care for.

This, however, was unmistakably a bar. One of the few things that would permanently keep me from earning my American citizenship. An arrest would be a scarlet A on my naturalization papers.

Sylvia had heard from Max too many times about deportation. She was saving me. I wanted to pull her into my arms and sob into her shoulder.

Handcuffs were placed on her wrists in front of her.

"No," I said. "This isn't right." I stared at Sylvia.

"It's a hazard of the business," she said. "What's the worst that can happen to me?" She placed an emphasis on *me*.

"Guys behind the counter too," the main cop said.

"Only one more pair of handcuffs."

"Then just the tall one." The officer moved toward Frank. Because he was a man, Frank was cuffed behind his back.

"This isn't right," I said.

"I'll be fine." Sylvia waved the handcuffs. "What a story I'll have." She winked at me.

"Don't worry about your friend," the cop said to me. "We book 'em, bail's paid, they'll be out in a few hours. We padlockin' the place?"

The squat one said, "Padlocking is a lot of work." He glowered at Frank and Sylvia till understanding settled over Frank.

"Otto," Frank said. "Could you grab money from the box? Leave it on the counter. Folks'll be coming by for it later."

Otto scurried off his stool and pulled out a wad of cash.

The first officer moseyed to the bar and set down his hand. When he lifted it, the money was gone. "There you go. Not even out of business."

The cops led them out. I grabbed my coat and all the cash from the lockbox in the back room and followed them. "Lock up, Vernon," I whispered as I slipped out the door.

Leo followed me.

"Go home, Leo."

"I'm not leaving you alone." He rubbed my arms. "You're trembling."

My entire body quaked, electricity running through me as if I'd stepped on a subway third rail.

"Let's go." Leo took me by the hand, and in silence we walked to the police station. His hand was warm. Comforting. His grasp helped me regain my composure.

We arrived at the police station shortly after they did. It took the entire night, but eventually I bailed them out. When everything was settled and it was only a matter of waiting for their release, I sent Leo home. He protested, but I knew how his father would be agonizing that he hadn't returned.

"You've been an incredible help," I said. "Tell your father he's raised a *mensch*." I kissed Leo on the cheek. My lips lingered just a whisper. "Thank you," I said softly.

After promising he'd be at the bar the moment it opened, he returned home.

A few hours later, Sylvia and Frank were brought out. They were disheveled but in strong spirits. Sylvia's excitement was boundless as we walked out of the station, the sun peeking over the skyscrapers. "I'll be milking that for the rest of my life! Wait till the girls at the office hear." She fluttered her fingers, which were still black from the fingerprinting ink. Indentations on her wrists signaled where the handcuffs had been.

"Won't that cause you trouble?" My chest huffed as I tried to swallow sobs.

"It might cause Minnie Goldwasser, American citizen, trouble, but not me! My little sister Minnie gets in all sorts of jams." She giggled.

"I can't believe you did that for me." The dam of tears broke, streaming down my face. "I—I—"

"Would you look at that?" Sylvia said to Frank. "Have you ever—*ever*—seen her at a loss for words?"

Frank laughed.

"Frank, I'm so sorry you were arrested."

He shrugged. "It happens."

"What's next? Will there be a trial?"

"Unlikely," Frank said. "Lansky should be able to fix this. You'll be out your bail money, but this should all go away."

"Money well spent." My nose ran. I wiped my sleeve across it. I wasn't sure I'd ever be able to stop weeping.

"Aw, Minnie," Sylvia said.

"I just can't believe it." I was a mess, both physically and mentally. These two had gone to jail for me. Jail!

"You would have done it for us," Frank said. "Besides, if you were deported, I'd have to concoct all those cocktail specials. Getting arrested is easier."

"Still . . ." I laughed through my tears, but the laughter soon turned into heaving sobs.

Sylvia put her arm around me and squeezed. "Minnie, you're not alone. We take care of each other." Sylvia turned to give me a full hug. "It's what we do."

~

After walking them home, I stopped at the bar to make sure everything was in order. Vernon, thankfully, had locked everything up. Once I saw the bar was copacetic, I headed home for a much-needed sleep.

When I left the bar, the morning rush was underway. Women shopping at pushcarts, men in suits, kids running, late to school.

Twelve years ago, when I had stared over the ship's railing, the skyscrapers had looked like so many Towers of Babel. Perhaps they were. Because here I was in the *Goldene Medina*, a mishmash of languages floating past—English, Italian, Yiddish, Hungarian. I couldn't even identify all of them.

All these people with their own stories, their own histories living side by side, whether they wore head coverings, crucifixes, or store-bought suits.

How frightening it had felt twelve years ago. How familiar it all felt now.

I thought I'd pass out as soon as I arrived home, as soon as I fell into bed, but my mind swirled with how much had happened.

First there was Duke.

That my consequences would stay with me hadn't occurred to me, that they'd weigh me down. But what had I actually done? I hadn't pulled a trigger. I hadn't pushed him from a ledge. I hadn't stuck a knife in his back. I had served him a drink or two. Of liquor he'd provided me. It was the same thing I had done a hundred times a day. He himself had said anyone going to a basement gin mill on the Lower East Side understood the risks involved. Who knew if it was even my drink that had done him in? Maybe it was a drink from another bar. Maybe he'd had a bad oyster. Maybe one of his own men had slipped him something. Duke wasn't well liked by a lot of people.

But I knew. Would ten-year-old me have been devastated by my actions, for breaking a commandment? Or would she be proud of me for doing what had to be done? My deed would shadow me, would sleep with me at night, wake with me in the morning. Duke may have been gone physically, but he'd live with me for the rest of my life.

Yet something else also shadowed me. Something that didn't feel dark and dangerous.

Max loved me even though my life scared him. Uncle Aaron helped the girls find a safe home. Sylvia and Frank saved me from arrest and deportation. Big Al took a shot for me. Rabbi Umansky and Leo kept watch over me. Toibe nursed me. Otto lied for me.

I worried so much about the people I loved. But, it turned out, they worried about me too. We took care of each other. I had people I could rely upon.

Bratsyana wasn't home; New York was. Mama was gone, Papa in jail, but that didn't mean I didn't have people who cared for me. *Home is where your people are,* Mama had once said. My people were here. In America.

And another thought.

With Duke gone, I was free.

My worries about Gertie and Louise—those lifted as well.

They were happy. That was a good thing, wasn't it? Did I want them mourning their past, looking backward? Their lives lay before them, an open road that could lead anywhere. Bratsyana was never their home. Our trip across the Atlantic wasn't their journey.

Gertie and Louise were loved. Leading a life where they didn't have to worry about protection or a father in jail or payments to the mob. They lived a life where no one teased them for their clothes or for the heavy accents they didn't have. They fit in.

They could be the Americans they were.

Gertie and Louise were safe.

I had made them so.

I would remember Mama and Anshel and Bubbe and Zayde. I would keep the memories alive. If I ever had children, I'd pass the stories on to them.

Mama, I thought. *Gertie and Louise are good.*

So am I.

And for that, I could rest easy.

Chapter Fifty-Two

December 5, 1933

Almost two years later, flanked by Leo and Toibe, I stood before the judge, reading from the paper in my hand.

"I hereby declare on oath that I absolutely and entirely renounce and abjure all allegiance and fidelity to any foreign prince, potentate, state, or sovereignty and particularly to the State of Russia, of whom I have heretofore been a subject; that I will support and defend the Constitution and laws of the United States of America against all enemies, foreign and domestic; and that I will bear true faith and allegiance to the same."

I'd answered every question the judge asked in schoolgirl proper English, and now the clerk was typing up my certificate of naturalization.

My legs were unsteady. A lump lodged in my throat. I wanted to scream it loud, for all New York to hear: *I am a citizen.*

∽

It was just a piece of paper. I knew that.

But it felt nice. The start of something new.

On the walk back, I floated, looking at the world with new eyes: the eyes of an American.

"So," Toibe said, "am I going to see this bar of yours before it closes for good?"

I halted. "What?"

"Might as well go while I can."

Sylvia and I had decided Toibe would make a better witness, just in case fingerprints were taken. Sylvia, albeit under the name Minnie, was still in the system, even though as Frank had predicted, there had been no trial.

"So. Your bar?" Toibe asked again.

"I guess you are."

"You going to make me a good drink?"

"Toibe, I'll mix you the best drink you've ever had."

She scoffed. "Not hard considering I've only drank wine."

"And we're not closed for good," Leo said.

"We?" Toibe raised an eyebrow. "So this is serious?"

Leo blushed. I laughed and grabbed Leo's hand. His cheeks turned a deeper crimson, but he didn't let go.

The day was cloudy, the weather mild for early December, but I swore the sun was shining. "Look at me!"

"What are we looking at?" asked Leo.

"An American!"

He squeezed my hand. After the night at the jailhouse, we'd started spending more time together outside of the bar. Leo was a calming presence. He made me feel warm, special. He felt like home.

Leo, however, wasn't quite a ladies' man, and I tired of his slowness. So last April, when he'd walked me home from his family's seder and moved to peck my cheek goodbye, I had pulled him close, kissing him, the kind of kiss that tickled inside. We'd been pretty inseparable since, though Leo and I were taking things slow; no matter how much he tried to fight it, Leo was still the rabbi's son, and he believed in waiting till marriage. That was fine. I wasn't in a hurry; Leo was worth the wait.

We reached the bar at 4:30 p.m., the evening darkening the sky.

"What is this?" A note on the door read CLOSED. "We don't have to shut down until midnight. What on earth—"

The door swung open before I could turn my key.

"Surprise!"

Candles on tables illuminated the room. Snow was falling. No, not snow. Confetti. "For she's a jolly good fellow," Otto sang. "For she's a jolly good fellow."

The others joined. "For she's a jolly good fellow! Which nobody can deny."

"Welcome, American," Frank said.

My mouth was salty. I was crying.

Everyone was there. Otto, Ben, and Walt each raised a glass. Frank, Vernon, Wesley, and Big Al, leaning on the cane he now walked with, stood to one side. On the other was Sylvia and her boyfriend du jour, Sammy. Max, with his girlfriend, Adina, and even Uncle Aaron and Rabbi Umansky.

"Stop your caterwauling," Sylvia said. "We have champagne! Honest-to-goodness champagne!"

"I hope it's champagne," Frank said. "I made a special request in our last order."

Garlands and silver tinsel decorated the bar, as if for the upcoming holiday. I saw Sylvia's touch in all of it.

"I'm making drinks for everyone." Still sobbing, I moved behind the counter and tied on my apron.

"I'm not sure I should do this," Rabbi Umansky said.

"This is your last chance to have a drink in a speakeasy," Leo said. "Don't you want something to tell your grandchildren?"

The rabbi shot a pointed look first to Leo and then to me. "Before the grandchildren, a wedding!"

"Tateh!"

I laughed through tears at Leo's mortification.

"Okay, okay, I'll have a drink," the rabbi said.

For the rabbi, I mixed a sweet brew, more fruit juice than alcohol. For Big Al, heavy on the bourbon, light on everything else. For Sylvia, one with as many different alcohols as I could fit in a single drink. For Toibe, a sugary concoction in a pale shade of pink.

I'm an American!

The feeling was similar to falling in love.

The radio played music, but at 6:00 p.m., I turned up the volume. A broadcaster spoke in a sonorous voice. "We interrupt this programming to bring you an announcement from Acting Secretary of State William Phillips."

The bar quieted, punctuated only by a shriek of laughter from Sylvia, which trailed off.

"Resolved by the Senate and House of Representatives of the United States of America in Congress assembled, two-thirds of each house concurring therein, that the following article is hereby proposed as an amendment to the Constitution of the United States, which shall be valid to all intents and purposes as part of the Constitution when ratified by conventions in three-fourths of the several states . . .

"Section One. The Eighteenth Amendment to the Constitution of the United States is hereby repealed."

A cheer rose, obliterating the rest of the proclamation. The thirty-sixth state, Utah, had ratified the amendment.

Prohibition was over.

"So what happens to you now?" Toibe asked.

"We close for a bit. I've put in a request for a permit to open the bar legitimately." Now that alcohol was legal again, having a speakeasy was not only redundant but more difficult. Going through the proper channels, I'd buy quality liquor without worry. There'd be taxes to pay and regulations to follow and, I was sure, graft to shell out, but I could stop worrying about deportation. Max could stop worrying about my safety. Papa would have a place to come home to.

"Either way," Leo added, "we'll be putting in a kitchen so we can turn this place into a restaurant."

"What will you do while we're closed?" Frank asked.

"Don't laugh." I sipped my bourbon. Straight, of course. "I'm thinking of night school. Get that diploma I missed out on. Wouldn't hurt to know some bookkeeping."

Uncle Aaron squeezed my shoulder. "Your mother would be so proud of you."

"I'm not sure about that."

"Your mother is looking down on you, saying, 'That's my daughter.' I have no doubt."

"You're getting maudlin," Sylvia said. "We need to toast. To the end of Prohibition. And the start of being an American."

"Hear, hear." I lifted my glass.

I looked around the room at these people. My people.

I'd never speak English without an accent. I'd never know my true birthday. I'd never be anything but a Jew from the old country.

But that made me no less of an American.

I was home.

Author's Note

The world was coming off a global pandemic. Race riots were breaking out across the country. Immigration quotas kept families apart. Those deemed undesirable were refused entry to the country. Deportations accelerated. Americans were scrutinized for their political beliefs.

The 1920s weren't all glamour and gaiety.

After the influenza pandemic of 1918, which killed ten million, people were antsy to rejoin their friends and experience life again. That's just one of the factors that led to the Roaring Twenties.

We tend to romanticize the 1920s, imagining the swanky life of drinking in speakeasies, dancing the Charleston, a world of flappers and fun. But a darker side existed, an underbelly of organized crime, violence, and fear.

The Eighteenth Amendment, also known as the Volstead Act, went into effect on January 17, 1920—the day Minnie arrives in America. It prohibited "the manufacture, sale, or transportation of intoxicating liquors." The banning of alcohol of course didn't eliminate alcohol in the US; it merely sent it underground, forcing people to buy their booze from bootleggers, make it themselves, or find it in the gin joints that sprouted all over the country. In 1929, when New York's police commissioner spoke at the Rotary Club, he estimated that there were thirty-two thousand speakeasies in New York City alone.

These bars were beholden to "syndicates," the mob organizations that supplied the booze. These same gangsters also provided "protection," which required substantial payments from bar owners. Who were the bars being protected from? Why, from the very mobsters they paid; fall behind on your protection, and they could destroy your bar. Prohibition was extremely lucrative for the mob, including the Jewish mob, the *Undzer Shtik*, whose associates included Arnold Rothstein, the man accused of paying to throw the 1919 World Series, and Meyer Lansky, who ultimately created a gambling empire.

While Minnie's bar on Baxter Street is fictional, the places she visits—the French Speakeasy, the Cotton Club, Moskowitz's Roumanian, the Cellar Speakeasy—were real. Despite the underground nature of drinking in the '20s, the *New Yorker* magazine published a semiregular column called "Speakeasy Nights," which I mined for details about the establishments.

While any errors in fact are mine alone, Daniel Okrent's *Last Call: The Rise and Fall of Prohibition* was my bible while writing *The Whisper Sister*. If you want an engaging and fascinating nonfiction look at this era, this is the book to read.

The 1920s was also a time when immigration became more difficult. In 1924, the Johnson-Reed Act severely limited how many immigrants could enter the United States. Had Minnie's family delayed coming by four years, odds are good they wouldn't have been permitted to enter the country.

How to Become a United States Citizen, by George Milburn, written in 1927, guided my understanding of the naturalization process. Would Minnie really be refused citizenship because of a small error on her form? Milburn tells us, "Before the alien files his declaration of intention, [. . .] he must take care that his information about his nationality is correct. In the remapping of Europe after the World War nationalities were reallotted to new governments, and boundaries were shifted. The alien is asked, not to renounce allegiance to the ruler or government under which he was born necessarily, but particularly to the ruler and government at present having jurisdiction over the place of his origin. [. . .] [This] mistake make[s] the first papers null and void, and if they occur it will be necessary for the alien to wait another two years before he can receive his American citizenship" (p. 13). So indeed, Minnie would be required to start again. Life has never been easy for immigrants in the United States.

Living with Minnie was pure pleasure for me, experiencing her highs and lows, following her into the bars of New York, helping her concoct her drink specials. Of course, for research purposes, I had to sample the many drinks Minnie mixes. The only one I skipped was the wood alcohol; I thought it would be better to use my imagination in describing the poison.

Poisonous drinks were a serious risk during the 1920s. Stills were often tainted with impurities that transferred to the liquor. But wood alcohol was the deadliest threat. Surprisingly, it was the US government that created this poisonous problem.

Industrial alcohol—alcohol used for purposes other than drinking, such as to make solvents and paints—was legal. However, it was high proof, and bootleggers would steal it to redistill into whiskey. To prevent this, the government ordered manufacturers to add wood alcohol—a lethal liquid—to the industrial alcohol, hoping it would deter people from drinking it.

It didn't.

Bootleggers sometimes passed it off in its deadly form. Sometimes they attempted to remove the poison by boiling it in stills, but removing all traces was impossible. A front-page article of the *New York Times* on December 30, 1926, declared "Government to Double Alcohol Poison Content and Also Add Benzine." The article states that the death toll that year from poison alcohol could be as high as eight hundred. Senator Edwards of New Jersey called this move by the government "legalized murder."

The 1920s weren't all glamour and gaiety.

I hope you enjoyed reading *The Whisper Sister* as much as I enjoyed writing it. In many ways, the 2020s are similar to the Roaring Twenties. Hopefully, though, with less violence and more cocktails (and mocktails). We can cheer to better times.

I'll bring the bourbon.

Acknowledgments

When the inklings of Minnie formed in my mind, I wasn't sure where the story was headed. The novel truly took shape the day I walked into my local library, Robbins Library, and asked the research librarian, "I'd like to poison someone with alcohol. How do I do it?" Without blinking an eye, she said, "I have the perfect book for you!" She put in my hands *The Poisoner's Handbook*, by Deborah Blum, and thus a novel began. Thank you both to Robbins Library and all the other libraries who give people so much more than just books.

So many wonderful people helped me bring this novel to fruition—most importantly, my agents. Most people are lucky to have one agent they love. I've had two. Laney Katz Becker guided me through the beginnings of this novel; Stéphanie Abou helped me bring it home. I couldn't ask for two better people to represent me. Thank you both for seeing the potential in this story and helping coax it out of me.

The Lake Union team has been a delight to work with. I'm forever grateful to Alicia Clancy, who saw the promise in Minnie and her bar. I thank Charlotte Herscher, editor extraordinaire, without whom this novel wouldn't be what it is today. Thanks also to Mindi Machart, Stephanie Chou, Danielle Marshall, Darci Swanson, Karah Nichols, Rachael Clark, Adrienne Krogh, and the rest of the Lake Union team.

Writing is a lonely task. Having friends to keep me accountable makes it a lot less lonely. I found my people in WAT, Writing Alone Together. Despite being an online group, these writers have become some of my closest friends in real life. A huge cheer for Kirsten Major, who brought this group into existence. The group is too large to mention everyone, but in particular, I would like to thank Abigail Beshkin, Amy Braunschweiger, Michele Midori Fillion, Susan Eve Haar, Wendy Hammond, Shirley Hilton, Maile Hulihan, Billie Lim, Sydney MacInnis, Nadya McGlinn-Krylov, Kate Motoike, Giavanna Munafo, Carol Murashige, Lisa Nackan, Nicole Reed, Jane Shufer, Laura Simms, Ruelaine Stokes, and Sharon Thomas.

For much of my research, I relied on the Tenement Museum's tours and online programs. The next time you're in New York City, a program with the museum is a must. The New York Public Library, the Museum of the City of New York, and the Center for Jewish History were also essential. I frequently referred to the EUVS Vintage Cocktail Books Free Digital Library. The online library has over two hundred digitized cocktail books, from around the world, from the 1800s through the 1900s. You can find it online and whip up your own cocktails.

So many people helped me when I had random questions. For all their help, I thank Josh Feldman of the Coopered Tot, who answered bourbon questions; Kathy MacDonald, who took care of my Jewish questions; John Adams, who advised me on bars; and Simon Leake, who always found the answers to my most random questions.

The Achayot Writers group nourishes my soul and encourages my creativity. I adore the women who lead this group: Talia Liben Yarmush, Erika Dreifus, Suzanne Reisman.

I can't even count how many drafts my fantastic beta reader, Holly Robinson, read. Her feedback and friendship were vital to the writing of this novel.

I owe appreciation to Henriette Lazaridis and her Krouna Writing Workshop, which allowed me to work on my novel in a gorgeous Greek setting. Ditto to Highlights Foundation, which provided me with a cabin to write in the most pastoral setting.

My writing friends are much loved. In particular I want to thank my dearest of them, Louise Miller and Lynda Cohen Loigman, who cheered me on when the doubts crept in. Other amazing writer friends have given a tremendous amount of support, both in my writing and personal lives. I'd like to thank Sarah Endo, Anjali Mitter Duva, Jennifer Fiore, Lindsay Hatton, Crystal King, Sarah Momsa-Billings, Elizabeth Preston, and Virginia Pye. Thank you to the Loft Literary Center in Minneapolis for allowing me to teach online. I've taken classes there myself, and it's an amazing, supportive community in which to hone your skills.

To the first person who fostered my love for creative writing, I am eternally grateful. Thank you to my kindergarten/first-grade teacher, Mrs. Ferrer. Yes, I know you said I could call you Deborah. No, I don't think I'll ever be able to do so.

I wouldn't be here today if it weren't for you, my readers. Every book club I visited, every email I received, every review that you wrote made my spirit soar. Thank you for spending the time with my characters. The Jewish Book Council was instrumental in spreading the word for my first book. The service they do for the Jewish book world is immeasurable. Also a shout-out to my local bookstores, who enthusiastically sold *Modern Girls*. Porter Square Books and Belmont Books, I'm lucky to have you both so nearby. And I can't forget my friends who championed the book and asked every time I saw them, "When's the next book?" Well, here it is! Thank you for your friendship and your love of books.

Family plays an essential role in *The Whisper Sister* as well as in my own life. I have so much love and gratitude for all of them.

Thank you to the Medros family for their warmth and support (and Maish's violin story!), notably Reagan, Claire, and Casey, mainly because I think they'll get a kick out of seeing their names in a book. Can we get those tattoos now?

My little sister, (Dr.) Melissa T. Brown, has put up with a lot from me. I wouldn't even know where to begin! I'm lucky to have her to keep me on the straight and narrow. My parents, Peter and Carol K. Brown, gave me my love of books and my curiosity about the world. I don't know where to begin in thanking them. I love all three of you.

Finally, to those closest to me, words are not sufficient. My husband, Adam Medros, lived through the writing, the grumping, the talking to myself. He is the family bartender and always ensured I had a fresh cocktail nearby. Thank goodness he hasn't poisoned me . . . yet. My kids, Nathan and Sadie Medros, never doubted I could write this book. They gave me not only encouragement but a stern "Just do it, Mom" when I needed it. And, of course, thank you to my constant writing companions who made sure there was no food hiding on my keyboard: Lansky and Bailey, you're the goodest dogs ever! My love to all of you.

About the Author

Photo © Sharona Jacobs

Jennifer S. Brown is the author of *Modern Girls*, which was a Goodreads Choice Award semifinalist for Historical Fiction, a Massachusetts Book Award "Must Read," and a *USA Today* bestseller. Her writing has appeared in *McSweeney's, Fiction Southeast, Southeast Review, Hippocampus Magazine, Cognoscenti*, and *Bellevue Literary Review*, among other places.

Jennifer has a BFA in film and television from New York University and an MFA in creative writing from the University of Washington. She loves writing historical fiction because the research lets her live vicariously in another time and place. Jennifer has two (mostly grown) children, two beagles, and a husband who won't let her get more dogs. You can find Jennifer on Instagram (@brownjennys) or at www.jennifersbrown.com.